David Brierley was ~~~~~~~~~~~~~~~~~~~~~~~~~~~~~~ is
early years in Sou~~~~~~~~~~~~~~~~~~~~~~~~~~~~~~~~~ er
graduating from C~~~~~~~~~~~~~~~~~~~~~~~~~~~~~~~~ le
spent fifteen years ~~~~~~~~~~~~~~~~~~~~~~~~~~~~~ es
before becoming a ~~~~~~~~~~~~~~~~~~~~~~~~~~~~~~~ ve
been set all over the world, from behind the former Iron
Curtain to the rainforests of Latin America. In 1992 he
moved with his wife to France where they now live in a
lovingly restored farm cottage.

Praise for David Brierley

'If you want espionage in the le Carré class, this is it'
Observer

'Brilliant description of a damp and cold life after Dubček
makes one want to read it by the fireside, and the paranoia
will keep you looking over your shoulder' *Sunday Telegraph*

Also by David Brierley:

Big Bear, Little Bear
Shooting Star
Czechmate
One Lives, One Dies
Cold War
Blood Group O
Skorpion's Death
Snowline
On Leaving a Prague Window

THE
HORIZONTAL
WOMAN

David Brierley

WARNER BOOKS

A *Warner* Book

First published in Great Britain in 1996
by Little, Brown and Company
This edition published by Warner Books in 1998

Copyright © David Brierley 1996

The moral right of the author has been asserted.

A CIP catalogue record for this book
is available from the British Library.

ISBN 0 7515 1997 9

Typeset in Berkeley by M Rules
Printed and bound in Great Britain by
Clays Ltd, St Ives plc

Warner Books
A Division of
Little, Brown and Company (UK)
Brettenham House
Lancaster Place
London WC2E 7EN

This is for Danny and Anna.
Green bush! Green bush!

CHAPTER ONE

This is the place they put murderers. Pickpockets and bigamists and other second-class citizens are escorted elsewhere. This is reserved for people who kill or force their way into women or make political statements with bombs. This is the waiting room for the aristos of crime, the true artists of crime. This is for me.

Tadeusz stood to one side of the door, his head high. This is the royal suite, he thought, room service by uniformed flunkeys, remote but watchful. I am safe in their hands.

The key turned, the bolt eased back, the door swung open. Tadeusz took a breath, filling his lungs. He smelt urine and unwashed male bodies and the smoke from a thousand cigarettes. A second breath brought old brickwork and disinfectant and despair. A hand was laid on his shoulder, encouraging him. He took two or three steps forward and stopped so abruptly he was bumped in the back.

'I beg your pardon,' Tadeusz said, though not to the person behind him. 'Intruding on your privacy like this.'

'Just bloody get in,' the man at his back said. 'Stop playing the fool.'

'I'm playing nothing but myself.'

'That's what I mean.'

A man lay stretched on the bunk along the left wall. His ankles were crossed and a pillow was doubled to support his head. His eyes were fixed on Tadeusz but he didn't speak.

Tadeusz came in another step and turned to look at the policeman. He was not a bad man, Tadeusz decided, and he was a noted collector of policemen of every stripe. He wasn't one of the new ones with uncut features, eager to impress his superiors with his zeal. He wasn't one of the old ones who'd done too much and done it to too many people. He was a middling sort of policeman. If he'd survived the big clear-out after the regime changed it was because he'd never been sharp enough to do the dirty work.

'This cell is already taken,' Tadeusz pointed out. 'That gentleman booked in first and now he's asking why we've come banging in, disturbing his daydreams. Still, it won't be for long.'

'They all say that,' the policeman said with a sigh. He was used to oaths and groans and tears, and this prisoner was altogether too light-hearted. 'A terrible mistake has been made, they say. Mistaken identity, they protest. I've got an alibi, they insist, I was with a woman but she never told me her name. I'll be out of here in two shakes of a lamb's tail, they promise, having a beer with my pals before you've even finished your shift.'

Tadeusz appeared deaf to all this. He addressed the man on the bunk again. 'Not long, not long at all. They'll have me off to Kleczkowska Street in no time. I'll be in a proper prison and you can have this accommodation to yourself. You see . . .' He made a brief pause for emphasis. 'I did it.'

There was a shocked silence. Tadeusz had sinned against the holiest tenet of life inside: Thou shalt not confess. If one confessed, all could confess. They would no longer be the unlucky bonded by adversity to the system, they would be robbers and rapists and drug dealers and murderers and embezzlers and other forms of low life. He appeared oblivious of the transgression, humming some snatch of a tune he seemed to have forgotten, smiling at a joke only he knew, straightening his shoulders from some invisible burden he'd been carrying.

'Guilty, are you?' the policeman said. 'Told them, did you? Well, it shouldn't take long to reach a verdict.'

The smile faded and doubt shadowed Tadeusz's face. 'They wouldn't listen to me. The evidence is clear, I deny nothing, I run to meet my fate, and they say: Hang about. Just a minute. Don't be in such a hurry. They said it was for them to decide if I was guilty or not. That was their job. It was presumptuous of me to decide my own guilt or innocence. Yes, pre-sump-tu-ous. There's a word to get your tongue round. You can go to prison for presumption, I have no doubt. I should have shouted in their faces: I am presumptuous! But it was too late. They all withdrew to chew over my fate. Have you ever heard such blathering? Have you?'

The man on the bunk had raised himself on one elbow to stare at Tadeusz. He frowned and shook his head to himself.

'See? This gentleman agrees. They only make this fuss upstairs because it keeps them employed, away from the stifling embrace of their nearest and dearest, prolongs their moment of power. A decision is the climax, you see, and they thrill too much to the foreplay to hurry it. I shall write a thesis about it: the verdict as orgasm. It's come to me in a flash. The accused – poor innocent – as the object of conquest. The prosecutor plotting the seduction. The defending counsel . . . well, defending. Hm, I'll have to work out the details. What do you say?'

'Jesus,' the man on the bunk said, lying back again and contemplating the ceiling, 'why didn't his lawyer plead insanity?'

This judgement on Tadeusz reduced him to temporary silence. The policeman promised dinner, if he was still here, and withdrew. And the man on the bunk fumbled a cigarette out of a packet, lit it with a cheap gas lighter and sent three separate smoke rings up into the air like the Sioux signalling the advance of General Custer to meet his fate.

This is my temporary palace, my autumn retreat from the cares of the world. Outside the common people work and love and quarrel. In here all is peace and I need never fear hunger or lack company or want for attention. I have only to raise my voice for the servant to come running. No need to stir – it's room service here. I could ask for anything. I could ask for cappuccino sprinkled on top with cinnamon. I could ask for Old Vodka. I could ask for quail's elbows in aspic. I could ask for angel's wings and fly over the wall and up to heaven and then . . . and then . . . behind some lumpy cumulus . . . on a bed of feathery cirrus . . .

'What's your name?'

Coming back to earth, Tadeusz looked at the man stretched out on the bunk.

'You spoke?'

'I asked your name, since we have been put in here together.'

Tadeusz considered, mouth pursed. 'Tadeusz,' he said, 'Tadeusz Lipski. Recognize the name, do you?'

'No.'

'Doesn't strike a bell? No hint of tintinnabulation? You're not a connoisseur of the arts – visual, dramatic, musical?'

The man stared, not answering.

'Not familiar from the newspapers?'

'I told you, no.'

'Just making sure.'

'Sorry I bloody asked.'

The silence ran for a bit. Tadeusz said, 'And you?'

'What?'

'What is your name?'

'Miler,' he said.

First name not given. He was never christened. He was never baptized, never took his first communion, never got married. He was left on a doorstep as a baby, wrapped in a blanket. He was kidnapped by gypsies, snatched from a pram. He was never a baby at all, he stepped fully grown from behind a tree, zipping up his fly. He was found in the cathedral, in a confessional, someone's sin. He was found under a stone, blinking in the unexpected light. He was found under a pile of rubble after the guns had fallen silent, gasping for air. Miler Miler Miler Miler. Spew it out fast enough and it is like the rattle of a machine gun. Miler Miler Miler. A soft machine gun.

'What are you muttering?' Miler asked.

'Prayers,' Tadeusz said.

'If you have to pray to get out, you've already lost. Of course, I forgot, you said you did it.'

'I did.'

Miler considered Tadeusz again. He was seated upright on the bunk. Can you sit at attention? He could be waiting for an army inspection.

'And the cops caught you?'

'I wasn't running.'

'What was it? What did they get you for?'

'Love.'

'Love?' Miler asked.

'Love.'

With that, Tadeusz stretched out on the bunk and gazed up at the ceiling. Love, he thought, love in the horizontal position. Love, passionate love, mother love, love of country, love of money, love of God, love of life. Love as possessing another person, love as giving yourself. Love is what you still have to lose when you've lost everything else. Love as an illusion. Love as self-delusion. Love as striving to reach the impossible. Love as giving your life for another. Love is lust, love is weeping, love is magic, love is trickery. Love is pleasing one person other than yourself. Love is a better version of yourself. Love is a cruel invention. Love is what man proposes, woman disposes. Love is a rejection of the world. Love is a whisper in the ear. Love is an eye at the keyhole watching another undress. Love is inventing another life. Love is destroying your former self. Love is jealousy. Love is betrayal. Love alters the past. Love invents the future. From love there is no going back.

'So they've made love a crime,' Miler said. 'First I've heard of it.'

'No, it's the things that are done because of love,' Tadeusz said.

Or because of a lack of love. Or because of trying to get love. Or because love has gone. Or because love is shared. Or because love was an illusion. Or because love grew cold. Or because love betrayed you.

'Do you speak English?' Tadeusz asked.

'No.'

'The English invented tennis. It has a crazy system of scoring which I very much like. You win a point, you score fifteen points. You win two points, inflation makes it thirty. Three points becomes forty – I don't know why. But zero – pay attention please – zero the English call love. Does that tell you something about the English?'

Tadeusz thought of Renton, who in a dull period had instructed him in the English oddness with tennis. He'd had a cold way with facts, a cold way of relaying the truth about betrayal. The English couldn't deal with emotions. Instead of having feelings for other people, the English had grabbed other people's possessions and called it an empire. And when they'd lost their empire, they'd taken to spying on the empire of others.

'Was she English, this woman you loved?'

After a moment Tadeusz shook his head.

'She have a name?'

The pause was longer before Tadeusz nodded. She had a name.

'But you're keeping it to yourself.'

This time the pause stretched and stretched until it was obvious that silence was the answer. Tadeusz turned on the bunk, his face to the wall, his knees pulled up.

She had a name. She had a face which was close to his. She had lips and eyes and a nose. She had breasts and ribs and a belly and then a darkness your imagination filled. She had hands that touched and caressed and brought him to life again. She was a diva of love. Her voice was her music. Her actions were her drama. Her body was her creation, moulded to her purpose, her art.

For a time Tadeusz closed his eyes. Sometimes you needed to keep the world out and keep your thoughts in.

From the corridor outside the cell door came the sounds of male laughter. Tadeusz heard it and wondered who found anything in this building to laugh at and what had been the cause. Was it a joke? Was it a banana skin? Was it mocking, teasing? Was it relieving tension? Ah well, making love was best for that but you needed a different room, a different mood and a different person from Miler.

No other sound came into the cell. Tadeusz had been brought from the courtroom, down stairs, along corridors, past doors that kept their secrets hidden. This was the bureaucracy of justice, a whole building devoted to it, and now he had to wait and think, or wait and try not to think. Which was a problem since his mind was a free spirit and liked to go off for walks on its own.

Think about something other than himself and his

situation. Think about these four walls, this high ceiling, this vast building, this factory farm of legal business. Next to it was an even vaster building which was the police headquarters. These hulks were built of brick, reddish-purple, an ugly colour. The buildings had been designed along the lines of castles, withstanding the sieges of a rebellious proletariat a century ago.

These twin bastions of law and order had survived the fury of the last war. The city had gone through many names – Wraclaw, Wrotizla, Pressela, Bresla, Breslaw, Breslau – before becoming Wroclaw. 'Which in case you didn't know', Tadeusz had instructed Renton, 'is pronounced Vrotswaf. Can you say it? Vrotswaf Vrotswaf Vrotswaf.'

'You crazy Poles and your crazy language', Renton had said. This was from the man who had instructed him that in English love was zero.

The very worst time in the city was when it became Festung Breslau. Hitler's orders. Breslau was to be a fortress that didn't surrender to the Red Army as it swept west. Breslau had been German until they pushed the frontier about a bit.

Miler Miler Miler, he said to himself. Miler. Of course.

Turning to face the other man in his bunk he said, 'Müller. That was your name, right?'

Now the pauses came in the other direction. Miler considered the question and answered, 'My father's name.'

Müller had looked at the post-war world and which side of the great divide he had elected to live on and how the sins of the leaders now in their graves were visited on the living and had draped his name in the protective colouring of the Polish flag. Müller became Miler. Like Stich became Stys. Like . . .

But Tadeusz was suddenly on his feet again, peering into Miler's face. There were lines at the eyes that people said came from laughter but could just as well come from screaming. Anger, fear, pain, any kind of screaming. There were furrows down his cheeks and a scar like a nailclipping on his forehead. This was a face that had seen a bit too much of the world and from a bit too close up.

'When were you born?'

Miler seemed to be pondering whether to answer. '1953.'

'A good year. You chose well.'

'What do you mean?'

'Year Stalin died,' Tadeusz said. 'Has to be good. Also it was the year I was born. Is that a coincidence or a sign?'

'Sign of what?'

Tadeusz shrugged. He could invent a dozen signs but he wasn't interested. 'You were born here?'

'Why do you want to know?'

'Well, what else have we got to do but talk?'

Miler thought about it. 'My family come from over there.' He jerked his head back. 'Small place down by the Nysa.'

Miler's father – Müller – would have called it the Neisse. A lot of the places had been ethnically mixed and the Poles who'd lived there spoke a dialect with German mixed in. *Water Polish*, they'd been called.

'And during the war?'

Miler swung his legs over the bunk and stood up so that Tadeusz had to step back. The lines in his face were deeper, his skin cracked like dried mud.

'What do you mean? What are you getting at?'

'He was in the *Wehrmacht*?'

The muscles along Miler's jaw bunched and relaxed and bunched again, restless like caged dogs. His brows were drawn together. The look said: And if he was? You want to make something of it? It was a look from the prison yard, from the prison showers, from the prison canteen. Tadeusz knew it.

'He fought the Russians maybe?' Tadeusz went on.

'He fought on the retreat from Russia. He fought at

Lwow. He fought at Przemysi. He was captured near Tarnov and escaped before they could kill him. He came to Breslau. He fought here until the end came. He went west, he walked. He went to Zgorzelec. Gorlitz he knew it as. He thought that was far enough to be safe, far enough from the Ivans, in Germany even if it was the Russian zone. But they had one more trick up their sleeve. They moved the border and he found himself in Poland. Other Germans packed their bags but he'd done with retreating by now. He stayed. He was seventeen when he began fighting. He fought the communists for a year and aged fifteen years. He killed as many as he could. And then it was over. No more German army, no more killing Russians. He met a girl, he became Polish, he got married, he became Miler. It's the story of our times. That satisfy you?'

Tadeusz thought of the cemetery in Wroclaw where the dead of the Red Army were buried. In the old days, under the old regime, people would say: The cemetery is very nice but it's not big enough.

Tadeusz sat down on his bunk. Miler, calmer now, sank back on his.

'When did your father arrive here?' Tadeusz asked.

'I don't know. Nineteen forty-four. In time for Christmas.'

'My father was here.'

Miler leaned forward to peer in his face. 'Your father was here? In the army? You mean your father was German? What did you say your name was – Lipski? What was he – Lipschitz?'

'He was always Lipski. There were Poles living here, even in Festung Breslau. Not many. A few hundred. A thousand maybe.'

'Right here? During the final assault?'

'The final act,' Tadeusz said.

CHAPTER TWO

What was it like, Papa?

You'll never know, Tadek. I pray you'll never know.

Tell me, tell me.

Later.

After supper, Papa?

Later – I mean when you're older.

I'll be older after supper. I'll be eight years, four months and three days, and four hours older than I am now.

Konrad Lipski wondered if his son would ever be old enough. How could anyone understand who hadn't been there? All your senses were overwhelmed. The sights were too awful to look at, too grotesque to ignore. The sounds replaced thought in your head. The smells invaded your nostrils when you were asleep. An acrid taste puckered your mouth. Even your sense of touch was altered, the feel of rough cloth, the cold and damp that seemed woven into the fabric.

He said to his son, When it started it sounded like the ocean far off.

What does the ocean sound like, Papa?

Konrad Lipski turned the corner and there they were, two of them in uniform. Military police were bad enough. At least not Gestapo. Their car was parked in the middle of the block, a scout car in camouflage paint. Even a small car used fuel. The Red Army had made a pincer movement so the city was surrounded. Since 15 February no fuel had got in.

Konrad felt the pressure rise inside his head whenever he saw police. State police, city police, military police, secret police – he hated their authority. They were an occupying force. They patrolled your life.

As he watched two more came out of a building. A first-floor window opened and a woman's head appeared. She shouted down, 'You can't treat us like that. You can't order us about. He's too ill to move.'

One of the military police looked up but didn't bother to raise his voice. 'He can stay there, Mother. Tell him from me, he can stay if that's the way he wants it. But if he stays he'll get moved all right.'

She was an old woman and the fight seemed to go out of her.

'But where do we go?'

'We told you. The trainee teachers' hostel. You'll get a room.'

'But how about the furniture?'

All four military police were staring up at her. One of them had unbuttoned his holster and rested his hand on his pistol grip.

'This is war. We're not furniture movers. You have until tonight to get out.'

The city had been under martial law since the autumn. A uniform was all the authority you needed to order people's lives. If they told you to go to the cemetery and dig graves, you did. If they ordered you to give blood, you did. If they ordered you to move house, you did. Hankego was the *Gauleiter*. He wasn't happy with the civilian administration he had to work with so he had the Deputy Mayor shot. Hankego was a true believer. He said the First Ukrainian Front would be broken when it attacked Breslau and the *Wehrmacht* would be in Moscow in time for Christmas. Somebody said that Hankego didn't salute the Führer, it was Hitler who shouted 'Heil Hankego'. When Hankego heard this he had the man shot. That was to encourage the rest to have total belief in Hitler.

The one who had unbuttoned his holster was frowning, not comprehending why the woman was still in the window. She was rambling now, something about this always being her home, she'd lived her married life here and she would die here.

'If that is your wish,' the military policeman said. He drew his pistol out and was raising it towards the window and the woman's grey head.

That is the moment when Konrad heard the ocean. He'd noticed it before, when the wind was in the right direction. He'd been to the Baltic two summers ago but the waves had been small, slapping on the beach. These were ocean waves that had come a long way and were crashing on the rocks. Yes, the tide of war was coming in.

He stepped forward and now the police attention was on him. The one with the pistol still held it but down along the side of his leg.

'Who are you?'

He answered, 'Konrad.' It was his name, on his papers. It could be German, it could be Polish, it could be a first name or a last name. If he said Lipski, the trouble started. You'd think it was a crime to have a Polish name, a Polish father.

'Why aren't you in uniform?'

'I'm classified unfit to fight.'

'You look healthy to me.'

'It's my kneecap. I was pushed off a tram and it was

smashed.' It was a soldier, drunk, who'd done it but he kept that to himself.

He walked slowly towards them, as you would towards a dog with its ears flat and its lips trembling. It was important not to show fear. His pace was uneven, short when he took a pace with his left leg, longer as his right leg swung wide, stiff at the knee.

'What work do you do?'

'I shovel coal at the power station.'

'Show us your hands.'

He held his hands out. The nails were rimmed with black, the skin was impregnated, calluses roughened his palms. They had been issued gloves but when the gloves were in holes there were no replacements. He looked at his hands and thought: One day this will be all over. There will be no police and no shovelling coal. Everyone will be free to take up his life again. Except me.

'I can't march,' he said. 'I can't bend the knee enough to sit in a tank or a pillbox. But I can shovel coal.'

And when this is over I can't take up studies at the Academy of Music because I can't sit at the stool of the piano and work the pedals. He heard the thunder of surf again, big breakers booming against rocks. It was outside the city but coming closer. The thing was, you couldn't stand against the ocean. It washed right over you, submerged you.

'Where do you live?'

Konrad pointed down the street. 'Number thirty-two.'

'This side?'

'Yes.'

'You have to get out by tonight. You can get a bed at the trainee teachers' hostel.'

'Is it permitted to ask why?'

'It's battle preparedness procedures.'

Konrad thought about that and still didn't understand.

'This side of the street is being razed to give a clear field of fire.'

Konrad looked at each man in turn. They'd finished with him and were about to leave.

'You mean you're going to blow the buildings up?'

'That is exactly what is meant. You have been warned.'

'And everything in the buildings?'

'Pack a bag.'

And my piano, Konrad screamed, you'll blow up my piano? But he only screamed in his head.

Konrad didn't watch that evening but he listened. He trusted his ears. He heard the tide of war right in the centre of Breslau, booming ten or eleven times. Afterwards there was an ache in his head. We should send a message to the Russians: Don't bother to blow up our city, we're doing it ourselves.

The ocean was much closer. The tide was coming in.

'One hundred and fifty seven this morning. That's what I heard.'

'That's not so bad.'

The day before it had been two hundred and sixty. For the whole week it had been over one thousand, one hundred. Soldiers, dead. Corpses brought for burial. Add to that the ones that disappeared, buried under rubble, disintegrated so that you didn't know which fragment belonged to which body. Sometimes a body had been buried with three hands or an unidentified extra bone. It tidied things up. That was before they switched to mass graves, pits.

Only soldiers were counted. Civilians didn't matter, civilians didn't fight.

Russian artillery was hitting houses and factories on the far

side of the railway. At night the sky towards the horizon
flickered like summer lightning. You could no longer see
the stars and by day the sky was greyed by smoke.
Buildings flamed and then smouldered until they burnt
out. No fire engines were working.

Now the shells were coming from the east as well.
Afterwards, when it was all over, people asked which were
the guns that had hit the cathedral but it was impossible to
tell. It was struck and struck again and its twin towers
came crashing down to half their height, and when the
stones had stopped falling you could hear the screams from
inside. They screamed for God to help them but He was
otherwise occupied. They screamed for the Virgin Mary to
save them but she'd gone deaf.

The zoo was empty. The carnivores had been shot. The
antelopes and monkeys and giraffes had been eaten. The
snakes were chopped into pieces and fried. There was a
tropical house with glass cases that were heated in winter;
they contained the collection of spiders from the Bolivian
jungle, some as big as a man's fist that hunted birds; a shell
blast blew out the glass and the spiders ran free.

Any dogs wandering the streets were shot. There was no
food for dogs.

Konrad's job disappeared. There was no coal to shovel.

He thought his father was dead. He wasn't Jewish but he
was taken to Gross-Rosen as slave labour and they worked
them to death at that camp.

He wondered about his mother. He thought she might
be at the camp right in the centre of town in Clausewitz
Street. It held Czech and French and Bulgarian as well as
Polish prisoners including women. If he got close he'd be
able to peer through the fence but when he reached the
corner of the block he saw machine gun posts and turned
away. He heard a voice raised, a shout, but he didn't stop.

He limped faster. Anyone could see his limp. The limp cried out for attention, the limp said I'm no danger to anyone. The limp said I can't kick you in the balls and run away. He heard a rifle shot, and someone crying out, and another rifle shot, and silence. But he didn't turn to look.

The trainee teachers' hostel was destroyed together with anyone who'd been sheltering in it at the time. Konrad had been out, walking the streets, limping. He knew there had been old people in the hostel. He knew there were mothers who kept their young children in because it was safer. He knew Sarstein was there because he'd been employed at the slaughterhouse and had no work now and spent his time stretched out on a camp bed. He knew Langhans was there because Langhans was a priest who spent his days comforting people. He knew Petra was there because she was a crazy old woman who had got it into her head that Konrad was her son. He knew other people were there but had never learnt their names.

Turning a corner in Breslau always promised a surprise, an unpleasant one. Konrad saw the trainee teachers' hostel reduced to rubble. Strangely it hadn't caught fire though there was wood enough in the floors and staircase and furniture. People were throwing bricks and masonry aside and on the pavement there were bodies lined up, some of them very small.

The tide of war was very close now, thundering, never completely dying away. It would sweep in and overwhelm them all. Units of the First Ukrainian front had reached Radwanitz. No, they weren't Ukrainians, at all, they were Mongolians, an Asiatic revenge on the master race. They were coming by boat down the Oder. They were parachuting in, dressed in fake SS uniforms, dressed in women's clothes, dressed as priests. Rumours grew, mutated, gained credence. They tied nuns to the front of their tanks. They cooked babies on their camp fires. Another rumour had it that Hitler was dead, he'd committed suicide. He blamed a Jewish-Bolshevik conspiracy for the catastrophe.

The sky darkened, the twilight of the gods.

In the dusk a plane came flying low, its machine guns raking the street where Konrad limped. He ducked into a doorway and stood waiting. The plane passed but he could hear other sounds of shooting. He pushed the door closed and went down the stairs to the cellar. I am an animal, he told himself, going back into its hole. At the bottom of the steps he stopped, the darkness total, and some animal sense told him he wasn't alone. His kneecap hurt from coming down the steps and he rubbed it, trying to place where the other person was. Or the other animal.

Animals is what we've become, he told himself.

But no, animals never behaved like this. Animals didn't band together in blind, battling armies. Animals didn't blow each other up, maim, torture. Animals didn't put on uniforms and strut and order each other about. Animals didn't slaughter other animals and award each other medals *Pour le mérite*. Only humans.

There was a small noise, a movement, the scuffing of a shoe on the floor. Over there. He brought out his box of matches. He'd kept them, hoping always to find cigarettes, and now he lit one and held it away from his eyes.

The girl looked seven or eight and had masked her face with her hands. If she couldn't see him, then maybe he couldn't see her. She stood against a wall that housed a floor to ceiling wine rack. At one time it must have been full for Konrad could see cards tacked to the wooden shelving giving the name and vintage of the wine. Maybe a dozen bottles remained.

'It's all right,' Konrad said, 'I'm not going to hurt you.'

The flame reached his thumb and finger and he dropped the match on the stone floor. In the darkness he heard the girl let out her breath and draw another one. She didn't see him, she wasn't breathing, she wasn't there. And then Konrad wasn't there. An explosion rocked the street, driving all thought from his head. The stone floor shivered, he felt it, and his brain worked again. Fortissimo, he thought, for a moment I didn't exist, I was dead.

He lit another match and saw the girl had her hands over her ears now.

'It's all right. We'll be all right.'

His voice wasn't his voice. The shellburst had squeezed his throat. He swallowed but had no saliva and his throat hurt. He tried again.

'We'll be safe here.'

He wanted to believe it. He wanted to be alive. He wanted to reassure the girl, but she had her hands over her ears still and couldn't hear. Before he had to drop the match again he saw there was a table and two chairs against another wall, and a candle in a china holder. With the third match he lit the candle. He saw a mattress on the floor, pillows side by side, blankets. The household had shrunk to this. He went back to the girl.

'My name is Konrad.'

He stuck his hand out. Without hesitating she took one hand from her ear to shake his hand. He grasped it, kept hold of it.

'My name's Konrad,' he said again, now she could hear. 'What's yours?'

She tugged at her hand but he gripped it tight. He asked her name again and she answered, 'Sigrid.'

'Well, Sigrid, I'm really pleased to have found you. It's good to be with someone when there's so much noise outside.'

She moved her other hand, slowly, to cover her mouth.
She pressed hard. Konrad could see her flesh dimpling.

'What's the matter?'

After a moment she loosened the pressure on her mouth
enough to say, 'Mummy told me not to talk to strange men.'

'But I'm not strange. I'm Konrad and you're Sigrid and
we're friends. Where is your mummy?'

'She went out.'

'Just now?' The girl shook her head. 'Today?' She
shrugged. 'Has she been gone a long time?'

'I don't know.'

'Did she sleep here last night?'

'I don't know when it's night.'

There was no window, no source of daylight. Outside
there was the briefest of screams followed by a crashing
explosion. The candle flame trembled. She snatched her
hand out of Konrad's grip and covered both ears.

This is the end, Konrad decided. The Red Army has moved
its artillery pieces up and is smashing the city centre, block
by block. German infantry are holding the suburbs but not
for long. Soon there will be nothing worth capturing.

Sigrid was sleeping. The candle was burning low but
he'd been upstairs and found a box with eight more. He'd
brought down a glass and a corkscrew to open a bottle. It
was a Nüssbrunnen from Hattenheim, fresh and fruity. He
decided he would simply drink through all the bottles –
eleven he counted – and by then he would be beyond car-
ing. He wondered who Sigrid's father was – had been – to
have such good wine.

'He's a doctor.'

'It's a busy time for a doctor. And your mummy – is she
a nurse?'

'She's a mummy.'

'Is she beautiful?'

'Yes. I hope she comes back soon. I'm hungry.'

Konrad said, 'If we had some spaghetti we could have spaghetti with mouse sauce if we had any mice.'

Sigrid thought about this. She said, 'I had a pet mouse once but it died.'

'What was its name?'

'Adolf.'

'Adolf is a good name for a mouse.' Konrad looked up from the bottle between his knees, corkscrew half inserted. The label told him it was Julius-Echter-Berg and came from Iphofen. 'It's the name for a mouse with rabies. For a pig, Hermann. Heinrich the Hyena. Josef I see as a goat. Martin is a skunk.'

He stopped. He wasn't being fair to the animals. He pulled the cork and poured another glass of wine.

'Tell me a story,' Sigrid said.

'Once upon a time.' Konrad stopped.

'Go on.'

'Once upon a time there was a mouse called Adolf. It ate bread and cheese but not meat. He had funny little black whiskers that grew down from his nose and when he walked his bottom stuck out like this.'

Konrad stooped slightly so that his backside was prominent and took a couple of steps. Sigrid laughed and said, 'Do it some more.' He turned and walked back, his right leg stiff and going in a loop. The girl laughed again and clapped her hands.

'Tell me more.'

Something bit the mouse, infected it, and not even Sigrid's father could cure it. The mouse began strutting. The mouse roared. The mouse went mad. He told Sigrid. The mouse began to bite, bite the furniture, climb the curtains, run along the ceiling and bite the central light. Konrad drank his wine and told Sigrid. The mouse went next door and said this is my house and bit everyone who tried to tell him it wasn't. It bit the cat next door and even the cat went away. He poured more wine and told Sigrid and she stared at him while he told her. The mouse invaded the very big house across the road and bit everyone. He told Sigrid, he did. He drank his wine, the Julius-Echter-Berg and went on. The bear and the bulldog and the eagle got together and they went after the mad mouse. And they roared and threw things and flew at him and the mouse was very fierce because he was mad with rabies. And the mouse was . . . the mouse was . . .

'Tell me. Why have you stopped?'

The mouse was crushed, exterminated, destroyed.

'Tell me, tell me.'

Konrad had told her, he'd told her all he knew. If she hadn't heard it was because she wasn't in his head.

After the Julius-Echter-Berg there was a Bockstein from Ockfen. It slips down, he thought, it slips and slips. Time to try the Falkensteiner. I should have spent the whole war here, got myself an education, become a wine expert.

He went upstairs to go to the toilet but the bathroom was on the floor above and that was too many steps to climb. He opened the front door and pissed out into the street. He saw people running. Some people were running from left to right, others were running from right to left. They have no place to run to, Konrad told himself. He saw soldiers throwing away their rifles and their helmets. He saw soldiers going into houses, tearing at their uniforms. He saw other men – or maybe the same men – coming out of houses, buttoning shirts, struggling into jackets. But what was the point? They couldn't change their army haircut.

'What's happened?' He was still pissing. It was the Bockstein, now it was the Falkensteiner. 'What's going on?' He buttoned his fly and went down the street, looking into faces, dodging people who were bumping into him. Or he was bumping into them. He spun round; reaching out, begging, imploring.

A man shouted, 'Berlin has fallen. The Reds are killing everyone.'

The man shook off Konrad's hand and Konrad went reeling. There was a noise in his head, roaring, the sound of the ocean crashing over him. There were gaps in the row of buildings and smoke and people picking at rubble where legs or arms stuck out. He found a building that was undamaged and patted it to see how solid it felt and leaned against it to stop it tumbling down.

So, Berlin has fallen. The Russians have cut off the chicken's head but the chicken, not knowing it is dead, keeps running about. Running from right to left, running from left to right.

If the war is over, he thought, there should be a celebration. It's a great victory. Everybody who died has lost, everybody who's alive has won. We must drink a toast to the end of the war. *Sekt*. Is there a bottle in that wonderful cellar?

He went in through the front door but he couldn't find the stairs to the cellar. Somebody had moved them. He opened a door and a woman he'd never seen was crouched near the wall.

'Are you Sigrid's mother?'

Her face was wild, stained by dirt, eaten away, hollowed by whatever had happened to her. A kitchen knife weaved in front of her.

'I'll kill you,' she breathed. 'I'll kill you,' she screamed. She spat.

'No more killing. The killing days are over.'

But outside there was the sound of shooting. Konrad went out to tell them to stop, they were too late, the killing was over for this war and they'd have to wait for the next. He couldn't see anyone. The stage had emptied and all the players gone home. He could still hear shooting though, a long way off, then all round him, then in his head.

He crossed the street to go in the building with the cellar and Sigrid but it had changed. He tried three doors and the rooms were empty. In one room there was a chaise longue and on this he stretched out. Peace, he said.

On 6 May Breslau surrendered. The Generals met in a building next to a sugar beet factory. If only Konrad had been there he would have appreciated how these old soldiers greeted each other, how they saluted each other, how protocol was observed. The Russians had won, the Germans had lost. But in their heads the German Generals hadn't been defeated – they had only lost this time.

Konrad wasn't there. He was still asleep.

Afterwards he could never find anyone who had been there to tell him what it was like. Did the Generals toast each other in vodka? Were they like footballers and swopped shirts?

He was never even certain where the sugar beet factory was. They wanted to discourage nostalgic old soldiers in tour buses and changed the name to Pszczenno.

Konrad woke, he stretched, he held his head. Then he went for a walk in the new world. He limped through streets where people stood, soldiers in strange uniforms patrolled, prisoners were led away. He heard explosions but were they shots or just ammunition going off in the fires that burned and burned? Flames and smoke rose from buildings in every block. The fires were leaking up from Hades.

He limped and limped until he found himself in the street where he used to live. The Germans had demolished the buildings on one side to get a decent field of fire. The Russians, to even the score, had demolished the other side. Konrad stood where number 32 had been. Now it was smoke-blackened bricks, grey plaster, cream window frames, rose-patterned wallpaper. And up there. . .

He clambered up the rubble, he pulled aside bricks and floorboards and broken glass and lumps of mortar. He uncovered the body of his piano. It was not a concert grand, of course, but an upright. Or had been until it lost one of its legs. It lurched towards Konrad, its keyboard open to him, its keys dusty but imploring him, Yes, yes, we've been waiting for you.

Konrad stood for several minutes, staring at his piano.

Yes, we're waiting.

He raised his hands and struck the keys and struck them again as hard as he could. He played the chords that open Beethoven's Fifth Symphony. He struck those four notes again and again, the rhythm insistent, his face turned up to the sky where the sun clothed the clouds in light. V for Victory rose up, fate knocking at the door, radiant and triumphant.

But, Papa, what happened to the little girl?

Konrad was off in his mind, standing on the rubble, poised like a statue at his piano. Why should the Generals have so many statues? Why should it be destroyers and not creators?

Papa, what happened to Sigrid? She was the same age as me. Papa?

Konrad's eyes came from far away to rest on his son.

I don't know.

Did you just leave her?

I went outside for only a few minutes but I couldn't find the way back. Then fate took us different ways. That's life, Tadek, you can never tell what's going to happen. If a drunken soldier hadn't pushed me off a tram and broken my kneecap I could have been put in the army and ended up dead.

Papa, you won't leave me. Promise you won't.

CHAPTER THREE

Tadeusz studied the face in the mirror above the basin. Hello, cheeks, you've flushed schoolgirl pink. Eyes, you've looked into the past before you were even born, not surprising you're haunted. Poor old forehead with that brain behind it, overheated from thinking too long, too dangerously.

Tadeusz splashed water again and again. Rejecting the towel, he wiped his sleeve across his face.

Miler, on his bunk, stared into the cloud of cigarette smoke above him. 'Your father,' he said.

Tadeusz's eyes changed focus to look in the mirror at Miler. 'My father?'

'He told you all this?'

'Over the years. Not all at once. It wasn't always the same either. Once he told me he had hidden for a week in a closet with a woman called Ulrike, who was a goddess with long golden hair and arms and legs like an octopus. Russian soldiers found them and raised their rifles to shoot when Ulrike began to sing. She was a soprano from the opera house, a prima donna, and she sang so magnificently that the soldiers spared their lives. But I didn't want that version. He was very angry.'

'Your father was? Because you didn't believe him?'

'I said I preferred it where he was in the cellar with Sigrid. He said I was a fool and when I grew up I would prefer to be in the closet with Ulrike.'

Miler stared at Tadeusz and then looked away. He had difficulty adjusting to the Lipski treatment of reality.

'My father didn't think like other people,' Tadeusz said. 'He told me: "If you think like everybody else, you'll be like everybody else – and have you looked at them?"'

'I see,' Miler said. It was what people said when they didn't see. He turned over on his side away from Tadeusz. After reflecting a bit he turned back again. 'And I'm like everybody else? Is that what you mean? I'm ordinary.'

'We'd neither of us be here if we were ordinary. My father was just disappointed I wouldn't buy his dream. I found reality amazing enough. Anyway, one day I was walking with my father and he said, "That's the house where I hid." He knocked at a door and a woman appeared. "Are you Sigrid's mother?" She mumbled something – "I don't understand. What do you want?" – something. My father said, "You've got a cellar down there with a wine rack along the whole of one wall. Is there any left? Any Bockstein? Any Falkensteiner?" Her eyes stretched wide and she looked as if she was about to have a heart attack. She thought we were the German owners come to reclaim our property.'

'My father would pause at the front door. "I'm going for a limp now." He was grateful to his limp. He said he owed it his life. He paid it attention, gave it treats. "We'll go to the zoo." I'd go with him and he'd instruct me. "Got to flush out the lies they taught you at school. Facts aren't the truth. Only the imagination is real. Einstein, Copernicus, Mozart, George and Wilbur Wright – their imagination created the world."'

Had his father said that? Maybe Tadeusz had said it. What difference did it make?

'The zoo is the world in one place. "Here's a piece of Asia. There's Australia hopping, Africa roaring." He'd take me into the building where they kept the snakes and spiders in their glass-fronted cages. Either they'd recaptured those big spiders or they'd sent for new ones. He'd stand with me in front of the glass. "Why are you looking at those spiders, Papa?" "I'm not, Tadek, I'm letting the spiders look at me. It's so they'll understand that although they can jump on birds, there's always someone bigger who can jump on you. There's always a bigger challenge in life."'

Miler squirmed on his bunk. 'I hate spiders.'

'They're all right. They're not going to bite you, not in Poland.'

'I don't want to talk about them. Just shut up about spiders.'

'No more spiders. We'd leave the zoo and limp across the road to the park and limp to the pond with its five-metre jet of water and the People's Hall squatting in front. He liked to come in the autumn, one of those October days when it is cold at night and you can sun your face in the day. We sat side by side on a bench by the long curving pergola. The leaves on the creepers were turning russet and mustard and scarlet. "Smell that," he said. I took a breath and another one. There was an elusive smell in the air. "The jungle," he said. Behind us were beds of rotting marigolds. "It's the Bolivian jungle." Have you smelled it?'

'Rotting marigolds? Why should I want to?' Miler asked. 'It's not the jungle.'

'Well, it's cheaper than going to South America to smell it. My father said, "People don't realize it but Poland is the Bolivia of Europe. Remember that, Tadek. When you look at our politicians, when you look at our Generals, when you look at our police and our economy and our whole crazy life and try to make sense out of nonsense, just whisper to yourself: Bolivia.'"

Four paces one way, five paces the other. High in one wall was a window that gave on to a courtyard though Tadeusz could see nothing but sky. The sky was hazed with grey as if light had leaked out of the cell. A patch of weak sunlight cut into quarters by bars fell across one wall. The walls were plastered and grubby. The ceiling was also plastered and cracks showed like rivers on a map. See, there is the Amazon and all its tributaries. To the south of it, that patch like a ball of crumpled paper, that's Bolivia.

Tadeusz stopped in front of the basin and looked in the mirror again. His face was a map and those lines were the rivers of his experience.

'Bolivia,' he whispered. 'Everything is Bolivia.'

'Why do you keep doing that?' Miler asked.

'Doing what?'

'That thing with your fingernails. It gets on my wick.'

Tadeusz stopped tapping. 'Odd,' he said. 'Beethoven's Fifth. Everybody knows V for Victory. And there's no V in the Polish alphabet. How do you explain that?'

Miler didn't. He rubbed an eye. 'Jesus,' he said, 'how much longer?'

Tadeusz considered Miler for the first time as a person with his own problems. 'They've gone out to consider the evidence in your case? Is that it?'

'Consider the evidence? The trial hasn't even begun yet. So why am I stuck in here as if I'm guilty of something? Pisses me off.' Miler swung his legs off the bunk and sat staring at Tadeusz. Indeed he did look pissed off. Then his lips twitched as if a little something amused him, perhaps his own slyness, and his expression changed again to wide-eyed innocence. It was a whole drama class in a single performance and it caught Tadeusz's interest.

'See, this is how it is,' Miler said. 'I've been out on bail. There was a bit of trouble and the police arrested me but I've been on bail until the trial. So yesterday I turn up at court because it's the day I'm to go before the judge. I'm in there, actually in the dock with this pig of a policeman sitting next to me, when the clerk rushes in and speaks to the judge and there's a big uproar. There's been a telephone call, someone giving a warning there's been a bomb planted in the building. Terrible, isn't it? Your Iranians, your Arabs, Russians, the mafia, maybe your bloody Bolivians and their cocaine – terrorists everywhere. Hell, you've seen the Russian market. Right on the cops' bloody doorstep. They should go out and ask questions there, clear them out.'

The Russian market was just the other side of the moat from the police headquarters and the court building. It was a maze of stalls which the city council wanted to bulldoze but which doggedly continued. There were Russians there with stalls of wooden dolls and trinkets and watches that died when your sweat got inside them. Mostly the stalls were Polish. Not your international bomb-planting terrorists here, more your local pickpockets.

Miler got up and stretched and coughed.

'So, you see, the courts have to be cleared, the offices have to be cleared, the building is sealed off while they carry out a search. So the lawyers bitch and go back to their offices, and the witnesses and jury are sent home. Trial postponed. Everybody's got busy calendars and the next time they can meet is ten days time, maybe not until November. So how about me? I'm on bail – why can't I go home? Why am I sent down here?'

Tadeusz didn't know.

'I'm not convicted. I'm not a criminal. I'm innocent until proved guilty. You can't just throw me in a cell. We got rid of that system. I complain to the judge, "Your honour, you should let me go home." "Mr Miler," he says. I don't think he's being polite, he sounds sarcastic to me. "Mr Miler, the first two times your trial date was set there were bomb scares and you were sent home. That's another two months you've been free on bail. This time you're going to be locked up." "But why? I didn't telephone. I was sitting here with this pi— pardon, policeman – next to me. Besides, if I'm down in the cells and the bomb goes off, where does that leave me? All over the wall." "Better send a message to your brothers not to keep ringing up with bomb scares."'

Miler lit another cigarette.

'Bloody judge. I don't have any brothers. Cousins, yes, but not brothers. I told the judge I'm not responsible for other people's phone calls and anyway I've got no brothers. And you know what he says? Do you?'

Tadeusz didn't know this either.

'He said, "Your brothers in crime." Jesus, I want my lawyer to sue him for slander, defaming my character, prejudicing my chance of a fair trial but the shyster just gives me a funny look and walks away. Bloody lawyer. What do you say to that?'

Tadeusz said Bolivia. But only in his head.

They'd eaten. A guard had brought chicken and vegetable stew. Perhaps-chicken and vegetable stew.

'Chicken from the old hen's home,' Miler said.

Tadeusz wondered what crime Miler was accused of. It seemed indelicate to ask but if there'd been three bomb scares . . .

Miler was using a tin lid as an ashtray. He dumped the

butts and ashes on the remains of his stew and lay back on his bunk with another cigarette.

'You know what I'd like?' Miler asked. 'Aside from being out of here? You know what?'

Tadeusz wished Miler would ask a question he had a chance of answering.

'I'd like to lie back and go to sleep and have a really good dream. You know the kind. You dream you open the door to your room and hey – there's this gorgeous blonde sitting up in your bed. She has the sheet drawn up to her chin but as you step forward she lets it drop as she holds out her arms and wow! You know what I mean? Melons. I wish I could order a dream, like, I want number twenty-seven tonight. Yes, sir, coming right up, sir, is that with or without the black lace? Last night I was here on my own and I thought I'd go out of my mind. So I said to myself: If I try hard, really concentrate on it, maybe I'll strike lucky, dream about Marilyn Monroe. You know, Marilyn and I romping in the sheets. Then I thought: Shit, what's the point, she'd be sixty-eight now.'

There was silence for a bit. To Miler, a vision of a younger Marilyn, skirt billowing above an airshaft. Tadeusz was struck by an image of Zuzanna, full length on the bed, lying on rumpled sheets, kicking one foot in the air, staring over her shoulder at him, her eyelids heavy from lovemaking. Oh Zuzia, Zuzia Zuzia Zuzia.

Five paces one way, four paces the other.

Tadeusz thought of prison and exercising round the yard and the pleasure of being released and being able to walk in a straight line.

'What are you doing?' Miler asked. 'Going for a walk with your father?'

Four paces, five paces.

'Or your mother. You never talk about her.'

Tadeusz stopped pacing. What should he say? It came to him in an instant. 'I never had a mother.'

'Everybody has a mother. It's a necessity.'

Tadeusz shifted his ground. 'Rather, I had a lot of mothers.'

'Ah-ha.' Miler, interested, faced him. 'Your father had a lot of mistresses?'

'He was an enterprising man even in the days when private enterprise was frowned on. The search, that was what was important. Somewhere in the world, he said, there was a woman who was destined to be the other half of his life. He kept searching.'

'That's a good line,' said Miler. 'Did it work? He had many opportunities?'

'He could never be a concert pianist so he learned to play the saxophone. He said it was the only thing he'd ever heard of that was invented in Belgium and he wanted to honour another small country in Europe. Also he said that Adolphe Sax lived to be eighty so possibly there were medical benefits to blowing into it.'

Miler was about to speak. There was such an obvious question to ask; but then he reflected there was no need, he knew the answer, Tadeusz always talked of his father in the past tense.

'For many years my father worked in the restaurant of the Monopol Hotel.'

'I've been there. One of my cousins got married and they had the wedding party there.'

'You must have seen my father. Medium sort of size, got a limp, played the tenor sax.'

Miler shook his head. 'I wasn't looking at the band. I had my eye on the bride's younger sister. Weddings make women feel randy and I was wondering if I could get in the saddle with her.'

'And did you?'

'I don't remember. There was this Soviet fizz-piss and Hungarian Bull's Blood and bottles of vodka in between. I don't think so. She's never looked at me as if we'd had a go.'

'Anyway, my father liked the Monopol. He said the restaurant reminded him of an old ocean liner. Perhaps you didn't notice that either. It has very high ceilings and huge mirrors and a chandelier and fat red pillars and long curtains draped across the windows to hide the Atlantic rollers. He used to play and couples would dance on the floor in front of the band. He used to look to see if some woman wasn't paying so much attention to her partner but was watching him. You see, he'd take a step forward for a solo and hold the saxophone in a special way, leaning over it, hugging it close to his body, fingers caressing the keys, and when he'd finished the solo he'd give the mouthpiece a little kiss and nod his head towards the woman. Sometimes at the end of the evening he'd find the woman lingering by the cloakroom. If not . . . well, he played six nights a week. Then he'd limp across the road and look at the opera house, at the posters outside, and think: It could be me playing here. But he consoled himself that playing a saxophone in the dance band at the Monopol led to more encounters by the cloakroom than playing a grand piano in the opera ever would.'

He remembered his mother. The other mothers, the ones who'd make a fuss of him at breakfast and call him 'my poor little darling', or the other ones who would put a hand to their mouths when he appeared and not know what to say, they all came later. His real mother, his necessity-mother as Miler thought of her, he did remember her. He remembered her vanishing, he remembered all the police.

CHAPTER FOUR

M others disappear.
Tadeusz's experience of mothers was not the common one, the rock to which the family clings. He thought of mothers as elusive, like mist, cloaking the world in mystery, embracing you; then in the sun's power, gone.

His father's mother, his own mother, Zuzanna who should have been the mother of his children, gone.

His father's mother had disappeared into a camp in Clausewitz Street. No longer wishing to commemorate an old Prussian warmonger, the city authorities had renamed it Hauke-Bosaka Street. Buildings were thrown up on the site of the old camp but like most buildings from the Ice Age of communism they were already crumbling. There was no hint of a camp, no roll call of names.

Tadeusz's memories of his mother were like fragments found by an archaeologist. Her hair was dark. Her breasts were squidgy under his hands. Her sigh was loud. She was tall standing over him. She smelled of perfume and Bulgarian vermouth when she bent to kiss him goodnight. His father was home most days while his mother went out to work. He liked the days when she came home and made a game of searching her handbag before giving him a slice of poppyseed cake wrapped in a paper napkin.

Sometimes he heard his parents arguing, his mother shouting, his father's voice rising in anger. Sometimes he heard them fighting in their bedroom, his mother's scream stifled, and even though he heard her giggle afterwards he was frightened. He stood inside their door, shivering in his pyjamas, until his father looked round: 'God, how long has the boy been watching?' His mother sighed: 'I expect he'll start young.' And little Tadek said: 'I want to make a puddle but it won't come.'

His mother disappeared when he was four.

A man came.

Little Tadeusz couldn't hear what he said but he heard the drone of his voice and his mother's responses. Papa had gone to play the saxophone at the Monopol so he was alone in the apartment with Mama and the man. Mama wasn't shouting or screaming or giggling and he wondered what they were doing in the kitchen. He wanted to look at the man. He could stand in the kitchen door and say he wanted to make a puddle and it wouldn't come, but then the strange man would know he was there.

His mother came into his bedroom.

'Darling.' She stroked his face. 'You should be asleep.'

'I see a dragon when I close my eyes.'

His mother paused. 'Well, that's lucky. Not many people see dragons. What colour was it?'

'Red. Dragons are red.'

He heard the man in the kitchen give a chuckle and he hated him. He didn't want the man to be listening.

'Good night, darling. I have to go out for a while but you'll be safe. Your mummy loves you very much and you are precious and . . .'

She had to stop. She kissed him, locked him in a long hug before turning away and leaving. He heard the man's voice and his mother's voice and then the click of the lock on the front door.

He closed his eyes and saw the red dragon. The dragon was going to come and get him and his mother wasn't here to protect him. He opened his eyes. He would go to sleep with his eyes open so the red dragon couldn't take him by surprise. He stared at the door which was open a crack to let in the light from the hall. Nothing could come in while he watched. He watched and he watched.

His father woke him. 'Tadek, where's Mummy?'

'I want Mama.'

'Where is she?'

The red dragon had taken her. He shouldn't have gone to sleep. He began to cry.

In the morning his father rang to say his mother wasn't well and wouldn't be going to work. Her job was at the telecommunications centre, in the restricted section. His father didn't go out all day except once, to buy more beer.

'Did your mummy call while I was out?'

Mama was with the red dragon.

His father took him to the neighbours in the evening and he was put to bed on the sofa with a stuffed rabbit to hug.

'I can't skip this evening,' his father explained to the neighbours. 'It's a special function. They've hired the restaurant for a gala dinner.'

'I saw something in the paper,' the man said. 'I didn't read it. Who are they?'

'The Forum of the Intellectual Workers for Peace.'

'Intellectual Workers? That's a bloody contradiction. Who's coming?'

'The usual.'

'Oh.'

'They say Picasso has been invited.'

'But has he accepted? It's easy to invite people.'

'I can't leave Tadek alone.'

'He'll be all right, bless him,' the woman said. 'And you haven't heard?'

They all looked at Tadeusz and then moved to the kitchen to talk and he couldn't hear. His father hugged him before he left to play the saxophone for the Intellectual Workers from Madagascar and India and the Congo and the People's Republic of Korea and Romania.

In the night Tadeusz found he wanted to make a puddle and it would come.

More men came.

'These comrades are policemen, Tadek. They are going to find Mummy.'

'She's gone with the red dragon,' Tadeusz said.

The policemen smiled and told him to run along to his room. They talked to his father for a long time and then the older one came into his bedroom and shut the door.

'Well, young lad, tell me about the evening before last and what your mummy said.'

'I want Papa.'

'In a minute. We don't want to trouble him just yet. You just talk to me and then your papa will come.'

So Tadeusz told the policeman about his mother kissing him and smelling of perfume and the man in the kitchen who laughed at the red dragon.

'One man?'

'Yes.'

'Did you hear him speak?'

'I could hear his voice and I could hear him laughing at me.'

'What did his voice sound like?'

'Like Papa's.'

'You mean a man's voice?'

'Yes.'

'Speaking Polish? Russian? Do you know?'

Tadeusz shook his head.

'You said she was wearing perfume?'

Tadeusz nodded.

'Does she always wear perfume?'

Tadeusz shook his head.

The policeman left the bedroom door open a crack and Tadeusz could hear what he said to his father, even if he couldn't understand it all.

'Bloody tough luck for you, that's what it sounds like. You never got a hint of the way things were going? She wasn't cold in bed? Nothing we can do if that's what it is. But you understand, comrade, with a job like hers, we have to report it.'

'These are more policemen about Mummy, Tadek.'

He didn't say they were going to find her. Why didn't he say that? Tadeusz looked at the policemen. They were not in uniform. Except their faces.

'Tell us what you heard,' one of them said.

'Be very careful not to leave anything out,' the other one said. 'We have ways of checking.'

Tadeusz knew just what to say because he had said it so often: to his father, to the neighbours, to the first lot of policemen, to himself.

'She's gone with the red dragon.'

'Tadek, that's –'

'Be quiet. Let the boy speak.'

This was still the time when you were supposed to address people as 'comrade' unless they were enemies of the state or parasites or foreigners. The police didn't call his father 'comrade'.

'A man came and talked to my mother in the kitchen and then she came to say good night to me and she was wearing perfume and she said I would be safe and then she left with the man.'

'You said earlier she went with the red dragon. Did the man speak to you?'

'He laughed at me.'

'Then he must have been talking to you.'

'He wasn't. He was in the kitchen.'

'You were in the kitchen and he was telling you what to say?'

The other policeman said, 'Or your father told you what to say.'

The neighbours looked after him for two months until his father came back. He limped more slowly than before and for some weeks he had trouble saying words containing 's'.

'You see, Tadek, I had an appointment with the secret police dentist and he took one of my teeth out.'

'Papa, when is Mama coming home?'

His father put one hand over Tadeusz's lips and with the other hand pointed at the telephone. He mouthed 'UB'. Later they went out. This was the time when his father Konrad began taking long walks.

'It's strange, Tadek, but sometimes the telephone works even when we're not using it. I think that is a great Polish invention. Out in the open only the birds can hear us. The birds sing but not when They put questions.'

'Where have you been, Papa?'

'I've been in a place where They could talk to me undisturbed. Gomulka is in power now and everything is meant to be better but I fear the Ubeks haven't heard.'

'Who are the Ubeks, Papa? Where do they live?'

'They are our very own secret police, Tadek. They live in telephones and behind trees and in walls and restaurants and factories and under stones.'

'I don't understand.'

'Nobody understands, Tadek. That's why They get so angry.' They went into a shop that sold ice cream. 'What flavour do you want? You can have vanilla or vanilla.'

'I want chocolate.'

'He wants the vanilla,' his father said.

They walked side by side to the River Odra, licking the ice cream when it threatened to drip on to their hands. Ducks were swimming on the water and Tadeusz wondered if there were Ubeks underneath with the fishes.

'Tadek . . .' He had to stop and give his attention to the ice-cream cone and his unruly feelings. 'Tadek, I don't think we're going to see Mummy again.'

'Why not?'

'It's difficult to explain. It's very difficult for me but I'll try to tell you. Mummy has gone away with that man you heard. That man had become a friend of Mummy's. He must be a very clever man because I never suspected and not even the Ubeks knew they were friends. At work Mummy had been using a special new radio and that man was very interested in how that radio worked. They say Mummy and the man took the night train to Dresden and then another train to Berlin. Then, They say, Mummy and the man took the S-bahn to west Berlin and then a plane flew them to America.'

'Can we go to America this afternoon?'

'They think that I helped her. I bloody helped my own wife to run away. They say I was part of a conspiracy with the imperialists and that was why I didn't report her missing at once. They think the Red Dragon is the man's name, his secret name. Sometimes They forget that story and try something else – that I've taught you that red is a bad colour. And the bugger of it is that this is going to stay in my file all my life. Probably in yours too.'

'Papa, I want to make a puddle.'

Tadeusz never saw his necessity-mother again, though after six months a postcard did arrive. Confusingly, it showed the Colosseum in Rome. The message read: *Long ago They used to throw Christians to the lions here. What has changed in the world? Tell Tadek I love him very much.* The card was unsigned but it was in his mother's handwriting and for a week his father looked ill and unhappy.

It took a little time but finally his father got his old job back, playing the saxophone at the Monopol. No more postcards arrived and there began to be temporary mothers.

When Tadeusz was older his father explained: 'In the eyes of the church I am married for life. Instead of having another wife I go to confession. God is happy, the Pope is happy, everybody is happy.'

Like mist, the mothers sometimes vanished with the sun. Others lasted longer, a few days, a week, two months once. An American tourist abandoned her group to stay for a long week-end. At school on Monday Tadeusz said his father had an American woman staying – black. His friend Jerzy was amazed. 'She's a Negro?' A Black person in Poland was wildly exotic. 'No, she's staying black,' Tadeusz explained, meaning illegally.

At school Russian was compulsory. At home Tadeusz studied English. He listened to jazz which was permitted because it was the music of oppressed Blacks. Hollywood films were shown provided the censors thought they portrayed the worst side of America: the depression, slavery, lynchings, poverty. Drunkenness could be shown, though this made America seem like home to many. Crime was inevitable in a capitalist society. Al Capone, gang wars on the street, drug dealing, corruption were rampant and shown in Technicolor. A certain section of Polish society frequented the cinema for its educational content.

Tadeusz took to studying his face in the mirror. Was that a shadow above his upper lip? 'When I'm grown up,' he told his face, 'I'm going to America to rescue my mother from Al Capone.'

Puberty kindled a fervent interest in the temporary mothers. Shielded by a hand, his eyes watched the movements under their blouses, followed them as they crossed the room, noted how their hips jutted out, how their buttocks shifted. He learned a phrase from one of his books and practised it with Jerzy: 'Your sister has a neat ass.' Jerzy looked up 'ass' in his English-Polish dictionary and punched Tadeusz for calling his sister a donkey.

It was just short of his sixteenth birthday, a Saturday afternoon when his father had gone to play at one of the inevitable wedding parties, when a mother who had been staying all week came into his room without knocking.

'What are you doing?'

'Reading. Learning English.'

'You're always studying. It'll stunt your growth. Hey, I've got an idea . . .'

She disappeared and returned with two blouses. 'I took both of these but I'm going to return one to the shop. Which do you think I should keep?'

She pulled the sweater she was wearing over her head and threw it on a chair. Her hair was in a mad disarray. Her breasts, whose movements had disturbed Tadeusz all week, thrust forward in her bra. She put on a blouse, cream with blue triangles.

'What do you think?'

Tadeusz swallowed. 'Well.'

'How about this one?'

She put on the second blouse which had an explosion of red poppies and had buttons to the neck, though she left the top three buttons undone.

'Which do you think is more sexy?'

She linked her hands behind her head and raised an eyebrow at Tadeusz. Her name was Alina and she said she was twenty-nine though a secret inspection of the identity card in her handbag showed she was thirty-four.

'I –'

She clapped her hands and her face lit up at another idea. 'I know. Since you can't seem to decide, we'll have a practical test.'

Alina put on the blouse with triangles again, pirouetted once and came over to Tadeusz. 'Well, let's see.' She reached down and laid her hand on his trousers. 'Mmm, not bad, could try harder.'

She switched to the blouse with the poppies and felt him again. 'My oh my, we certainly know the winner.'

She was standing next to Tadeusz, her breasts almost touching his nose. He could see down the gap of her blouse, the valley between her breasts, the delicate curves. The skin was milky white with a tracery of fine blue veins. The bra's frilly edge promised no resistance to hesitant fingers. She moved a shoulder to rest against him and the flesh quivered. She lifted her hand to stroke his cheek.

'Come on,' she said.

She helped him off with his clothes and put him on his narrow bed and lay on top of him. He had no idea it would be like this. He'd had endless talks with Jerzy and they agreed the woman's bones would stick into you, her hips and her ribs would make it impossible to get close. But Alina was soft against his body from shoulder to knee. She put her mouth against his, parted her lips and invited his tongue in. Pulling back, she studied his face.

'You've never done this before?' she said. 'But I think you'll do it again.'

He would rather spend a week in a closet with Alina then in a cellar with Sigrid.

'I love you,' he said. He knew a woman expected you to say that. He could think of nothing else to say so he said it again. 'I love you,' he said. 'Alina,' he added, just so she was certain.

'Well,' she said. Then she smiled. 'Certainly you'll remember Alina every time you see a photo of a fashion show.'

How could he trust Miler with his memories? Miler was a cabbagehead who imagined Marilyn could grow old.

CHAPTER FIVE

Footsteps swelled down the corridor, two pairs, and stopped outside the cell. The door was unlocked. The guard who'd brought the stew and an official with a clipboard came in. He consulted a sheet of paper.

'Lipski, Tadeusz.'

'Yes.'

The official looked at him. 'You'll be here for the night. The judges and jury have packed it in for the day.'

'What does that mean?'

'They are considering the evidence, they are studying the law and they are consulting their consciences under God's guidance.'

'I know all that,' Tadeusz said. 'But isn't it obvious?'

'Nothing is obvious to the legal mind.'

The official turned to go.

'What about me?'

A glance at his clipboard, a frown, and the official said, 'You are Miler, Al—'

'Yes, yes,' Miler interrupted. 'Why am I stuck here?'

'It's typed here: "Bail approval withdrawn."'

'Shit, what's my lawyer doing?'

The guard said, 'I'll bring you supper.'

'Bloody *zapiekanki* like last night?'

Zapiekanki was toasted cheese without the gourmet excitement.

'Do you want a beer?' the guard asked.

Miler seemed to have empty pockets and Tadeusz paid for them both. The beer was served in plastic beakers. A broken bottle made a potent weapon in the hands of someone who seemed on good terms with the bomb-planting class.

Miler held the plastic beaker upside down over his head and gazed up into it like a plaster saint towards heaven. Oh crap, Tadeusz conceded, not a saint.

'Is one beer better than none? It just gives you the idea of what you're missing.'

The great philosopher caught a final drop on his tongue. In a moment, Tadeusz knew, he's going to bring up Marilyn Monroe again, how looking at a photo of her sucking a lollipop gave him ideas.

'What I say is,' Miler said, 'it's no good stoking the furnace if there's nowhere for the heat to go. The same, you know, as . . .'

Mile's voice went on like a radio in the background. Tadeusz was stunned by a memory, an image that Miler's words had created.

Zuzanna was as lithe as a gymnast. In one flowing motion she swung her legs off the bed and came towards him, clothed in her own glory, nothing else. Four, five easy strides, tossing the hair out of her eyes. She stood at his shoulder, looking at the easel.

'Tadek, no, no. There is no heat in me, not how you've painted me. My nipples are electric, my thighs are burning, my skin is hot, I am a woman consumed by fire. On the canvas you make me look like the Report of the Party

Congress, faithfully done, full of statistics but no passion. Feel me, feel me here, that's what you must paint.'

His fiercest critic, wanting more in his work, more depth, more life, more passion; less of the outside world, less drabness, less of the Ice Age.

And later.

'Yes, Tadek, yes. The heat, the fire. Feel the flames licking your body.'

His fiercest lover.

'I said, "Were you in the army?"' Miler said.

The image went to dust.

Tadeusz looked at Miler who was now using the plastic beaker as an ashtray.

'I did my army service, yes.'

'What did you do?'

That was too boring. 'What I *wanted* to do,' Tadeusz said, 'was drive a tank. You remember that German a few years ago – I think his name was Rust – flew a small plane right across Russia and landed it in Red Square and Gorbachev got so mad he sacked his Defence Minister? Well, I had the idea years before, only it would be a tank. I'd climb into it and go, crash the border near Brest. "Don't worry, comrades, this is a fraternal Warsaw Pact tank, the kind that went to Prague in '68." I'd drive along the highway, never give a damn about the potholes, see Minsk and Smolensk, wave to the crowds, wave to the KGB. Need to refuel? No problem. Stop in at a service station and say, "Fill her up and send the bill to God." Who'd argue with a tank? I'd get to Moscow, drive into Red Square and stop the tank with its gun facing the Kremlin. I'd flip the lid and stand up with a loudhailer. "Okay, Brezhnev, come on out, the game's up. I've got a message from Party Secretary Gierek. He says, Give Poland its freedom, stop bluffing, he knows those eyebrows are false." Yep, that was my dream.

Action, patriotism, a place in history and film rights.'

There was silence. Miler was staring at him. He said, 'They never let you drive a tank, did they?'

'I was a stubble-kicker like everybody else. I carried a rifle that weighed as much as a sack of potatoes and couldn't shoot straight. At target practice I hit the bull's-eye next door.'

Miler believed it.

'Army service was a waste of my life. They never found out what I could do. If they'd found out that I'd studied the saxophone, they could have put me in a band. If they'd found out I painted, they could have had me doing May Day posters. If they'd found out I could act, they could have made me General Secretary of the Party. But nobody asked.'

'Well,' said Miler, determined to get a grip on their talk, 'I asked if you were in the army because I was. We're the same age, must have been doing our service at the same time.'

'I don't remember seeing you. Perhaps you saw me?'

'No, never. You see, they did find out something about me, I spoke German as well as Polish. So I was sent to Potsdam with this officer who was supposed to be liaising. By the way, that's a great career to be in, liaising, you have an easy life, get to see places, liaise with girls. Me, I had to shine his shoes and post his letters to his wife and change his sheets. In the evenings what I used to do was go to a beer cellar, pick up some fräulein with big German boobs, get her cross-eyed, take her round the back where they stack the empty barrels and give her a good time.'

'So that's what you did in your army service.'

'Yes. *No*, not all the time. I got Saturdays off so I'd take the train into Berlin and then I met some very interesting people. You could pick them out in their leather jackets and genuine Levis when all I'd ever seen were Polish jeans called Blue Moon. The Wall had been up six, seven years, and these big tour buses like greenhouses used to come in from West Berlin. You could see the faces at the window of the bus, all these Cold War tourists from Ohio and Nebraska, gaping at Checkpoint Charlie. The buses would cross over and they'd park somewhere so the tourists could look at the Brandenburg Gate and walk down Unter den Linden and then these boys in leather jackets and Levis would fall into step beside them. They'd speak out of the side of their mouths, see, like this: "Change dollars? Deutschmarks? Best price." I watched and thought: So why not Poland? Why not Wroclaw? After all, they make a good living, they can afford to buy Levis.'

'So that's what you did when you got out?'

'Did I say that?' Miler was suddenly suspicious. Perhaps they'd put an informer to share his cell. 'Maybe I did, maybe I didn't.'

He crushed out another cigarette. Tadeusz sometimes felt he was the only person in Poland who'd never taken up smoking. By now Miler's lungs must look like smoked herring.

Miler shook his head. 'But I'll tell you, when they freed the currency market here, made changing money anywhere legal, it made a lot of people on the street unemployed.'

Tadeusz saw a newspaper headline: DEMOCRACY BAD FOR BLACK MARKET TRADERS — LEVIS SHARES FALL.

Five paces one way, four paces the other.

What had Tadeusz got out of his time in the army? A short haircut and a hangover the day after he left. Whereas Miler had travelled abroad, even if it was only to East Germany, and started a career.

Four paces one way, five paces the other.

When he went home his father said to him, 'What are your plans? What are you going to do?'

'I've only just got out,' Tadeusz said. 'Let me grow my hair a little.'

'Did you practise the saxophone in the army?'

'They didn't appreciate it in the barracks.'

'Well, practise now. I'm not going to play at the Monopol for ever. I can get you in.'

So that would be things sewn up for life. He'd play *The Beer Barrel Polka* and *Alexander's Ragtime Band*, he'd watch the couples circle the dance floor in the restaurant that looked like an old Atlantic liner, he'd eye the ladies, he'd have temporary lovers. His father, his father's friends, the neighbours, people he scarcely knew would say, 'When are you going to settle down?' They meant, 'When are you going to get married?' He'd be introduced to some Teresa or Izabela, a country cousin on a visit. He'd hardly catch his breath before he found himself in the Saturday afternoon queue at the cathedral for the nuptials. They'd have the wedding party at the Monopol and his father could play. Teresa (or Izabela) would be waiting at home for him every night. The Pope would be watching how they behaved so a baby would come before the year was out. Then two. Four. Lech Walesa had seven – when did he find time to be President?

'I want to do something different with my life,' he told his father.

'What? Is this the younger generation rebelling against the older?'

'What have I got to rebel against except everything?'

'Then what are your plans?'

'I have no plans. I'm rebelling against five-year plans, that's what.'

Five paces one way, four paces the other, walking through mirrors.

He turned and was face to face with Miler.

'What are you doing?' Miler asked.

Tadeusz had a close look at the grin on Miler's face. He pictured Miler practising the grin in the mirror, thinking it was honest but fun. It was dishonest and stupid.

'I'm walking,' Tadeusz said.

'We'll exercise together. I'll walk behind you.'

'This is different,' Tadeusz said, and put himself on the bunk. Movement brought the memories. He was walking through the past, down a long line of mirrors, the faces he saw were his own but younger. He'd see different expressions: eager, optimistic, puzzled, frightened, amazed, angry, frustrated. Is it possible to be all these things at once? During the Ice Age it wasn't just possible, it was necessary.

'When you got out of the army,' Miler asked, 'what did you do?'

'I went to Warsaw. Everybody has to go to the big city when they're young.'

'What did you do?'

'Nothing.'

'You can't have done nothing.'

'All right, I lived. I stayed at the flat of an army friend. I pushed a wheelbarrow on a building site. Then I came back here.'

'Why?'

'Stalin drove me out.'

'Stalin was in his grave the year you were born.'

'You know how the Pharoahs built pyramids? Stalin built the Palace of Culture. His body was in Moscow but his spirit soared above Warsaw. Everywhere I went I saw it. I'm having a piss in the morning, I look out of the bathroom window and Uncle Joe is watching. I'm kissing a girl and

Stalin is over her shoulder, glowering like some heavy father. So one day I went to the Palace of Culture and kicked it.'

'What for?'

'Two cops saw me and came over and said, "What are you doing?" "I'm kicking Stalin's Palace of Culture." Like you they couldn't understand why. I said, "Hasn't every Pole always wanted to? Don't you want to?" They looked round and no one was watching, so they set to. There we were, three of us kicking Stalin's Palace of Culture. Then we shook hands and I went and packed my bag and got out from under Stalin's shadow.'

Enough.

Tadeusz stretched full length, facing away from Miler. Enough of talking to Miler. How could anyone embrace life with so little imagination? Unless – now here was a possibility – unless he was something else. A spy. Say he had in reality been an East German sent to report on a Polish officer seconded to Potsdam, a classic piece of fraternal spying from the days when no one was trusted. The Cold War was so deep frozen that people died of double paranoia.

Tadeusz eased himself over to watch Miler who was now doing some purposeful walking. Five steps one way, four steps the other. He didn't swing his arms, he wasn't a soldier. His hands were clasped behind his back and his face was set in concentration. Exercising like this required intellectual effort.

No, no spy.

Once more, enough. Enough of Miler.

After Warsaw, Wroclaw. That was the beginning of the rest of his life. It all started then and didn't stop until he ended up in this cell. And still it hadn't stopped.

CHAPTER SIX

It was the summer of 1976. All Europe was hot, even Poland, even Wroclaw, especially the room Tadek had taken. It was at the top of the building, open to the sky at the end of the war, reroofed but not modernized. He froze in winter, he baked in summer. I am an artist, he told himself, it is necessary to freeze and to bake. This is my Montmartre and Toulouse-Lautrec is walking on his knees to the corner café. I am an undiscovered genius in a garret.

He had a problem being an undiscovered genius: he wasn't certain which way his genius was pointing. He'd had two years of art school and left it, feeling discipline was the enemy of genius. He'd had a year on his own trying to decide: Was he a painter? Did he have a distinctive vision? Was he a musician? Jazz for its free expression? Was he a composer? Was melody the refuge of the insincere? Was he an actor? A sculptor? A writer? Sometimes he was awed by the possibilities his talents suggested. The blank paper, the blank canvas, he told himself, were the expression of total honesty because they were from a time before the compromise of ink or paint. Sometimes at night he'd turn off the light and when his eyes had grown used to the dark he could see the blank canvas, the blank page. Finally they no longer seemed a challenge waiting for his creative inspiration, they *were* his creation. One morning he put a gilt frame round a blank canvas and pinned on it a title card: Pure Perfection.

He took the picture to one of the little galleries that at that time were to be found in Odrzanska Street. The owner, a lesbian in a trouser suit and a long cigarette holder, inspected the picture. She eyed him to decide whether he was a hoaxer. 'You haven't signed it.' He borrowed a felt-tip pen and wrote Tadek in one corner. 'No surname?'

'If a genius like Van Gogh could sign his canvases Vincent, I can sign mine Tadek.'

She took a long pull on her cigarette holder, blew out a lot of smoke and said, 'Now listen to me, Tadek, pay close attention to what I say. You are a Satirist. You are a founder member of the Wroclaw Satirist Movement. I'll put the canvas in the window. The West Germans are starting to come again after the oil shock – they'll buy anything they are told is the latest trend.'

A lawyer from Kiel bought it to give a little intrigue to the reception area of his office. He paid five hundred Deutschmarks, telling the gallery owner it was a pleasure to do business in a cheap country like Poland. The gallery owner gave Tadeusz half.

'I'm a Satirist,' Tadeusz whispered into his beer.

He bought a beret. 'I'm satirising Montmartre,' he told his reflection in the mirror.

He had a roofscape for a view. Across the street a pretty girl with funny reddish hair had a room but she was uncooperative about undressing and closed the curtains. Tadeusz had smiled at her and she had scowled. He had blown her a kiss and she closed the curtains with a snap. This warm evening, 24 June, she had the curtains and the window open in hope of a breeze. Tadeusz could hear her radio and then her scream. She was leaning out of the window and when she saw Tadeusz she yelled, 'The bastards want us to starve.' She disappeared before he could ask her to explain.

There were voices down in the street, people coming out of doors, standing in little groups. When Tadeusz went out to find out what was going on he met the girl with the funny reddish hair.

'What's happened?'

'They're going to starve us to death,' she said.

'Who are?'

'Those bastards.' Her cheeks were flushed but it was an entirely different red from her hair. 'In Warsaw. The government. Gierek. The Party. All those bastards.'

It wasn't an evening to be guarded. Who cared who was listening? Tadeusz heard it in bits and pieces from people in the street. The Prime Minister had given a talk on the radio. Prices were leaping up.

'Seventy per cent for meat. So we have to give up meat and eat more bread. But they've thought of that. Bread is going up too.'

'What's your name?'

'Ewa,' she said.

'Ewa, why don't we go and have a drink before they put that up.'

'What do you do?' Ewa asked.

'I'm part of the Satirical Movement.'

'I've never heard of it.'

'You will.'

'Who else is part of it?'

'We've had no publicity yet. Soon.' Tadeusz ran a hand through his hair and put his beret back on.

'What do you do, being a Satirist?'

'I paint. I play music. I compose. I write. I sculpt. I act. But I don't dance.'

'I like dancing.'

'The kind of dancing I don't do is different from the kind of dancing you do do.'

'Are you being satirical now?'

'That is what I do.'

'Well, even if you don't dance, you do a lot of other things.'

'I'm a Multi-Discipline Artist.'

'Oh.'

'Yes.' Tadeusz drank some more beer.

There were raised voices in the bar. This was anger that had been rehearsed again and again: during the Stalinist Ice Age in the early '50s, the uprising in Poznan in 1956, the protests and violence in 1968, the agony when Czechoslovakia was invaded, the price rises and violence in 1970. There would be strikes and demonstrations and protest marches – what other way was there? It would be met with violence – what other way did They know?

'Your hair is amazing,' Tadeusz said.

'Does that mean you like it?'

'Where did you get it?'

'What do you mean? It's mine. I work on the cosmetics counter at Centrum and sometimes bottles come my way. If you know what I mean.'

'It's unbelievable.'

'No, it's Texas Red, one of the new range of shades.'

Her hair was a reddy-brown but at the ends the colour faded to a sort of pink. It frizzed round her skull and put Tadeusz in mind of cartoons of someone getting an electric shock.

'I'm getting an idea,' Tadeusz said. 'It's to strike a blow against those price rises. I want to paint you.'

'Where are we going?' Ewa asked.

'Across the stream, then towards the trees.'

'Why do we have to go so far?'

'So I can paint in peace.'

'I'm hot.'

Tadeusz began to feel that asking her had been a mistake. She had a whine to her voice. It meant: Go on, surprise me, be the first man in my life who isn't a big disappointment. He remembered her scowl as she drew her curtains.

'You'll soon cool off, Tex.' Get hot, cool down. Life and love, all in a phrase.

'Why do you call me "Tex"?'

He stopped and when she was by his side he patted her head. 'The amazing hair. And you wouldn't like it if I called you "Red".'

'Tex . . .' She tried it out and shrugged.

There were stepping stones across the stream. He'd been here before and knew there would be stepping stones. He'd brought other girls, she decided. She didn't say anything. She could bring it up later if she wanted to accuse him of anything.

Across the stream Tadeusz said, 'One moment.' He took two bottles of Piast beer from his backpack and left them in the stream.

Their car, a borrowed Polski Fiat, had been parked in the shade of a tree. The road, and any traffic, was now out of sight. The trees and rocks were dramatic, the stream made a pretty tinkle, the sky was as perfect as the first day of creation. This was certainly the place to bring girls, if that is what he did.

'Okay, Tex, this is it.'

He carried a stretched canvas and a sketchpad in one hand, a collapsible easel wrapped in a rug in the other. He set up the easel and canvas and handed her the rug.

'This is for you. I'm going to paint you naked.'

'Now just one minute,' Ewa said, 'I don't know you. That kind of thing might work with the other girls you've brought here, but I'm not falling for any cheap tricks.'

'Not you, me. I am the one who's going to be naked.'

'You? I suppose that's being satirical, is it?'

'They think They own us body and soul and can run our lives just the way They want. Out here I am free to do what I want. You needn't look.'

At first she didn't look. She'd thought of going straight back to the car but if he didn't follow she'd have to wait and anyway Tadeusz had explained he only wanted to paint her head so that was all right. She lay on the rug but he said he needed to have her head upright so she had to sit. Her face was half turned away so she didn't have to look at him. After a while she had a little peep. Well, he wasn't entirely naked. He wore his beret.

'Is it satirical, wearing the beret?'

'I don't want sunstroke.'

'It's hot, isn't it?'

He didn't reply. He was standing behind the canvas, which hid quite a bit of him actually. Then he took a step to one side as if he wanted to see her more clearly and she saw him more clearly. Oh.

'It really is hot,' she said.

Being painted was boring. She'd imagined it would be glamorous, being the centre of attention, or at least her hair would be. It turned out she wasn't the star, Tadeusz was. He grimaced, frowned, sighed, swore, flung down his brush, scratched himself without any delicate feeling for her presence.

'Do you think it's getting hotter?' she asked.

In his creative intensity he didn't hear her. She considered taking her blouse off. He'd notice that. She would still be wearing her bra. Would she have to tell the priest at confession? Oh dear, was she going to have to tell the priest she'd had the thought even if she didn't do it? Being with Tadeusz complicated life.

Tadeusz announced a lunch break and fetched the beer.

'Can I see what you've done?'

'Not until it's finished.'

They sat on the rug and ate salami and gherkin sandwiches. Tadeusz hadn't thought of glasses so she drank from the bottle. They do that in Texas, she told herself.

'Suppose someone comes,' she said.

'Who?'

'Someone. You know, anyone. You're on the rug naked and I'm fully clothed. They'll think that, well, not right.'

'Take your clothes off too. They'll know what to think then.'

'Tadeusz, we are not married. We're not even engaged. I'd have to go to confession again, and I've only just been.'

'Anything interesting to confess?'

'That's not the point about confession. Take it back.'

'You know what this reminds me of?' he said. '*Déjeuner sur l'Herbe*, only in reverse. I like that concept very much.'

Ewa didn't know about concepts but she felt hotter than ever. She undid another button of her blouse. She leaned back on the rug and fanned her face. 'What's going to happen now?'

'Back to work.'

About five o'clock, the heat leaving the sun, Tadeusz announced he was finished and she could come and look. She shrieked.

'You've painted me naked. I might just as well have taken

my clothes off. Everyone will think I did.'

'It's only your head, Tex. It's not your body. I did that from memory.'

'I can tell it's not me. My breasts aren't as big. Who was she? Don't say your mother.'

'No, my mother's in America, I think. From my imagination.'

'Well, I think your imagination has a lot to answer for. And that's Gierek.'

'I used a photo from the newspaper. I painted him last night.'

'A nude photo of Gierek?'

'It's his face. For the body I stood in front of the mirror.'

'Yes,' she said, 'I can tell.'

He stood back to consider the painting. It showed a nude Gierek, General Secretary of the Party, handing a red apple to a nude Ewa. A green and yellow snake coiled round the branches of a tree. A speech bubble came out of Gierek's mouth:

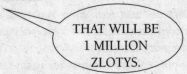

THAT WILL BE 1 MILLION ZLOTYS.

Ewa's hair stood out from her head, reddish-brown but with pink ends as if it sizzled with electricity.

'I'd thought of calling it Garden of Evil, but a better title is Price Shock. You can see why I needed to paint your hair.'

'You've painted the snake covering its eyes with a hand. Snakes don't have hands.'

It was the second day after the price rises were announced. At Gdansk the shipyard workers besieged the managers in their office. In Radom the Party building was stormed and the secret police took swift retribution. In Warsaw the workers in the Ursus tractor factory tore up the rail tracks that passed through their grounds. No trains could run to Moscow, and they smiled at this and blockaded the line for good measure.

In Wroclaw workers walked out at the Pafawag railway coach factory, from construction sites and printing works. Leaflets were printed demanding the withdrawal of the price rises. This was during the time before Solidarity was formed but badges saying CCR were to be seen.

'What's that stand for?' Tadeusz asked.

'Creeping Counter-Revolutionary,' he was told.

He wore a CCR badge pinned to his beret.

He collected two friends, Zbigniew Bacewicz and Zdzislaw Kucharski. Carrying the painting wrapped in newspaper they walked through streets that were new to them. There was little traffic, fewer people than usual, far fewer people. Walking up Swidnicka they paused as a car did a U-turn and came back past them. It slowed and four faces were turned in their direction. The four men, even the driver, were eating ice-cream cones. These were the worst, the ones who weren't in uniform. The car drew away ahead of them. Tadeusz found his sense of hearing was altered. His head seemed to ring with the kind of silence that comes after a scream.

They crossed Rynek, the old market, and saw how everything was altered today. This corner, at the back of the City Hall, was where the amateur painters propped up their pictures for sale. At least rumour had it they were for sale though Tadeusz had never seen money change hands. The paintings were of bowls of pears, houses in the snow, a crucifixion, a vase of dahlias. Today there was no one.

'Where is everybody?' Zdzislaw asked.

They're at home under the bedclothes, Tadeusz thought. They're actually under the bed. They're out in the country, on the other side of the stream, painting in the nude.

'Should we just have a look around first?' Zbigniew asked.

Like spies checking the safety of a rendezvous, they did the circuit of Rynek. There was one stall doing no business in the flower market. Two uniformed city police turned their heads as they walked past. A café had people huddled over inside tables as if sitting outdoors was too exposed. A mother grabbed a howling child by the wrist to drag him along. There should have been dozens, hundreds of people about. Pigeons took off with claps like gunshots and the police were very quick to look. Distant shouts came from the direction of the university. A car's engine could be heard racing.

They finished the circuit of the square and stood close to the railings that fronted the Gothic building. The clock above their heads read 10.40.

'If there's nobody around,' Zbigniew said, 'what's the point of showing the painting?'

'Let's wait until eleven,' Zdzislaw said.

'And then?' Tadeusz wanted to know.

'We'll see.'

Tadeusz was wondering about the spirit of his friends. They weren't even Creeping Counter-Revolutionaries. They were Absolutely Stock Still Counter-Revolutionaries. But then, before there could be any more talk about it, the counter-revolution began. At first it was a distant noise. No, at first it was no noise at all. Then Tadeusz became aware that a sound had been fading in; he noticed it, turned his head in that direction. People had come down from their concrete towers, the socialist realist blocks of flats for a sleeping proletariat, and crossed the Grunwald

Bridge. The sound swelled but the slogans they chanted were still indistinct. Then a hymn caught hold and grew louder until the procession appeared down Wita Stwosza and turned into Rynek, going clockwise round the square, carrying banners with crude letters: DOWN WITH PRICES and IF WE CAN'T EAT, WE CAN'T WORK and THE PEOPLE CAN'T PAY. From the north side of Rynek appeared students from the university, a phalanx, a bodyguard of youth surrounding grey-haired men in professors' gowns. As the crowd surged past, Tadeusz ripped the newspaper from his painting, held it above his head for people to see and joined the march. Zbigniew and Zdzislaw were caught up in the crowd as it swarmed into the square and halted in front of the City Hall.

'Down with prices! Down with prices! Down with prices!'

Tadeusz joined the chanting. He was in the very front with the painting over his head, twisting it to one side, then to the other so that everybody could see. He turned to check if Zbigniew and Zdzislaw were close, a grin beginning to force its way on to his face. This was life, painting with inspiration, a Satirist, a girl who'd smiled before she closed the curtain last night, at one with the people of Wroclaw, shouting defiance at a hated government. The faces in the crowd showed none of his exhilaration. It struck him, it was a revelation, that the price rises weren't an excuse for shouting and slogans and satirical pinpricks; they were a matter of substance, of real pain and hardship. The faces were rocks of contempt and determination and sheer simple outrage. How dare the communists deal another blow to the people they were supposed to be leading to the promised land?

Tadeusz lowered his canvas and held it to his chest.

The chants and shouts died away, and only after the

tumult had stopped did he seem to hear the gunshot that had brought it about. Heads were raised and on roofs round the square, silhouetted against a midsummer sky of cornflower blue, were the figures of men in uniform – ZOMO as it turned out – holding rifles.

A shot had been fired in the air, not as a warning, but as a signal as personnel carriers approached from side streets and riot police jumped down and came at the crowd at a run. They wore steel helmets, carried riot shields and swung long truncheons with eagerness at the soft targets so generously provided. There were screams of pain from women and men, screams of fear, screams of hatred, abuse and fury. But all the time the screams were punctuated by the drumbeats of truncheons cracking bones, thudding on shoulders, heads and arms. People were scrambling to escape the square, stumbling on bodies knocked to the ground, slipping on cobbles glistening with blood.

A truncheon jabbed Tadeusz in the stomach. Doubled over with pain, he was set just right for a swinging blow to the head that should have concussed him. His beret soft-ened the impact but went flying. He sunk to his knees and found himself being dragged away by one of the ZOMO and shoved into a van already stuffed with other prisoners.

'Try to escape and you'll be shot.'

'Strip,' the ZOMO shouted.

Tadeusz didn't know where they'd been taken. It cer-tainly wasn't the police headquarters next to the courts of justice. That housed the national police and the secret police. It was a facility somewhere outside the city, possibly the barracks of the ZOMO riot police.

'Strip, I said.'

'There are women present,' a prisoner protested.

These were cells like cages filled with prisoners, a dozen

or more in this cell and Tadeusz didn't know how many cells there were in this block, how many blocks there were.

'Everybody must strip, women as well as men.'

There were angry shouts at this and the ZOMO reached through the bars, grabbed an arm and pulled a man close. The ZOMO cracked his truncheon down on the head of the prisoner until he was crying out for him to stop in the name of God.

'Take your clothes off, all your clothes. You are enemies of the state, vermin. Vermin don't wear clothes.'

'You have no right to hold us,' another man shouted. 'We were demonstrating peacefully. The violence is all from you. The constitution guarantees—'

He didn't finish. Two ZOMO unlocked the barred gate to the cell, snatched the man and dragged him into the corridor. They beat him with truncheons until he lay unconscious on the concrete floor. They pushed him back in the cell.

'If he can't take his clothes off, you do it. If any of you are wearing clothes in five minutes time you will all be punished.'

Of all that happened that day, this was the worst. It wasn't that they felt shame at being naked. It was intended as humiliation, but it wasn't that either. What was terrible was the unspoken thought in everybody's mind, of Oswiecim which the Germans had called Auschwitz, of Treblinka, of Gross-Rosen so close to Wroclaw, of trainloads of prisoners arriving and being told to strip naked for the showers. The shadow of the past was very dark.

It was night. Tadeusz wasn't certain what time because the ZOMO had come back and shouted at them, 'I said take everything off. That includes your watches.' Then all their belongings had been loaded into large laundry baskets and wheeled away. 'You can sort it out later,' the ZOMO said, 'find your own things or take someone else's.'

They'd been given no food or drink. There was a bucket in a corner to urinate into. There were three women in the cell and when one wanted to go the other two stood in front of her as a shield. But the men took pride in their situation and wouldn't have looked anyway. They sang the hymn *God who does defend Poland* and sang the last line 'Lord, return our homeland to us free' which was how it was always sung in the exiles' churches in the West. The ZOMO, furious, beat on the bars with their truncheons.

Why were they kept so long? Perhaps nobody in authority had said what was to be done. As best Tadeusz could tell it was the middle of the night, before the early midsummer dawn, when all the cells were unlocked and the prisoners herded down corridors where men with drawn pistols ordered them to hurry. Outside the stars hung ripe in the sky but there was no moon. They processed in a long line – how many? A hundred and fifty? Two hundred? There was no telling. The line disappeared through the open double doors of a building like an aircraft hangar. There the yells and screams began. The prisoners looked at each other, fear of the unknown widening their eyes.

'Keep moving, keep moving.'

At the far end of the building figures emerged into starlight, running, stumbling, crying, cursing. Just before Tadeusz reached the double doors there was a hold-up as a woman tried to break away. She was caught, beaten with batons as she was hauled back into line. They edged forward until Tadeusz saw what was ahead. There was a double line of ZOMO, perhaps thirty in all, and the prisoners had to run, walk or crawl between them while the ZOMO flailed at them with their truncheons.

'Go, go, go,' a ZOMO was yelling. 'This is the Path to

Good Health. Beat the anti-state shit out of you.'

He sounded drunk. Most of the ZOMO were drunk, laughing drunk, eager drunk, lashing out drunk, but also slowed drunk, sometimes missing as a prisoner hustled past. The men ran with one arm covering their heads, one hand protecting their genitals. The women nearly all covered their breasts with a forearm because if they didn't that was the soft swaying flesh that attracted vicious blows.

'God may forgive them,' a man growled in Tadeusz's ear, 'I never shall.'

A hand gripped Tadeusz's arm and he was hauled out of line. Did they think he was the one who'd spoken defiance?

'You're to come this way,' a man in a dowdy suit said. 'For you special treatment.'

First impressions as Tadeusz was pushed into the office: a man in a dark blue suit with his tie off, a slew of folders on the desk, an angle-lamp shining on to some paper he was reading. Then Tadeusz's eyes jumped to the canvas leaning against the wall. It was the back that he saw but he recognized the size and shape of it.

The man looked up. 'You are . . .?'

'Lipski, Tadeusz.'

Everyone's name had been written down on arrival and here was the result: a pile of folders that had slumped under its own bulk. The man searched and picked one out. He opened and read a moment before looking up. 'Son of Konrad.'

Tadeusz said nothing. It hadn't been a question.

'You speak when you're spoken to. Konrad Lipski is your father?'

'Yes.'

'Until now there has been no separate file on Tadeusz Lipski. We shall have to start one. It has an impressive opening. Mother: a spy for America, defected with state secrets, adopted new identity, untraceable. Father: abetted her escape by concealing it for forty-eight hours. Denied the offence even after rigorous interrogation. Tadeusz: anti-state activities including . . .'

He gestured at the canvas.

'I was on the roof of the post office. We knew there was trouble coming, you see. We watched you arrive with two associates, saw you go round the square, saw you wait for the crowd to arrive. We had these twenty-X binoculars, army field glasses, so when you held up that painting I was interested. We all had a good look at your face too. You've stepped into shit, boy, and wherever you go you'll leave a smell we'll know.'

His eyes inspected Tadeusz. What he saw was a male of twenty-three whom he'd called 'boy', though less of a boy than yesterday. Slim, dark hair, quick brown eyes veined red by lack of sleep, pale skin with purplish patches of bruising, uncircumcized, and a face as naked as his body showing plain terror at his situation.

And Tadeusz? What did he see? His Nemesis, though we never realize that on first acquaintance. Or if Nemesis is over-dramatic, then certainly the scourge of his life in the future. The person behind the desk was in his late thirties, hair prematurely receding to leave a lake of skin on top that reflected the desk lamp, protruding lips that made him look sensual, eyes . . . eyes . . . Here Tadeusz faltered. He could never paint such eyes. They saw him, saw inside him, saw his past, saw his future.

Those eyes now travelled down Tadeusz's naked body to his knees, and up again to his genitals, a penis tiny, shrunken by fear. The eyes fixed on his penis, judged it, speculated on its history until now.

'Are you a virgin?'

'No.'

'I thought not. Have you known many women?'

'No.'

'You don't know what I mean by "many", but I suspect you have not been successful. You're a boy, not a man. I recognized Gierek' – he gestured with his head at the painting – 'but the girl is new to me. Tell me about her.'

'No . . . That is to say, she's no one. An imaginary person.'

'You lie.'

'I—'

'To lie is to want to protect her. Posing for you makes her as guilty of anti-state activity as the artist. What is her name?'

'No, no one.'

'You'll tell me. It's my job to find out, you could say my speciality.' His eyes fixed on Tadeusz's face. 'You've not known many women but you've painted a body that is normal in every respect. Men in prison who have not known women for many years paint from their dreams, a riot of curves and provocative poses and body hair. You didn't. And then there is the head, her hair, so particular.'

Tadeusz swallowed. He saw the hair, not in this room but in the sunlight. He must not think of her. Tex. No, not even that. Her real name, his name for her, her Texas Red dyed hair, nothing existed.

'Walk,' the man said.

'Where to?' Tadeusz asked.

'Over there and back.'

Tadeusz went four paces to the wall and four paces back. When he got back the man was standing close in front of him.

'According to the file your father limps. Nothing to do with us. But we could make you limp. Is that what you want – to limp like your father?'

Tadeusz made no answer. That was not allowed and the man shouted in his face, 'Is that what you want – to limp like your father?'

'Of course not. I—'

A hand slapping his head to one side finished Tadeusz's sentence.

'There is no "of course" in here. There is just you and me. Do you understand?'

'Yes.'

'What is your work?'

'I'm an artist.'

'People buy stuff like that? Do you make money?'

'A little.'

'Then how do you get money to eat?'

'There's a shop in the market I work some days.'

'What sort of shop?'

'It sells records and cassettes.'

'So, a place young people come. Does she work in the shop?'

'I imagined her.'

'Is she a customer? Did you get to know her that way? Maybe a cousin? A girlfriend – that's worth protecting? You wouldn't want all the world to know that was her body. An ex-girlfriend?'

Tadeusz shook his head to each question, kept shaking and shaking his head that ached from the truncheon blow, while the man shouted in his face.

'Tell me, tell me. I think a girlfriend. Perhaps a sister-in-law? A waitress you met? A neighbour?'

'No, she's not.'

The man stopped and considered. That denial was blurted out.

'A neighbour. Quite possibly a neighbour.'

Tadeusz said, 'No.'

'I'm not ZOMO, you know. My job isn't to crack skulls, just to crack people's defences. I'm SB.'

He let that sink in. People still thought of the secret police by their former initials UB. Ubeks had no friends except other Ubeks. Ubeks kept no laws except the ones they made. Ubeks answered to no one for what they did.

There was a knock at the door which the man ignored.

'Not far from here,' he said, 'near Katowice there is an Academy where SB recruits are trained. I could continue interrogating you or I could send you there. The recruits need someone to practise on. At first all recruits are too eager. They get results but at a cost. Even fatal. "Excesses of legality" it's called, like in the Stalinist time. Places like that still exist, Lipski, in Poland.'

The knocking came again.

'So what is your neighbour's name? Well, I can send someone to look, knocking on doors, asking around, then have her brought in.'

The door opened and a uniformed man stood there.

'Excuse me, Captain Baran. Excuse me for butting in, sir, only they said—'

'I didn't tell you to enter.'

'Excuse please, sir, but we've just had a message from Warsaw. They said: Tell Captain Baran at once. Apparently they are going to announce the cancellation of the price rises some time today. Sorry to interrupt, sir.'

The man, a ZOMO messenger, stood at attention. He'd delivered the news but didn't know what else was expected of him. He looked at Tadeusz, looked at his genitals, then back at Baran. Baran had gone very still, not even breathing for a few seconds. Then he took a deep draught of air and colour darkened his cheeks.

'Get out,' Baran ordered, 'get out, go.'

Baran went round the desk and sat down. Tadeusz stood,

stiff, aching, and still petrified. He had no idea what his fate would be at the hands of a man who was more powerful, more experienced, more astute, and more cunning. What Tadeusz didn't realize was that he was privileged, as few were, to see one of the secret police deflated. It would only be temporary, and doubtless Baran was exhausted at the end of a long night, but for now the steam had gone out of him. He said nothing at first. The eyes that had looked in and through Tadeusz gazed at the wall as if they could penetrate it and see as far as Warsaw where the untrustworthy politicians had shifted their ground. Abruptly his arm made a clean sweep of the files on his desk. 'Damn, damn, damn, damn. They've got no balls. Rabble march on the square and are sent running – and the politicians go and show weakness. What were the rabble armed with? A few banners. And you with a painting.'

Then his eyes came back, settled on Tadeusz, and he seemed to regret letting his authority slip.

'You better get out too,' he said to Tadeusz.

Tadeusz stood a moment too long.

'What are you waiting for? Do you expect me to kiss you goodbye? Shoot you?'

We've won, Tadeusz told himself. He finally took in the message that had been brought. We've won. A uniformed man prodded him on the way to the cell block but Tadeusz paid him no attention. We've won. The cells were empty, the people released. We've won. He found his shirt and shoes with his socks tucked inside but his jeans had gone. No matter, we've won.

They hadn't won, of course. Just a tactical withdrawal.

Two ZOMO agents dropped him outside the railway station. 'You can walk from here. We're not a bloody limo service.'

'Without trousers?'

But they drove away.

It was seven in the morning and people were going to work. Tadeusz stood in his socks and shoes, with his shirt tails hanging front and back, and debated what to do.

I'm a Satirist, he told himself. Since leaving Baran his self-confidence was returning. This is how you satirise the lack of goods in a communist economy. He strode boldly away from the station and at the corner had to wait at a red traffic light. To the men who were staring, the girls who giggled behind their hands, he said, 'This is the latest fashion. It is the ZOMO air-conditioned style.'

Nobody stopped him, nobody screamed, nobody arrested him. He reached his room without trouble and lay down on the bed. In his overheated brain images flashed of a crowd marching, of truncheons flailing, of a line of naked bodies, of eyes he could never paint taking the measure of his own nakedness.

Baran, he said to himself. Baran Baran Baran.

Later he would go to see Tex, tell her how he protected her identity. Baran had thought he'd painted her naked body and he was wrong.

Baran Baran Baran.

CHAPTER SEVEN

'Where do you suppose the holding cells are for women?' Miler asked.

His voice was faint. It came from a long way off – the present – and Tadeusz had to drag himself out of the past to listen again to Miler's words inside his head.

'You see, I was wondering if we could get the turnkeys to arrange a swop. Better than being two of a kind in the same bloody cell all night.' When Tadeusz didn't respond with enthusiasm, Miler looked round. 'Unless . . . Oh-oh, you're not the other way inclined, are you, friend?'

In Tadeusz's experience people who laid casual claim to be friends seldom were. He thought of telling Miler about the time he'd been locked up with a dozen other men and women, all naked. Miler would ask: An orgy? That had been a party thrown by the ZOMO, all the booze drunk by them, all the sadism and flagellation laid on by them.

'Shy to admit it? Got to watch my back door all night? Eh, chum?'

'I'm an artist,' Tadeusz began.

'Is that another word for it?'

'I paint, I play music, I compose, I act, I write. Remember I told you?'

'Sort of. You said a lot of stuff.'

Stuff, Miler called it. The stuff of someone's life.

'I've been thinking about a girl I knew way back, let's see, eighteen years ago, just when I was starting to get involved in everything that led right up to here . . .' Tadeusz took a moment to swing his thoughts back to what he'd been going to say. 'Her name was Ewa but I called her Tex. I painted her.'

'Yes? In the nude?'

'I didn't dare suggest it. I was young, a boy, pretending sophistication and cynicism and cleverness and world-weariness. I wasn't a virgin but I was still in awe of actual warm female flesh. But I wanted her. I wanted to lure her into a passionate situation. So I hit on an ingenious scheme. I painted her head, her face and particularly her hair which was very striking. Bizarre, in fact. She said the colour was Texas Red, which was why I called her Tex. But the actual body I painted, it was a sort of composite of the two – or three if you count the whore I was given as a birthday treat in the army – that I'd known plus photos and paintings and imagination.'

'You mean, you never saw her naked? But you did a nude painting of her?'

'Exactly, friend Miler, you've got it. My plan was this. I would paint her naked. I mean, I would be naked while I painted her. She would be dressed but when she saw how I'd painted her without clothes, and how I was without clothes, she would feel liberated and strip off and then the two of us would be Adam and Ewa, as it were.'

Miler stared at him. He waited, frowning, and said, 'Sounds crazy to me but did it work? She joined you in a nude party?'

'It didn't turn out like that. And then there was an anti-government protest, I was arrested and the authorities got hold of the painting which as well as nudity had a political message. A few days after my release some Ubek went round my quarter, knocking on doors, looking for Tex, wanting to get her name for their files. She opened the door to this stranger carrying my painting. He asked her name, wrote it down. Then he looked from the painting to her and said, "I like a woman with big tits but I see your boyfriend exaggerated." She was so furious – not with the Ubek, with me – she came round to my room and hit me over the head with the canvas. "I told you those breasts were too big."'

'What did you do?' Miler asked. 'Thump her one?'

'Why should I do that?'

'She whacked you with your painting, didn't she? Well then.'

'No,' Tadeusz said. 'She was my first critic. I admit I was a bit hurt – my pride, I mean. Now of course I'm used to critics. I'm told some of them are even human in their off-moments.'

But it hadn't ended quite like that. There was a bit more he hadn't told Miler.

Ewa smashed the canvas on him, on the head that still ached towards the end of the day from the truncheon blow. He finished with the painting round his neck like some clown's ruff. She burst into tears.

He put an arm round her shoulders and looked round for somewhere to sit. There was only the bed.

'Losing my temper, hitting you with the painting, means I have to go to confession again.'

'You must tire the priests out,' Tadeusz said.

He comforted her, stroking her shoulder, feeling some good was after all going to come of this, leaning together on the bed.

'He said – that Ubek – he said I had to report on you, any anti-social behaviour, political talk, meetings with subversives. I don't know what subversives look like. He said people who talked a lot, people who read foreign books and listened to rock and roll. Jews were a high risk. Look out for Jews, he said.'

'Does he think I'm a Jew,' Tadeusz asked.

'I don't think so. Well, he certainly wouldn't if he'd had a good look at you like I did.'

She blushed. More for the confessional.

'Suppose,' Tadeusz said, another plan unfolding itself in his head, 'we invent some stories for you to tell him. That will satisfy him, you'll be safe and we can see each other. Let's see now. You were at your window, it was night, your light was out so you couldn't be seen. You were able to look across the street into this room, the light was on here, the curtains and window open because of the hot weather, and you saw these people arrive. Two men. You hear laughter and voices all mixed up. Then you hear me say, "When's the next protest, Icchak?" And he says, "Call me Isaac, it's more Western." But you don't hear any more because they start playing a Rolling Stones record very loudly. Would that satisfy your Ubek?'

She looked at him sadly. 'I don't have a Ubek. We – all of us – have the system against us, all the Ubeks. You're still a boy, you think it's a game. He's going to come once a week to check what I've got. Either you'll get hurt or you'll get me in danger.'

She left him. Tadeusz didn't see her after that. Presumably to get herself out of an impossible situation, she found somewhere else to live.

For a while Tadeusz had kept the painting. Unfortunately she had smashed that side of the canvas which had her head and the imaginary woman's body on it. Then he thought: What's the point in keeping Gierek's unlovely face? I can see that any day in the newspaper. And the body? I can see that any day in the mirror. He determined to throw it away. But first he cut the canvas into small pieces so it wouldn't arouse suspicion and then divided the pieces among several bins in the Copernicus Park. People were always sifting through rubbish bins in the hope of finding something useful. A rubbish bin, Tadeusz decided, was a communist supermarket. And vice versa.

Ewa had called him a boy. He'd kept that from Miler, chopped the scene short as if he were guilty of something. Or ashamed. It was no more than normal, suppressing someone's criticism, concealing it even from oneself. He examined it again now. Baran had said the same: a boy, not a man.

He remembered how puzzled he had been at the time: how do I cross from boyhood to manhood? How do I acquire authority, make my will prevail – snap my fingers or give a hooded look and people come running? He had considered possibilities, and impossibilities too. Should he go out and find a Ubek to kill? Seduce dozens of women? Or men? Drink vodka by the litre? Escape Poland and join the French Foreign Legion? Throw away the beret – well, that had been done for him – and grow a beard? Get married and breed?

I must suffer, Tadeusz had thought. Manhood is not achieved without pain. It is not a question of physical growth and physical attributes but of moral growth. He considered suffering which seemed almost as various as love. Suffering through physical deprivation, suffering through persecution, suffering through isolation, through ridicule, through rejection, through self-criticism, self-sacrifice, self-denial. Death was the ultimate denial of self. The world was an unpleasant prospect viewed through suffering eyes and he abandoned it.

They don't want me as I am, Tadeusz agonized to himself, they want me to hurry into middle age. In eight months I shall be twenty-four. By next summer I shall be fifty. By the winter I shall be in my grave. I shall insist on them chipping on my headstone: Here lies a man.

Perhaps the shortcut to manhood was not to fight the system but to join it. In his head he directed a short film, starring himself. He banished all thought of a replacement beret and strode confidently into the ugly police headquarters. Rapping with imperious knuckles on the reception counter, he demanded: 'I want to be a Ubek. I want to take on the substance of a man as well as the form.'

I want to know how to trick my fellow citizens, lie to their faces, cheat them of their lives, swear everything they believe is false, live by no laws known to decent people, learn all the deception and double-talk and cock-eyed thinking and upside-down and inside-out logic that this perverted society demands. I want the smell of death about me. Will that make me a man?

There was no need actually to say all that out loud because They already knew it.

He decided he knew the secret of being a man: it was to know dreadful truths and yet be able to function.

So where does that leave me now, Tadeusz thought, stretched out on his bunk. I know the dreadful truths but I've stopped functioning. Perhaps I had it wrong. The secret of being a man is to know dreadful lies and yet be able to function.

Or maybe it's all bullshit.

It was amazing to him how seriously he had considered, in his prolonged adolescence, these magical passages to manhood. One or other must work. And all the time Zuzanna was approaching, Baran was preparing, and the pressure that would lead the whole of Poland to manhood was building up.

Looking over at the other bunk he saw Miler had his eyes closed. Was he asleep? He looked like the kind of man who would snore but he was breathing gently. The light was still on in the cell. Tadeusz could turn it off – they were allowed that much freedom of choice – but he felt the light kept away memories that were too dark. At least, he hoped so. His watch had stopped. He had never invested in a quartz battery model and his watch was frequently neglected. Do you regulate creativity by the clock, he asked himself.

His watch said something past two, but it had been saying that since the afternoon.

It had been this time of night fourteen years ago – fourteen, he marvelled – that fate took hold of his life and shook it so violently that its pattern was quite altered from then on.

CHAPTER EIGHT

Concrete, Tadeusz said to himself. Concrete, concrete concrete.

Concrete is the essence of communism. Concrete is heavy, ugly, brutal, devoid of humanity. Concrete hurts when it meets your body. Concrete lacks elegance. There is no poetry in concrete, no music, no colour, no excitement. Concrete doesn't mellow with age, it weeps weather streaks. Concrete is the style of the bosses. When people refer to the party leaders they call them *bétons*, the French for concrete.

Tadeusz celebrated summer 1980 with a poem.

CONCRETECONCRETECONCRETECONCRETE
CONCRETECONCRETECONCRETECONCRETE
CONCRETECONCRETECONCRETECONCRETE
CONCRETECONCRETECONCRETECONCRETE
CONCRETECONCRETECONCRETECONCRETE
HELP!

He painted the poem in bold ugly block capitals on canvas and took it to the lesbian gallery owner. She blew a stream of cigarette smoke in the air and said, 'Don't tell me – it's called Concrete.'

Tadeusz said, 'It's called Party Secretary Gierek.'

She said, 'You're mad.'

Tadeusz said, 'I'm mad. You're mad. Everybody's mad. The whole country is as mad as hell.'

She said, 'If I put that in the front window, the Ubeks will burn the canvas, smash up the shop and throw me in a cell. Who would buy it? Someone with a death wish?'

Tadeusz said, 'Put the canvas in the window. Put a price tag: zero zlotys. Put a title card with Party Secretary Gierek in a sealed envelope. You give away the painting but the buyer has to pay for the envelope. How much do you think?'

'The Kiel lawyer would probably go to two thousand Deutschmarks.'

'Make it five. If he can't open the envelope until he's paid, he'll pay.'

The lesbian gallery owner gave him a long searching look and sent up another cloud of smoke. 'You're learning.'

It was August 1980, the morning of the fourteenth, when workers at the Gdansk shipyards went on strike. Their demands, at first, were the release of political prisoners, the reinstatement of sacked workers and a pay rise. By the third day the strike had spread to offices and factories and the original demands had grown to twenty-one. On the fourth day, Sunday, a mass was held inside the shipyard gates. The strikers claimed God was on their side. A rough wooden cross was erected and later a sheet of paper was nailed to it with a quotation from Byron:

> For Freedom's battle once begun,
> Bequeathed by bleeding Sire to Son,
> Though baffled oft is ever won.

Hoping to avoid violence, however, they left out the word 'bleeding'. By the next week five hundred firms were on strike. The government tried to isolate Gdansk, cutting telephone and transport links, but the news spread. Strike committees were set up across the country.

A knock came at Tadeusz's door. It was not a Ubek knock, that hammering eagerness to get at the figure inside. He'd had a visit from them only a week before. They gave no reason but he assumed it was because of his CON-CRETE canvas. They'd taken possession of his room, shaking books to see if any secrets floated out, flicking through papers, dropping cigarette ends on the floor and crushing them with a heel, inspecting paintings with their heads to one side. Was the subject matter counter-revolutionary? Were the brush strokes anti-Party? They spoke little to each other and nothing to him until they were leaving. Then one, laying a fist tenderly against Tadeusz's nose, murmured: 'We'll be back.'

They hadn't come back now. This was a light knock, a secret for-your-ears-only knock, that couldn't be heard elsewhere. He opened the door and saw Natalia, the gallery owner. She slipped inside and locked the door and even as she did that her head swivelled round and her eyes made a survey of the room. Tadeusz, unused to conspiracy, took this in quite the wrong way. She was dressed all in black, a tall slim figure, no hips, no breasts to speak of, but with allure none-the-less. 'You don't get a handful, but you get a mouthful', Zdzislaw had said, inspecting her through the plate glass window of her gallery. People said that Natalia was lesbian but seeing her as she stood before him, her back arched like a bullfighter strutting into the arena, Tadeusz had other ideas. Why had she come to him, locking the door? Why were her skin tones overlit, her eyes so bright? He reached his arms out to gather her into an embrace and with one hand she pushed him away.

'Men are such clichés. They see a woman and their only thought is fucking.'

Tadeusz pulled back.

'There's a woman in Gdansk,' she went on in a rush, giving him no time to deny what had been in his mind, 'works in the shipyard – used to work in the shipyard. Drove a crane, God help her. You'd try to get her into bed, wouldn't you? Yes? Maybe up in the air – sex in a crane driver's cab. And her a grandmother.'

'Have you finished?' Tadeusz asked.

'She's called Anna Walentynowicz. You haven't heard of her? Really? And there's a man called Lech Walesa. You haven't heard of him either? Talk about an ivory tower . . . The strike was about getting their jobs back, in part. But more than that, much more now. One day people will ask: What were you doing when you heard the news about Gdansk? And you'll say: I was trying to fuck Natalia.'

'Have you finished now?'

'The government's censored the radio and television, and there's nothing in the papers of course but don't you listen to the BBC? You sit here playing with yourself.'

Something had wound up the spring in her and she seemed able to run on and on so Tadeusz sat in a chair. Indeed he'd glanced at the newspapers and they'd said nothing about strikes. He'd learned the potato harvest was going to be good and the holiday weather was good and steel production was good, and that Gierek had returned from his annual holiday in the Crimea. Returned early, people speculated, on the orders of his masters in the Kremlin. Tadeusz had heard people discussing strikes in Gdansk, but there'd been strikes before in Warsaw and they weren't as pressing as the empty shelves in the shops and the price of sausage. He stared out of the window at a sky deepening to a cerulean blue. There'd be the first stars soon. One couldn't see many stars from the centre of town but if he stretched out of the window and looked to the right the Plough would wink at him.

'That thing between your legs – I'm not interested.' She was silent a bit and said, 'All right, I've finished with that.' She stood next to him by the window but it wasn't for stars she looked but down at the street, both ways. She closed the window though no one on the pavement could have heard her voice now that she had it under control. She stuck a cigarette in her holder and lit it. She regarded Tadeusz, considered the slight tantrum she'd just thrown and decided on a simple and direct approach.

'This strike in Gdansk,' she said. 'They've occupied the Lenin shipyard and the Paris Commune shipyard and I don't know where else. They're not marching through town, they're not inviting the riot police to waterhose them. They decline to be charged and beaten up and shot at like before. They are holding the shipyards hostage, if you like. Someone's learned a little cunning at last. It is our holy duty to support them in every way we can. We have decided, on my recommendation, that you are someone who can help. We think it's time you found some serious use for that talent of yours. You are on the lazy side, to be honest. You've got the ideas, Tadek, and now is the time to put your gift to work. That is what we think.'

Tadeusz found himself straightening in his chair and looking at her with sharper eyes. *We think?* Who was this *we*? The gallery owner was showing a side he never suspected.

'Oh yes,' she said, reading the look on his face. She pulled a straightbacked chair up so she could sit alongside him. 'I do more than sell stuff to people with pretensions to culture. There is a group of us who have been meeting for some time. We are academics, trade unionists, theatre people, a priest, writers, someone in the city administration. We just call ourselves the Klub, nothing specific. Talk, talk,

talk. All the problems of Poland: the government, the cen-
sorship, the police, the prices, the big neighbour next door.
These are people whose lives revolve around talking.
Nothing more, until now. Now we feel we must act, must.
It is the chance for you to join and help us. I don't mean
merely help us the Klub. I mean Poland, Tadek, a chance to
help *Poland*.'

She pulled on the cigarette holder, blew out smoke and
looked to see what effect she was having. Tadeusz, stunned
by this sudden approach, asked the first question that came
into his head.

'Why me? Why choose me?'

'Certain people remember a painting you did, how you
marched with it, how you were beaten up for your pains.
That is like passing a test. And as for your ability, I spoke
for that.'

She was quiet again, waiting for Tadeusz to grow accustomed to the notion, to catch up with her. She opened the
window a fraction to drop the cigarette out and prepared to
wait again.

An extraordinary sensation took possession of Tadeusz.
He straightened his spine and rolled his head round to
relieve the knots in his neck muscles. Me? My talent? He
had the impression that the walls of his attic room were
falling away and the whole of Poland stretched out on all
sides of him. Out in the deepening dusk waited the preda-
tors of the night, Ubeks and riot police and army and
tanks. And he was needed. He would do battle using the
only weapons he had: his paintbrushes. He wasn't afraid.
Why not? Didn't he have the imagination to be afraid?
Imagination was not necessary, he'd seen the reality, he'd
experienced the violence of the state's thugs at first hand.
He was sustained by the belief that others had in him.

He took Natalia's hand – she didn't resist that – and

looked at the back. She was perhaps fifteen years older than he was but the skin was still smooth, showing none of the little diamond patterns of middle age. He turned the hand over to study the palm. One of the lines was her love line and he wondered what a palmist would make of it. He laced their fingers together and she still didn't resist. He felt her squeezing his hand with surprising strength and when he looked at her face she was smiling, a thing he'd never seen her do before.

'Good,' he said.

'Of course,' she said. 'You are a Pole. What choice did you have?'

'What do I do?'

'Meet the Klub. Then you will be told.'

'When?'

'Now. Do you imagine there is time to waste? I have something for you to take.'

From her bag she took half a pottery pig, a piece of folk art. Tadeusz remembered the pig. It had stood on the desk next to the telephone in her gallery.

'What happened?'

'It had an encounter with a Ubek's shoe.'

Pig meets pig, he thought.

'Go to the station,' she said. 'You must hurry. At twenty past ten stand under the departure board leading to the platforms.'

'Where am I going?'

'You'll find out. Hold the pig against your chest. Waldemar will meet you. He'll have the other half of the pig. He'll make the pig whole again. That's how you'll be sure of each other. You must go now because there's no time to lose. I'll wait five minutes so we're not seen leaving together.'

At the door Natalia stopped him and kissed him lightly

on both cheeks. Tadeusz folded his arms round her – and she didn't resist that either. It could pass as a comradely hug he gave her though he was aware of trying to feel the outline of her, Zdzislaw's mouthfuls. Tadeusz felt his heart racing as if they had consummated a secret love affair. She looked in his face and smiled. She was one of life's unobtainable desires.

Tadeusz stared at the indicator as if puzzled by the destinations. He was jostled by men lugging suitcases tied with string and women with bundles. A train from Warsaw was due in five minutes and it was going on to Prague. Other night trains were posted to Krakow and Szczecin and Jelenia Gora, but the 01.25 to Gdansk was cancelled. But perhaps he shouldn't be so blatant about taking a train so he lowered his head and surveyed the dim station with all the caution of a novice conspirator. He was aware of more police than was surely necessary. He supposed there were others he wasn't aware of. There were men who stood in pairs and looked about. At whom? At him? Why was he still standing under the indicator? Was he perhaps a troublemaker thwarted by the cancellation of the train to Gdansk? He'd never realized how many ways there were in which a guilty man could give himself away.

The half pig rested in his hand. He clutched it to his chest as if he felt a pain in his heart. He remembered the Creeping Counter-Revolutionary badge he'd had in his immature youth, lost with his beret, thank God. That wasn't something to boast of if you were trying to disguise the real thing. A man was approaching him. He seemed to have appeared out of the shadows of the tunnel and at once Tadeusz was alert to a trap.

'Do you have the time?'

'There's a clock up there. Why do you ask me?'

The man looked exasperated. 'I think that clock is wrong. What time does your watch say?'

To look at his watch Tadeusz had to move his hand away from his chest and a pig's snout peeped out between his thumb and forefinger. The man opened his own hand and showed the tail end of a pig. Gently he relieved Tadeusz of the front, fitted both parts together, then dropped them into the pocket of his baggy jacket.

'Are you Waldemar?' Tadeusz asked.

The man considered him a moment, frowning.

'It's best not to use names in a public place like this. No, don't look round to see who's watching. Don't shake hands either. Come on. We should hurry.'

Tadeusz checked the indicator. The next train was the one to Prague.

'Where are we going? I haven't got a ticket.'

'We don't discuss things like that either.'

Waldemar set off for the exit. Tadeusz, who had just made his first ever covert rendezvous, hurried to catch up. He felt the eyes of half the secret policemen of Wroclaw on his back. Thank God for his jacket, which covered the sweat patches on his shirt.

They crossed under the railway line, Waldemar setting a fast pace. Neither talked. Pausing at kerbs, Waldemar checked for traffic to the right, then to the left with his head twisted a little further so he could see behind them. Once, in shadows, Tadeusz saw two fireflies hovering in a mating ritual, and the fireflies brightened on the faces of the men watching. They advanced into Poludnie, a district as uninspiring as its name, which just means South. This had been flattened in 1945 by the First Ukrainian Front of the Red Army and there were those who thought they ought to be invited back to perform the service again.

Some buildings moonlight deals kindly with. But Bierut Apartments was no Taj Mahal. The name was not a misspelling but that of an early Party hack. It was one of the perversions of communism that it was thought an honour to a man to give his name to such a dump. It had been a slum in the making from the day unfortunate families had been moved in. The light of the moon could not disguise its greyness, its crumbling entrance, its chipped paint. Seemingly it was squashing itself into the ground under the weight of its concrete.

Waldemar, assuming it was Waldemar, led the way up dark stairs to the first floor, then down a short corridor. The ceiling pressed down on them. Doors barely taller than they were led to the so-called apartments. Tadeusz, in his heightened state, saw them as caves. To live here you had to become a troglodyte. The achievement of Polish socialism was to have put the development of civilisation into reverse, like a film being rewound. Today the troglodyte caves, tomorrow the stone age, next week dinosaurs, next year primeval mud. There was a smell of cat and mould.

Waldemar knocked at a door. A voice on the other side demanded to know who was visiting at this hour of the night. Waldemar said, 'Don't keep us hanging about. I've got both halves of the pig.' The door was unlocked and they stepped inside. 'I've brought Tadek.'

They were in an entrance hall large enough to hold a bicycle propped against the party wall to the next flat. One door, closed, led presumably to a bedroom. Another door, ajar, showed a toilet, basin and shower. They walked through the third door into the living room/kitchen.

'This is Tadek,' the flat owner said, 'Natalia's Tadek. I'm Eugeniusz. Waldemar you've already met. Henryk, with the grey hair. Say hello, Henryk.'

'Welcome,' Henryk said. 'Your ears should have been burning from what Natalia said.'

'Hello,' Tadeusz said, uncertain whether to demur or look pleased.

'You probably recognize Rafat.'

Rafat was dark and handsome, possibly thirty, possibly forty, possibly many things. He peered through half-closed eyes while a hand carelessly thrown back smoothed his hair.

'I know the face –' Tadeusz began.

'That's quite enough on a first acquaintance.'

'The Contemporary Theatre. On a poster.'

Rafat brightened. 'I was in "The Plough Must Hurt the Earth". *A bravura performance*, the critics said. Dear Jasiek, such a sweetie. You saw me?'

'I saw the poster. I am a severe critic of posters but I approved.'

Rafat made a *moue* but said nothing.

'I've saved Justyna until last. My wife.'

Tadeusz bobbed his head to her. She looked like a mother, but not one of the temporary mothers. Plump, with greying hair in a bun, her hands clasped in front of her floral print dress.

'Others were here earlier,' Eugeniusz said. 'They left after the decision was democratically made.'

Five people plus Tadeusz seemed to fill the room. How many more were in the Klub? How had they crowded in? There was a two-seater settee and four wooden chairs. People would sit on the floor against the wall with their knees drawn up, or stand in the little hall.

'Do we have coffee for Tadek?' Eugeniusz asked.

'We have tea.'

'I want nothing, truly.'

'We have real tea.'

Now Tadeusz had the sense to pause a moment. Tea and coffee were already as scarce as hen's teeth. Most people gathered blossoms from the lime trees or went to the country to search for camomile. To be offered imported tea, a tiny unobtainable luxury, was to be given a sign: Welcome, you are one of us.

'Later, please, if there is time,' Tadeusz said. 'First I must do what I have come for.'

He was rewarded with a mother's approving smile from Justyna.

'Right then,' Eugeniusz began and was interrupted by a knock on the door. The knock was soft but it was familiar and he remembered Waldemar had done the same. That tattoo was what his father had played on the piano rescued from the rubble at the end of the war, the opening beats to Beethoven's Fifth. Eugeniusz returned with a priest.

'Father Michal, this is the man Natalia talked of, who will design the poster. His name is Tadek.'

Father Michal took Tadeusz's right hand in both his and grasped it firmly, as if this was the hand that was going to do God's work and needed strengthening. In Tadeusz's experience priests were divided into two categories. There were the ascetic ones, so thin they seemed to be denying the existence of the body and its unruly demands. Then there were the plump ones who seemed to say, Well yes, God has seen fit to give us bodies and their appetites. Father Michal was plump but his eyes were haunted by what he had seen, and his jowls were weighted down as if they were burdens he was forced to carry. So he was his own category of priest.

'We should say a prayer together,' he said. All, even Tadeusz who was no regular communicant, stood with heads bowed. 'Lord, we ask Thy blessing on this enterprise we are embarking on. We ask Thee to protect our brothers and sisters in Gdansk and Gdynia, to hold them in the palm of Thy hand, to guide them according to Thy wisdom, to bring them safely through this time of trial to achieve the justice and liberty which are the rights of mankind. We ask Thee to guide the destiny of our land so that Poland may be Poland through centuries of centuries.'

'Amen.'

When Tadeusz glanced at the priest, his eyes were nearly closed as if he'd seen too much and feared what he might see again. He looked round at the others. Justyna's face was radiant, with a half-smile. Rafat's eyes were pressed tight and his lips were parted to let an actorly sigh escape. Henryk's head was so bowed his face was invisible. The silent Waldemar, to Tadeusz's embarrassment, was watching him. Eugeniusz said, 'You have news?'

'Not much,' Father Michal said. 'Walesa is inflexible, I'm told. Very strong, some say stubborn, if there's a difference. It seems as if the most important thing for him is the monument to the martyrs of 1970. You know who I'm talking about?'

Now everybody looked at Tadeusz.

'I was seventeen,' he said, as if that explained any lapse. 1970, he remembered with a shiver, may have been the year of the martyrs of Gdansk, but for him it was the time he'd tried telepathy to bring Alina, that temporary mother, back to his bed. Adolescence was an age of futility.

'Hundreds of people were shot down. The government admitted twenty-six but there were hundreds. Walesa insists there has to be a monument and it's got to be forty metres high. The bosses say the site they want for a monument is where a supermarket is going to go up. This chap Walesa says: What do we need a supermarket for? They can find somewhere else to put their empty shelves. No, a plaque will not do, a monument. Got to be forty metres. Forty, no less.'

Then, while Tadeusz waited for instructions, there was a digression into the significance of forty. Was it a sly allusion to Ali Baba and the Forty Thieves? Did it refer to the forty days and forty nights in the desert? It was Tadeusz's first encounter with a committee, where the talk canters off in different directions, dragging the beast apart.

Eugeniusz consulted his watch and said, 'I have to leave in an hour's time.'

This brought them back to Tadeusz. And what he could do. Indeed, what could he do? They had left it too late, talked too long before deciding to invite him into the Klub, expended more time in recruiting him and giving him a rendezvous at the station and walking to the flat and talking and praying and speculating. Now, abruptly, Eugeniusz had presented a deadline.

Eugeniusz worked at the Preema Print Works, a one-time union representative before realizing the sham of the official unions. Now he was hot for free trade unions and was destined to be an important figure in Solidarity in Wroclaw. He was leaving in an hour to work on the grave-yard shift. Now there was no time to do more than a typographical poster, no time to get plates made, no time for anything but to run off the five thousand flyers they decided were necessary.

'You can have coloured stock,' he conceded.

Black on yellow was the most visible, though hideous.

They gave Tadeusz a pad and pencil and gazed expectantly at him as if creative sparks would leap from his eyes.

'There's nothing I can do,' he protested.

'Then just lay out the type and suggest the font and size,' Eugeniusz said.

They wanted him for reassurance but more importantly to commit him for further use.

'But hurry.'

He turned the pad round to give a landscape effect and then blocked out: MARCH FOR POLAND

He used different type sizes to give the impression of bodies of different sizes in a procession. Eugeniusz said there was a typographical dingbat, a crusader banner, he could use as if being carried between the M and the A. The total effect was really quite similar to the design for Solidarity that became so famous throughout the world. The march was to take place in the afternoon at 17.00, from the Cathedral of St John the Baptist as far as St Adalbert's on Dominican Square close to the centre of the city.

'Even our stormtroopers respect churches,' Father Michal said.

Tadeusz was still working, writing in the time and the day and the date, a line about supporting the strikers in Gdansk, a plea to come in peace and love that the priest insisted on. Finally, in the bottom right-hand corner, he signed himself Tadek.

Rafat, who had taken the pad and held it at arm's length to run a critical eye over it, stiffened. 'What's that?'

'My name.'

'What for?'

'This is the poster you all asked me to do so I've put my name on as I do on my paintings.'

There was a pause.

'Your real name this would be?' Rafat continued.

'Yes.'

'My dear fellow, you must use a stage name, a secret name, a codename. Otherwise you will be arrested.'

Tadeusz thought about this. 'Will everyone know it's false, a codename?'

'Yes, of course.'

'In that case the Ubeks will believe Tadek is a codename

and my real name is something else. They'll look for someone whose name is anything but Tadek.'

Baffled, no one contested this logic.

Eugeniusz took the design for the poster, folded it and
stowed it in an inner jacket pocket. He kissed Justyna and
went into the hall to his bicycle. Tadeusz asked, 'How will
the posters be distributed?'

There was silence.

They didn't leave the flat in a bunch but in ones and twos.
Tadeusz went last with Rafat. They descended the dark
staircase in silence, taking care where they placed their
feet. Approaching the entrance Rafat spoke.

'It still worries me, putting your name up in lights.'

They went through the door.

'Of all people you should understand about getting
billing on a poster,' Tadeusz said.

They were on the steps leading to the pavement. Rafat
had not responded. Thinking he might have given offence,
Tadeusz softened his remark with a joke.

'And I did give myself the very lowest billing.'

'Oh my dear fellow,' Rafat said, laying a hand on his arm.

A car was parked at the kerb where no car had been
when Tadeusz arrived. It showed no lights, no parking
lights, no interior lights, and the night was dark. But a face
turned as they stepped on to the pavement and it appeared
luminous. A woman's voice floated out: 'All my life I've
been waiting to meet a dear fellow.'

Tadeusz stopped in his tracks. The voice reverberated
inside his head, inside his body. A few words, a tone of
voice, a face: whatever comes next in my life, he told himself, is up to me.

CHAPTER NINE

Sometimes he remembered her saying, 'I'm dying to see your dear fellow.'

Or, 'Your dear fellow has kept me waiting.'

Even, 'Should I be jealous of your dear fellow?'

He would pretend he wasn't certain, but it was only play. He always returned to the one true version.

'All my life I've been waiting to meet a dear fellow.'

Simple, even banal, but a tease. She could be his match, a satirical artist in words.

That light tone had already wrapped itself round him. There are some voices that can seduce you, no matter what they say, and hers was one. It wasn't deep like a man's but it had depths. It could also play games with itself, with pauses that made you wait, and tripping up and down the scale, and at the height of love-making fall suddenly into a little girl's breathless 'aaah'.

But that wasn't yet.

'You've got yourself a good one.'

Who said that? Where was he?

The interior vision faded and Tadeusz found himself stretched on the bunk. Miler was grinning at him.

'I've been watching your face. As good as bloody television, you know, where they have a close-up of the actor and he's really earning his money putting on these expressions. You can see what he's thinking: Who's there? I'm not scared. I'll get you, you little shit. Know what I mean? Well, your face . . . Your brows lift, your brows tighten, you take a breath, your face relaxes, you have a little smile. Aha, that smile, I say to myself, our Tadeusz has a tender memory.'

There was too much light in the cell. Miler wasn't sleeping. Miler was watching him instead. Tadeusz swung his legs off the bunk.

'Shall we have the light off? Try to get some sleep?'

'Get a bit of shut-eye. Try to dream of her, entice her into your arms.'

A narrow shaft of light still came through the judas window in the door but Miler and Tadeusz were only shadows on their bunks now. It seemed that Miler wasn't ready for sleep. The darkness had created a confessional mood. Secrets could be murmured.

'What was her name?'

Zuzanna. Zuzia. Miler had asked her name hours ago but Tadeusz still wouldn't speak it or Miler would be full of questions. Besides, Zuzanna was still only a face in a car window, a voice.

'I won't tell your wife on you. You married at all? I asked, are you married? Ever been?'

'No.'

'Well, everything's all right then. It's just you hesitated so.'

'No, I'm not married, never have been married, never had a wife, not likely to.'

He hadn't meant to say *not likely to*. It just slipped out. But Miler didn't pick it up.

'All right, all right. It was a perfectly straight question. Me, I've been married. Well, I still am married. That's what the Pope says. For someone who's never endured wedded bliss, His Holiness is ever so certain that a marriage is for ever, even when it's as plain as piss that it isn't. Take my wife, for instance. Well, you can if you like and no hard feelings. But take her attitude. Where have you been to? Why are you so late? You've been drinking again.'

Miler had a voice for his wife though it wasn't her voice. It was just the way men pretend women nag. Tadeusz looked over and by the ghost-light from the judas window he saw Miler was perched on the edge of his bunk. Memories of his wife had roused him.

'I mean, what's wrong with a glass? Come to that, what's wrong with a bottle? Don't tell me you say no because you drank your beer well enough. A drink, a laugh, they go together, don't they? But my wife didn't drink and laughing wasn't on the menu either. Well, you know as well as I do what a drink and a laugh put a man in mind of. Yes? Am I right? That certain someone whose name you won't mention. It's all right, I respect your reticence, you want to protect a lady's name. Maybe she's married. Could be that. Could be your best friend's wife. All right. You see, you and me, we understand each other.'

Miler had reached this conclusion by some devious route that had nothing to do with Tadeusz. He was searching for a cigarette and finding the packet empty he tossed it on the floor.

'You don't smoke, do you. But perhaps you keep a packet in your pocket to offer your lady? No? I'll give up again. Actually I stop smoking about thirty times a day. Anyway, anyway, one dismal morning my wife said to me, "Where were you last night? You didn't come in at all." "Do you care?" I said. "Felt like a bit of bumps-a-daisy for once? That would be a bloody miracle." She didn't like that, didn't like me for criticising. She could dish it out but have you ever heard of a woman who could take it? News to me if you have. I don't care to be bullied myself and she was setting out that way. "Who was she? Give me her name and where she lives and I'll go and settle with her." "You'll settle with me," I said and showed her this.'

Miler clenched his hand. It made a big fist.

'She cooled down then so I said, to make peace like, "I wasn't in some trollop's bed, I was driving round all night." She went very still which usually meant she was preparing one of her attacks. But she kept her mouth shut. Afraid I'd shut it for her.'

Miler lay back on his bunk again. When he spoke there was sly satisfaction in his voice. He was dropping a hint but keeping a secret.

'Right, driving all night, I told her. Not *all* bloody night, mind. It wasn't the whole truth, but close enough.'

Tadeusz closed his eyes, shutting Miler out. He wanted Miler to go away. Miler wasn't to be trusted. Miler spied on him, imposed on him, and God help him even seemed to have a parallel dream. Driving all night. Well, not the whole night. But close enough as Miler had said.

Driving, the road ahead penetrated by headlights, the darkness pressing in on them, the enclosed space creating its own intimacy, a life can change with the finality of a card turning over.

CHAPTER TEN

'Zuzia, this is Tadeusz,' Rafat announced, flourishing a hand in the direction of each. With a bit of theatrical business he crossed the hands over. 'Tadek meet Zuzanna. There. Consider yourselves oldest chums.'

There was no doubt – though Rafat showed a rough politeness – that he was put out to see Zuzanna in the car. Was she meant to be a secret? Or was it Tadeusz who was supposed to be under wraps?

Zuzanna's head moved a degree or two so she was staring at Tadeusz. A hand crept out of the window, not a stiff formal hand presented for shaking, but palm down, fingers rounded, offered like a gift. Tadeusz, in a moment of perfect understanding, ducked his head and kissed the hand. The skin was smooth and cool to his lips. Lifting his eyes to her face, which was very close, he saw how round and large her eyes were, unblinking, wide open to take in every detail of him. She made a little sound in her throat as Tadeusz pulled back.

'I told you not to come,' Rafat said.

'I had nothing to do. Am I supposed to sit and wait for you?'

'How long have you been here?'

She turned her face towards Rafat but Tadeusz could swear her eyes were still on him. 'Long enough to excite the interest of a pair of policemen. Police boys really. They asked what I was doing. I said I was waiting for my lover.'

She turned her face back to Tadeusz so he had the full benefit of a mischievous smile. 'I said, "He's just inside saying good night to his wife." One of them choked on his cigarette smoke. The other asked if he was going to be long and the one who'd choked said, "Would you be?"'

Rafat said, 'You shouldn't say things like that. They'll remember you were here.'

Zuzanna said, 'You mean they wouldn't remember me otherwise?'

Rafat said crossly, 'What they'll remember is you parked in my car outside this apartment block, waiting for somebody. They won't believe that story you told.'

She opened the door so the interior light came on, casting a glow on her. She swung her legs round and got out of the car in one flowing movement. They didn't welcome each other with an embrace. No reason they should but Tadeusz knew he'd help himself to a kiss at every opportunity if he had this woman to call his own. Her voice, her smile, her hair the colour of an August cornfield in the car's feeble light, the silky movement of her body, her spirit – everything was etching itself into his brain. They stood slightly apart. Was this the marital tiff of the unmarried?

'Should I call you Tadeusz or Tadek? To call you Tadek . . . Sometimes it is a little familiar on a first acquaintance.'

'Friends call me Tadek.'

'We shall be friends then – Zuzia and Tadek.'

It was a small thing but when your imagination is taking feverish leaps small things seem significant. There was no common diminutive for Rafat – though a visiting American director had privately tried Rat – so that he seemed excluded.

They were driving out to the country. You cannot sit in a parked car for three hours – Rafat said – or you attract the sort of attention Zuzanna already had. They were due at the Preema Print Works at four to collect the flyers for distribution. There was too much electricity in the air tonight to try to sleep for a couple of hours, or to sit round drinking camomile tea or toasting the Gdansk strikers in vodka. Also, news had come that the strikers had sworn off alcohol and any bottles smuggled through the shipyard fence were emptied on the ground in a poignant silence.

Zuzanna wanted to know what the latest news was from Gdansk and what people felt about the news. 'Angry,' Rafat answered and peered into the tunnel of the headlights.

Rafat drove because – Zuzanna said – he tensed up if she drove. He said she was colour blind, didn't see red lights. 'Besides, if I sit in the back and you two sit in the front I can compare your profiles. Rafat's right profile is the one he favours.'

This little sally was greeted with silence. They drove on the road towards Jelenia Gora, not to reach it but just to be going somewhere while the clock's hands moved.

Zuzanna tried conversation again. 'What's the plan for this afternoon?'

'We march,' Rafat said.

'Where from?'

'The cathedral.'

'Where to?'

'St Adalbert's.'

'And then?'

'Speeches. A prayer. Displaying solidarity with the strikers, showing contempt for the authorities, pledging defiance.'

'Whose idea was it?'

'Whose idea? What difference does it make? It was a joint decision. The Klub's.'

'Someone must have suggested it.'

'Waldemar did. Or that Professor Henryk.'

The conversation had an edgy quality. It was the night before a battle, when sleep was out of the question. Nerves were too close to the surface.

'Your idea?' she asked. 'Wasn't it yours?' She kept probing for the tender spot of his ego.

'Maybe I suggested it. For God's sake, we didn't keep minutes.'

A police check put an end to the talk – two cars at the roadside, striped barrier, waving lanterns. Papers, papers for the driver, papers for the passengers. Rafat, Tadeusz and Zuzanna sat in silence. They've raided the Preema Print Works, Tadeusz thought, they've raided the troglodyte flat looking for the abandoned wife, they're looking for Tadek Codename Tadek. Where are you going, one of the police demanded. To Strzegon, Rafat said, to my aunt who has a glut of plums. In the middle of the night? It won't be the middle of the night by the time we get back to Wroclaw. They sat alone and separate until Tadeusz felt a hand creep on to his shoulder and give it a gentle squeeze. That was Zuzia wanting reassurance, wanting human contact, wanting to be in touch.

They drove on, past the place where in pre-troglodyte days Tadeusz had painted Tex in the nude. Who was Tex? A nobody, a fantasy. He could recall nothing of her.

'You're not married?' Zuzanna asked, breaking the silence. 'No Mrs Tadek worried why you haven't returned home?'

'No,' Tadeusz said. That was too bald an answer so he added, 'I live on my own.'

'What do you do?'

'Tadek is a great admirer of Wroclaw theatre,' Rafat said. 'A connoisseur of our posters, isn't that so?'

Tadek, finding no useful reply, ignored that. He said, 'I

paint. I play music. I compose for the Moog synthesizer. I write. I create sculptures. I practise *feng shui*. I act. But I don't dance.'

The other two spoke together.

'What's *feng shui*?' Zuzanna asked.

'What have you acted in? I don't believe I've seen you in anything.'

'You haven't. I act what I've written. There have been no public performances.'

'Oh yes,' Rafat said.

'What's *feng shui*?'

'It's the art of arranging the objects in a space – say a room – to encourage good energy to flow through it.'

'That's brilliant.'

'You think so?' Rafat said. 'Where's it sprung from? China? Japan? Outer Mongolia?'

'It's a Chinese discipline.'

'Give me one practical example of *feng shui* at work so I'm convinced it's not a sham.'

'A theatre empty is dead. A theatre with people filling the rows of seats exerts a force, an energy, you can feel on stage.'

The sound of soft clapping from the back seat punctuated the silence.

'And what do you do?' Tadeusz asked.

'Oh, I exist,' she replied.

Rafat had a different answer. 'What she does, she does very well.' But he didn't say what it was.

The car took a sudden lurching turn on to a road to the right and Zuzanna said, 'Where are you going?'

'Back.'

'Why this way?'

'So the police don't look in the car and ask where the plums are.'

Tadeusz had no idea what Rafat was like as an actor or as a lover but he seemed well equipped to run a secret life. Was he trained by theatrical intrigues? By a love life of levantine complexity?

They drove back in near silence, arriving at Preema before dawn. Who needs sleep, Tadeusz demanded of himself. Sleep is boring. Sleep is for people who achieve nothing. Sleep is for the profligate who throw away their lives. But to sleep with someone, that is *feng shui* at its most sublime.

They met eight or nine others at Preema. The whole business was cloaked in unreality. They gathered in some secretarial office with the lights off and with the only illumination coming through the window from a security lamp out in the delivery yard. Eugeniusz appeared from the factory wheeling a trolley with a layer of handbills advertising an athletic track meet covering the flyers for the march. Voices were lowered, words cut to a minimum. The sound of the presses drummed inside them and affected them in different ways. To Henryk that drumming had echoes of the war that had rolled over his childhood farmhouse. To Tadeusz, too, it had echoes of war but as portrayed in films. Rafat lifted his head and listened to Shakespeare, Henry V before Agincourt. Or perhaps, Tadeusz changed his mind, it was a scene from a Hollywood B movie, black and white, the gang taking delivery of bootleg hooch, tommy guns rattling out of sight.

The flyers were in batches of five hundred, still warm and damp from their birth. No leader gave orders but it was quickly decided. Two hundred went to Henryk who would cover the university area. Five hundred to Adam, who worked at the Dolmel factory. Justyna had come and would borrow Eugeniusz's bicycle and would go south with five hundred. Someone would take the Gottwald estate, someone else to the cathedral and then up through Olbin. To the east was Biskupin where a woman called Maria lived. Tadeusz, Rafat and Zuzanna were accepted as a unit, whether Rafat wished it or not. Tadeusz picked up a pile, Zuzanna another and hugged it to her chest. Careful, Tadeusz warned her in his head, you'll squash those breasts; and when she shifted the pile he saw printer's ink had come off in smudges on her blouse as if dirty hands had been fondling her.

They drove west from Nowy Swiat, from where Tadeusz could not quite point out the building where he froze and baked in the attic though he and Zuzanna squirmed round in their seats and squinted out. Rafat stared in front and finally shouted, 'Watch for bloody police, for God's sake.'

Then Zuzanna wound down her window and stared out like a passenger in a stagecoach fearful of raiding Sioux. A minute passed, two minutes, and she called out, 'There, beyond that tram stop. In that car. Doing nothing. Who sits in a car and does nothing at this time of night except cops and drug dealers and there are no drug dealers in Wroclaw.'

They turned a corner and Rafat stamped on the brakes so Zuzanna was slammed into the back of Tadeusz's seat and cried out. Rafat hauled round and shouted at her, 'It's not a bloody game. You're like a child, or you like to pretend you're a child. It's not a march round the playground we're organizing, it's real, like the police are real and the Ubeks are real, and they have real guns and real batons and real boots. You want to get out and walk or you want to grow up?'

There was a car coming towards them. In the brightness of its headlamps Tadeusz saw the slashes that ran down between his brows, the eyes that were holes into his churning anger, the way his lower lip was braced over his teeth and how his cheeks had tightened. Moving his head he saw Zuzanna close to the back of his seat. Her face was caught in the advancing headlamps and he saw in it the light of battle and a half smile of something like triumph which he didn't understand at all.

Rafat turned to the front again and got the car going. As for distributing the flyers, there was no great plan. They simply tossed them out of the window as he drove. There was no time to go pasting them on buildings or tucking them under windscreen wipers so they scattered them for people to pick up, to be blown by any breeze, for children to run home with. That was what they did and no one spoke.

When Tadeusz returned to his room he found a note left by Natalia. He took it to the window to read by the early morning light. She had written in her scrawl, 'A whole pig is better than two halves unless the halves wear police uniform.' It was a bit of nonsense she had left as a welcome but for a time he was lost to any significance at all. Pig? Halves of a pig? Then he remembered. But so much had happened to him, to his dreams and his emotions during the night that standing in the railway station clutching the broken pig was a scene from a different life entirely.

Tadeusz lay on the bed and tried to sleep and couldn't. He got up and went to the window and saw the sun sparkle on the window pane opposite where Tex had ignored him. He looked round his room, at the artistic disorder he had created. He saw Zuzanna staring at the abandoned canvases, Zuzanna fingering the keys of the saxophone, Zuzanna turning the pages of a novel in progress, Zuzanna admiring sketches he'd made of ideas for sculptures, Zuzanna touching books and a pot of dried flowers. Mostly he saw Zuzanna lying on the bed.

He went back to the bed and left room at his side for her to stretch out. She was at the window, naked, leaning on the windowsill to breathe the morning air, her back to him but not in rejection, one hip cocked, buttocks beautifully rounded and inviting to his hand. Now she lay down next to him, resting on her side so her breasts arranged themselves like two soft buns. The rise from her waist to her hip and down the length of her flank was sculpted like a sand dune. And he whispered *Zuzia* and she answered *What is it?* and he said *I want you* and she said *I'm always open to you, to embrace you, to take you deep inside me and hold you.*

When he thought of being in the car he thought of it as a play. It was the final act of *Rafat and Zuzanna* and the first act of *Zuzia and Tadek* rolled into one. Rafat was an actor and Zuzanna too had been acting a part. Only, she wrote her own lines.

The cathedral has a daunting atmosphere which warns that God is not to be trifled with. There is none of the exuberance and erotic fantasy of the baroque churches of Bavaria or Bohemia. None of the clarity and simplicity of Greek chapels. None of the bargains you can strike with God in Italy. The Polish experience of God's will is severe, as He seems to punish them for their very Polishness. And yet they love God. The cathedral is busy at all hours of the day and night.

So, at something after four o'clock it was no surprise to see men and women coming into the cathedral. They pray, they light a candle to the BVM, they queue on benches for the confessional stalls. This afternoon, after doing all these things, they did not leave. By four-thirty there were no seats left in the pews. Then minutes later the aisles and two entrance porches were blocked. By ten to five the pretty square in front where at dusk a bearded young man comes to light the gas lamps was filled. The crowd spilled round to the narrow alleys to the north that lead to the Botanical

Gardens, and finally to the square to the east where the hospital is.

Anyone who was there would confirm the unity of the crowd. The movement called Solidarity was hardly born but the word was everywhere. Another word, a gift from the English, was 'strike'. The official radio talked of 'certain interruptions of production'. Radio Free Europe gave harder news. Strike, strike, strike. The government was sending a minister to negotiate.

There was a crowd of perhaps three thousand. If the fly-ers had been printed earlier, even half a day earlier, there would have been many more. A huge banner had been roughly painted: MARCH FOR POLAND. Eugeniusz held the pole at one end of the banner, Adam the pole at the other end. Priests were grouped behind with Father Michal at his most inward and severe. Rafat had determined on a place in the very front row. Others of the Klub were masked by the crowd. But Tadeusz was absent.

The bells rang five o'clock and the procession didn't begin for another fifteen minutes. This was the 'Polish quarter of an hour' during which nothing happens. Father Michal was observed speaking but his words were lost in the rumble. What did he say? What did he say? The message was passed back, 'He said "Peace and solidarity with the strikers."'

While the crowd was gathering at the cathedral, Tadeusz was making last-minute preparations to join them. He was shaving, a chore he might have left until tomorrow except that, well, you never knew. Never knew what, he asked himself. You never knew what you never knew. He had scraped the soap and bristles off his cheeks and chin and had only a white sudsy Hitler moustache when Zuzanna came. There was a knock at the door and he answered it and there she stood, scowling when she should have been smiling.

'What have you done to your face? You look quite ridiculous.' But she seemed distracted and paid no attention to his reply. She peered past him at the room, going on tiptoe to see better over his shoulder. 'Why are you half naked? Who else is here? This time of the afternoon you should either be wholly naked or wholly dressed. Am I disturbing something?'

This was a woman who fired questions like a machine gun, confident that some will hit. Tadeusz, still startled by her appearance, treated the questions as frivolous.

'How did you know where I lived?'

'Easy. I just asked for the man who lives in a pig sty.'

'Pig sty?' He was confused by that, remembering the broken pig. 'What?'

'Don't be dull.' She laid one finger on his naked chest and pushed him back so she could have a proper look at the genius artist's garret and said, 'It's disgusting. Where can I sit? Is the bed safe? No shy little friend hiding under the covers?'

'But how did you find me?' he asked again, wanting an explanation for this miracle.

'I asked for the shop with the basins and the baths in its window. You said you lived above.'

Had he told her that? He was sure he hadn't. Well, almost sure. He didn't care. He didn't care that she scowled and thought his room chaotic or worse. She was here. He went to the basin and was wiping off the shaving soap when his gaze in the mirror shifted and he saw she was scowling twice as hard at his back. Alarmed, he turned.

'What's wrong?'

'For a moment . . .' She stopped and gathered herself. 'Rafat, when he's shaving in the morning, stares at the mirror and smiles. He's seen his own face and it's the best thing in the world to him. I mean, five minutes before he had my face on the pillow to look at and he never smiled like that. Actors are narcissistic. How are artists?'

This glimpse of her domestic life seriously disoriented Tadeusz. She left him and turned to his paintings, half a dozen of which were stacked against a wall. She bent down and pulled them forward one at a time to inspect and Tadeusz felt it was not just his paintings but he himself who was being given the critical eye.

'Oh yes,' she said, 'oh, you *are* talented.' A little song started in Tadeusz's heart. She selected a canvas and placed it on the vacant easel. 'One day, Tadek, you are going to be famous. But . . .'

But. The song went off-key. He hated *but*. *But* snatched back what had just been given. *But* was a mugger who ignored your wallet and tore out your heart. *But* strangled generous impulses. *But* was offering a kiss with the lips tight closed. I love you *but* I won't. *But* was Romeo without Juliet. *But* was a beautiful face darkened by a scowl.

'Who is she? Girlfriend?'

'She was someone on a bench, no one I know. I think she was waiting for a boyfriend and he never turned up.'

'Another one. The world is full of faithless men. Are you sure it wasn't you who jilted her?'

'I told you, she was just someone I saw.'

'Name?' Zuzanna kept trying to force a confession.

'I never asked. I had a sketchpad and I got her lines, the curve of her body, the way she had twisted to watch the path. Then I put her on canvas when I got back here.'

'Tadek, you see, it's all there.'

She paused. It wasn't an ending, Tadeusz knew, she was considering her options. He quite absurdly wanted her good opinion. He wanted her to be his champion and ride out in front of him and defy any hostile critics. She was younger than he was and yet seemed immeasurably older. How could this be? It was her sexuality, he decided, from thousands of generations of women dealing with men. She lifts a finger and I want to please her. I want that finger and all the rest of her.

Her head was to one side, studying the picture. Then her attention was all on him. Her voice was slow and throaty. It shared a secret between them. 'Tadek, I see a girl, wistful face, young, pretty without question. You've got the lines, the twist to her body to bring her breasts out, eager. You got it all up there.' She touched his forehead. 'But you didn't get it down there.' Lightly, with one finger, she touched his groin.

For a second or two she looked him straight in the eyes.

Tadeusz reached for her, his arm stretching to encircle her waist and draw her close, but she'd already turned and moved away to the window.

I love you *but* you won't.

The crowd had flowed down the Cathedral approach. They didn't march – they were no army, no militia, no trained force. A small island divides the river Odra and they crossed over the wooden bridge and they turned past the dark Gothic church and the library and then over the next bridge on to the large island which is the heart of Wroclaw. Stragglers joined all the time. To the left was the market hall, to the right the university buildings. Trams were forced to halt and people saw the MARCH FOR POLAND banner and got out to join.

Rafat, right at the front, was recognized by some people. Retman, Rafat Retman – he caught his name in the air. He had the strange feeling he was on stage and part of the audience at the same time. It was the biggest stage and the biggest audience of his life and he determined to speak.

Father Michal would say prayers but this day demanded speeches. He had no prepared text but the mood of the people would lift him. In communist methodology intellectuals join and lead the proletarian masses and this had provided their revolutionary thrust. Now it was for people like him to lend their voices to mobilise the workers against the communist hierarchy.

There had been a shower earlier, the cobbles glistened and the tram lines gleamed like silver laid on a table. There were faces at windows and Rafat raised an arm in an emperor's wave. He sent a silent cry up to them: Men of Poland, women of Poland, join us. We are one people, united under God, in defiance of an alien creed. Those who oppose us believe in force. They have no self-respect without force. They know they are inferior without force. If they cannot use force they are filled with fear. But we have the moral strength to defeat them without force of arms. We are united by love – love of God, love of our country, love for ourselves, true love. We are many, too many to defeat. We are a river running into a sea and finally an ocean – yes, an ocean of us who . . . who . . . huddled masses, suffered long enough . . . children yet unborn will say, This was their finest hour . . .

For all his vanity, this was from the heart. He knew, when the moment arrived, when the crowd was hushed, the speech would come and the sincerity with it.

Dominican Square has yet another of Wroclaw's blackened churches, and the crowd flowed out, spreading over the pavement and the grassy areas and the empty plot waiting for the builders' scaffolding and cement mixers. There is a road along the south side of the church but no traffic could pass. It was here, with their backs to the church, that the leaders of the rally took up positions.

'We should have brought beer crates to stand on,'

Eugeniusz said, 'and a microphone and loudspeakers.'

'There was no time.'

'You must project your voice,' Rafat said.

Forming a nucleus by the church were members of the Klub, Waldemar, Adam, Rafat, Natalia, Henryk, Father Michal and four other priests.

'You're alone,' Natalia said to Rafat.

'What? How can I be alone among thousands?'

He laced his fingers and cracked his knuckles, rotated his head to loosen the neck muscles and in an automatic gesture checked his flies. He felt the familiar quickened pulse of first-night nerves.

'No Zuzanna?' Natalia said. 'I thought she shared everything with you.'

'God, you stand here and gossip while history is being made. Got your eye on her, have you, darling? She's yours. She's always bitching.'

Natalia said, 'She's too much of a woman for you, is she?' And thought: Now I'm bitching, today of all days. She looked into the crowd, recognising a face here and there, Jurek, Stasrek, Elzunia jumping up and down, Skibiriska, whatever her first name was. Faces on bodies in front, faces on shoulders behind, then faces, faces, faces all the way back, the faces of Poland, faces stretching like a beach. Tadek should paint them. Where was Tadek? Tadek was not in sight. And no Zuzanna.

'Everybody's here,' Rafat said, as if the seats in a theatre were filled. 'What are we waiting for?'

'For loudspeakers,' Eugeniusz said. 'Henryk has sent to the university for them.'

'That will take for ever. Never keep an audience waiting or they'll turn against you. Can't you feel it – the energy? Does Father Michal need loudspeakers? I've never heard of a priest who couldn't shout a sermon.'

'We'll sing the national anthem.'

'For half a bloody hour?'

'What's your idea?'

'Speak! Speak from the heart! Speak for Poland, loud and clear!' With both hands Rafat cleared the people in front of him, gave himself space and stood very straight. He raised both arms high in the air, a gesture borrowed from de Gaulle when he claimed to understand the French *colons* in Algeria. 'Men of Poland! Women of Poland! Listen to the truths I speak to you. I dare not use the word "comrades" – though we are dear to each other – because They have stolen the word from us and perverted it for their own use. But we are men and we are women and they cannot steal our humanity.'

He had never spoken with such force and dignity and even those at the back who missed the words caught the mood and the sense. Rafat, confident of their attention, lowered his arms.

'They use violence against us – but we are not afraid. They use violence against our minds, swearing something is true when it isn't – but we are not deceived. They use violence against our faith, saying that God does not exist, God is a fairy tale – but we pray that God may forgive Them. They use violence against the strikers in Gdansk, threatening their jobs and intimidating them – but we stand here in solidarity with them. They use violence against us in our daily struggle for existence, denying us and our children decent food and clothing and homes – but They cannot break our spirit. They use violence against our neighbouring countries, sending tanks to confront civilians in Hungary and Czechoslovakia – but They only succeed in making all oppressed people determined to gain their freedom. They use violence against our own country, treating it as a colony – and we tell the imperialists to get out. They use violence against our history, distorting our past, making enemies out of our heroes – and we despise Them. They use violence against our intelligence, claiming their system is a triumph and the envy of the world – but we know only the failures we must endure in our everyday lives.' Sensing it was time to change the rhythm of his rhetoric and involve his audience, Rafat punched out a fist. 'Are the failures ours? Are they?'

'No,' came shouts from the crowd.

'Are the failures theirs?'

'Yes,' came shouts, stronger, more heartfelt.

'Are we afraid of Them?'

'No.'

'Are They afraid of our determination?'

'Yes.'

'Are the strikers in Gdansk alone and forgotten?'

'No.'

'Do we stand together with Lech Walesa and Anna Walentynowicz and the thousands who demand justice in Gdansk?'

'Yes,' came the shouts like a roll of thunder. The chanting began, as was happening in Gdansk, at the mention of Walesa: 'LESZEK! LESZEK!' Knowing he could not outshout the crowd, Rafat drew himself even taller and contented himself with conducting it with both arms; 'LESZEK! LESZEK! LESZEK!' His mind was slipping ahead to what he should say next. Shakespeare had the speeches, no doubt, Shakespeare was the model to follow. In his head he tried: Men in Wroclaw gone home early will hold themselves accursed they were not with us on this day.

This was when the helicopter came. It appeared from the north, as if it had followed them from the cathedral; but in fact seeking a note of surprise it slipped low over the church roof. Its clatter, suddenly and frighteningly loud, stilled Rafat and turned everybody's head. It was painted in army colours and was large enough to hold twenty men. It hovered above the crowd and began to sink. It was obvious it cared nothing whether it landed on the road or on bodies and panic struck like lightning. Screams, urgent shouts, warnings, then the crowd was breaking, scattering, scrambling to give the helicopter space. It landed perhaps thirty metres from where the leaders of the demonstration had been standing. The doors opened to let out not soldiers but men in leather jackets.

At the same time, cued by the helicopter, riot police appeared. They had been waiting behind the Panorama Hotel and in the pedestrian tunnel under Olawska and in a side street towards Rynek. Eye witnesses say they came forward like Zulu warriors, at a trot, batons across their chests, chanting in time with their step. Some swore they chanted 'Wesza, wesza, wesza', and maybe they did, though it would have been odd. It means 'Lice, lice, lice', and normally their language was more violent and more obscene.

The crowd's screams redoubled, and they split into groups as the batons swung, and the groups splintered further, and people were running and stumbling and being beaten to the ground.

The confusion was total. The leaders of the rally held fast for a few moments and then they too turned to escape. Natalia, Adam, Eugeniusz were just more stumbling figures swallowed up by the crowd. Father Michal and the other priests retreated into the church. Only Rafat stood, legs astride, the words and deeds and visions of heroes holding him firm until he was surrounded.

The helicopter rose. When it went, Rafat was no longer there.

CHAPTER ELEVEN

Tadeusz lay becalmed on the bunk. It was that time of night in the cell, it was that time in his life back in 1980. He felt the same now as he had then. He was waiting for the wind to spring up, fill his sails, swing him round and start a new course.

The wind was Zuzanna.

She'd stayed in his room, drunk some of his precious store of coffee, stretched and turned and moved so that Tadeusz grew very aware of the body under her clothes. But she sensed when he was about to reach out and by a slight tightening of her brows she made him hesitate. No, she was saying. But since she didn't leave it was really: No, not now, not yet. Then her eyebrows relented and she switched on a smile: Soon.

So why did They take Rafat? Tadeusz had often asked himself this question and the answer he gave depended on his mood. Because Rafat was the one who was speaking. Because Rafat Retman, actor, was the one with a public profile. Because the other leaders had dived into the crowd and the priests had taken sanctuary in the church. Because he simply stood there waiting to be scooped up.

Tadeusz found these answers dull and tried brighter alternatives. It was an extreme form of dramatic criticism. It was an early death experience, assumption into heaven in a rising helicopter. But he only tried these possibilities out of muddled feelings of guilt because he hadn't been there.

He remembered the knock at the door and how it opened before he got halfway there and Natalia appearing. She was panting and each breath pressed those mouthfuls against her shirt. Dishevelled? Hair mussed? Maybe. He remembered how she stepped into the room and stopped as she saw Zuzanna leaning against a wall. Natalia's eyes went from Zuzanna to Tadeusz and made the short hop to the bed. At least the bed was virginally tidy. But still . . .

'Now I understand.'

'Understand what?' Tadeusz asked.

'Why you skipped the rally.'

Tadeusz had not known what to say. He hadn't gone. He hadn't forgotten. It had been in and out of his mind, but what are the words to say: I was trapped here by that old black magic. There are some truths that cannot be spoken.

Natalia had gone on, 'I came to tell you the rally was broken up and the Ubeks snatched Rafat. But that probably doesn't worry you.'

There was a silence before Zuzanna said, 'Grabbed Rafat?' Feeling her reaction lacked urgency she came off the wall and said, 'You mean They've taken him away? Rafat's been arrested?'

Natalia gave a long thoughtful look at Zuzanna. This was the woman that Rafat had casually offered to her as if she was a holiday paperback that could be passed on, its pages well fingered. No, Natalia decided, not for her. She considered many replies, but in the end contented herself with, 'That's right.' And left.

Zuzanna had seduced him that day, no doubt about it. It's just that it wasn't consummated. She'd left shortly after Natalia, saying, 'I must find out about Rafat.' But it was his cheek she'd given one kitten's stroke to before making for the door.

In the days that followed Tadeusz had worked. The police raided various buildings and arrested people at random and he stayed in his room waiting for the boots up the stairs and nobody came. He remembered how he'd worked all the hours and all the reasons he gave for the frenzy of creativity. I'm a multi-discipline artist, he'd whispered to himself. He wrote the first pages of a new novel about a Nazi who fled to the Bolivian jungle; in his womanless state the man fell in love with a monkey but committed suicide when he discovered it was a Jewish monkey. He gave serious thought to a sound composition. He drew elaborate sketches for several unrealized sculptures. He painted.

It was because he hadn't gone to the rally, because Rafat had disappeared, because Natalia was angry. But he never thought, never, that he filled his days with creative fury because Zuzanna didn't come back and he didn't know where to find her.

When he left his room, he left reality behind. Only his created work existed. The outside world was a dream, the men and women had come from a different planet, a different galaxy. See – he'd told himself – a shop is for selling things and these have nothing to sell so they are a hoax, a joke. The factories are for making the things that should sell in the shops but they're making nothing so they are a hoax. The police are for protecting the citizens but instead they beat them up so they are a hoax. He saw a discarded flyer advertising a MARCH FOR POLAND and signed in a bottom corner Tadek – but Tadek was a codename for Tadek so he was most definitely the biggest hoax of all.

'Hello, pal, you awake there? Are you alive?'

Tadeusz, coming from a long way off, focused on the

dim figure sitting up in the other bunk. Miler, that was the name. He'd forgotten the existence of Miler.

'You'd wake the dead,' Tadeusz said.

'I was having a bit of shut-eye when I had this wonderful dream and I thought: I must share it with my pal Tadeusz. He'll laugh out loud.'

Tadeusz had a horror of other people's dreams and said nothing.

'So I'll tell you. I was in court, you see. I suppose being in here makes it natural to dream of something like that. There's this girl, see, who says I got her up the spout and am the father of her bouncing baby boy. Naturally this is something I deny. Okay, maybe we'd had a little rattle together but for all I know half the street did as well and she's just picked on me because I have a kind face. Anyhow, this judge says: "Lift up the baby, let's have a good look at it. All right now, accused, drop your trousers and let's have a good look at your willy. Well, it's obvious, his willy looks nothing like the baby and can't be its father. Case dismissed."'

Miler laughed, and after he'd stopped and thought about it he laughed again.

'Perhaps I'll get a judge like that next time. Have you got children, Tadek? Any babies you acknowledge as all your own work?'

'All my own work? Doesn't the woman play a part?'

'You know what I mean.'

'Friend Miler, we have a few minutes fun but it's the woman who does the work for nine months.'

'Don't try and get smart with me.'

'I don't even have to try.'

'I'm warning you. You try to get smart, that's not smart. You understand?'

'Understand?' Tadeusz was sick of Miler, sick of being

locked up with him. Like boys in a schoolyard, anger flared over nothing. 'What I understand is it's the middle of the night and I don't want to listen to your dreams or your Hollywood tough guy talk. So why don't you just shut up and go back to dreamland. Go and make another baby.'

Tadeusz heard movement and felt knuckles jammed against his mouth. 'Feel that? You'll get a taste too then you'll be the one who's shut up. Got that?' The fist twisted against Tadeusz's lips so that he couldn't have replied even if he'd wanted to. 'Of *course*, I was *forgetting*.' Two extra twists of the fist added emphasis. 'You said you were here because of love. You're the great lover. Probably you have nine months fun and the woman has just a few minutes work and out pops the baby. That's what it is.'

The fist was removed; Miler, laughing, returned to his bunk.

I wasn't the great lover, Tadeusz thought, I was the great lover frustrated. I was the monkey mourning in solitude in the Bolivian jungle. But not for long. Not for too long.

On the fifth day after Rafat was arrested and Zuzanna disappeared and Natalia left in a draught of disapproval, there was a knock at the door. There'd been no boots up the stairs so it wasn't the police. In fact the footsteps had been so light it could only be . . .

CHAPTER TWELVE

Father Michal wore the expression he surely wore in the confessional: his jowly face a mix of steely goodwill and weary puzzlement at the human capacity to screw life up. The face became more bemused by the sketch done on a piece of card propped on the table. It showed planet earth drawn on the naked buttocks of a fat man bending over, the split up the buttocks neatly cleaving Russia and something plopping from Moscow.

'Tadeusz, what have we here?'

'It's obvious.' Tadeusz was abrupt, still feeling the stab of disappointment it wasn't Zuzanna.

'Does one have to have one's nose rubbed in the obvious?'

'It's a symbol.'

'You're instructing a priest about symbols? Tadeusz, a symbol gains its power through suggestion. The viewer or listener or reader makes the connection. With the connection made there comes the light and satisfaction.'

Head to one side, Tadeusz considered the sketch. Then he took it, folded it and tore it in half, folded the two pieces again and tore them into quarters, and in silence presented the pieces to Father Michal. The priest accepted the gift with both hands and looked for somewhere to dispose of it.

'If I am arrested, I would prefer not to be found carrying criticism of a fraternal socialist ally – I believe that is the accepted term.'

They sat in two straightbacked chairs and Father Michal

clasped his hands on the wooden table.

'Natalia told me where you live,' he said in answer to a question Tadeusz hadn't asked. 'We need another poster. I said that just because you didn't attend the last rally, it didn't mean you weren't still committed.'

'Of course,' Tadeusz said.

Father Michal was looking him full in the face. Then by a dreadful power of attraction, his eyes darted to the bed and came creeping back.

'Tadeusz, we need your God-given talent. The strikers in Gdansk have reached agreement with the government and got more than we ever prayed for. Yet here in Wroclaw the authorities are still holding Rafat. So we plan another protest.'

'Despite what happened at the last one?'

'Because of what happened. To do nothing is to admit defeat. We shall march, we shall protest, we shall organize, we shall sing and raise our voices until they are heard, above all we shall pray until our prayers are granted as they surely must be. The church cannot stand apart from the troubles of our people, and if we are to stand together it is necessary to act. Oh yes,' Father Michal said, nodding in agreement with himself. 'The authorities will have to arrest us all like They have arrested Rafat. Once They have arrested the whole nation They will understand how many we are and how few They are. They have imprisoned Poland already so what difference does it make if They put us behind bars? We are not afraid of that. They are the ones who are afraid.'

Abruptly Father Michal stopped his speech. There was a silence where applause should have been. His hands that had been beating the air sank back to the table. He blinked and looked round the room as if surprised to find it empty. Then he came back to Tadeusz.

'We shall gather together to show our strength.' It was

like repeating a piece of church dogma. 'Rally, march, demonstrate.' This was no clandestine conspiracy. 'Put up posters, meet in public, speak aloud.' The plan had the simple logic of the novice. They had nothing to conceal because there was no need to hide virtue. They were not plotting in the shadows. 'So, Tadeusz, you will help?'

Father Michal had asked for a symbol and Tadeusz knew exactly what was needed. He used his sketchpad which he propped on the easel for he liked the sense of working in space that the easel gave him. He could step back and see his work in a wider context: is it simple enough, strong enough to stand out from the clutter of the real world? Yes, he decided, even including the time, the place, the message, the new Solidarity logo.

He had finished the rough layout when he caught a creak from the floorboard outside his door, or possibly a boot scuffing the wood, then the silence of men preparing to burst in. They followed the priest here, Tadeusz thought, that's how They know. He jammed the lay-out under some other sketches, which would delay Them for about five minutes if They made a search, and stared at the door. He should go to the door, jerk it open and surprise Them himself, but he found he couldn't move. He strained to catch the sound of a whispered order and heard only his own breath. Come on, he urged Them silently, don't keep me in suspense. He saw the handle turn, the door ease open a crack, and pause. They are listening, trying to work out what I'm doing. He thought of the things he should have done – drop the pieces of the buttocks into the street, make a paper dart of the lay-out and launch it – too late. The door opened wider, a head appeared, then a body, and the door was closed again as Zuzanna came forward to greet him, eyebrows raised.

'Tadek, why are you looking at me like that?'

Tadeusz didn't know how he was looking or how he was feeling. He was conscious only of heat swelling his head and burning his cheeks and the thump of his heart.

'Why have you been avoiding me?' she asked.

It took Tadeusz a moment to work out the question was the wrong way round. 'Me avoiding you? I don't know where you live. Where have you been?' The words burst out of him, much louder than he intended.

'What have you been doing?' she asked. She always seemed to have a question to bounce back at him. He searched for the lay-out and put it back on the easel while she came and stood close. She reached a hand up to his shoulder and boldly leaned against him while she considered it: bars, as in a prison, stretched the depth of the page and were wrenched apart as if by Superman. 'That's good. I like it. One problem.' She pointed to the headline Tadeusz had roughed in: RAFAT – CHARGE HIM OR FREE HIM.

'Problem?'

'Rafat's been put on trial and convicted.'

'Nobody knows that. A secret trial?'

'Well, I was there. The prosecution accused him of trying to overthrow the state which is ridiculous when you consider what Rafat is, full of wind and poses. That really scared him because he could have been hanged. The charge was reduced to anti-state propaganda and he's been given three years. So . . .'

That's terrible! That's wonderful! Tadeusz's emotions surged one way and back again. Three years . . . It was a long while to be put away. He was conscious once more of Zuzanna's closeness, her watchful eye on him, her waiting for his reaction.

'Three years in prison for making a speech is not acceptable,' Tadeusz said, sounding pompous in his own ears.

'We must demonstrate. I must do the poster. I'll change the headline: FREE RAFAT! FREE POLAND!'

She nodded and walked away a little. 'Yes,' she said and Tadeusz had the idea he had passed some test though what was a mystery to him.

'Zuzia, have you ever posed? Been an artist's model?'

'No.'

'I'm going to do the artwork for the poster. But if there are boots running up the stairs, Ubeks mounting a raid for Rafat's accomplices, I'll hide the poster and pretend I'm painting you. If They come, if the Ubeks raid, you must take all your clothes off very fast. You'll be my nude model.'

Zuzanna perched on the edge of the bed, then decided she would be more comfortable stretched out. She lay on her side, her chin propped in the palm of one hand and gazed at Tadeusz while he worked. After a few minutes she decided on a new position and snuggled lower on the bed, using her forearm as a pillow. She said, 'Tadek, do I have to wait until there's a raid?'

Tadeusz was blocking in the prison bars, dark grey shading to light grey. He didn't answer though his brush hesitated in its stroke. He didn't look to the side where Zuzanna lay but straight ahead at the easel. He heard a thump and hesitated again, waiting for the thump of the second shoe.

There were four bars to paint. He began with the bars at each side because they were straight and quick and easy. Zuzanna didn't speak but he could hear her sometimes take a deeper breath, sometimes shift her position. She seemed to grow restless but he refused to look. I need my eyes to paint, he reasoned, but he sent his ears out on patrol. There was a rustling and then a sound like drifting sand, or the soft sigh that cloth might make landing on the floor next to the shoes. She had been wearing a shirt in yellow and grey stripes and he decided that was just the noise that yellow and grey would make hitting the bedside mat.

He started on one of the Superman-bent bars. It must look absolutely right, shading, gradations of light, reflections. His ears picked up the sound of bedsprings as she shifted position and a little grunt as of someone twisting an arm back to reach something. The tiniest metal click – if his ears weren't on sentry duty he'd have missed it – such as a metal hook makes being attached to – or rather detached from – a metal eye. A small metal hook and eye, very small, for something small such as a bra.

He finished the bar and began on its twin, its un-Siamese twin, not joined but bent away, and the silence was torn by another metallic sound. A zip. The zip of a pair of dark blue slacks, to be precise. Then came another protest from the bedsprings and the sound of cotton material being slid over limbs, first one leg, then the other, and an altogether more substantial clump as if the slacks had been thrown on the floor.

There was more shifting on the bed, of a body moving itself out of the way as blankets and sheets were pulled aside. The last sound was a tiny indrawn breath.

Tadeusz's hand holding the brush had come to a standstill. Seduced by the audible striptease he turned to look at Zuzanna. She lay on her back and even in that position her breasts were not flattened. What she was doing, Tadeusz saw, was running a fingertip round and round a nipple to make it stand erect. Seeing Tadeusz at last turn her way, she gave a lovely smile.

'Would you help me do this, please?'

Natalia had a flat above her gallery. Just before nine o'clock Tadeusz presented himself with the poster. The table was set for two, with cold meat and salad and a bottle of Egri Bikaver wine, but the other person either hadn't arrived or was in another room. Natalia drew on her cigarette holder and gazed at the poster and nodded.

'It's powerful, direct, striking yet subtle. Eleven marks out of ten. Why have you signed it TCT?'

'A little private joke.'

'Which you're sharing?'

'Tadek Codename Tadek.'

She blew smoke at him.

'Natalia, I've heard that Rafat has been put on trial and sentenced to three years in jail.'

'How did you hear this?'

'A friend told me.'

'Does this friend have blonde hair, blue eyes and big tits?'

Tadeusz didn't answer.

Natalia reached out a finger and ran it over lips that were bruised and suffused with blood. 'It's just as well she's found someone new then.'

Tadeusz lay on his back, Zuzanna on her front, sprawled half over him. The night still held the warmth of the day and the covers were thrown back. The moon was riding high and staring in through the uncurtained window, a round moon with a bite out of it, a mad Bolivian moon.

'I love you,' Tadeusz said, whispering his secret.

'Louder.'

'I love you, I love you, I love you.'

'Only three times.'

'I'll love you some more and then I'll love you again and then again.'

'Promises, promises.'

'I can't have enough of you.'

'I don't satisfy you?'

Reaching out a hand, Tadeusz tipped Zuzanna's face up

and kissed her with his bruised lips and marvelled that there seemed another Zuzanna that lived in her mouth, a tongue that had its own existence and fluttered all round his tongue and explored his mouth. When he came up for air she said: 'More.' They kissed and kissed and she was stroking and bringing him alive once more.

'What a hero,' she said.

She squatted astride him and the feeling as she guided him inside was so exquisite he made her do it again.

It was her turn to whisper. 'Keep still. You're tired from all you've done. It's my turn.'

She moved on him with a slow rocking motion.

'Tell me what you like, Tadek.'

He opened his mouth and caught his breath before he could say, 'That.'

Her hand burrowed down between their bodies so she could fondle him. 'And this?'

'Oh. Ohhh.'

He'd known that she would be the best lover in the world, in the whole of creation, but he still marvelled at the feel of her body, her movements, her whispers, her convulsions as electric currents passed through every part of her, her sudden dive to find his mouth, the urgency of her tongue, the rearing up, the hair flying as she shook her head from side to side, her voice rising, 'Oh God, oh yes yes yes.' And her final ecstatic wordless cry.

'Zuzia,' he shouted as his fingers dug into her, clutched her as if he was clinging to a mountainside and was about to tumble into space. 'Zuzia Zuzia Zuzia.'

She put a hand on his cheek to steady his head and then pressed so his mouth came away from hers.

'Every part of me is made for kissing.'

She put a finger in his mouth and touched his tongue

and let him chase the finger round and round. When he looked in her face he saw her eyes were closed but the corners of her lips were lifted in a half-smile.

She pushed her blonde hair aside and offered him an ear. When his tongue was inside she suddenly shivered and broke free. 'You feel as if you're inside my thoughts, taking me over.'

She turned on her side and crooked her arm. 'Even my elbow.' It was the only rough skin of her body and his tongue smoothed it.

She cupped her right breast so the nipple stood proud. 'It's the way you lean over – you only ever caress my left nipple. My right one is jealous.' Tadeusz took the nipple between his lips and found it hard, a tiny volcano of flesh. 'Suck, suck as hard as you can.'

'My feet,' she said. 'Feet aren't just for walking and treading the grapes. Slip your tongue between the toes.' Between the big toe and the next was a gap just the right size for the tip of his tongue. He was kneeling on the bed with his head bowed, a truffle hound searching for buried treasure.

She turned over to lie on her stomach. 'The back of my knees, Tadek.' Yes, Zuzia, the back of your knees, he thought, I shall never again walk behind a woman without making love to the back of her knees.

She turned again and spread her legs. 'My lilybud. Can your tongue feel it? Yes, oh yes, don't stop.' He didn't stop.

I won't stop, I'll do this for ever, he told himself, this will be the rest of my life, doing what Zuzia tells me, tasting her body, all the parts that are yet to be kissed.

But Zuzanna had other ideas and pulled him up so that they lay face to face. She reached down to feel him and said, 'You are amazing, a hero.'

He said, 'It's because of you.'

When Tadeusz woke it was towards morning, a faint light

showing the damp patch on the ceiling. The bed was cold and when he put out a hand he found Zuzanna had gone. He turned over in a convulsive movement and found she hadn't gone far. She was perched on a chair by the window, her knees drawn up and her chin resting on them. She had pulled on one of his sweaters but so far as he could tell she wore nothing else. He pictured her sitting on a boulder on a headland staring out to sea, to the horizon, to hopes and dreams that are beyond reach. He went to stand close to her, putting a hand down inside the sweater to cup one of her breasts.

Her face tilted to him and by the dawn light he could see the upturned lips of her smile. She said, 'Thank you.'

Tadeusz felt a surge inside him, of what he didn't know. His life seemed to turn over. He thought he understood what she meant. It was not just for the pleasure, it was for the consideration. She didn't say *You're not like Rafat* but perhaps that was what she meant by her thanks. Not like Rafat who appreciated no beauty so much as the sight of his own face in the mirror in the morning.

'I came to sit here and watch the darkness go so I could remember,' she said. 'I wanted to fix everything in my memory before the day brought anything new. I wanted no fresh experience before last night had set solid.' She tapped her temple.

It was our wedding night, Tadeusz thought, you want memories of that. Aloud he said, 'Come back to bed.'

She did. 'Just hold me in your arms.'

She fell asleep like that and he watched as the growing light gave life to her features. She's beyond me, he thought. Even in our most passionate time there is some last part of her I don't possess. I can possess her breasts and her lips and between her toes and deep inside her but something eludes me. Whereas she, on the contrary, possesses me absolutely. I am lost in her.

Perhaps it was always so in love. Tadeusz didn't know.

CHAPTER THIRTEEN

We put up a statue to a great man, but a woman we remember in the horizontal position.

What would Miler say to that? From the sound of breath sawing in his throat, nothing. But maybe Miler's great accomplishment was to snore when he was awake.

Tadeusz went to the toilet partly concealed by a half partition, splashed water on his face from the basin and never looked in the mirror like Rafat. There were hours of the night left, with none of the glimpses of dawn that silhouetted Zuzanna after their first night.

There's only ever one first night, in the theatre, in a love affair, in prison. There is only ever that one discovery, that hand unfolding to show its secret, that bomb exploding inside you, destroying your world until now, and in a blinding flash showing you a new one. There is only ever that one certainty that this is the best, the unique, the everlasting.

But he remembered how even in those first days she would dress and go to the door.

'Where are you going?'

'Out.'

'What are you going to do?'

'A woman can have her secrets.'

'Wait – I'll come with you.'

'No.'

'You're tired of me already. You're going to see another lover.'

It had been something to say, something of a tease, a prelude to renewed kisses. She stared at him for an eternity, five seconds at least. She said, 'That's not funny.'

To bind him closer.

When she returned from wherever she'd been, from whatever she'd done, from whoever she'd seen, she would kick off her shoes and start in a rush. 'What have you been doing? Painting? Drinking camomile tea? Thinking of new ways to love?' She'd come to him, stand very close if he was sitting and writing or sketching or reading. 'What's this?'

But she didn't expect an answer. She expected his touch, his hand on her calf, on the back of the knee he had kissed, moving higher up the inside of her thigh.

He remembered those days, the first three or four, with clarity. Call it their honeymoon.

Tadeusz had dozed off. What woke him was the flushing of the toilet and Miler's return to his bunk.

'How are you doing?' Miler asked.

'I drifted off to sleep.'

'Sweet dreams?'

'I don't remember.' Tadeusz had wakened with a jolt and the dream had fled.

'I had a dream,' Miler said.

'You told me.'

'No, another dream. Featured a girl I know called Marcelina. I dreamed she walked in here naked and went to lie down in your bunk. You weren't there, you see. When I woke up I thought, I'll just go and check.'

'I'm glad you checked first.'

'Yes, I saw my mistake at once. No boobs. She's got big ones, with really big nipples like big brown saucers. You know what Marcelina said to me one day?'

'No, I don't know what Marcelina said to you one day.'

'She said, "Do you know the reason women have brown nipples?" No, tell me, I said. "It comes of having men sitting bare-arsed on their tits." How do you like that?'

'I'll remember that one. Marcelina you said her name was?'

'Right, Marcelina. She said, "It comes from having . . ." No, she said, "It comes from men sitting on their tits with bare arses."'

'Bare arses?'

'Yes.'

'And I always thought it came from stirring their coffee with their nipples.'

There was silence for a bit. 'Jesus,' Miler said, 'I think you're crazy, you know? No offence, pal, but I do. Stirring their coffee . . .' Miler lay down and turned his back. It was a minute or two later when he heaved over. 'Hey, how about the ones who don't take sugar in their coffee and don't stir?'

'They have white nipples.'

'White nipples? What are you talking about, white nipples? I've never seen a woman with white nipples.'

'That's because they all take sugar.'

Miler sat up and shouted, 'And I have never seen a woman stirring her coffee like that.'

'They do it at puberty when their breasts start to swell and it stains the new soft skin. You know how cheap red wine can stain your teeth? It's the same with girls at puberty and coffee.'

'You're bullshitting me.'

'Listen,' Tadeusz said, 'haven't you ever said to a woman, "Come back to my place and have a coffee." And she gives you a funny look and says, "No." That's because she knows what you're thinking. You want to watch her stirring her coffee.'

'She knows I'm not thinking about coffee.'

'All right, you believe Marcelina's theory and I'll stay with mine. But I tell you, I think Marcelina's theory is a lot crazier.'

Someone once told Tadeusz: We have clean ideas outside, we have dirty ideas inside. Nowhere was more inside than a prison cell. He wished he could go to sleep, really sleep for the rest of the night, not just doze and have his mind wander. There were places he didn't want it wandering.

When he tried to white his mind out, what he got was a blank canvas, and then a figure began to develop on it. The figure appeared in pieces, like a landscape at dawn. First was a flowing line from shoulder to ankle, with the hip making a hill. A breast caught the light, now the second one. A foot lay twisted. Eyes suddenly open, with depths, which was not usual with blue eyes, eyes that stared back at you, gazed while your own eyes slipped to the breasts again, to nipples the colour of milky coffee.

The figure on the canvas turned into a living woman. Zuzanna swung herself off the bed and came to stand beside him. There was no way to tell her that an artist's work in progress was private, that he needed to experiment, to make mistakes, and not be always anticipating criticism. She was very close so that he was overwhelmed by the warmth of her, the scent of her body, the sound her hand made as it swept hair from her eyes to let her see with total clarity.

She stood so close he could no longer focus his mind on his work. Is that what she intended? His resolve melted, his mind and his body turned to her, he was caught. It was a secret power she enjoyed, revelled in.

She'd conquered him. When Renton appeared, she conquered him too. Had she guessed what Renton's real job was?

CHAPTER FOURTEEN

'**Y**es . . .'

The word hung in the air, the sentence unfinished, a *but* looking for a tender target. Tadeusz flung his paint-brush at the wall. The brush had been dipped in bright red – whatever the label on the tube said, Tadeusz knew it as Mexican Whore Red – which he'd been going to dress her nails with. Those nails were talons that drew a man's blood.

'*But*. I don't want to hear your *but*. What do you think – you're a world famous critic? Curator at the National Museum?'

They'd had their first night, their first fury of love, now their first quarrel. Zuzanna's eyes widened, a glow was on her cheeks.

'I'm a woman, Tadek. What do you know of women?'

'I'm an artist. What do you know of art?'

'So you're painting art. I thought you were painting a woman.' She cupped her breasts. 'You've caressed these, so you think you know a woman.' She gave two rhythmic pushes with her pelvis. 'You've gone in here so you think you know all about women. All you know is your man's view which in reality is a boy's view, a prurient boy peeking through the bathroom keyhole at his big sister in the shower. You want to see everything in a bright light. You want every detail, every hair, as if then you'll understand what makes a woman. Yes?'

'I paint what I see. What I see are breasts, nipples, navel, pubic hair, thighs, knees, one foot crossed over the other.'

'And that defines me?' Zuzanna tossed blonde hair from her face. 'You poor boy. Look at me.'

'I'm looking.'

'I'm naked and you can inspect everything but I don't see you aroused.'

'I'm working. Correction. If I wasn't arguing, I'd be working.'

'But in your head, in your imagination, you should be making love. Why do you think you close your eyes when you kiss me?'

'You're going to tell me.'

'Because you think I'm ugly? Maybe you're tired of looking at me? Or you want to go to sleep? Why don't you answer?'

'I'm listening.'

With a gentle touch she closed first his left eyelid, then his right. 'Imagine. You're in a locked room. The window is open but the shutters are closed so you can't see out. But you can hear the outside world. You hear the siren of a police car, then an ambulance, then a fire engine. What's going on? In your mind you build different scenes. You picture an apartment building on fire, smoke billowing, people leaping from windows, babies being thrown into blankets. Or a multiple crash, a petrol tanker in flames, people trapped in cars, beating on windows, screaming. Your imagination runs wild. And that, Tadek, is why you close your eyes when you kiss. The imagination goes further.'

Tadeusz answered nothing. Well, no words. Instead he picked up his palette and squeezed from a tube called Midnight Blue, and deciding that wasn't sombre enough added from one called Total Black, then a lightening from Apple Blossom Blush, and muddled the cocktail together to a haunting dark shade before turning his attention to the canvas. With bold brushstrokes he created a shadow to hide her body from knees to ribcage, leaving just a rim of skin, a

fair silhouette. It was what she wanted, what she was telling
him to do. More darkness, more, she urged, giving it out like
an order. Darkness defines sexuality because darkness hides
secrets. A nude on a beach is banal, too much sunlight, too
much openness. Someone undressing in a halflit room across
the street makes your breath come faster, isn't that so, Tadek?
As if she knew about Tex and how he'd waited with longing
at the window. Tadeusz felt Zuzanna wasn't giving art
lessons, she was instructing him in other mysteries. If there
was a theatre of love, she was the leading lady. How had she
learned her part? How had she auditioned for it?

Why she did it he never understood. Why did she say:
These are my tricks. Why say: This is why I like the light
dim. Why say: These are whore's tricks with underwear.
Why say: I go out so you will have time alone to fantasize.
Unless . . . unless there was one final secret she hid.

I should write a play for her, he thought. She will be
alone on stage and it will be dark except for a single spotlight. The light will be on her face, her perfect face in its
blonde frame. But when she moves across the stage and the
spotlight follows, suddenly a breast or a flank or a secret
darkness between her thighs will alert you that she is naked.
A flash of pale flesh before the spotlight fixes once more on
her face. And the audience will be part of the darkness. It
will be a conspiracy between Zuzanna and the audience.

That is what the painting had become with its glimpses
of her flesh, a conspiracy between Zuzanna and the viewer.
You ached to see more of her, you begged. And she said:
Later, possibly.

'Art is a conspiracy between the artist and the viewer,'
Tadeusz informed Zuzanna's left breast. 'The artist, the
viewer and the model,' he amended. Sweat stuck his cheek
to her skin. He put out his tongue to lick the underside of

her breast and felt her stir. 'My style has evolved. I used to
be a Satirist. Now I am a Conspirator.'

'Love is the biggest conspiracy of all,' Zuzanna told him
as her hand explored the corrugations of his spine.

'Darkness hides its secrets.'

'And the Ubeks are baffled.'

Zdzislaw and Eugeniusz stood in front of the canvas. There
was silence and Tadeusz watched their faces. They are the
public, the first ones exposed to my new creative spirit.
Speak. Say Yes yes yes. Don't say Yes but.

Zdzislaw cleared his throat, he shuffled his feet, he
seemed generally ill at ease. This was his friend's woman
and he shouldn't be staring at her like this. It was
Eugeniusz who spoke.

'It's like after the sun sets, in the dusk, when you strain
your eyes because you want to see more. I'm a plain working man so I'll speak my mind. Tadek, I would like to see
more.' He laughed and clapped Tadeusz on the shoulder.
'And where is she?'

'She had to go out.'

'Good. We have Klub work and we shan't be disturbed.'

'Can we turn the canvas round,' Zdzislaw asked. 'I won't
be able to concentrate otherwise. Stone the dogs, Tadek.'
He shook his head in awe. 'Stone the dogs.'

A couple of thousand – nobody kept a tally – came to the
demonstration. With the longer warning there should have
been more. But the events at Gdansk had for the moment
lulled people. A great victory has been won, some said,
mistaking ceasefire for surrender.

Outside the western cathedral porch a low wooden dais
had been erected from dismantled packing cases. With four
people standing on it there was a dangerous sag. The

cathedral's internal sound system had been extended, two loudspeakers rigged to the outside wall and a standing microphone placed on the platform. As a backdrop a banner demanded: FREE RAFAT! FREE POLAND! Late afternoon sun lit up the blue and yellow lettering. The sun still had warmth but Tadeusz could feel it was pulling back, heading south, leaving an emptiness in the air after the immediacy of summer heat.

'Citizens, fellow Christians, friends, we are gathered together to protest the monstrous injustice that has been done to one of our brothers.'

Father Michal had the microphone, Eugeniusz and Natalia were to one side of him, Henryk to the other. Tadeusz, standing on the doorstep of a house across the little square, saw others grouped round the platform. He didn't know them but they stood like organizers, like people who wanted to be thought leaders, facing the crowd. Tadeusz searched faces and couldn't see Zuzanna. Next to him on the step stood a man who also scanned the crowd. Zuzanna's most secret lover whom she went to visit when she'd exhausted Tadeusz? One of the Ubeks?

Father Michal was saying a prayer.

Solidarity badges studded the crowd. They showed the jumbly marching figures that made up the letters. The red splashes on lapels were like bullet wounds.

'*The Red Badge of Courage*,' Tadeusz murmured, saying the American title, and the man next to him moved his head a fraction and a narrowed eye stole a look at Tadeusz.

Father Michal was saying Mankind is born free and the chains he finds himself in are of his own making.

This was a young crowd, people gathering in a swell of hope, children hoisted on shoulders. Tadeusz saw mainly the backs of heads, then one would turn to nod Yes to a neighbour and a face would shine. He caught a face he knew, Zdzislaw, but Zdzis didn't see him. Then a woman's face as she turned to hand a two year old to the man next to her. It was Ewa, no longer Tex. The hair had turned mousy, no more the electrified marvel he'd painted when he was a Satirist. Married, a mother, life's pattern of cooking and washing and pregnancies and confession had settled over her. She had become ordinary, which is what she had always longed for.

The man on the step beside him was straining to catch Father Michal's words which had become indistinct. Then, like some dreadful action replay on television, a helicopter swung into view over the cathedral, dipped down and hovered above the craning heads of the crowd. Father Michal's face was also turned up and he was shouting into the microphone which provoked an electronic howl from the loudspeakers. He was shouting something about God but Tadeusz thought he would do better to invoke the devil. The door of the helicopter opened and a figure could be seen struggling with a sack, lurching and regaining his balance, then tipping the sack out over the crowd. A rain of small objects struck heads and shoulders and fell on to the cobbles. Squeals penetrated the clatter of the engine and children were darting between legs, parents calling out and blundering among the chaos for their offspring.

'Shit,' the man beside Tadeusz said. In English.

'No shit,' Tadeusz said, 'not yet. They are still straining at Party headquarters to get that out.'

The stranger swung round on him. 'So?'

'Sweets,' Tadeusz said, 'a sackful of sweets.'

'Confrontation Polish style.'

More Bolivian style, Tadeusz thought. But talk had become impossible. To the pandemonium in the square and the noise of the helicopter's engine was added a blast of music. Someone in the helicopter was playing a tape of 'Carmen', as if this small square was a *corrida* and there were *picadors* and a chanting crowd and a strutting *matador*

and a bull. No bull. No bull charging or being dragged
away for the butcher's slab. The helicopter dipped lower,
the music was louder, children began crying, the banner
behind Father Michal was swept free by the draught from
the rotor, the crowd was breaking up. Children were gathered up in arms, some people began to run. No riot police
were needed this time. Opera for the grown-ups, treats for
the kids – that was the new style of crowd control. No
trucks of uniformed men waited down alleys. Tadeusz
looked to the north side of the cathedral where a car had
appeared. People were scattering from it, one of the figures
being Zuzanna who was dodging through the crowd
towards him before veering aside and being swallowed up.
His eyes went back to the car, to the man behind the
steering wheel whose face was partially obscured by reflections on the windscreen. The man leaned forward as if to
see more clearly. Tadeusz recognized a bald head that
gleamed like a wet stone and the protruding lips of some
fish in its glass bowl. No, not a goldfish, more a shark by
nature and last met in a riot police barracks while the prisoner Tadeusz Lipski stood naked in front of him. Baran was
watching another tactical victory with satisfaction.

Fearing a baton charge, people had taken refuge inside the
cathedral. There was no escaping the clatter of the helicopter or the blaring of the opera. In the cathedral it was
normal for the priest's voice to be raised and the congregation merely to follow. Now a woman's voice cut the air.
Natalia was saying, 'Why doesn't the Pope excommunicate
them? What good is a Polish Pope if he's not fighting with
us?' Her audience was Father Michal and Eugeniusz.

   Tadeusz was looking towards them, then back to the
stranger who'd spoken English outside.

   'Do you speak Polish?'

'I admire Poles immensely for mastering Polish. To me it is like climbing in the Himalayas: it is all around me and a challenge.'

Tadeusz brightened. Here was someone with a viewpoint to respect. 'My name is Tadeusz Lipski.'

'Robin Renton.'

'R.R.,' Tadeusz said, 'as in the car.'

'You flatter me,' Renton said. 'Like that man who was briefly American President said: I'm a Ford, not a Cadillac.'

'You're a tourist here?'

'I'm posted to the British embassy in Warsaw. On the cultural side.'

'The Cultural Ambassador.'

'The British don't rank culture that highly. Merely Assistant Cultural Secretary. And you?'

'I paint. I compose. I write. I practise *feng shui*. I sculpt. But I don't dance.'

'Then you are cultural too.'

'Because I don't dance?'

A glance, a fleeting smile, like lovers linked, and their secret was intercepted by Zuzanna. 'Who is your new friend? Why does he speak English? What were you smiling at? Why were you hiding in here from me?'

She tossed out questions like fruit. Here, catch an apple, an orange, a hand grenade, a pear.

'I wasn't running from you, from the helicopter.'

The music still blared. Zuzanna's eyes inspected him for telltale signs of lying, such as shifty eyes or too steady eyes, such as evasive answers or too ready answers. 'And your new friend?'

Tadeusz told her.

'A cultured Englishman – that's wonderful. And from the embassy. Well, well.' An eyebrow was raised and then a smile made her whole face glow. 'Does he understand

Polish? Of course not. So you must translate. Tell him how honoured we are to meet someone so distinguished from the country that has given the world Shakespeare and the BBC and the Rolling Stones. No, don't bother. Tell him about your work instead. Tell this cultural gentleman he must come to see your paintings. Tell him you are a Conspirator.'

Tadeusz said, 'I am a Conspirator.'

'Ah, a conspirator,' Renton said. He had a tone of voice perfected at the embassy social functions he couldn't escape. 'How absolutely fascinating.'

The crowd had melted away leaving a few loners, adrift, looking for lost companions, missing the camaraderie and sense of purpose. These stragglers stood singly and in pairs. Were they hoping for something more to happen? Were they Baran's foot soldiers? Tadeusz eyed them and felt Zuzanna's tug at his arm.

'What brings your new friend to Wroclaw?'

New friend? Tadeusz wasn't certain of the description. Renton was on the far side of Zuzanna and Tadeusz had to speak across her. 'She is curious why you have come here.'

'Culture. Why else? Is the Cantans Festival going ahead? I couldn't get any sense out of anybody in Warsaw so I came to find out. Culture is a two-way street so I must get to know Wroclaw's great traditions, your fine Gothic build-ings, the Aula Leopoldina, the opera, the art galleries –'

'What's he saying? What's he saying?'

'He's come for the culture.'

'The culture?' Zuzanna gave Renton a long look as if culture was something discreditable or at least peculiar. 'He chooses his time, doesn't he? With everything in Poland in a ferment.'

Tadeusz translated and Renton replied, 'What would she

have us do? Close the embassy shutters and play games with the secretaries?'

To this Zuzanna said, 'I thought that was what secretaries at embassies were for.' Seeing Tadeusz staring stupidly at her, she added, 'To keep the diplomats from playing games with us natives.'

Tadeusz spoke across her breasts to Renton, 'She hopes you are enjoying your visit.'

Renton smiled. It was the smile of someone who hasn't understood what's being said, showing good will. That was how Tadeusz took it. Maybe Zuzanna thought that too. She linked arms first with Renton, then with Tadeusz, and marched them across the square away from the cathedral.

'Did he find the rally to be culturally interesting? Folkloric perhaps?' She gave a tug at Tadeusz's arm. 'Go on, ask him.'

Renton's reply was more of an apology. 'I was admiring the Gothic arches in the cathedral when the crowd began forming. Naturally I stayed to see what was happening.'

With life in the square returning to normal, an artist had appeared. He squatted on a stool with a dozen of his watercolours of city landmarks propped against the wall of a house.

'Look, culture,' Zuzanna said.

It was a word that didn't need translating. Renton glanced towards the paintings while Zuzanna forged on, dragging the men with her. They reached the bridge over the river. On the willows the first yellow leaves of autumn brightened the late afternoon.

'Is she leading us somewhere special?' Renton asked. 'I should really be getting back.'

'Where are we going?' Tadeusz asked.

Was she angry with them? Upset? She hurried them in front of a clanking tram and turned into a street lined with grey stone university buildings. 'Look,' she commanded again, nodding at a poster stuck to the wall. 'Culture of a different kind. Tell him what it is.'

'I designed that,' Tadeusz said.

Renton pulled them to a stop to inspect the prison bars pulled apart. 'Signed: TCT. Your initials?'

'Tadek Codename Tadek.'

'Of course, you are a conspirator.'

Was it a joke? Renton's head eased round so he could see if anyone shared it with them.

'There is a Klub – certain people meeting to decide what actions we should take – and I do the design work for them.'

Zuzanna watched their faces, catching a word or two, before pulling them forward. They came to a statue outside one of the university entrances. She said, 'Well, are you going to tell him?'

Tadeusz stared at her.

'It's culture he's interested in, isn't it?'

Tadeusz's attention stayed on her a moment longer. From the start, now he came to consider it, she had taken control of their lives together. But not with this edge to it. Something antagonised her or made her nervous. Or she picked up some vibration from Renton. Or she didn't like not following the talk in English. Or it was the time of the month – Tadeusz had become aware that a woman's life had a rhythm to it. Or it was his imagination.

He said, 'There is a legend that a young man of noble family came to the university to study but fell into bad company. He drank wine and he knew women.' Tadeusz frowned as if himself was beyond such things. 'He went to a casino – no, that is not right. He went to a betting place –'

'A gambling den?'

'He went to a gambling den where he lost everything: first he lost all his money, then his books, finally he lost all his clothes. All they allowed him to keep was his sword to defend what was left of his honour.' Again Tadeusz frowned as the romantic legend took a swift plunge into bathos. 'Every first of April the students cover his nakedness with underpants.'

Like three voyeurs they craned their necks to inspect him.

'Nothing to boast of,' Zuzanna said.

'The statue is very special because he is a symbol,' Tadeusz said. 'Noble, Polish, stripped naked of all his possessions, yet still he grasps his sword to defy the world.'

On, on, Zuzanna led the troika down Odrzanska and pulled up short in front of Natalia's gallery.

'There,' she said. 'I brought it when you went out after lunch.'

The window had been swept clean of its usual clutter so that nothing detracted from the canvas resting on an easel. It was the painting Tadeusz had done of Zuzanna stretched on the bed, face serious, eyes speculating, hand palm up offering or maybe imploring, nipples the colour of *café au lait*, then a silhouette flowing from ribcage by way of waist, hip and flank to knee, the darkness textured with impassioned brush strokes, one foot tucked behind, the other foot extended, and between the big toe and the next toe just space enough to insert a tongue. A small placard read: *The Horizontal Woman*.

'I would say Natalia finds me interesting now,' Zuzanna said. Renton gazed and gazed so Zuzanna prompted, 'Ask him what he thinks.'

Renton replied, 'It makes me want to see more.'

Tadeusz hesitated and then translated. Zuzanna stretched her body inside her clothes, rolling each shoulder in turn. She said, 'I think Mr Renton approves of the cultural side of Wroclaw. I think Mr Renton will return.'

'Definitely I shall.' Under the spell of the live Zuzanna

and the painted Zuzanna, Renton forgot to wait for the translation.

Naked, standing with legs apart and bending over, Zuzanna's forehead was visible from behind ringed with the pale fire of her hair. She said, 'I can't see much of you, feet, ankles, knees, legs to half way up your thighs. I don't recognise you. You could be anyone.'

She didn't say whether this possibility excited her, that he might be a different man, and Tadeusz hesitated to ask. Whole areas of her life, her thoughts, her dreams, were a mystery.

'Where do you come from, Zuzia?'

She bent lower so she could peer at his face from between her legs. With her head upside down he couldn't tell if she was quizzical or angry or wary. 'The darkness on the other side of the moon.'

'An angel, is that what you are?'

'An angel from hell. A devil from heaven. Isn't that what a man wants in a woman?'

Now she was reaching behind with both hands to pull him close and Tadeusz couldn't answer.

'Gently,' she said, 'gently. Wait, I'll help you. Wait, impatient boy. There. Oh *yes*.'

For a time that Tadeusz wasn't conscious of, seconds, minutes, infinity, there was no more talk. Words yes, sounds, exclamations, urgent orders, his, hers. Tadeusz cried out – or Zuzanna – and they sank to their knees. Finally they were lying on the floor, Tadeusz spooned behind her, feeling the moisture on her skin, clinging to her, keeping himself afloat as the tide went out. Zuzia, he called out in his head, Zuzia Zuzia Zuzia. She gave a convulsive heave, an after-shock of love, and lay still.

Maybe there's nothing else to life, he told himself. We

shall stay here and never go out. Archaeologists will find
us, skeletons in each other's arms, dead of starvation and
loving.

The afternoon had darkened into a Conspirator's dusk.
Zuzanna took Tadeusz's hand and laid it on her breast, the
right one, the neglected one.

'What did you talk about when you disappeared with
Renton?'

Tadeusz had led the way to the Monopol Hotel. Partly it
was to celebrate Natalia's clearing the window of her gallery
to exhibit his painting. Partly he wanted Renton to admire
the trappings of the place where his father had played the
saxophone and made his assignations. But the restaurant
was booked for a wedding party and they'd had to go to the
coffee shop instead. When he'd visited the men's toilet,
Renton had accompanied him.

'He said how beautiful you were.'

'So you went to the toilets to snigger over me. Men!'

'He *did* say that. Also stunning and other English words
I didn't understand.'

She stretched and fitted herself closer to him.

'All right. And then? What did he say?'

'He was interested in the Klub.'

'Why?'

'He didn't say. I didn't ask him. He just was. Is that its full
name? Where does it meet? Does it have regular members?'

'And you said?'

'I said it wasn't like that. The Klub was people getting
together to discuss the crisis, plan tactics, support each
other, decide on actions.'

'You were gone a long time.'

'Were we? Well, he also asked about my work and asked
when I was having a one-man exhibition and to be sure to
invite him to the vernissage.'

She lowered her shoulder so she could look at his face, a long wondering look.

'You must get to work then.'

Sensing a tension in him she clamped his arm tight against her side so he couldn't move his hand from her breast.

'Not this minute. Another thing, Tadek. I've been thinking and I've decided you need a bigger space than this to work.'

'Move?' he said. 'Where?'

'You'll see.'

CHAPTER FIFTEEN

W here?
Tadeusz, confused and drifting, surfaced to full con-
sciousness. Had he been dozing? Dreaming? Overwhelmed
by memories? He peered at his watch but that was useless.
Some time before dawn. The worst hour, the very worst.
Even whores and thieves have gone to sleep. Insomniacs
own it, and suicides, and secret police, and betrayers public and private, and the condemned man willing his last
sunrise not to happen.

'Tadeusz? Pal? You in the land of the living?' Miler's
voice seemed to have dropped half a register, as if he'd
been crying.

'What is it?'

'Do you ever get to wonder what the meaning of life is?'

That, too, was the trouble with this hour: it was the time
to think the unthinkable.

'Why does life have to have a meaning?' Tadeusz asked.
'It just is. Like a stone. Or a cabbage. No one in his right
mind asks what is the meaning of a cabbage.'

'I'm not a good Catholic,' Miler said. 'In fact, some of the
things I've done make me a very bad Catholic. But I listen
to what the Pope says. He flies off to some country – maybe
it's India – and kisses the runway. Of course now he's getting so old they have to lift a piece of the runway up for
him to kiss. And he says prayers and blesses all those

Indians and there are millions of them at the airport and hundreds of millions more of them out in the jungle and the rice paddies. And he says contraception is wrong so there's got to be billions more even though they've got nothing to eat. Doesn't matter, he says, life is sacred. What is he on about? What's so sacred about life with an empty belly?'

'Write and ask him.'

'No, what do you think?'

Slowly Tadeusz got his legs over the bunk and sat upright. He felt stiff and tired and older than he should have.

'You know about time,' Tadeusz said.

'Time?'

'Time. Time is what keeps everything from happening all at once. All right then, fix that in your mind. Now, can you see my hands?'

Tadeusz held his arms in front of him, the hands apart as if he was telling a fishing tale about the one that got away.

'There is time beyond my left hand before you were born and time beyond my right hand after you have died, and your life is between them. Your life is what keeps the eternity of time separated. Without your life . . .'

Saying that, Tadeusz clapped his hands together and lay back on the bunk.

Miler was silent.

There was a Conspirators' gloom about the cell, no doubt of it, and Miler was staring at him. He could feel Miler's eyes on him, exploring him, taking his measure. Miler's eyes were resting on his hands that had clapped together and made a life vanish. Miler's eyes were moving over his throat, his mouth, his nose. What was Miler locked up for? Miler had violent friends. You choose your

own kind to be your friends. Miler wasn't his friend but
Tadeusz felt he better make an effort.

'Miler,' Tadeusz said, 'Friend Miler since you haven't told
me your name.'

'Friend Miler is okay. I like the sound of Friend Miler.'

'Friend Miler, have you ever kissed a woman between
the toes?'

'Eeugh, no. Feet are smelly.'

'Depends on . . .' Don't say: on the kind of woman you
know, or Friend Miler might come over and put his hands
round your neck and strangle you. 'Depends on the
weather. All right, picture a hot summer day, languid and
sexy, and this woman you meet invites you to come
upstairs. She disappears into her bathroom for ten minutes,
fifteen minutes, and when she comes out . . . Well.'

'Yes?'

'She's had a bath and her skin is still a little damp and
she's used Lux the Beauty Soap of the Stars and Evening
Primrose Million Bubble Bath Oil and Tropical Island Silver
Sand Talcum Powder and Christian Dior Eau de Cologne
and – have I missed anything?'

'Jesus, she must smell powerful.'

'Fragrant is the word. You're lying on the bed waiting for
her and she walks across the room towards you –'

'Naked is she?'

'Naked as Eve before the fall. But not so innocent. She
knows you are watching her body move. She sees how
excited you are getting, how much you want her.'

'Yes, go on.'

'She comes to the bed and lies beside you.'

'And?'

'And the first thing you must do is kiss her between the
toes. You see, there's a little space between the big toe and
the next toe.'

'Don't tell me,' Miler said. He sounded pleased with himself. 'I know what the space is for. It's like you said life is what keeps time apart or something.' He clapped his hands together. 'That little space is what keeps the toes apart.'

'Exactly, Friend Miler. So you kiss her there before you do anything else, put your tongue in that little space. But if you can't get your tongue in . . .'

'Why not?'

'Because there is a solid web of skin there. Then you know she's not a woman at all but a frog and you don't want to fuck a frog, do you?'

'Jesus, no.'

Here was a cell. Here was sharing an unending night with a man like Miler. Here was telling tales and waiting for tomorrow, or waiting longer if they hadn't reached a decision. It took an effort to banish the here and now.

Then was a different world, no, a different universe. Then was leaving his garret room where he'd ogled Tex and painted and written and composed and been a Satirist and a Conspirator. Zuzanna had decided for him. She could change your life like that, alter things in a moment, with a word, a look. She could draw a breath through parted lips and her body could move and her eyes could slip inside you like an invading army and you'd say: Yes Zuzanna, yes Zuzia. She could have been a leader: Joan of Arc, Alexandra the Great. No, Cleopatra was her style.

He remembered that evening when she had said he needed a bigger space, that he should move. He supposed they had dressed because they couldn't have walked through the streets naked. But he remembered nothing except shock at the idea of leaving his life behind.

Where? Where are you taking me?

Just come.

She'd taken possession of him, her arm through his arm, and led the way. The streets, in his memory at least, had been empty. If there were people about, people watching even, he was unaware. Lamps lit the streets in patches and the darkness in between could have hidden lovers and spies and murderers.

Where are you taking me?

He'd asked it again and for an answer she'd tugged at his arm to hurry him. They'd walked right through the centre, passed the Monopol for the second time that day, through the city park almost to where the Nazi High Command had had its underground bunker, then veered across the old moat.

To the station?

Not to the station. They hurried down Kosciuszko Street. He was a General who'd defeated the Russian army, but that had been two centuries ago. To show impartiality he'd also fought alongside the Americans against the English. They passed shops and a bar or two and small businesses, and the area was taking on a depressing meanness. Zuzanna steered him round a corner.

There? He'd cast a look at Zuzanna and then at the tenements. Over there was the quarter known as the Bermuda Triangle. Things sank there without trace. Cars, television sets, crates of vodka, carpets, meat trucks, fur coats – the Bermuda Triangle swallowed them up. Shake hands there and your rings would be gone. Electricity wires tiptoed round the meters. Women were spirited up unlit stairways and never seen again. Police went to ask questions and people laughed in their faces, laughs of beer and garlic and derision. They unzipped their flies and pissed on the cops' shoes. They hauled down their trousers and mooned in their faces. The police retreated.

Not there, Zuzanna.

She tugged at him again and they moved into calmer waters. There were apartment buildings put up on the rubble of Festung Breslau. Nothing fancy, not for the Party élite, but decent. Between two blocks stood an old house that had by a miracle survived the destruction of the war.

Zuzanna already had a key in her hand.

CHAPTER SIXTEEN

Zuzanna opened the door and Tadeusz walked into a new life. He took a couple of steps and came to a halt.

'Here?'

'Here,' she echoed.

'But, Zuzia, it's huge.'

'It is not huge. It's normal. To starve in a garret pretending you're Van Gogh is not normal. Besides,' she rattled a handle to show a door on the left was locked, 'this side is where the Brandts live. They have their own entrance round the side.'

'Who are the Brandts? Are they German?'

'I don't know who they are,' she said. 'They have dogs, big dogs,' as if that explained them.

Tadeusz went another couple of steps. A door was ajar to a sitting room. Beyond was another door, closed. Beyond that was a kitchen. Before the kitchen was a staircase leading presumably to rooms with beds where the evening sacrifice took place.

'Is it yours?' Tadeusz asked.

'Do you think I stole it?'

'It belongs to you, I mean?'

'Perhaps I got it off someone in the Bermuda Triangle?'

'Did you inherit it?'

'Why do you think that?'

The game of questions: serve a question and a question came whipping back over the net.

She relented. 'I have money,' she said simply and Tadeusz did not know what she meant. Had she inherited money, been given money, earned money, found a suitcase stuffed with money?

'How . . .' he began and stopped.

'How did I earn it? On my back, do you mean? We all earn our money on our backs. We're all whores, only some of us are called postmen and others are called butchers and others schoolteachers or train drivers or factory workers or politicians – particularly politicians – or streetsweepers or writers or a thousand other jobs. We all whore for money even if we call ourselves Satirists or Conspirators.'

Tadeusz had lifted his hands to his ears but he could still hear her voice hammering at him. She was speaking right into his face, her eyes wide open. Her body was thrust at him too and she used that, knowing its effect on Tadeusz, knowing she could speak like this and he wouldn't turn away.

'When you have your one-man show and Natalia comes and fawns on you and the Englishman comes from Warsaw and smirks at you and all the darlings and loves creep up and stroke you and say how wonderful you are and you stand there and nod your head – you'll be the biggest whore of the lot.'

There was silence.

Leave, get out, Tadeusz told himself, don't take her shouting and her rudeness. But she was so close he could feel the heat of her body. And if he left she might follow and go on shouting at him in the street. Or worse: she might not follow. So they stood and Tadeusz had a strange feeling she had got inside him and was testing him. She seemed to know all about him: his weaknesses, his desires,

his fears, his pretensions. Even his future. It was a troubling sensation.

Abruptly she clapped her hands and said, 'Come, see
where you'll be working.' She took hold of his hand and
when he stared at her, startled by this swing of mood, she
kissed his lips briefly and said, 'Don't be so snooty.'

'Snooty?'

'Haughty then.'

'Haughty?'

'Oh stop picking on me. Aloof, critical, sulky, disapproving, whatever you are. It's just my way. I hate you
when you look like that. Kiss me, then you'll feel better.
No, we'll do that later. Come on.'

She dragged him down the passage. The closed door
opened into a room about five times bigger than his garret.
It had a desk and a chair along one wall and a chaise longue.
Otherwise it was bare though the paintwork showed the
dusty outlines where bookcases or cabinets once stood.

'There, Tadek, can you work here? Enough space, the
right vibrations?'

His eyes had gone to the tall windows that gave on to the
night. Beyond a low garden wall was a concrete apartment
block with lighted windows. Zuzanna was pacing about
the room and came to a halt in the centre.

'I shall tell you my theory about this house. Long ago,
half a century ago when the city was Breslau and it was in
the Third Reich, a highly esteemed professor of psycho-
analysis lived and practised here. Herr professor sat at his
desk and wrote lofty books on the naughty adventures of
the id. You notice the chaise longue with its carved legs and
its brocade covering? That was his version of the more
clinical Viennese analyst's couch. The windows had velvet
drapes held back in swags and net curtains ensured no
peeping toms looked in. "Frau Biederman," he says, "be so

good as to stretch out on that chaise longue and tell me
what is troubling you. Oh, you mean you have an uncon-
trollable desire to take off all your clothes. Please, it is
damaging to your psyche to thwart such primitive urges.
One moment while I turn the key in the lock and we shall
not be disturbed for an hour. Dear lady, I want to put you
at your ease so I shall follow your liberating example and
remove all my clothes too." *Voilà*,' she said, clapping her
hands, 'that is the shocking history of this house, in my
version. What do you think?'

Tadeusz thought: so it didn't belong to her family, she
didn't inherit it. But he kept that to himself. He'd seen her
temper once this evening.

He said, 'And us? Do we use the chaise longue or is
there a bed upstairs?'

Zdzislaw, who worked at the Dolmel factory, had acquired
a decrepit van. Much loving evening and weekend work
had got it into running order. 'It's got a smoker's cough,'
Zdzislaw said, 'but it's not ready for the graveyard yet.'
Four days after Tadeusz had seen the new house – the half-
house – he felt ready to move his possessions. Together the
two men loaded the van. They packed a suitcase but that
didn't hold all Tadeusz's clothes. So they piled the rest into
a sheet and tied the four corners together.

'Eugeniusz has made a flying visit to Gdansk,' Zdzislaw
said. 'He went to see the Great Moustache in person. A bit
like going to Lourdes, expecting a miracle.'

'I've never been to Lourdes,' Tadeusz said. 'Have you?'

'All right, Czestochowa then. I asked Gienek if the
moustache had grown, whether it got star treatment, was
fed special beer and so on. He got angry and said I was
childish. I said I admired Walesa but did I have to worship
his moustache? He said the moustache was worth more

than all the Party hacks put together, so we shook hands on
that. Stone the dogs, Tadek, are you really taking all these
canvases?'

'Yes.'

'Even the old ones?'

'I can paint over them.'

'Eugeniusz had gone about the Solidarity branch here.
He's head of the print section and they're joining up with
the engineers and metal workers for a parade. Here – can I
have this one?'

'No,' Tadeusz said.

'It's her, isn't it?'

'Yes.'

'You don't mind my looking, do you?'

'Why should I? It's a painting. Art is meant to be looked
at.'

'Yes, but it shows every hair on her body.'

Together they peered at the reclining nude, Zuzanna
with her legs raised on to the metal rail of the bedstead. It
was done in the pre-Conspirator style, very explicit.

'Stone the dogs, Tadek, you're doing all right for yourself.' Zdzislaw sighed. 'And to think in my work I look at
electric turbines all day.'

They went downstairs and loaded the canvases into the
van.

'Eugeniusz heard Walesa make a speech to some of the
lads from Nowa Huta. He tripped over his sentences and
forgot the tenses of verbs. But then he got to the part about
setting up Solidarity and he punched the air with his fist:
IN-DE-PEND-ENT SELF-GOV-ERN-ING SOL-I-DAR-I-TY. Gienek said
you could see the lights go up in everybody's eyes. He said
they were like kids at Christmas, these big steelworkers.'

They climbed the stairs and collected armfuls of note-
books and sketchpads and sheet music and a skeleton

made out of electrical flex that had for its head a 40 watt
bulb that lit up and a saxophone. Tadeusz took a final look
round the room and locked the door.

Tadeusz said, 'Zdzis, do you remember that first march
we went on four years ago?'

'You were wearing that stupid beret,' Zdzislaw said.

'And the ZOMO beat us up and took us away and made
us strip naked. I was questioned by some big secret policeman called Baran. I saw him again last week at the rally at
the cathedral. He was seated in his car staring.'

'And nobody got beaten up.'

'No. We've made some progress.'

'That's the point that Eugeniusz makes. Now there are
ten million of us in Solidarity we count for something.
They can't ignore us any more.'

'We're going to win, aren't we?' Tadeusz said.

But they looked at each other and neither spoke.

I shall write *The Story of Z*, Tadeusz thought, and it will be
set in her bedroom. In the Half House.

It was a Conspirators' bedroom. Had it always been like
this or had Zuzanna got hold of rolls of paper and pasted
them up? The paper was dark midnight blue flecked with
the tiniest points of silver, like stars in the night sky.
Ceiling and walls were equally covered and to enter even
during the day was like ducking into a cave.

'We can be anywhere we like in here,' Zuzanna said. 'We
can be shipwrecked on a tropical island. Or lost in a desert.
Or we can be Neanderthal man and woman in the time
before sex got civilised. I could wear a wolf skin, you could
carry a club. We could mate on the floor and forget all our
inhibitions.'

It was the first Tadeusz had heard of Zuzanna's
inhibitions.

'Or we could be in the jungle,' Tadeusz said, 'in Bolivia. Can you hear the wild animals roaring?'

'To be honest . . .' She cupped an ear with a hand to listen. 'Tell me about them.'

'Those are the most dangerous ones, the silent ones that drop without warning from the branches of trees.'

'What happens then?' she asked.

'They leap on you.'

'And then?'

'They make the beast with two backs.'

'What does this beast do?' There was one lamp in the room, with a dim bulb under a pink shade. It lit the contours of Zuzanna's face, highlighting her cheeks, her nose, her lips. Her eyes were in sockets of darkness, twin spots of light that switched off-on when she blinked. 'Tell me.'

'The beast paws naked flesh. Its talons run over limbs. Its tongue licks warm skin.'

'Like this?'

'Yes.'

'And this?'

'Yes. Oh yes.'

'And then?'

'The beast writhes and bites and struggles and tears itself apart until finally it cries out in desperation and then . . . it is silent. The beast sleeps in the watching breathing jungle.'

For a while the fury was over in the Conspirators' bedroom in the Half House.

In November the Klub shifted its meeting place from Eugeniusz and Justyna's flat. It was at Father Michal's prompting. Or Henryk suggested it. Maybe it was Tadeusz's own idea. No one knew how the idea gained acceptance. Eugeniusz was certainly in favour.

'They're always hanging about outside watching me,' he

said. 'It's because of my organizational work. They know too much about me. They don't know about Tadeusz's place yet. And I think They may have put a microphone into the wall. How else could They have known about that last leaflet?'

The Ubeks had raided the Preema print works and it was sheer good luck that Eugeniusz had stuffed the copy for the leaflet into the pocket of the wrong coat before he left home.

'God was looking after you,' Father Michal said.

So far as Poland was concerned, it was Eugeniusz's opinion, God had been asleep on the job the last forty years. Ninety-nine per cent of Poles might be Catholic, the priests might have a mighty hold in cities and villages, Walesa might wear a badge showing the Madonna of Czestochowa, but Eugeniusz was a sturdy free-thinker.

'And besides, the flat is so cramped,' Eugeniusz said, 'while I hear you have this big house now, Tadek. You've gone up in the world while the rest of us struggle.'

'Zuzanna says it's not big, just normal. I call it the Half House.'

'This is what that woman calls normal?' Eugeniusz muttered in an aside to Father Michal. They were in the sitting room which was large enough for a settee, three overstuffed armchairs, five straight-backed chairs and a big pouffe which Zuzanna made her own perch. There were enough seats for the regular attenders of the Klub and if extra people came – Witold from Pafawag, Dorota from the City Hall administration – chairs were brought from the kitchen.

Through the long Polish winter the Klub met at irregular intervals to talk, to argue, to plan. Eugeniusz and Father Michal overcame their spiritual differences and in effect formed a dual leadership. There were wildcat strikes over petty grievances and it fell to Eugeniusz to sort the trouble out. He banged heads together. 'For God's sake,' said the free-thinker, 'we can't put all the corrupt officials in jail. How could we afford to keep them?'

There were demands made for an investigation into the activities of the secret police. Who were the informers, the spies? What hold did They have over otherwise blameless citizens? The notion of investigating the secret police struck at the very power base of the regime. Alarmed, Moscow moved several divisions up to the eastern border. Tadeusz designed a poster: 'Visit the Soviet Union before the Soviet Union visits you.' Someone slipped this into the window of the Orbis travel agency in Rynek where it stayed fully twenty minutes before the sardonically grinning faces outside alerted the manager.

In January Walesa went to Rome for an audience with the Pope. Father Michal, who claimed some small acquaintance with John Paul II when he had been plain Cardinal Karol Wojtyla of Krakow, decided he wanted to go too. 'You'll never be given a passport,' Eugeniusz said. To general amazement the passport was granted in a matter of days. A photograph appeared in *Solidarity Weekly* – though not in the state-owned press – of a smiling Pope talking to a hugely pleased Walesa. Just beyond Walesa you can see the head of Father Michal bowed forward to eavesdrop.

'Tell us what happened,' Eugeniusz said on Father Michal's return. 'What did they discuss? What did our Pope advise?'

'Steadfastness,' Father Michal replied; 'Faith in God. Faith in Poland's future, free and democratic. Patience to wait for the inevitable crumbling of godless communism.'

'It is easier to be patient,' Eugeniusz said, 'when you are cosy in a palace in the Vatican.'

'So what would you advise?' Father Michal retorted, his

own patience for once exhausted. 'Immediate civil war? Invasion by the Red Army? Armageddon?'

Eugeniusz didn't respond. What reply was there?

'Artistically I have said everything I have to say as a Conspirator,' Tadeusz announced.

'You have?' There was a post-coital drowsiness to Zuzanna's voice. She seemed not to appreciate this was another creative turning point in Tadeusz's short career.

'The spirit of imagination which infused my work has become sterile.'

'You've been listening to critics again,' she said. 'It's a mistake. They are the ones who are sterile. No, really they are eunuchs: they can't perform themselves, they can only look on and squeak with second-hand emotion.'

Tadeusz was quiet for a moment, digesting this. He kissed her big toe, which he had been speaking to, and looked up the length of her body. He saw it as a landscape, the long ride up her legs, the ridges of her hips, the flat plain of her belly, the hills of her breasts, the jungle of her pubic bush, and hidden in the blond thickets a moist warm cave.

'Man is a dichotomy,' he said.

'I didn't know you were that way inclined.'

With a finger he tickled the instep of her left foot. She wriggled.

'Don't,' she said.

'Is that *Don't – yes* or *Don't – no*?' Tadeusz asked. 'Woman too is a dichotomy.' His finger trailed over her heel, her ankle, her calf, the back of her knee, up and up her thigh. 'As a Conspirator I have explored the dark areas of the soul, I have expressed the texture of desire, the unobtainable, the unknowable, the haunting echo of lost visions, the . . .' Running out of words, he let his finger convey his feelings. She stirred. 'You see,' he went on, 'the logical end of being a Conspirator is to represent human beings, life, the world, the universe as a totally obscured canvas. But that is very much as I began as a Satirist. It is the circularity of all human endeavour. The big O.'

Not knowing what to make of this gibberish, Zuzanna parted her legs to ease the way for him. 'Go on,' she said, 'don't stop.'

'The dichotomy,' Tadeusz announced, like the title of a poem he was about to recite. He sat up and laid a hand across her breasts. 'On the one hand I am a Mammaist. This does not mean that I am in search of a mother figure, absolutely not. To be a Mammaist is to acknowledge the importance of the mammaries. The breast, source of pleasure, source of the milk of life. On the other hand,' he raised his left hand and pulled, like one might pull a lavatory chain, 'I am a Cacaist, depicting the *caca* of politics that stains and dirties our lives.'

'I like your Mammaist side,' she said. 'I like it very much.'

Tadeusz threw himself into a creative frenzy. Within a week he had painted a dozen new canvases. It's spring, he told himself, the juices are flowing, the sap is rising, the buds of Mammaism are bursting.

He lined the canvases against the wall in his studio and sat in the chair behind the desk. He tilted the chair back while he studied his creations. They were of breasts, all of them. Perhaps they were Zuzanna's breasts, perhaps they were the forbidden breasts of smuggled copies of *Playboy*.

Breasts as tropical islands, lapped by azure seas, capped by cumulus.

A breast as a sand dune where sunbathers took their ease under parasols.

Breasts as animals behind bars in the zoo. And then hands wrenching the bars apart to let the breasts free – an echo there of his Free Rafat! poster. (Whatever had been Rafat's fate? Nobody talked of him any more.)

Breasts as volcanoes erupting into a sky of swirling storm clouds.

General Jaruzelski's Breasts – at least according to a card pinned to the canvas – with dark glasses over the nipples.

Breasts as theatrical masks of comedy and tragedy with the nipples as noses, and eyes above and gaping mouths below.

A breast as a hen's egg with a new-born chick breaking out.

A breast as a fruit being offered by Eve to Adam.

A nuclear explosion with a breast for the top of the mushroom cloud.

Tadeusz surveyed the paintings for a long time. Then he fetched a paintbrush and a tube of paint and set to work.

'I came as soon as I could,' Zdzislaw said. 'Is it safe to leave the van outside?'

'Who would steal it?'

Zdzislaw jerked a thumb in the direction of the Bermuda Triangle. 'One of them.'

'Baffle the cops – use it for a slow get-away.'

Tadeusz led the way to the studio and locked the door behind them.

'The message said *Come quickly – it's urgent.* What's the matter?'

'I'm finished.'

'Finished?'

'Finished. Mammaism is a false path. As an artist I've said all I have to say.' He paused, struck by the memory of saying the same about Conspiratorism a week ago. 'It's a sign of maturity to know when the creative well is dry.'

Zdzislaw stared at the wall where the canvases were ranged, all of them painted over black.

'I'm in mourning for my dead genius,' Tadeusz said. 'Soon I shall be dead too.'

'What do you mean?'

Tadeusz went to a window-seat in one of the bays. He used a pair of scissors in the lock of the cupboard built under the seat not so much to turn the lock, more as a hook to drag the door open. Stooping, his back obscuring Zdzislaw's view of what he was doing, Tadeusz fumbled as he unwrapped something. When he stood up he held a pistol in his hand.

'Stone the dogs,' Zdzislaw whispered.

At the war's end the ruins of the city were littered with guns of all kinds, rifles, pistols, machine guns, also boxes of ammunition and grenades, bayonets, helmets, unexploded shells, Iron Crosses, unfinished letters beginning *Liebchen*. Some of the rougher children had played Cops and Robbers using real weapons. It had taken the authorities until the late forties to pronounce the city gun-free. Here was one that had been missed.

'Luger,' said Tadeusz. 'I suppose this had been an officer's house and he stuffed it in there. Or his widow did before getting out.'

'Is it loaded?'

Tadeusz turned the pistol on its side so that a little lever on the grip was visible. It said *Geladen*.

'Does Zuzanna know about it?'

'No,' said Tadeusz, 'just you and me.'

'Don't you think you should hand it in?'

'Why? Haven't They got enough guns already?'

Tadeusz stared at the pistol. There was no doubt that holding it made him feel different. People said that to hold a gun gave you a feeling of power but that wasn't quite right. Or that it was a penis substitute but that was plain silly. He knew perfectly well what his penis was for and this pistol wouldn't be a substitute at all. The closest he could define what he felt was that the gun in his hand seemed to be alive – and that was daft for something whose sole purpose was the taking of life.

He raised the gun and pointed it at the caricature of Jaruzelski done in his Cacaist mode. The General was all dark glasses and prim mouth. Jaruzelski had been prime minister now for a couple of months.

Tadeusz shook his head. 'I'm not handing it in. You can never tell when it won't come in useful.' He closed one eye and steadied his aim on where Jaruzelski's brain should be. 'Bang.'

'What shall we drink to?'

'Spring.'

'That is banal,' Tadeusz said. 'Death.'

'Don't talk like that.'

'Death to Mammaism.'

'All right.'

They drank. They'd gone to a bar near the station. Although it was only mid-afternoon, the smoke haze in the bar made it seem like dusk.

'I've concluded I was premature in abandoning Conspiratorism. Conspiracy is everywhere, in women's eyes, in politicians' mouths, in bars by the station, in friendship, in a cupboard under a window-seat. Conspiracy is life.'

'You're going to be all right now?'

'Yes, Zdzis.'

With a friend called Zdzis, you sounded drunk after one beer.

'Listen,' Zdzislaw said, leaning closer.

'A conspiracy?'

'If you do die, can I move in with Zuzanna?'

'You randy bastard, planning my death just when I've been reprieved.'

'No I'm not. It's an if.'

'Dear old friend, I regret to say you haven't got what it takes for Zuzia.'

'The balls?'

'The madness.'

CHAPTER SEVENTEEN

M adness?
Why did he think Zdzislaw didn't have enough madness to satisfy Zuzia? Everybody was mad. The entire country had been entering a time of supreme madness.

Take the General. Dark glasses defined Jaruzelski. His eyes had been scorched by Siberian snow. Now here he was, leader of a fraternal socialist state. Were the dark glasses to protect his retinas or to hide the madness that fuelled him?

And Walesa? Didn't madness ferment in the shelter of that moustache? To take on the might of the state, the militia, the secret police, the army, the armed forces of the Soviet Union and its satellites could not be said to be the actions of a sane man.

And the Polish people? They were as mad as mad could be. They were mad with their demeaning poverty, mad with the ruling élite, mad with frustration, mad as lies were succeeded by lies.

And Eugeniusz riding past militia cars on his bicycle with two saddlebags stuffed with leaflets urging another strike? Mad or what?

And Father Michal taking a service in the cathedral when the bishop was indisposed? To preach a sermon urging a fresh start to the nation's affairs, an open society, democratic elections, a free press, respect for individuals . . . The congregation sat as if turned to stone, petrified that such madness would enter their ears and infect them. But when the sermon was finished and in the pause before the next prayer, the immobility shattered. There was a hum as of some huge dynamo starting, a crackle in the air, heads bobbing to left and to right. The truth, spoken aloud in God's house. Amen.

In this madhouse Tadeusz had been the sanest person he knew. He had his art, his woman and his gun. What more did a man need? A little food – well, there was a little. A little drink – there was that. As for Ubeks and ZOMO and Party apparatchiks, what were they? Poland, with its partitions and movable frontiers and invasions, was not so much a state as a state of mind. And in his mind, They had no place.

Gazing up from the bunk he saw the window had lightened. Pale grey sky was quartered by the bars.

'I am a good Pole,' Miler said, as if doubt had been cast on his reliability. He had lain so still Tadeusz had thought him asleep. 'Every year on Christmas Eve my wife cooks a carp. Like every Polish family. We have vodka, we have wine, we have candles. Out in the kitchen I wash one of the big scales from the carp, dry it and place it in my wallet. That way for the year ahead my wallet will never be empty.'

A tradition has to start some time. Who had first done this? A cynic? A Jesuit? A court jester? The tradition didn't promise that for the coming year your wallet would be stuffed with zlotys, just that it would never be empty. It would have a carp scale.

'Last Christmas,' Miler said, 'my wife was late to market and the carp had all gone. What a slut! She bought a *sandacz* instead. So now I am punished. My wallet is empty and I am in a cell.'

'Friend Miler, it's dawn, a new day. You know what they say – With morning there is always hope.'

But what to hope for? That was Tadeusz's problem. It seemed to be Miler's too. In the grey morning light his face had aged.

'I don't want to go to prison. That fool of a lawyer couldn't defend the Pope against a charge of bigamy.'

'Prison isn't so bad now. You get television in your cell. If you don't like watching that, you can have a goldfish bowl. There's a special suite so you can enjoy a conjugal visit from your wife.'

'Please.' Miler was not mollified. His brows contracted in obvious pain.

'Try converting to Islam,' Tadeusz suggested. 'Have your choice of four wives.'

Miler stared wide-eyed. Should he be four times afflicted? Madness.

Tadeusz had read of the feeding frenzy of sharks and piranhas and currency speculators. Could there be a madness frenzy? The year 1981 stood out. Shipyard workers went on strike and were arrested and the rest struck again until the imprisoned men were released. Coal miners occupied the mines while their wives lowered food to them. Farmers met and demanded their own union; in turn they had their skulls cracked and their ribs broken. The whole country decided on the massive earthquake of a general strike and pulled back from the abyss with minutes to go. Soviet war memorials were daubed with graffiti, and who knows whether it was crazy Poles or maddened Stalinists trying to provoke a showdown. Meanwhile the fraternal wolves of the Soviet Union padded up and down the border, smelling blood, their muzzles pressed between the barbed wire, hungering to join the feast.

And Tadeusz, sanest of the insane, had his own plan. He would go to Warsaw, he would see Renton.

CHAPTER EIGHTEEN

'What is this, Tadek? What are you doing?'
From the doorway Zuzanna watched Tadeusz, his sleeves and trousers rolled up. He poured water from a jug into a bucket. He'd spread copies of old newspapers on the floor and dumped a pile of sand on them. Uplifting stories clamoured to be read: 'Bicycle production to be increased', 'Weightlifters make extra effort.' A smiling girl next to a cow was headlined, 'Chopin nocturnes help cows increase milk production.' The lid of a wooden packing case made a platform on which he'd laid a couple of dozen cobblestones.

'I'm mixing cement.'
'What for? Why are you making a mess in my house?'
'Our house, I thought. The Half House. My half of the Half House.'
'Tadeusz, stop at once. Explain it to me.'
'I can't. I'm busy. Cacaism lives.'
'What's in that big bag?'
'Come back when I've finished.'

'I've been neglecting sculpture,' Tadeusz explained to

Zuzanna. They sat on the chaise longue with a bottle of vodka on the floor. With the economic crisis vodka was as scarce as horse feathers – a Polish nightmare – except for Zuzanna.

'Oh, it's a sculpture,' she said. Her tone was flat and she seemed to be restraining an impulse to hit him.

The cobblestones were cemented firmly in place on the wooden platform. A battered dustbin – one that looked as if it had itself been thrown away – sat on the cobbles as it might on the street awaiting emptying.

'Take the lid off and look inside.'

'Is this a trick, Tadek? I warn you I shall be very cross.'

'Go on, have a look.'

Zuzanna crossed the room, lifted the lid and screamed. 'Oh my God.'

Inside were the heads of Marx, Lenin and Brezhnev jumbled together.

Tadeusz poured vodka and raised his glass in a toast. 'To the Dustbin of History.' He drained the glass and in Russian cavalry officer tradition tossed it over his shoulder where it smashed against the wall. A Polish cavalry officer, it is said, would have held out the glass for a refill.

In 1815 Jan Potocki finished his great novel *The Manuscript Found in Saragossa*. It had taken him eighteen years to write and in between whiles he had wandered far from Poland, adventuring in Asia, fighting pirates, contracting two marriages and other liaisons less legal, writing history books. Count Potocki believed that self-interest was the motive of all human action and that his own interest was best served by his death. He took the lid of a silver teapot, moulded it into a bullet and put it through his brain.

What, Tadeusz wondered, had become of the rest of the teapot? Could it be found and sent to the Central

Committee of the Party, a gift from the Polish people? Would it make enough silver bullets?

There was a short path from the Half House with oblongs of grass on either side, a place for dog turds and tossed cigarette packets. Zuzanna had had plans for flower beds and had planted tulip bulbs. The blooms had long gone to brighten some room in the Bermuda Triangle, and the plan had languished. Zdzislaw and Tadeusz turned left from the path into the street heading towards the station. As they moved off two men got out of a van.

'Where is it?' Zdzislaw asked.

'It's before we get to the station. It's a hairdresser's and the man is called Zanussi.'

'Why can't a hairdresser have a good Polish name? Why can't he be called Szczepanski? That sounds honest.'

'Mieczyslaw Szczepanski, how about that? That sounds so honest he would cut your hair with sheep shears.'

They paused at the kerb to let a tram go past. Its overhead rod ticked against the power cable like a disapproving click of the teeth.

'Why doesn't Zuzanna get them?'

'She had to go out,' Tadeusz told him. 'What we do, she said, we go in and ask for Mr Zanussi and say we've come about the basket, and he takes us into the back room.'

'The country is going to shit,' Zdzislaw said.

'That's what the government says, all the Party hacks. They all say Poland has no chance because of all the troublemakers in Solidarity.'

'You think I'm backing the Party? It stands to reason the country is collapsing. Next winter we'll be burning the furniture because the miners are on strike. We'll be eating nettles because the farmers haven't got the harvest in. I ask you – who ever heard of going to the back of the hairdresser's to buy potatoes?'

'They're from his cousin's farm. New season's.'

'I love them when they've just been lifted. They taste of the earth, not warehouse dust and mouse droppings.'

England had stations like cathedrals. Germany had stations like banking halls. But Wroclaw had a railway station like a Moorish castle that had slipped out of someone's dream. It stood just ahead, complete with twin towers from which the muezzin could summon the faithful. Tadeusz came to a halt, slapping first his pockets then his forehead.

'Idiot,' he said.

'I agree,' Zdzislaw said. 'What is it?'

'Do you have money?'

'Before pay day?'

'I left my wallet behind.'

Without a word they turned to retrace their steps.

'Look on it as practising for the future,' Zdzislaw said. 'When there is nothing to buy in the shops you naturally go out without money.'

'The advanced stage of communism.'

Rounding the corner into the street where Tadeusz lived they both came to an abrupt halt. A van parked at the kerb had its loading doors open on an interior stacked with canvases. Two men were coming crabwise down the path staggering under the weight of the Dustbin of History on its platform of cobbles. The front door of the Half House stood open.

'Burglars,' Tadeusz whispered. 'Stop, thieves.'

How do you shout for help when your vocal chords are shocked into paralysis? Zdzislaw, seeing more clearly, laid a hand on his friend's arm to stop him running into trouble.

'Ubeks,' he said.

Tadeusz shook the restraint off. He ran forward. That was his creation being carried away, his work stacked in the van, his life being stolen. Zdzislaw followed, not knowing whether he was trying to hold Tadeusz back or support him.

'Put that down. Put it down at once.'

Tadeusz had recovered his voice. In a miracle of obedience the two men did just that, crushing withered tulip leaves under the load of cobblestones. Tadeusz and Zdzislaw were at the beginning of the path when the two men turned towards them. They didn't have the features of burglars but of men with long experience of dealing with people, of looking for weaknesses, of anticipating moves, of deciding on moves of their own, their eyes darting from faces to hands to pockets and back to faces. One was drawing a pistol from under his jacket. His colleague said a word and the gun was slipped back out of sight. Instead both produced flick-knives, so much quieter apart from the victim's screams.

'Tadek,' Zdzislaw warned. They both turned on their heels and ran. At their backs were shouted orders to stop, to stop right now, to stop or they'd shoot. But Tadeusz and Zdzislaw were beyond the effective range of a pistol. Footsteps behind them echoed their own. They ran from the Half House, from the van, from the Ubeks. Run! It didn't matter where – they had the whole of Poland to choose from. But at Pulaskiego Street a burst of traffic held them back before they launched themselves in front of a truck that slammed on its brakes and gave a protesting blast on its horn.

The Ubeks began shouting again, ordering pedestrians to stop them, they were criminals escaping. But in this district that was to proclaim them honoured citizens and no one put out a hand as Tadeusz and Zdzislaw dodged past. Empty shops and gimcrack little businesses that mended spare parts for ancient machinery and cafés with grimy windows passed in a blur. Rising behind these were the tenements of the Bermuda Triangle.

'Double back to the station,' Zdzislaw shouted. 'Disappear in the crowd.'

'How far behind are they?'

Zdzislaw turned to look over his shoulder and a broken paving stone sent him sprawling. When he scrambled to his feet his knee buckled beneath him. 'Stone the dogs,' he was muttering through his teeth as Tadeusz turned back to help. He draped Zdzislaw's arm round his shoulder.

'In here.'

They turned down an alley that gave on to a courtyard with two gutted wrecks of cars, a bin spilling rubbish, bottles, rusted metal rods, rotten wood, a skinny mongrel. Gaping entrances led to staircases. The tenements rose five storeys. Open windows let out conflicting radio stations. Boys stopped kicking a ball to stare.

'Over in the corner.'

A low building on the far side of the courtyard looked as if it let out into another street. But they'd only limped halfway when the Ubeks caught up with them.

'You dumb shits, you shouldn't have come back so soon,' one of the Ubeks said. He had the kind of square face you expected to see behind a plough horse but with nicks and white scars picked up on the street.

Tadeusz swung round on him, ignoring the blades that caught the sun. 'Why were you stealing my sculpture?'

'That pile of crap? Evidence of anti-state activity. Imperialist propaganda.'

'Where did you get the cobbles?' his colleague asked. 'Theft of state property.'

The one with the ploughman's face was sidling round to the back of them and Zdzislaw turned to launch a kick at him, crying out with the stab of pain in his knee. The Ubek made a feint at his eyes and as Zdzislaw jerked his head back stabbed at his stomach. Zdzislaw threw a punch and the Ubek pulled away.

Tadeusz spat at the man in front of him which provoked a wild swing of the knife. Tadeusz aimed a shoe at his groin but he jumped clear.

So far so good. But Tadeusz knew that two professional thugs armed with knives would always beat two unarmed civilians. It was a question of time before he or Zdzislaw made a mistake. The Ubek in front of him was feeling his blade with his thumb, testing it for sharpness or to distract Tadeusz's attention. There was a special horror in the idea of steel slicing one's flesh.

'Who told you to go to the house and remove my stuff? You had no orders to attack us.'

'You made a mistake coming back. That changed things.' He lunged and Tadeusz knocked into Zdzislaw and there was a shout. But it came from a window.

'The scum, the scum, the scum,' a woman was screaming.

It was like kicking an ants' nest. Men and women appeared from doorways, leaned from windows, came in from the alley. They were jeering, shouting, picking up half-bricks and metal bars, flashing knives of their own. The Ubeks turned away from Zdzislaw and Tadeusz and one of them produced his pistol. Far from intimidating the crowd, the sight of a gun excited them. Here was a trophy worth having.

The crowd formed a ring round the four men, jostling, muttering threats, daring each other to lead the attack. When a Ubek turned to threaten with a knife or pistol, a man or woman out of sight edged forward. Finally a man let out a hoarse cry and pointed at the sky and with this diversion causing confusion the mob rushed in. The pistol went off before it was wrestled free, the knives were clubbed from the Ubeks' hands, and the mob swarmed over them, kicking, gouging, pummelling. The Ubeks, and Tadeusz and Zdzislaw as well, were overwhelmed. In the Bermuda Triangle all outsiders were fair game and Tadeusz felt blows raining down. He protected his head with his arms and struggled to break away. One Ubek was on the ground with two women sitting on his legs while two men stripped off his leather jacket. The other Ubek had made the tactical error of ripping away a woman's blouse and the bare-breasted fury was clawing for his eyes. The brawl stopped with equal suddenness, as if the mob had satisfied some primitive lust. They stumbled away, dodging final kicks.

'Whose side were they on?' Zdzislaw said, rubbing his ribs.

'Their own.'

Zuzanna entered a studio that seemed to be holding its breath. Her eyes swept across walls that were bare, paused over the Dustbin of History that had been brought back inside and ended on Tadeusz and Zdzislaw who sat side by side on the chaise longue.

'What's going on? Your canvases . . . Your face . . . My God, what's happened?'

Her cheeks had gone pale. She came to Tadeusz and touched the dark bruise under one eye, the scratch that ran across his forehead.

'We had guests,' Tadeusz said.

Her eyes widened. Her mouth opened but she said nothing.

'And we didn't get Mr Zanussi's potatoes,' Zdzislaw said.

She ignored him. 'Who . . .' She faltered. 'Tell me, Tadek.'

'We came back early and disturbed Them removing all my work.'

'Who?'

'They introduced Themselves with pistols and knives so we can only assume it was . . .' He leaned closer and lowered his voice to a conspirator's whisper, '. . . you-know-who.'

'And this?' She touched his face again. 'How did this happen?'

'That was the work of honest Polish citizens over there.' He nodded in the direction of the Bermuda Triangle. 'We were guilty by association.'

'They took my wallet,' Zdzislaw said, 'though there was nothing in it.'

'You can always sell a wallet.'

'What we were puzzling about when you came in was how They knew about the canvases and the sculptures.'

Zuzanna went to the chair behind the desk. On one corner of it, overlooked by the secret police, stood a silver teapot – well, silver in intent though made from a large can that once held plum jam. The teapot was missing its lid. 'To the Politburo', read a card, 'it's teatime.' The two men still sat side by side on the chaise longue. They could have been supplicants and she the judge deciding their fate. She sat with her head to one side, waiting for their suggestions.

Zdzislaw said, 'Was someone in the Klub a bit careless in his talk? Or her talk? We can't believe anyone deliberately told tales.'

'Or,' said Tadeusz, pointing to the other half of the house, 'could the Brandts have found out? Do they have microphones, peepholes?'

Zuzanna swivelled in the chair to nod through the window. 'Or did someone look down from one of the flats and watch what you were doing?'

*

Zdzislaw and Tadeusz walked down the short path beside dying and battered tulips. Zdzislaw had been unable to get diesel for the van and was going to the tramstop. Tadeusz stared up at the block of flats. A woman carrying a rifle crossed one of the windows. He blinked and pictured the brief scene again. On second thoughts it was a broom.

'Someone in one of the flats could have reported what I'd been doing,' Tadeusz said. 'That's certainly a possibility.'

'Or you were seen taking the cobblestones.'

'Or the big dogs next door have big ears.'

At the end of the path they stopped.

'Does Zuzanna go out a lot?'

'Yes. I don't like being watched while I work.'

'Where does she go?' When there was no answer he said, 'What does she do?'

'I don't know.'

'Don't you ask?'

'It's not possible to question Zuzia. Try asking a tiger what it's doing.'

'Tadek, pardon me for saying this, but do you think she goes to see someone else?'

'Another man?'

'It could be a woman friend.' He paused. 'Or of course a man.'

There was something of an awkward silence. 'Sometimes when she comes back she is . . .' Tadeusz broke off. 'It's hard to explain. Withdrawn, doesn't want me to touch her. I tell myself she is a woman so she will have her moods. Now I'm not spying on her but a week or so ago I was looking in her coat pockets for some change and I found a cigarette packet. She doesn't smoke any more. She stopped back in the winter.'

'Did you ask her about it?'

'What's there to ask? A half-smoked packet – she could

have picked it up anywhere. To ask her is to accuse her of having another lover. Am I not enough for her?'

There are some truths one doesn't want to know.

True, she wasn't always there. Even now it caused him the odd worry that she wanted to go out without him. She had explained to him that lovers needed time apart – like a breathing space – to keep their longing for each other strong. There was truth in this and in any case it gave him time to see people from the Klub without her brooding presence. Eugeniusz worked an evening shift, Zdzislaw worked in the afternoons. He could usually see one or other of them. Or Father Michal.

Their union was not regular in the church's eyes but Father Michal had a curious gloss to put on matters. 'When you are married,' said the unmarriageable priest, 'you spend your time together, the family as a unit. The church encourages this and naturally the church is correct. But is it by chance that Polish men drink so much? I think vodka is the Polish divorce. Tadeusz it is good you see different people and not be closed up together. That may not be God's truth but it is mine.'

Some truths are dangerous. Some truths are contradictions. Some truths are paranoic. Some truths are elusive. Some truths come damp with the sweat of fear. Some truths are lies.

Take Roman Bacewicz, for instance. Call me Romek, he says, as if you were old schoolchums or worked together on the production line. Was he what the Americans call 'a regular guy', Tadeusz wondered? Yet he had a Rolls-Royce for everyday use and a Mercedes as a weekend runabout. He had a palace in Warsaw rebuilt from the ruins of the ghetto uprising in 1944, marble floors, chandeliers, a fountain in the master bathroom. He had a castle in the Tatra mountains. He had a private jet. He never travelled with fewer than two secretaries to attend to his business and personal needs.

In the workers' state he was a capitalist.

But hush. Some truths are too secret to share.

While the princes of communism feasted, the people of the people's democracy queued for half a loaf. And when that was eaten they wet their fingers and chased round for crumbs. We're anteaters licking up termites, Tadeusz decided. They have anteaters in Bolivia.

Tadeusz could no longer buy canvases. He cut up sheets and stretched them over wooden frames and redid the paintings the Ubeks had spirited away. He created new sculptures. One was a wooden panel large enough to accommodate twin shanks of black hair in the form of a great moustache; under the moustache cowered a tiny figure in a General's uniform and dark glasses; the caption read: 'The shadow over Jaruzelski.'

Zuzanna asked, 'Where did you get the hair?'

'From an old cushion I found.'

'How old? From the war?'

'Possibly.'

'You know they used to stuff cushions with hair shaved off women at the camps. Auschwitz, Majdanek. Gross-Rosen is close.'

Tadeusz stared at the great moustache. Was it true? Had some woman given up her life to the mad ideology of an earlier era and her hair to his art?

'She's come alive once more. She's in the struggle for freedom again.'

In early autumn Solidarity held its first Congress. Across the other side of the Gulf of Gdansk the Soviet navy began manouevres. Destroyers, submarines and assault vessels took part. Helicopters hung in the sky. The Kremlin growled. Tadeusz looked long and hard at his paintings and sculptures and knew it was time to act. Zdzislaw had sweet-talked a supervisor at the Dolmel factory into giving the van a full tank of diesel. They loaded pictures and sculptures into the back while Zuzanna watched from the door. She looked as sour as if Tadeusz was running off with another woman. When Tadeusz went to kiss her goodbye she turned aside.

'It's only a few days.'

'You're going to cause trouble,' she said. 'And you're going to get into trouble.'

On the advice of Eugeniusz they did not take the direct route to Warsaw through Lodz but secondary roads via Pietrkow. 'Otherwise you'll meet roadblocks and They'll check the back of the van and beat you up and They'll throw you into some "health farm" and beat you up some more.'

Even off the major routes there were checks. Before Opole two cars and a striped wooden pole barred the way. The militia officer looked at Zdzislaw's papers.

'Where are you going?'

'Pietrkow. We're doctors and there's an emergency there.'

The militia man frowned as he checked the documents again. His head snapped up. 'It says here you are a metal worker at the Dolmel factory.'

'Ah, but our patient is a synchronous hydrogenerator,' Zdzislaw said and slapped a carton of cogs and copper tubing on the floor between him and Tadeusz. 'It keeps coughing and they're afraid it'll die. A spot of spare part surgery is needed.'

Zdzislaw had an open face and a puckish grin, and the militia man's frown lifted to wrinkles of amusement. 'On your way, doctor.'

When they rounded the next bend Tadeusz put out his hand and silently they shook. In the payload area of the van the great moustache quivered. The skulls in the Dustbin of History rattled. They were as good as in Warsaw. Only another 370 kilometres to go.

At night they took a sidetrack to a farm cottage and knocked at the kitchen door. A man in shirtsleeves with a nose like a walnut answered. A lantern on the table lit the faces of his wife and two teenage sons. The Pope beamed from a wall. They had finished supper, the plates cleared away, but they appeared to be simply sitting until it was time to go to bed.

Tadeusz said, 'Good evening, uncle. We're on our way to Warsaw but now it's night it's too dangerous to drive.'

The farmer inspected them. 'You have no headlights?'

'Indeed yes. And they light up the brass buttons of the militia at every crossroads. Could we sleep in your barn until daybreak?'

'Have you eaten?'

'No.'

'Come. We have soup.'

Towards noon they stopped at a public telephone in the Warsaw suburbs and Tadeusz rang the British embassy.

'I want to speak to the Cultural Ambassador.'

'There is no Cultural Ambassador.'

'I want to speak to Mr Renton.'

The line went dead. Or comatose, breathing heavily. There were sounds like someone using a toothpick, sounds like someone frying sausages, sounds like a sparrow chirping.

'Secretariat,' a woman's voice said abruptly.

'I want to speak to Mr Renton,' Tadeusz repeated.

'Mr Renton is out. If you give me your telephone number Mr Renton will call you on his return.'

'No.'

The silence, or near silence, ran for a bit.

'What do you want to speak to him about?'

'Certain cultural matters of interest to us both.'

'I see. You are Mr . . .?'

'Tadek. From Wroclaw.'

In half a minute Renton was on the telephone. 'We met outside the cathedral, correct? Then looked at the naked statue and a certain painting. What was it called?'

'The Horizontal Woman.'

Satisfied, Renton said, 'I advise you not to come to the embassy. Our situation has taken a turn for the worse today and we have many of your countrymen posted outside. Some are in uniform, some are not. They will look at your papers and since you do not have a British passport they may be obstructive.'

'Obstructive?'

'Like a boot can obstruct you, or a hand on your collar. Why do you want to see me?'

'I have something for you.'

'Of, how shall I put it, of cultural interest?'

'Oh yes.'

'This is what you must do.'

The Grand Hotel is not particularly so, its bar even less. But Zdzislaw and Tadeusz looked like the provincials they were among the American tourists, the Swedish and French businessmen, the Ministry officials, the interpreters and the pair of hookers left over from the night before or preparing for the siesta trade. Tadeusz had left a message at Reception, saying he was expecting a call. Finally an elderly boy in a maroon uniform came paging 'Mr Krupowicz'. Tadeusz got up.

'You've changed your name?'

'Stay here,' Tadeusz said. 'If that blonde gets any closer, tell her she couldn't afford you.'

In the vestibule he was shown to a telephone and turned his back on the receptionists.

'This is Tadek.'

'Welcome to Warsaw. You chose a fine time to come. The General is flexing his muscles. We hear there are troops moving out into the villages. He is preparing for something.'

This was a new Renton, more direct, more focused. The languid fellow of the Assistant Cultural Secretary had been put aside. Now, as if peeping between curtains, Tadeusz glimpsed the man.

'There were a lot of militia on the road from Wroclaw.'

'That is normal. The army fanning out into the country is unusual. Now, you cannot come to the embassy. You would simply get yourself into trouble.'

For a moment Tadeusz had a vision of Zuzanna's face frowning. She'd said he would get into trouble. Listening, he caught the sound of traffic from which he decided that Renton was speaking from a public telephone.

'But I must see you.'

'Are you alone?'

'Zdzis came with me. An old friend.'

'Good. Collect your friend and come back to the vestibule. As you are crossing as if to go out, stop suddenly and tell him you're going to the toilet. Make a performance of it. Point to the sign to the toilets. That is important so that even the dimmest person understands. Don't look round now but you are being watched. Your friend stays standing in the middle of the vestibule, waiting for you. The watchers will also wait. You go to where the toilets are, go to the end of the corridor and there is a Fire Exit to the alley at the side. Go through that.'

'You're sure?'

'Believe me, if you live in Warsaw any length of time, you get to know your Fire Exits.'

Renton had wanted the anonymity of Central Station – perhaps that was where he had been calling from – but Tadeusz said he was coming in a van, repeating he had something to show him. The escape from the Grand Hotel went smoothly apart from Zdzislaw's bewilderment.

'But I want to go to the toilet too.'

'Wait. You can wait five minutes, can't you? Then you can sit in the vestibule until I come back.'

'Where are you going?'

'I'm not telling you.'

'Why?'

'If They ask you, it's better you don't know.'

'How long will you be gone?'

'You nag worse than a wife.'

'Tadek, I didn't know coming to Warsaw would be like this.'

Nor did Tadeusz. There seemed nothing to say.

Tadeusz picked up Renton outside Central Station and drove round the side to park. With the engine cut there was the ticking of cooling metal and a low hum of traffic. In Wroclaw there would have been the chatter of office girls and students. Here people seemed quieter, subdued by Stalin's Palace of Culture. It stood watch, waiting to fall on deviant talk. Renton kept his eyes on the door mirror.

'You're clean,' he said.

'Years ago,' Tadeusz said, 'when I was young I came and kicked the Palace of Culture.'

'When it falls down some day, they'll say you were the one who first weakened it. They'll put up a statue to you.'

'To my right foot, maybe.' Who worked in the Palace?

What function did they have? A thousand windows gazed at them. Were a thousand pairs of eyes watching? 'You know all about making exits. Is that culturally necessary?'

'You mean leaving after the first act? You know those sort of plays. You'd die if you had to sit through any more. Bulgarian folk dancing, Hungarian avant garde, that sort of stuff.'

They both smiled.

'How is the lovely Zuzanna?'

'She is thinner, tighter round the hips,' Tadeusz said, as if that defined her.

'The way you paint her, that won't show. Conspiratorial art you called it? Do you have trouble with the authorities over it? Not socialist realist enough?'

'I was raided in the spring.'

Two women went by wheeling a pram. A man stood reading a newspaper. He folded it up and stuffed it in his pocket and walked away. Renton's gaze followed him. He shifted in the seat so he could watch the mirror more easily.

'What happened?'

'Zuzanna was out. Zdzislaw and I went out to buy something and They were waiting for that. We came back early and found Them stealing my paintings and statues.'

'They were waiting outside? How could They know you'd go out?'

'I didn't get a chance to ask Them. When we surprised Them carrying the Dustbin of History They brought out pistols and knives and chased us.'

'And?'

'They followed us into some tenements in the Bermuda Triangle and were beaten up.'

Renton was impressed. 'Feelings in Wroclaw are that strong?'

'You just don't hear about it.'

'Except from you.'

A pair of policemen were walking along the path at the edge of the park in front of the Palace of Culture.

'Shall we go for a stroll? Two men talking in a car or a van always invite attention.' They set off at an angle away from the police. 'How is your Klub?'

'Active.'

'Meetings, marches, that kind of thing?'

'And strikes. You know we use the English word "strike"? It has been your country's gift to us. And now Thatcher. She is strong. We Poles admire that.'

'She is also against strikes,' Renton said, 'except in Poland. So she must be pleased just now. Another big strike coming – and that is when the General will strike.'

'Then we must strike back.'

'Tadek – I may call you that? Tadek, he has the army and the police in all their forms.'

'We have our own weapons but they are different. Come.'

Tadeusz led the way back to the van and unlocked the cargo doors. Renton reared back as if it was a furnace that had been opened and a rush of hot air had singed his eyebrows. Deliberately he turned his back on the paintings and statues but it was to check if anyone else could see inside the van.

'What is this, Tadek?'

'Weapons to fight the police.'

'They can bring axes and hammers and smash everything to dust. That teapot They can flatten. Those cobbles They can set into the road.'

'The original canvases They took away. I repainted them. They can't destroy truth. I've brought all this to Warsaw to give to you.'

Renton looked at him. His eyebrows asked why.

'So you can have an exhibition at the British embassy. *Poland – The People Speak*. It will attract many visitors, many, many. The international press will come. It will be known throughout the world. Even in Moscow what we really think will be known.'

'Particularly in Moscow,' Renton said. He lifted the lid of the Dustbin of History and made a thoughtful pursing of his lips as if blowing a kiss at Lenin. He replaced the lid and closed the van doors. Linking his arm with Tadeusz's, he strolled to a bench.

'Well?'

Tadeusz sat on the bench but Renton positioned himself rather differently, his legs between the seat and the back, his arms resting on top of the seat. He faced the opposite way from Tadeusz, his gaze on whoever approached them from behind.

'I am flattered – truly I am – that you thought of the embassy as the right place to carry on your struggle. But . . . You must understand that for the British embassy to mount such an exhibition would be akin to a declaration of war, trying to bring down the legal Polish government.'

'Not legal. The government was forced on us by the Russians.'

'It is recognized by the whole world as the legal government. Secondly, even if we mounted the exhibition, no one would be allowed in. No one. Any foreign reporters who wrote about it would have their visas cancelled. As for Poles, the police would simply turn them away.'

Tadeusz stared up at the sky, palest blue with some cumulus that had been blown south from the Baltic. Why had he been so naive? The West wasn't going to help Poland. The West would watch the gallant democrats of Poland while they battled the might of the state. It would be September 1939 all over again: cavalry against tanks.

The message was clear: Don't look to the British or the Americans for help. Sadly he said, 'So you won't help us?'

'On the contrary. I propose something more exciting: I am asking *you* to help *us*.'

Renton began by talking of what he called 'Poland in the European context'. The Soviet satellites he likened to a mummy found in a Pharaonic tomb. The mummy was being restored to life and everywhere it was straining to escape its shroud. What was happening in Poland was vitally important because of its effect on its neighbouring countries East Germany and Czechoslovakia.

When Renton had been in Wroclaw he had been impressed by talk of the Klub, by the rallies, by the commitment and 'not least by the posters signed Tadek Codename Tadek. I thought – this fellow could help us, he knows what is going on, he has contacts. So I initiated certain enquiries, here, in London, with other people with whom we have friendly relations. Nothing but good things did I hear about you. Tadeusz Lipski, son of Konrad and Elzbieta. Elzbieta – your mother – a woman of great spirit, eloping to the West and bringing with her as a dowry some very interesting information. With such a pedigree the son is bound to be a good 'un. Liz is well, by the way. I thought you'd like to know.'

Tadeusz stared with stupid eyes at him. 'Liz?'

'Like Taylor. That is how your mother prefers to style herself. Liz Munton.'

There was silence while Tadeusz came to grips with this piece of news. His mother? He'd thought both his parents were dead and now one was suddenly waving across the years at him. His own mummy out of a Pharaoh's tomb was restored to life.

Tadeusz said, 'But Munton . . .' and stopped. He said, 'Where?'

'In America. In Florida, a classy condo. You know what a condo is? Your Bermuda Triangle with a swimming pool and widows from New York walking poodles. She apparently had an adventure or two and her last adventure was with a Mr Munton who manufactured speedboats in Minnesota. When he suffered a cardiac arrest on the golf course he left her well off. She moved to Florida where Polish snow is just a memory. So there you are.'

Renton decided that movement would help Tadeusz digest this rewriting of his personal history. He wished they were walking in the country or on cliffs overlooking the sea, somewhere with a wide horizon rather than with Stalin's oppressive presence. But maybe the awful legacy of Stalin would be helpful.

Tadeusz had questions – health, money, new ties – which Renton tried to answer. And then brought the talk back to Poland. Or something a little different.

'You see, if we mounted your exhibition it would inevitably come out that you were the artist. The authorities would link you to the mother who escaped with state secrets and then your life would be hell. At any rate no one has ever said that a UB cell is a fun place. But you can still strike a blow for freedom – and on a significant scale. From time to time you see Soviet troops in Wroclaw?'

'No.'

Renton looked puzzled. 'I thought –'

'Sometimes a truck loaded with Russian soldiers comes into the city but we don't see them. They do not exist. We look straight through them.'

'Ah, I understand. But what I want – if it is possible without drawing attention to yourself – is for you to take a close interest in them. There is a Soviet garrison city not far from Wroclaw –'

'Legnica,' Tadeusz said.

'As you say, Legnica.' He paused, his eyes fixed on two men who altered course to walk towards them. 'And now, I think, it is better that we speak Polish. *Mam nadzieje, ze panu nie przeszkadzam. Moze zjemy razem obiad?*'

Stunned at this unexpected fluency, Tadeusz could only mutter, '*Przepraszam.*'

'*Czy ma pan czas w piatek wieczorem?*'

'*Moze tak.*'

'*Wspaniale.*'

The men had stopped by Renton. Tadeusz, twisting, saw two men in their early thirties wearing Polish jeans and lumpy jackets. One of them said, '*Czy moze mi pan powiedziec dokladnie, ktora godzina?*'

Renton pulled back a sleeve. '*Jest prawie drugiej.*'

'*Dziekuje bardzo. Czesc.*'

When they were out of earshot Renton said, 'One can never be too careful.'

Tadeusz looked at the backs of the receding men. Why did they have no watches? Normal life was impossible without knowing when to work, when to get up, when to start queuing for life's necessities. Did they have Soviet watches which had broken? Did they just want to hear Renton's accent?

'I had no idea you spoke Polish. You hid it from me.'

'As I say, one can never be too careful. As in the matter of Soviet troops in Legnica. We have heard a rumour in the last days that the Soviets are revolving their troops, posting the previous lot out of Legnica and bringing in a new division. These are from East Germany. Or so we hear. One of the assault divisions with which they would invade the West. Perhaps. Only in this case it is Poland they would be invading. From inside Poland.'

'I don't understand.'

Renton spoke slowly, leaving gaps for Tadeusz to think.

'If Jaruzelski cannot keep control . . . If Solidarity turns openly political . . . If the "leading position" of the Party is eroded . . . If a communist state on the Soviet border threatens to be overthrown . . . Then Brezhnev would order the Red Army to roll in from the Soviet border, and at the same time order the division in Legnica to fan out and secure southern Poland and the Czech border.'

'But it is impossible. It would mean war.'

'Certain analysts tend to agree with you. If, of course, it is true. Here we move on to what we could call "the higher mathematics of the balance of terror". The Americans are already paranoid. They see Poland engulfed in civil war, the Russians invading, Czech and Hungarian divisions in revolt and refusing to obey their officers, and when sabotage spreads to East Germany and affects the Soviet divisions there . . . Europe is destabilized. Hawks in the military establishment in America say: Go nuclear now while the Kremlin's decision-making élite is distracted. In Moscow hawks are warning: America will take advantage of this situation – better order a pre-emptive nuclear strike. And in America certain super-hawks say: the Sovs are about to order a pre-emptive nuclear strike – better we should have a pre-pre-emptive strike. When the hawks and the super-hawks agree, watch out. There are no doves cooing around Washington and Langley; they are all hiding in deep shelters. That is the hypothesis at its simplest – I repeat simplest. What they call "the worst case scenario". Or doomsday.'

'You expect me to stop a war?'

Renton gave a thin smile. 'Nothing so heroic – though I'm sure you would if you could. We are trying everything we can to find out what is happening. Satellite pictures, electronic eavesdropping, monitoring railway and aircraft movements, all the usual. And human resources. In the jargon you are a human resource. One of several, I may say. If you agree to help.'

'Stone the dogs.' Zdzislaw was furious. 'Where have you been? Those goons threatened to beat me up to make me tell. What have you been doing?'

'Finding out how to stop a war.'

'You're crazy, do you know?'

Tadeusz's mind was reeling: a lost mother returned from the dead, the worst case scenario, the practical details Renton had gone into such as what insignia to look for, the difference between the 100-seater Antonov An-12 and the newer Ilyushin Il-76, a 'hot line' telephone number that was secure and the code to use in case it wasn't. 'It was Jan's twenty-third birthday yesterday' meant the 23rd motorized division of the Soviet army had transferred to Legnica. 'Aunt Maria sends her love' meant nothing ominous was happening. How would he remember not to give Aunt Maria a twenty-third birthday?

He nodded to Zdzislaw. 'In a totally crazy world, the crazy man is normal.'

In the turmoil of his mind he'd already decided what he must do. And he knew the gravest danger he ran was if Zuzanna got wind of it. She would claw his eyes out.

CHAPTER NINETEEN

'You – a spy?'

Tadeusz could still, after years, recall the tone of voice though he'd never been able to settle on a single word to define it. Surprised certainly – but surprised was too banal. Interested? Intrigued? Sceptical – he had to admit that Zuzanna didn't sound convinced of his ability. Amused even? Baffled? Taken aback? There were so many ways to interpret the way she said 'You – a spy?' and none of them, frankly, paid him too much of a compliment.

He'd told her about his meeting with Renton and she'd straightened her body against his – they were in bed, of course, celebrating his return – and called him a spy. He hadn't thought of himself as a spy. Spying was what Russians did in Poland. What a Pole did in Poland was being patriotic.

'Renton is a spy for the British,' Zuzanna had said. 'You are a spy's spy. Oh, do that again.'

He'd licked the underside of her breast, the slope that was like a cantaloupe melon. He'd moved his tongue to a nipple that seemed as ripe as a berry. His hand had lost itself in a tangle of moist curls. The moment of doubt about Tadeusz being a spy had passed. Making love removed doubts, cured evils, assuaged pangs of jealousy, soothed anger, bonded friendship, melted enmity, brought forgetfulness, killed despair and made one a spy on one's object of desire.

*

Footsteps swelled in the corridor, the door was unlocked and a new officer came in. He was young and seemed cheerful as if the day had got off to a good start. Tadeusz remembered mornings like that with Zuzanna when they'd breakfasted on love and dozed and woken to find the sun streaming in through uncurtained windows and glinting in her blonde hair and they'd enjoyed a second breakfast.

'Breakfast will be ready in ten minutes. The coffee's heating, the bread is fresh – or freshish – and there's sliced cheese.'

'I had the same yesterday,' Miler said, 'and even yesterday the bread was yesterday's.'

The officer was thrown off kilter working this out. 'You must be Alfons Miler.'

Miler frowned and darted a glance at Tadeusz and back to the officer. 'Miler, yes.'

'Good news for you. You're appearing in court this morning.'

'Shit,' Miler said.

Alfons, Tadeusz thought, Alfons Alfons Alfons. No wonder he kept quiet about his name. Not many parents baptized their sons Alfons any more. It caused the boys nothing but grief. Out on the street an 'Alfons' was a pimp.

And yes, from Tadeusz's sole experience of a pimp, Miler had the same tough outer skin, bluster and leering camaraderie, the same petulance and swiftness to take offence at imagined slights. Pimp and girl came out of the same box.

Some memories are complete in themselves. Nothing leads up to them, nothing follows on. They exist like short stories. It was how Tadeusz remembered his visit to Legnica.

The town was seventy kilometres west of Wroclaw, well positioned for a Soviet garrison, within striking distance of Prague and Berlin. Tadeusz hadn't told Zuzanna he was

going there, even less who he was going to see. If she
thinks I'm a spy, he'd reasoned, I'll have a spy's secrets. It
took an hour by train. At one point the line passed close to
a stream and a grassy patch between rocks and trees where
one hot summer's day a Satirist dressed in a beret had
painted a woman with amazing red hair. But Tadeusz
looked out on the other side of the train. He wasn't going to
spy on the past.

 At Legnica station Tadeusz saw all manner of police,
civilian, military, Polish, Russian and without doubt the
ones with no uniforms but a certain way of checking left
and right without moving their heads. He went into the
buffet and bought a beer. There were no Russian soldiers.
He tried to remember what Renton had said about the
insignia – did the assault troops have shoulder patches
with lightning flashes or had that been Nazi stormtroopers? Renton had said to buy beers for the Russians and try
to be friendly. Soldiers posted abroad were lonely. Also soldiers liked to boast of their skills, especially if they had
been relocated to Poland. Tadeusz could manage a few
words of Russian remembered from school but the idea of
pumping soldiers for information made him uneasy.

 A young woman sat at a table alone. She caught
Tadeusz's eye and smiled and when he smiled back she
walked over to join him.

 'For a while you were looking lonely,' she said. 'Far from
home, are you?'

 'Far enough.'

 Far enough for Zuzanna not to walk in and surprise
him. What would she do? Scratch the other woman's eyes
out and then go for his?

 'Are you going to buy me a drink?'

 'What do you want?'

 'What do I want? I want champagne. Or whisky. Even

vodka. You must come from more than far enough. There's
beer. If you don't want to drink that, there's always water.'
She picked up Tadeusz's glass and drank some. 'I don't like
beer. Don't waste your money buying me beer. Give me a
cigarette.'

'I don't smoke.'

She sighed. 'I don't get a drink. I have to smoke my own
cigarettes. But I bet I know something we could do
together.' She put a hand on Tadeusz's knee, slid it up his
thigh and began picking at a trouser seam with her finger-
nail. Tick, tick, the nail went as it caught the ridge of cloth.
Her eyebrows were plucked into thin lines and one of them
was raised as she leant closer. 'You want to come with me?'

'Where would we go?'

'I have a room. It's not far.'

'Not far is far enough,' Tadeusz said.

She frowned. 'What's that supposed to mean? Oh, come
on if you're coming.'

At the station entrance a pair of military police stood like
statues in a patch of sun. Were they Russian?

'Do they bother you?' Tadeusz asked.

'You mean, do they ask for a free ride? Sometimes.'

'Do they stop you going with Russian soldiers?'

'Don't worry. You don't look particularly Russian and
you certainly don't look like a soldier.'

Was this a compliment? She'd linked her arm through
his and was steering him across the road and down a side
street where two teenage boys kicked a ball. One shouted,
'Woo-hoo, your pants are bulging.'

The woman shouted back, 'So would yours if you were
men. Fucking kids show no respect,' she said to Tadeusz.
They turned into one of a row of houses. The moment
they were inside a door opened on a man in a plastic-
leather jacket who looked an older version of the boys in

the street. The woman said to Tadeusz, 'Give him a couple of hundred so we won't be disturbed.'

Was this to stop others interrupting? Or to stop the man disturbing them? He didn't look the type to argue with.

At the top of the stairs she led the way into a room whose drawn curtains kept in permanent night time. She switched on a light and Tadeusz looked round. The usual framed print of the Pope welcomed him from a chest of drawers. In one corner was a portable plastic bidet, a sponge and a pitcher of water. The bed was wide enough for one and a half people to sleep, or for two people in a close encounter. Above it on the wall were magazine photos of a young Elvis Presley, John Kennedy and what could best be described as 'a bare-breasted dusky maiden' on a palm-fringed beach. A dressing gown hung from a hook on the door. A closet stood open on three or four dresses, slacks, shoes and shelves of blouses and underwear. A bedside table held a lamp, an empty glass, an ashtray and a small radio. A magazine lay on the floor.

'And it'll be five hundred to me before we go any further.' She was already unbuttoning her blouse as she spoke. 'Put your clothes on top of the chest.'

Tadeusz looked round the room again. There was only the bed to sit on. The woman had put the money in a box in one of the drawers and was stepping out of her skirt.

'I want to talk,' Tadeusz said.

'Oh yes? One of those?' She came to stand close to him. 'Dirty talk excites you? Is it you who's going to talk dirty? Or me? Do you want me to help you off with your clothes?'

'No,' he said.

'Suit yourself. Shall we get better acquainted? You can call me Marysia. And down here is little Myszka.' She patted her knickers where Myszka lived. 'What's your name?'

He was going to say Tadek and was surprised when it came out 'Tex.'

'Tex?' Marysia said.

'Tex is American. Rhymes with sex in English. You know what sex is, don't you? Do you speak English?'

'Why should I? I live in Poland.'

'Russian?'

'I can say "Darling" in Russian. Also I've picked up some other words, basic ones. Is that what you want?'

She sat beside him on the bed, her bare leg laid carelessly against his clothed leg, her bare shoulder against his clothed one. She wore a white bra that had grey patches at the top of its cups, grubby from lack of washing or from fingering. Her breasts – what were on show – were the poor relations of Zuzanna's. The skin of her chest and thighs was mottled. Her skin looked dead, he thought. And her face was a mask. Zuzia's face lived her emotions, Marysia's face hid hers. Powder made her cheeks white and accentuated twin spots of rouge. Lipstick had been spread beyond her lips so that her mouth appeared bigger. Her eyes were grey and she'd outlined them in black so that she seemed to stare at Tadeusz from ponds of brackish water. Who would be so desperate as to want a woman like this? Some Ivan, he told himself.

'You have Russian soldiers from the garrison?'

'Now we're getting to it: you want to watch me do it with a Russian boy?'

'No, I want to talk about the Russian soldiers.'

Marysia stared at him for a long moment, her grey eyes showing nothing. Abruptly she pushed herself off the bed and from the door yelled down the stairs, 'Krzysiek!'

It was the same man he'd given two hundred zlotys to when they came in. He'd flung off his jacket somewhere along the way and came through the door in a hurry, like someone used to dealing with the rough trade.

'He's causing trouble?'

'He's asking about Russian soldiers.'

Krzysiek jerked his head towards the door. 'Out. We don't want trouble-makers.'

'I'm not causing trouble. I paid for her time and I want to talk. It's none of your business.'

The pimp was suddenly furious. 'Her business is my business. I'm not having some do-gooder ordering me about. Out! Out through the door or I'll put you out through the window.'

His nose had met a wall or a fist at some time and it pointed at an angle towards the window.

Marysia said, 'Russian soldiers are no different from Polish soldiers: their privates stand to attention when they're with me. Maybe they smell a bit more. What I do, I make them keep their socks on because their feet stink. Some are a bit jumpy like it was their first time.'

'Let me handle him,' Krzysiek said. 'What are you? Church holy roller? Trying to reform her? Take her living away from her? You'd be putting her out on the street if she wasn't already on the street. We've had your type before. Got down on his knees and it wasn't to say hello to Myszka. He was shouting to the Lord to save her. When I get him outside he begins singing a hymn. How can she do a bit of business with some Bible-puncher outside singing "The Dear Lord Jesus loves a Sinner"?'

When he'd finished, Tadeusz said to the woman, 'Do they speak German?'

'You're always on about speaking bloody languages. They're Russian so they shout a bit in Russian. They're stuck here, conscript boys a long way from home, they want their mum and a bit of comfort. That's what I give them, comfort.'

'Are you going? You start your bloody hymns, I'll tip the bidet on you.'

Conscript boys who were homesick for mum had sounded nothing like élite assault troops. Tadeusz had telephoned the number Renton had given him. Bit eerie it was. The ringing tone stopped but nobody spoke. 'This is Tadek Codename Tadek.' He waited but there was no response so he blurted out his message into the void: 'Aunt Maria sends her love.' Which all in all was ironic because Marysia was a pet name for Maria, and Myszka – the Mouse – even more of a pet name. About a fortnight after that he had received a postcard on which was scribbled: 'The birthday party has been postponed but could still be on. He watches over us still.' Mischievously the postcard was of Stalin's Palace of Culture.

Tadeusz had never gone back to Legnica. Finally the Soviet occupying force had packed up and retreated to Russia. They'd stripped the houses and barracks, torn out even the plumbing. They'd have pulled up the roads to ship home if they could. But they'd left something behind.

If you went to where the fuel bunkers had been, dug a hole in the ground and sunk a bucket, it would fill up with diesel. Not even a thistle would grow in soil so polluted. But a farmer who went there got enough to run his tractor. Thanks to the Russians, Poland was an oil-producing country. Why not apply to join OPEC?

'Don't worry,' Tadeusz said, 'your secret is safe with me.'

Miler, facing the wall, shrugged a shoulder just like an *Alfons* or his girl would have done.

'To me you'll always be Friend Miler.'

A friend is someone who doesn't betray you.

CHAPTER TWENTY

For the first time Tadeusz truly appreciated the weight of November. It was heavy with the winter ahead, the sky growing lower under the burden of snows to come.

In her sleep Zuzanna had wrestled off the blankets and turned towards him, head cushioned on one arm, a single breast exposed. Breathing, her breast swelled like the ocean. Pale moonlight and shadows defined its slope and valley, made it into a wave that rose and fell. He'd never seen the ocean. What would it be like to sail over the horizon, perhaps to Florida, to a mother he didn't know? Like certain *parfumeurs* who can recognize each field in Provence by its scent of musk roses or lavender or jasmine, his only memory of his mother was of the mingled smells of vermouth and perfume that stayed with him when she kissed him goodnight, goodbye. But she'd become Liz and lived in a condo which he imagined as a stockade surrounded by swamps with alligators. The shock of hearing she was alive had subsided. She had no hold on him.

He could sail further south to warm seas where fish were said to fly and birds to swim underwater and snow didn't exist. He pictured it as the flag of some tropical country, in bands of blue, green, white and turquoise – blue sky, green jungle, white sand, turquoise water. He saw Zuzanna under palm trees wearing a necklace of orchids that swung between sun-bronzed breasts. Her head was tilted to one side, her lips just parted in invitation. It was the image from Marysia's room.

As he slipped out of bed Zuzanna stirred and mumbled something. It could have been 'Love you' or 'Idiot' or some-one's name. He pulled the covers over her and went downstairs. There was no coal for the boiler so he put on his overcoat against the cold. The door to the sitting room stood open and the smell of cigarette smoke was still heavy. It hung in the air like the smoke of battle. The Klub had met in the evening. All the tensions, divisions, fears, uncer-tainties and accusations of Poland had been present in this one room. People gave and received labels. Reformer, con-servative, radical, appeaser, confrontationist, moderate, negotiator, bully, provocateur – the Klub was splintering.

Henryk had urged caution, a step by step approach that wouldn't force the government into violent repression. Father Michal was increasingly radical and out of tune with the Church's traditional conservatism. 'If we don't act, we will starve. The future is that stark. We will be dead by the end of winter. Have you seen the black market opposite the Hall of Justice? I recognized a High Court judge there, bargaining for three eggs for his family's supper. Even a judge!'

Adam's brother, who was a conscript in the army and due for release, had had his period of conscription pro-longed into next year. Zdzislaw said he'd seen army officers coming out of the director's office at Dolmel. Witold said that at Pafawag they were determined on a warning strike. Eugeniusz said warnings were useless; all that the previous warning strikes had achieved was economic collapse and a General in charge. Henryk said there were sixty-five sepa-rate strikes going on in Warsaw at the moment and that was why the Soviet Union was pressing ever closer.

Waldemar said:

'You're silent, Tadek. What do you think we should do?'

Why the room had gone silent for his view, Tadeusz didn't understand. They all looked towards him. Zuzanna, quiet on her pouffe, waited for him as if his judgement was crucial.

Tadeusz said, 'As an artist I am naturally a dictator, that is to say I rule my own anarchy. As a Pole I am naturally a democrat and I will do what we collectively decide, design the posters if a strike is called, design the posters if a rally is to be held, design the posters if dialogue with the authorities is what we think best.'

'That is admirable as far as it goes,' Father Michal said. 'But we need fighters for our cause as well as artists. As a Christian I follow my conscience under God's guidance. I must preach.'

'Then I shall design the poster that advertises your sermon.'

And that, reflected Tadeusz as he entered his studio, was as much of a conclusion as the Klub had reached.

He tried the switch and was blessed with electricity. On the easel he set up the piece of plasterboard he had been reduced to using. He stared at it, head tilted to one side much as the dusky bare-breasted maiden had looked. 'It is God versus communism', Father Michal had said. 'In the end as at the beginning, that is what it comes to. That is what I shall preach.' Tadeusz didn't know how he would paint the Apocalypse. The poster wasn't urgent. Father Michal wouldn't preach until the bishop was away in Krakow in December. So for now he would paint something else.

When Zuzanna found him at dawn he was just finishing, the anger and fear for the approaching winter all expressed in the painting.

'Tadek, you left me. What is it?'

Shivering, she insinuated herself inside his overcoat to look at the painting. The plasterboard was four-fifths grey clouds, heavy with the menace of winter snow. Crouching underneath was the tiny figure of a woman, possibly Zuzanna, holding a baby to her naked breast.

'It's a calendar for next year,' Tadeusz said.

A strip at the very bottom said January. It began 1, 2, 3, 4, 5, 6, 7, 8, but the dates grew smaller and more cramped and changed into a row of dots and the dots grew smaller and stopped.

'It's called Happy 1982,' Tadeusz said.

Zuzanna had cooked pork chops and arranged them on a plate with separate little heaps of beetroot, carrot and cabbage salads. Tadeusz prodded the chop with his knife.

'Where did these come from?'

She cut a piece of meat, put it in her mouth, chewed and swallowed. 'From the taste,' she said, leaning back in her chair to give him the full benefit of blue eyes that had become chips of ice, 'I would say from a pig.'

'There's no meat in the shops.'

'From a friend of a friend.'

'Who? What friend? What friend of a friend? Do I know him?'

'Him?'

'Or her?'

She thought about this. 'I would say,' she cut another piece of meat and lifted it towards her mouth, 'no.'

Nobody bought Tadeusz's art any more. Even German buyers kept away from a country sliding towards the abyss. For money, Tadeusz dipped into her handbag. There was a stigma attached to being a kept man but he comforted himself: I am an artist; in Renaissance times artists had patronage; it is like that.

Money? Pork chops? Did it matter? It seemed a difference in kind. Money could have come in a dozen ways. Pork chops had to come from an individual. What did she do in return?

The next afternoon he followed her when she went out. She turned left and headed towards the station. She turned right and crossed over the moat then left again to walk beside it through the park. Ahead were the monstrous hulks of the Police and UB headquarters and the Hall of Justice. She's going to the black market, he thought. It was early December and the sun had already sunk below the roofs of buildings. Bushes and trees stood naked and he held back so she wouldn't catch sight of him. People sat on benches, huddled in coats. Or picked among the odds and ends in litter bins. Or walked in pairs, talking in low tones, falling silent when they passed anyone.

Then she turned in towards the centre of the city, the opera house on the left and the Monopol Hotel. She has a friend in the kitchen, he thought. But she went on until she reached Rynek. There was a police station in one corner and people staring in shop windows for something to buy, anything that could be bartered for food.

She turned the corner of the City Hall and when he reached it she had vanished. She had to have gone into the museum and Tadeusz ran up the steps. He followed a sign that pointed to the Exhibition. The Exhibition was of the World Congress of Intellectuals for Peace. The Congress had been held in August 1948 but the authorities had decided to rerun it.

In the first room Tadeusz stopped in some bewilderment. Large display panels divided the room and she could be concealed anywhere. He passed by a huge map of the globe with illustrations of how delegates to the Congress had evidently arrived: the Australian had come in the pouch of a kangaroo; some unfortunate who was swimming from Latin America was being eaten by a shark; Americans wore cowboy hats and six-shooters; Africans dressed in loincloths did a tribal dance.

The next room had photos of distinguished peacemongers. Bertrand Russell's white hair blew in the wind. Feliks Topolski looked inscrutable. Picasso wore a tie and a three-piece suit and a cigar was clamped in his mouth. No Zuzanna.

Another room was a jumble of broken tree trunks and ancient machine guns and photos and still more photos: Boers on horseback, the trenches at Verdun, Bulgarian atrocities, that Spanish Republican soldier being hit, American bombers over Vietnam, Pearl Harbor, the Hammer & Sickle being hoisted over the Reichstag. Reeling past a curious stone statue of a bear playing the bagpipes Tadeusz went out into the fresh air. Zuzanna had been nowhere. In fact nobody had been there except him.

That evening, uncertainty gnawing at him, he said, 'I was having a walk this afternoon when I saw you.'

Her eyebrows lifted but she said nothing.

'You went into that exhibition at the City Hall but when I followed I couldn't see you.'

'You were spying on me.'

'No,' he lied. 'I just caught sight of you and—'

'And you thought you'd follow me. When you couldn't find me, you decided you'd question me. A spy's questions.'

He said nothing.

'But I suspect you didn't check in the women's toilets. That's where I went, Tadek. Did you check in there?'

'No.'

'Don't follow me, Tadek. Don't spy. I give you my love but you don't own me.'

It's just that he needed to know that she gave him all her love. The idea that he might be sharing her was more than he could bear.

In bed, in the dark before the moon had risen, she relented.

'Tadek, if you had followed me into the women's toilets . . .'

What was coming next? What hand grenade tossed into his face? Edgily he replied, 'Yes?'

'You would have seen a scribble of graffiti on the wall.'

'I thought only men did that.'

'I think this was not done by a man. It reads: "Tadek Codename The Great Lover."'

A fantasy like this made him love her more.

At midnight, as they were sinking into sleep, Tadeusz heard the grinding of heavy engines from Krasinskiego Street. It sounded like a procession of lorries. Bringing food? Bringing coal? Shivering at the window he saw nothing. From bed she said, 'Come back. I'm cold.' She called him 'Darling' which she almost never did, and 'My greatest lover', which pleased him though not as much as if she'd called him 'My only lover'. She said, 'You are amazing,' and 'What a hero,' and coaxed him to life again. He thought: Marysia would not know such tricks. And wished he hadn't had the thought. She wrapped her arms round him and held him tight as if he were a log that was her only hope of safety as they were swept through rapids, with currents and eddies snatching at them, whirlpools threatening to drown them, until at last at the journey's end they lay stranded, aching, overwhelmed by sleep.

It was morning but still dark when the knocking woke them. On the step Tadeusz found Eugeniusz, back to the door, scanning the street. In his hand he held a small overnight bag. He pushed past Tadeusz and shut the door.

'Thank heavens you're safe,' Eugeniusz said. 'I didn't know where else to come.'

Drugged by sleep, Tadeusz stared stupidly.

'You haven't heard? The General has struck.'

Eugeniusz went into the sitting room. Something about it, perhaps a memory, displeased him and they moved to the studio. He stared at the shanks of hair over the small figure in dark glasses.

'He's not in Lech's shadow any more.'

He told his story in pieces, as someone in shock will do, backtracking to chunks he had missed. He was determined to get it all out.

'The trouble is they were asking for the moon. Let's have a referendum. Let's have free elections. Let's ask the people if they think the Party is fit to rule.' Seeing Tadeusz still puzzled he explained, 'I was at the meeting of the National Commission. Someone would get up and shout, "Let's appoint a Solidarity government." Big round of cheers. "Let's go for a national strike starting on the seventeenth." Then I was called away.'

He'd been passed a message that his wife Justyna had tripped and broken a leg. He caught the night train from Gdansk to Wroclaw and was stiff from sitting up the whole way.

'At the station you'd have thought I was visiting royalty, so many uniforms everywhere. It was still dark and half the station lights were out but I could see people being stopped, their papers inspected, some being led away. So I dodged through the side exit into the parking lot.'

He stopped, looking over Tadeusz's shoulder. Zuzanna stood in the doorway. She'd pulled a couple of sweaters over her head, tousling her hair. It made her look untamed, something from the wild.

'Do we have any coffee?' Tadeusz asked. 'Gienek's been travelling all night.'

She hesitated, then went without a word.

'Coffee?' Eugeniusz said. 'I remember that. What do you have to do to get coffee?' But he didn't wait for an answer. This was not a morning to worry about the black market. He went to the window and bent his body to peer towards the street. The sky was paling. It was that early dawn light when everything looks grey. Is that a tree trunk? Is that the shoulder of a man standing behind it? Or the knob of a branch? Nothing has substance. 'Outside the station . . .' He broke off to peer again. Satisfied for the moment he came back to Tadeusz. 'Outside the station, army lorries with troops. You could see their cigarette ends. I thought: that's what soldiers have – a last cigarette before they go into battle. There was a squad of ZOMO in helmets. Helmets – that means business. There were militia on motorbikes. Everybody had come to the party. There was a car with three men in – more militia – but they had the radio on and were concentrating on that. It was the General broadcasting. Still dark and I thought: Maybe he's announcing the sun is going to be rationed. He was declaring martial law. Six in the morning. Catch people at their lowest. A couple of people off the train stopped to listen. The General said the Polish People's Republic was in a state of war. One of the men didn't hear properly or didn't believe his ears. "What's he saying?" I told him, "It's war." "Where?" "Here in Poland. The General has declared war on us." The heads in the car turned and the militia looked out at us and you know – they did nothing. I think they were ashamed. They're not like the ZOMO or the Ubeks. Not all of them.'

He switched off the lamp and stood by the window again. Lights were going on in the building opposite. Neighbours were waking each other, spreading the news:

The General has declared war on us.

Zuzanna came in with a tray, stumbling in the half-dark.

'Why did you turn the light off?'

'Because it's war. You stand a better chance in war if no one knows you are there.'

'War?' she said.

'Martial law,' Tadeusz said. There was no difference in Polish. The phrase for 'martial law' was 'state of war'.

'The station must be one of the places they were told to make a show of force. I got away and found a telephone. I wanted to ring Solidarity in Gdansk, ask what was going on, what we should do. "The number you have rung is not in service," a man's voice said. "Who is calling?" Bang down the phone.' Eugeniusz peered towards the street again, using his sleeve to clean the glass. He turned back, taking three or four deep breaths. 'I went to my flat. Correction, I got to the corner and saw there was a car parked outside the building. ZOMO again. I could see one of them holding his helmet, twisting it like this, like that. Like you admire something. Who were they waiting for? Me? Going to beat me up? I heard a rumour yesterday they've had their truncheons lined with lead. You can crack open a skull with that. So I backed away. I ask you – if I go to the hospital to see Justyna, will they be waiting by the bed?'

Everybody has their Martial Law Day story.

Eugeniusz left his overnight bag with Tadeusz. 'Otherwise,' he reasoned, 'some overzealous fellow will think I'm running away to hide and take me in. They'll open the bag and the Solidarity letters and leaflets will hit them in the eye.' He paused, frowning, glancing at Tadeusz. 'You can always burn them.'

'Don't insult me,' Tadeusz said.

'We could hide them under my clothes,' Zuzanna said.

'Searching through women's clothes is their special pleasure,' Eugeniusz said. In the end the bag was shoved in
among boxes of old brushes, loops of wire, pots of glue and
a partly used bag of cement.

Justyna had been taken to the hospital in Jantarowa –
'Maybe not the most suitable but the closest to where she
fell.' He approached with caution but assumed nobody
would be waiting for him out in the cold when they could
be comfortable inside. He used the entrance from the
ambulance bay, following a bleak corridor. He even put on
a bit of a limp as a threadbare excuse for being there. He
chose a middle-aged nurse – one who had some authority
and wouldn't be easily frightened and explained the situation. This, of course, would be her Martial Law Day story:
how she had helped a Solidarity activist into a doctor's
gown and even added a nose-and-mouth mask and cap as
if he'd just come from surgery. Then she said, 'You need a
clipboard. A clipboard means you are working. It shows
you have patients to see and are busy and mustn't be
detained.'

She led him to the ward where Justyna lay sedated. And
indeed on chairs just inside the door two militia sat waiting. Not all the militia were bad but they obeyed orders. He
did the round of the beds, asking 'How are we feeling this
morning? Making progress are we?' When one woman
complained of pain passing water he said to the nurse, 'See
to that.' He reached his wife. As he bent over to feel her
forehead he was conscious of the militia's eyes on his back.
He whispered, 'Don't worry. They won't get me. I'll go into
hiding.' She smiled, pleased to see him, though her eyes
showed some confusion. The drugs, he told himself.

Only when he was outside, walking away, did it strike
him she might not even know about martial law yet.

*

Witold had a confused impression of Martial Law Day. He hadn't heard the General's proclamation on the radio. The baby, who was teething, had woken him before six. He'd turned on the radio but hearing what he described as 'brass bands marching through my head' he'd switched it off. There was enough noise in the flat as it was. If he'd caught the bus to work he'd have been told in seconds. But he cycled, a recent hobby of his. He did pass a lot of uniforms and army lorries, but to his mind there was no logic to the way the military worked any way.

When he reached the Pafawag factory he got off the bicycle but still didn't take in the enormity of what was happening. The crows that usually scavenged in the yard were wheeling in the dawn sky, angry at being disturbed. The morning shift was arriving but instead of entering the gates had formed a great crowd. Pafawag produced railway carriages, locomotives and good wagons but what he could see looked very different.

'Have we gone into the arms business?' he asked some-one.

'It's the bloody army.'

Blocking the gates, gun turrets facing the crowd, were three tanks. Behind them was a line of soldiers. When Witold had been conscripted into the army they'd been issued with Soviet rifles. Czech would have been fine but the Russian weapons weighed a ton. It was, barrack room myth had it, to punish them for not having defeated the Wehrmacht single-handed in 1939. These soldiers were issued with weapons that looked more like soldering irons, light, lethal at a touch.

Pushing forward for a closer look, perhaps still not alert after a disturbed night and no coffee, he reached the front row. He was face to face with a group of men standing beside one of the tanks. Plain clothes. Ubeks, he supposed.

Someone with a loudhailer was reading out from a piece of paper that the factory was closed today. Sit-ins were a favourite tactic and this was being avoided. Standing with the Ubeks he saw the foreman from his line. Unfortunately Jablonski the foreman saw him too, pointed him out, and a snatch squad of Ubeks dragged him away inside the gates.

He heard protests from his workmates but also an order shouted and the clatter of military metal. Would Poles fire on Poles? Maybe they weren't regular units but the Army Security Service. Then his attention was snapped back to the foreman who was saying, 'He's one of them, a provocateur.' Someone tripped him up and he found himself staring up at wheeling crows. He rolled over as the Ubeks began to kick him, forming himself into a ball, knowing otherwise they'd kick him in the groin.

Then a voice he knew said, 'Stop that at once, you've got the wrong man.' Twisting his head he saw the production manager for the locomotive works pointing to the foreman. 'He's got a grudge against young Witold. Witold is a good worker. Let him go. Jablonski is the one who needs a lesson.'

To his amazement, Witold was let go while Jablonski was led away, struggling as the Ubeks put handcuffs on him. To his even greater amazement, he saw the production manager raise a hand and, as it shielded his face, give him a deliberate wink.

In fact Witold's freedom was brief. Ubeks came to his flat two days later and arrested him as an 'anti-state element'. With the teething baby bawling and his pregnant wife in hysterics, he was hustled out. In the cell he was taken to was the production manager, face swollen, blood dribbling from his mouth, two front teeth missing.

*

Zdzislaw's Martial Law Day story was that of Henryk.

Zdzislaw called on Tadeusz in the late morning in shock, which was normal for the day. Zuzanna made more coffee and they tried the radio but it alternated between military marches and Bach so they switched it off.

Zdzis had heard the radio news early but had gone to the Dolmel factory none the less. Tanks, he said, and soldiers. And nasty men in hats and belted raincoats who'd crawled out of the woodwork. He hadn't taken the van to the factory owing to a lack of fuel. He caught a bus back to the centre and reasoning that Solidarity activists were in danger he went to the university to warn Henryk.

Chaos. Well, students can cause chaos just changing lecture halls but this was worse, shouting, chanting, jeering at soldiers. He asked where Professor Henryk Radnicki's office was, but he was already too late. A military commissar had arrived at the main building with a couple of truck loads of troops carrying rifles with bayonets fixed. Bayonets! Henryk tried to barricade the staircase, demanding they respect academic freedom and was threatened for his pains. With a bayonet. Henryk pointed out this was the Faculty of Moral Philosophy not a barracks and was ordered to stand aside. Henryk addressed the students backing him up: 'Chairman Mao said that power grows out of a gun. In Poland today morals come from a bayonet.' He was arrested. Several students who thought to protect him were clubbed to the ground. Fortunately the soldiers used the butt end of their rifles.

Father Michal came. Because the Klub had met in the Half House, it was natural to go there hoping for news or comfort. It never occurred to them that the authorities might raid it. It was a curious oversight, perhaps the confusion of the day, that the house was left in peace.

'I must preach,' Father Michal said.

He drank the coffee that Zuzanna handed him but was so distracted he didn't remark on it. Coffee! In Poland!

'The bishop has given permission?' Tadeusz asked.

'I am sure His Lordship would give my sermon his blessing.' Father Michal chose his words with care. 'He is a Pole. As is the Pope. I am sure he would.'

But in case caution overcomes him . . . Tadeusz thought. Better not to say that out loud.

'There will be more funerals this winter,' Father Michal said. 'From cold. From hunger. And I fear from conflict. The duty of the church is plain. It is to preach God's law. What I shall say is this: Go on your knees before God not before a General.'

'They will arrest you.'

'I shall have company. You know what the General has ordered?' Father Michal took hold of his thumb. 'A curfew from ten to six.' He took hold of a finger and followed it with another finger for each prohibition: gatherings banned, strikes banned, trade unions banned, through the dreadful list of what were now called crimes. He ran out of fingers on his two hands and had to start again. 'Sporting and public entertainment banned. All we may do together is work, stand in a queue, and pray. The church is the only place of resistance left. You will do me posters?'

The printing presses had been stopped so Tadeusz turned himself into a copyist, churning out the simple message: 'The church speaks for Poland.' Tomorrow morning after curfew ended but while it was still dark they would scatter these as widely as they could. Waiting until morning would leave the army less time to lean on the bishop to forbid it.

And Tadeusz? Did he have a Martial Law Day story? Two actually, though the first was very minor and seen by no one. He went to the cupboard under the window seat and took out the pistol. It still said *Geladen* but he made himself open the magazine to check it really was. He rehearsed how the safety eased off. If they try to raid here, he thought . . .

Better not to finish the thought.

Zuzanna, too, had her Martial Law Day story, though it only came out later.

In the afternoon she left Tadeusz at work on the posters. She was going out to see for herself what was happening, she said. She came to give him a hug, pulling him fiercely against her, and was gone. She never returned.

It was after dark, just gone seven, when Eugeniusz returned.

'I have a message for you,' he said. 'Urgent. Father Michal wants to see you.'

'Where?' asked Tadeusz.

'In the cathedral. He thinks it is safer.'

CHAPTER TWENTY-ONE

When the officer appeared at the cell door again, his early morning glow had already been dusted over by the chores of the day. He heaved a sigh as if these remand prisoners did not know their luck in escaping the cares of the world.

'Well, Alfons Miler –'

'Miler, yes.'

'I'm having to disturb you from your daydreams. Sorry. Never knew anyone in a cell who wasn't having pleasant thoughts about girls or a glass of something cold. You are due in court this morning but first I am taking you to see your lawyer. A consultation, he called it. Gave a lick of his lips, he did. A consultation is more expensive than a talk, see.'

And he winked at Tadeusz. Remand prisoners were not convicted prisoners and were due a joke or two.

'Good luck, Friend Miler.'

Miler nodded as he left. He had other things on his mind. As did Tadeusz.

There were so many 'what ifs' in life. But this was the biggest one. Eugeniusz had told him to meet Father Michal. There was something in his voice as he said it, also some pinching of his brows. Call it Martial Law Day fever. The symptoms were shock, fear, doubt, mistrust. Eugeniusz had glanced at the party wall with the Brandts. Brandt was something to do with rail transport and was away a lot. The dogs were company and protection for his wife. Why? No other wife needed protecting. There had always been some hesitation about Brandt.

So Eugeniusz had given his message and turned aside. Whatever was troubling him he kept to himself.

But what if he'd said more?

The past was a book in which Tadeusz had lost his place and he kept flicking through the pages. He'd discover a memory he treasured, another memory that puzzled. And the end came racing towards him. The pages turned in a blur. He couldn't stop them though he'd lived and relived it too much. If only he could take hold of the story and push it in another direction, rather like the communists used to rewrite the past. Beria good, Beria bad, Beria airbrushed out of the photos. Stalin the deliverer of the Great Patriotic War, Stalin the creator of the gulag and genocidal monster, Stalin in the Dustbin of History, now joined by communism itself. To give yourself a different history, that would be a wonderful gift.

Tadeusz heard whistling approach, *Dimanche à Orly*, Polish pop, never mind the French title. Foreign was sophisticated, foreign was an escape from dull care, though he doubted that in Paris they fantasized about Sunday at Okecie airport in Warsaw.

The officer came in to collect the breakfast dishes.

'You're on your own now. You want something to read, book, magazine, help pass the time?'

Tadeusz shook his head. If he stared at a page, the words re-formed themselves, thousands of letters swarmed like ants, the sentences ran backwards, the subject turned into the object, his understanding became grammatically challenged.

'Well, it was just a suggestion because of having no one to share a joke with. Takes people differently. I know I couldn't stand solitary. I'd be out of my mind in half a day. Got to have a face to talk to. Now to be honest, I suspect you won't be seeing that fellow again.'

'Friend Miler?'

'He's a pal of yours? Friend Miler did you say?'

'I called him Friend Miler because he kept his first name to himself.'

'Alfons. Stands to reason he might. And Miler he calls himself. Outside it was Müller. I don't know which name he'll be charged under. His lawyer might have a bit of fun over a confusion of identification. It's complicated enough as it is.'

'What's he done? What's he charged with?'

'You don't know? It's been in all the papers. Where have you been hiding?'

'Bolivia.' A different cell from this, anyway.

'Surprised it wasn't there too.' The officer put down the breakfast dishes. Miler hadn't finished yesterday's bread. The officer stuffed a slice in his pocket before settling himself on the bunk. 'I keep chickens. You can't beat a fresh egg. Right Miler/Müller. He arrived three or four months ago, presented himself at the City Hall and demanded to see the President of the Council. Had he received the telegram from Bern? No matter, here he was in person, Heinz Müller, presenting his credentials. He had a Swiss passport, afterwards found to have been manufactured in East Germany when it was under the communists. Also a letter on the headed notepaper of the Swiss Ministry of External Affairs – the paper likewise found later to be a forgery. He had been appointed Swiss Consul. In Wroclaw! The President of the Council was speechless and then he was full of speeches. The honour, the recognition of

Wroclaw's industrial strength, its cultural vitality, so forth. Well, you know what these political types are.'

The officer got out his cigarettes and companionably offered one to his prisoner. Tadeusz shook his head. Even shaking his head didn't help his understanding: Miler as a Swiss Consul!

'He rented himself an office. He advertised for a secretary and had himself some fun interviewing them. Two or three girls later came forward as witnesses. Müller had told them a tale that a Consul's secretary had to double as his hostess and it was necessary to interview her on the couch to see that she possessed the right social qualities. He had headed notepaper printed. As with everything, a Consul naturally was given credit. Then he issued invitations to a grand Polish-Swiss Friendship Reception. Hired the restaurant at the Monopol. On credit, of course. Champagne, smoked salmon, the lot.'

'Miler did? The one who was in here?'

'The very same. He sent invitations out to dozens of people. He invited bankers, he invited certain political leaders in the community, a couple of big landowners who'd returned after the changes. To brighten things up he asked a number of actresses who were reputed to look favourably upon the gentlemen. Also he asked some of our Captains of Industry. Included among these industrious men were certain managers from Dolmel. This was very careless of him. You see a Swiss company has bought Dolmel and two of the managers who came were Swiss, naturally delighted to make the acquaintance of their Consul. Afterwards, they told the police that though Müller spoke German all right, he had no knowledge whatever of the dialect they speak in Switzerland. That he was no more Swiss than I am. Or you are.'

'Was it a big hoax? A practical joke? He didn't seem to have much of a sense of humour to me.'

'While these people and their wives and mistresses were at the reception, a gang visited eight of their grand houses. Four had servants at home, as they found out by ringing the bell. The other four were burgled. The gang knew which properties to go for, they knew where the wall safes were, where the silver was kept, they knew how to switch off the alarms. And they got away with their loot. Müller was packing his suitcase when the police called on him. He has his alibi, of course. Fifty of Wroclaw's most upstanding citizens could vouch for his presence. The police cannot break his story. He admitted only to an overpowering urge to discover what the diplomatic life was like. So he is being charged with deception, impersonation of a diplomat, activities threatening relations with a foreign state, so forth. Whenever he comes up for trial, there are these bomb threats.'

'Miler could never have organized something like that.'

'Exactly. That's my view, that's the police view, that's the prosecution's view. He just had his part to play. Mr Big got away. Mr Big seems to get away with a lot in Poland these days.'

Tadeusz would have loved to have seen Miler as the Swiss Consul, hosting his reception. Did he wear evening dress? Did he sport obscure decorations, honourable member of the Order of the Leopard, Class 2, from Zaire?

Then, leaning back in his bunk, an idea took shape in his head and demanded to be spoken. He said, 'Rich people like to have private security arrangements to guard their houses. I wonder if they all used the same company. Have the police followed that up?'

The officer gazed at him, the beginnings of a pitying smile twitching at the corners of his mouth. Amateur sleuth, his lips said, bumbling into the professionals' preserve. But the longer he gazed, the more thoughtful he became. In Wroclaw there were only two security firms of any size: Recom and PAX. The officer gathered up the dishes. In the corridor he began humming *Dimanche à Orly*, at first softly, then with a great deal more conviction as his footsteps retreated.

CHAPTER TWENTY-TWO

The street was dark when Tadeusz came out of the Half House. There was starlight but no moon. It was cold enough to shiver. Or it might have been nerves. The General has declared war, he told himself, I am going into battle. In some small way he understood how the cavalry must have felt in September 1939 when they saw Hitler's panzers rolling towards them.

This is Poland, he rallied himself. There is no need to feel nervous on the streets. Crime cannot exist in a socialist society except among unreformed elements where capitalist freebooting ways linger and lack of social justice leads to violence. Such as in the Bermuda Triangle to his right from where he could hear shouting. He turned left.

This is Poland. The army, the police and the vigilant secret servants of the state are here to protect us. The honest citizen has nothing to fear. In the upside-down thinking of the workers' state the beatings and incarcerations made people free, the empty shelves in the shops were evidence that people had satisfied their needs, and Solidarity was banned because logically it was unnecessary.

This is Poland, repeating it again, a statement so resoundingly simple it grew to have a resonance in his mind. This is Poland on the first night of the war which General Jaruzelski has declared on his citizens. At this moment while its future hangs in the balance any doubt, fear, truth, myth or conspiracy is possible. You can view the world through any glasses you choose – dark, short-sighted, distorting, rose-coloured. You can declare Jaruzelski a patriot, saving the country from Soviet invasion. You can maintain the opposite, that he is dancing to Moscow's tune. You can even think he is Washington's puppet, ensuring the communist regime stinks in the nostrils of the world.

This is Poland, betrayed, oppressed, invaded, dying, reborn, living, struggling. It is a stage where other nations' dramas are played out.

Tadeusz turned in towards the city centre.

The lamps were mainly out, unreplaced bulbs or lack of electricity or policy he didn't know. The few down the main street created pools of light and sent flashes off military metal. It had rained in the afternoon. A passing militia car threw out a sheet of spray from the cobbles. The car drew into the kerb and two officers got out. They stood on either side of him, handing each other his papers, inspecting them by the light of a torch, turning the beam in his face to see it matched his photograph.

'What is your name?'

It was in the documents in their hands but they stuck to their ritual. He told them.

'Where do you live?'

He told them.

'Where are you going?'

He told them. 'To the cathedral. I shall say a prayer for Poland.'

There was nothing they could say against that. Instead they warned him the curfew started at ten. 'If you are on the streets then, you risk being shot.'

He set off again, across the moat, walking fast. Ahead rose St Adalbert's where the Solidarity rally had been bro-

ken up by the ZOMO. It must be a favourite haunt of theirs
because half a dozen young men came suddenly running,
shouting 'ZOMO! ZOMO!' and disappearing into the night.
Tadeusz shrank behind a tree trunk as the ZOMO came
pounding in pursuit, hampered by helmets and riot shields
and heavy truncheons. After they passed he advanced more
cautiously, detouring on a route that took him towards the
central square.

He walked up Swidnicka and passed the Gothic City
Hall. There were people about but the mood was sombre.
Here in the heart of the city he was struck by how immac-
ulate the streets were. There was no litter. It wasn't civic
good housekeeping. People had nothing to throw away.

A man stepped out of a doorway and fell in beside
Tadeusz. He had an unlit cigarette between his lips.

'Can I have a light?'

'I don't smoke.'

'Where are you going?'

Not trusting the man, Tadeusz didn't answer.

'If we got matches,' the man pursued Tadeusz, 'we could
set fire to the Savoy. Pile of old newspapers under the
drapes, a match and slip out while they're all shouting
orders at each other.'

Some thought had gone into this. The Savoy was a hotel
dedicated to putting up visiting police, those in uniform
and their other darker brethren.

'What do you say?'

Tadeusz swerved across the road to get away. Patriot,
provocateur, it wasn't a night to find out. This is Poland, a
country destroyed by warring dictators, impoverished by
ideology, occupied by foreign divisions. It is a country
where a stranger suggests insurrection and it seems quite
normal.

He thought he was being followed. Now he considered

it, he thought he might have been followed almost from the Half House. He wasn't accustomed to checking over his shoulder. Now, when he turned, there seemed to be two or three men trailing behind him. Or was the cathedral a magnet on this evening? He took turnings at random, ducked down dark alleys and lost them. It is a mark of honour to be followed, he told himself, a mark of folly not to lose them before he met Father Michal. If, of course, they had been following him.

He turned north again, passing university buildings. He caught the sound of singing. It wasn't students, drunk on beer or youth. This came from further off. '*Zeby Polska byla Polska,*' the voices sang, haunting, thin on the night air. It was the battle hymn of Solidarity. Let Poland be Poland. Let there be no more foreign troops on Polish soil, no more alien theories foisted on them, no more tribute paid to Moscow. A truck passed him, its back crammed with uniformed and helmeted men, heading in the direction of the singing.

Closer to was a shout, short and urgent, followed by the sound of breaking glass and the patter of running feet. The feet ran towards him, then stopped. Tadeusz stopped too. When he went on, cautiously, he saw no one.

He'd never crossed the bridge over the river Odra before and not been passed by a tram. There were no buses either, and private cars had been forbidden. Headlights signalled the army of occupation. As he drew near to the cathedral he shrank into a doorway at the approach of a car that seemed to crawl as if searching for someone. It passed. The gas lamps that jutted out from buildings were lit, great glass globes casting a soft light. The mass of the cathedral was in front of him, its twin towers black against the star-pricked sky. To one side of the front entrance was a heap of builder's sand, a cement mixer, a jumble of bricks. In the

final battle of the last war the cathedral's roof had gone
and its walls had come crashing down. It had stood
marooned, half its original height, a fire-blackened skeleton. It had been a matter of devotion to rebuild it, even in
the days of desperate privation. There always seemed work
to be done even now, a fissure to be patched, a buttress to
shore it up. The cathedral never closed, people coming at
all hours of the night. Constricted by the approaching curfew, would the cathedral be empty? Or would the devout
spend the curfew hours in the pews?

Tadeusz pushed open the door and entered the porch. If
there was dim light out in the open from the stars and the
gas lamps, here there was nothing. He stopped dead, not
knowing which direction to take. He tried to recall his last
visit: was the door straight ahead or to the side? The question was answered. A door to the right creaked open and
two women, heads covered with scarves tied under their
chins, shuffled forward. Tadeusz stood aside to let them
pass out. He went through the door they'd shown him into
the cathedral proper. For some minutes he stood at the
very back, letting his eyes adjust to the gloom and the per-
spectives. The roof above the central nave was so high it
was lost in blackness. It might never have been rebuilt and
Tadeusz stared hard as if to make out stars. To each side the
roof was lower and arched, the ridges of the arches darker
against the white plaster. A little light was reflected from a
row of four bulbs set into pillars. Other illumination came
from candles, dozens of them, guttering in sandtrays
placed beneath paintings and statues. On the right was the
chapel of the Blessed Virgin Mary with a phallanx of votive
candles and three kneeling figures.

Somewhere someone was murmuring. Tadeusz couldn't
make out who it was or even where to look. The acoustics
of the cathedral made the droning voice surround him.

Was it an incantation, a prayer, a command by a priest to reform? On it went, on and on, the tone rising and falling but always mournful. Surely no one's life was so filled with grief. He decided it was a woman's voice but even that was uncertain.

At this moment, with that damned recital of woe and the general graveyard air, he might have been tempted to retreat. A sense of duty – which in Tadeusz's view was a fancy way of saying stubbornness – made him go on. The nation was in crisis, Father Michal had something important to tell him. End of hesitation.

Peering about he saw other shadows that seemed to move. But were they people or wavering ghosts set jostling each other by the candle flames? A man coughed and the sound echoed and died. The air was cold enough and damp enough to set a whole congregation coughing. Tadeusz could feel it clammy against his cheeks, like mist rising off the Odra. Dampness was inside his clothes too, moisture crawling over his chest and under his arms. He advanced a few steps and was alarmed at how loud the grating of his shoes was against the stone floor, though no one five metres off would have heard him.

'He'll be in one of the confessional boxes', had been Eugeniusz's parting instruction, 'the ones on the left.'

On the north wall, near the side entrance into the cathedral, were two double confessionals, with stalls for the penitents to kneel on each side of the central cubicle where the priest sat and listened.

'There are two confessionals. He'll be in the one closer to the side door. Don't go to the other one. The one nearer the door. Got that?'

Yes, Geniek, I may be an artist who lives too much in his dreams but I have managed to get my brain round what you are saying.

Tadeusz began crossing, as softly as he could, over to the north side of the cathedral. He could see now there were three muffled figures waiting on benches. But they were waiting for the confessional further away from the side door. Did penitents have favourites among the father confessors? Priests who knew their whole history of sinning and would make allowances? On this night of nights there must be many who'd had the most extreme impulses. 'Father, in my heart I want to kill Jaruzelski and the Ubeks, every single one.' 'To want to take human life is a grave sin, my son, but . . .'

Tadeusz passed on to the stalls nearer the door. They were substantial wooden constructions, fine lattice work. In the central cubicle was a small light the priest switched on to show he was in and ready to receive. The light was off. But that could just be Father Michal trying not to advertise his presence too much. The door to the priest's cubicle was cut in half and the lower half was closed with the end of his stole draped over it. *I am in*, the stole said, *waiting for you, Tadek*.

Tadeusz was something of a stranger to church, as Father Michal well knew. Looking at the stole Tadeusz could grasp the attraction of obedience and the comfort of ritual. The church's traditions had an aura that engulfed him. Was that why Father Michal had chosen the cathedral for a rendezvous? To entice the strayed sheep back to the fold? No, that was too cunning for a straightforward man. It was for reasons of security.

Nobody occupied the confessional stalls to either side of Father Michal. Tadeusz entered the first one and got down on his knees. He would have felt more comfortable sitting but penitents weren't there for the ease of their bodies. Only the priest was given a seat to perch on. He pressed his forehead against the wooden panel, his mouth close to the grille to which the priest directed his ear. He cannot take two confessions at once, Tadeusz registered. He can only lean one way. No confusing a young man's sins with a widow's wishes.

'Father Michal,' he murmured through the grille.

How many confessions had been whispered here? The gaps in the fretted wood were so meagre while the sins had assumed such proportions in the penitents' consciences. Father, I have sinned, I had impious thoughts about a boy, a young man really. I saw his body naked except for a beret. Though I was tempted, I resisted. But Father, how my fancy was stirred.

Is that what Tex had confessed long ago? Since then sins had sifted down until the confessional should have been a thick mud of lust, envy, bitterness, blasphemy, violence, theft, hopelessness, doubt and whatever else was troubling the faithful.

'It's Tadeusz, Father.' He might know many people by that name. 'Tadek Codename Tadek.'

No sound came, no movement, no recognition.

'Father Michal? You're not asleep, are you?'

But of course if he had fallen asleep he wouldn't answer.

Tadeusz got off his knees, went to the front of the cubicle and reached in to tap Father Michal on the shoulder. 'Father Michal?' This having no effect he gave a gentle shake and then a more vigorous one and Father Michal began to tumble forward. Tadeusz struggled with the priest's garments, trying to slip his hands into his armpits to support him. The stole became entangled with his wrist and jerking it he felt wetness. He pushed the priest's chest to get him upright and his knuckles rapped against a hard something sticking out. Fumbling to get a grip, his fingers grasped the hilt of a knife sticking out from Father Michal's chest.

'Dear God,' he cried out.

The shadows that had been so insubstantial turned into figures hastening towards him. The penitents waiting their turn on the bench rose to their feet. A figure slipped in the side entrance and took swift steps towards him.

'I need help,' Tadeusz said. 'Father Michal has been stabbed. I think he must be dead.'

He had one hand under a shoulder, the other still gripping the handle of the knife when there was a flash, blinding in the gloom of the cathedral.

'Got him,' a man said.

'Take another one.'

A second flash caught Tadeusz, still holding the body and the knife, with his head turned towards the camera, his face white, his features sharp in every detail.

'Help,' Tadeusz said, 'or he's going to fall. He's heavy.' Dead weight, he thought.

But nobody helped him. They stood round him, eight men in a semicircle, blocking his way if he thought to run for it. The man with the camera took another shot, kneeling to get an angle up at Tadeusz's grimacing face, all teeth and gun-slit eyes, looming with menace. Other people in the cathedral were turned in their direction, women disturbed in prayer, men who had been having a private word with God. The man who'd slipped in the side entrance drew closer. He wore a belted raincoat and a hat he hadn't taken off.

'What has happened?'

Two of the semicircle gave him room, treating him with a certain respect. Turning his head, Tadeusz saw the gleaming forehead and protruding lips of Baran.

'It's the priest. He's been killed. This is the man who did it. We weren't in time to stop him.'

It was spoken like a bad school play, the lines stilted. But the man raised his voice so that others in the cathedral would hear.

'We suspected something might happen,' another man said. 'A conscientious citizen gave us warning. We hurried but this man was quicker.'

There was a pause. Nobody had written them any more dialogue.

'What is the name of the priest?' Baran asked.

'They call him Father Michal. He is one of the ringleaders of the anti-state Klub.'

Tadeusz's understanding had come slowly through this performance. Blame it on Martial Law Day. He had been punch-drunk from Eugeniusz's pre-dawn arrival. Add the constant flow of callers with their stories. Top it up with his walk through the streets, the uniforms, the shouting and the singing, the unearthly light of the cathedral, the corpse that fell into his hands. Now Baran. Now his cohorts. Now the handcuffs. Now the accusation of murder. Now he was being taken away, prodded like a pig into the abattoir.

'No!' he yelled, furiously wrestling himself free of the hands. He turned back to the onlookers. 'They've killed Father Michal. They've murdered him. They got me here so—'

He was hit in the stomach by one of Baran's men. When he doubled over his chin met the man's knee. His head snapped back, his mouth filling with blood from his tongue. There were other blows but he hardly felt them. Giddy, spitting blood, with the scene drifting away from him, he was half carried, half dragged towards the entrance, his heels scraping along the stone flags.

'Baran,' he called out. 'Baran Baran Baran.'

They hustled him more roughly hearing him shout the name. But to the people watching did it mean anything?

Baran was his name but in Polish a *baran* was a ram. Why did he cry out Ram Ram Ram?

From behind him, and it seemed to come from far off, he heard Baran's voice. 'Liar. We'll teach you some respect for the guardians of the state.'

Strangely, it was Baran who stopped them beating Tadeusz.

'No, only if he tries to escape. But watch him. His family has a history of escaping. Your mother got away, didn't she?'

Baran gave him a long look. Tadeusz wasn't seeing clearly and the light from the gas lamps was feeble round the north side of the cathedral. So far as he could tell Baran wasn't angry with him or hostile. The look he gave was without emotion much as one might look at a sheet of paper or a pair of pliers that could prove useful.

Three of the men accompanied him in the back of the van, unmarked, without even a revolving light on the roof. The glass panels in the rear doors had been blocked with plywood so he couldn't see where he was being taken. Private vehicles were forbidden according to martial law which meant four times they were stopped while the driver spoke to soldiers or militia, showing official papers.

'What are you doing?' one of the men asked. 'Don't try shouting for help. It won't do you any good.'

'It might do you a lot of bad,' another one said.

They laughed.

Tadeusz didn't speak. He was trying to wipe the blood from his mouth on to the collar of his coat. His tongue had stopped bleeding from where he'd bitten it. It was just that when he licked his lips he could taste blood.

How long did they drive? Forty minutes? He couldn't see his watch and he wasn't timing the journey anyway. But out of the city. He heard the labouring of passing diesel engines but nothing more. Abruptly the van swung to the right and stopped for more talk. A muffled thump could be a gate lifting. The van drove in, stopped, reversed into position, the doors were opened from outside and he was hustled out with only a glimpse of what looked like barrack huts.

'Blindfold him,' Baran said.

He was pushed down a corridor, round a corner, up some steps and into a room. The blindfold had a slight gap at the bottom which let him see he was sat down at a desk, one of a row.

'How long will it take?' Baran asked.

'It's being done now.'

Tadeusz waited in silence then blurted, 'Why me? Father Michal I can understand because he was a focus. But why frame me?' Nobody answered. Tadeusz yelled at the top of his voice, 'I asked you a bloody question.'

There was movement. An arm went round his neck so that his windpipe was constricted in the bend of the elbow. When he tried to get up, other hands forced him down. As shooting stars began to slant across his vision, the elbow was relaxed and he gulped air.

'Shout again,' Baran said, 'and you'll be gagged.'

Once more they waited in silence until footsteps came into the room.

'Here you are,' a voice said.

'Good.' A pause. 'They're excellent. How much longer do we have to wait?'

'Not long. He's on his way.'

Tadeusz thought to count the seconds. He'd nearly reached a thousand when more men entered the room and there was murmured conversation. A voice was raised, 'There should be a flag. That shouldn't be difficult to find here.' There was another delay until the same man said,

'Take off his blindfold. The court is now in session, Judge Skibska presiding.'

Tadeusz blinked because of the light and the confusion that broke inside him. This was a court? Court martial? But no one wore uniform. The judge wore a poorly cut suit and a nondescript tie. He was an old man whose neck had shrunk inside his shirt collar. As the judge began polishing a pair of spectacles on a scrap of chamois leather, Tadeusz's eyes swept the room. Not a school classroom but a lecture room of some kind. Army, ZOMO, UB, Militia, take your pick. There was a blackboard rubbed clean. A filing cabinet had a globe turned so that South America faced the room. General Jaruzelski's unsmiling features looked down from a framed photograph. A dais held the desk and chair where the judge sat. A small Polish flag stood in an old pickle jar to one side.

Having jammed his spectacles on, Judge Skibska cleared his throat and asked, 'Who is the prosecutor?'

Baran came to the front row of desks but remained standing. 'I ordered the prisoner's arrest. I am charging him.'

'Very well. Accused, stand up.'

Tadeusz kept still until he felt someone's hot breath on the back of his neck and a whisper, 'Do what he says. Don't make life for yourself hard later.' He rose to his feet.

'Name?'

'Tadeusz Lipski.'

'Occupation?'

'Multi-discipline artist.'

The judge pondered this.

'I paint. I write. I sculpt. I compose and play music. I practise *feng shui*. But I don't dance.'

'He also,' Baran said, 'designs posters for a banned organization.'

'Solidarity wasn't banned when I designed them.'

Baran opened a file, produced a sheet of paper and unfolded it. Craning his neck Tadeusz saw the poster: THE CHURCH SPEAKS FOR POLAND. So They've raided the Half House, he thought. What else will They bring in evidence? The Dustbin of History? 'You were doing these today. Several dozen of them. However, he is not being charged with anti-state propaganda but with murder.'

The judge looked at Tadeusz. 'That is a very grave crime. You should have legal representation.'

'Under martial law,' Baran said, 'we are bidden to put aside such legalisms. This business is urgent. The security of the state depends upon respect for its authority. The facts are very plain and none of the obfuscations that lawyers introduce will help the prisoner.'

'But I would never murder him,' Tadeusz burst out. 'He was a friend and colleague in the Klub. What reason could I possibly have?'

'Because you found out he was an agent of the state, reporting to me. That is why you went to the cathedral to meet him: to kill the man you felt was a traitor to Solidarity. We were concerned about this rendezvous which is why there were several of my men close by. Unfortunately not close enough.'

Tadeusz sat down and no amount of prodding would get him back on his feet. The proceedings were a sham. The truth was the opposite of what Baran said. But the case was presented as if there could be no reasonable doubt about Tadeusz's guilt.

According to Baran there was also a history of some personal feelings. Hadn't the prisoner been living in sin with a woman? Hadn't the priest spoken to him about this?

But the nub of the case was the discovery that the priest

was an informer for the state – 'as many upright and honest citizens are', in Baran's words. He said Father Michal had secretly been taping the meetings of the Klub. He even played a tape as if this was conclusive evidence. Tadeusz listened to the voices arguing and scarcely bothered to wonder how they'd been taped: a recorder hidden by one of Baran's men, a microphone poked through from the Brandts' side of the house. No matter.

'When did you discover Father Michal's links with the organs of security?'

Tadeusz gave no answer.

'He does not want to convict himself out of his own mouth.'

Evidence was given by two of the men who swore they'd seen Tadeusz plunging the knife in. Photographs were shown – still damp from printing – of Tadeusz bracing the body so it wouldn't slump out of the confessional and gripping the knife. Fingerprints on the knife handle matched a filing card of the prisoner's in every particular. When had they stolen those, Tadeusz wondered. Was there any part of his life that wouldn't be put on show? A film of Zuzanna and himself making love?

'Show Judge Skibska your hands.'

When Tadeusz made no move, Baran grabbed a wrist and thrust it at the judge.

'Of course he shrinks from showing you. The priest's blood is still on them.'

The judge looked from the hand to Tadeusz's face.

'What do you have to say against this charge?'

Nothing.

'Two men say they saw you stab the priest. A photograph shows you apparently driving the blade home. Your fingerprints are still on the handle. Do you deny this evidence?'

What was the point? This play-acting had taken less than forty minutes.

The judge let his eyes travel slowly round the room, at the men who sat like sacks until they could crack open a celebratory bottle of vodka. He gazed at the photograph of Jaruzelski in whose name the prosecution was taking place. Maybe Jaruzelski stared back but the dark glasses kept their secret. His eyes could be closed or angry or glancing anxiously towards Moscow. There was no telling.

'For a charge as grave as this,' the judge said, 'I should not be sitting alone.'

'The times are not normal. The country is at war.'

'What punishment are you calling for?'

'For murder, there is only one punishment that is appropriate: execution.'

Tadeusz heard but had difficulty in understanding. Was it really his death that was being discussed so matter of factly? I didn't do it, he screamed, but only in his head because there was no point in protesting aloud. Every single one of them in that room knew he was innocent. Even the old judge whose head was now bowed must be fully aware this was a mock trial carried out for other reasons. Why didn't he object? Was he a Party bigwig? In their pay?

The judge said, 'You have the papers for me to sign?'

Or, looking at how his hands trembled as he unscrewed his fountain pen, what guilty secret did the judge have in his own past?

The man behind Tadeusz leant forward. 'In the night, when you're asleep, I'll come for you.' Tadeusz could feel the man's hot breath on his ear as he whispered. 'You'll wake up and it'll be my hands you feel round your throat.'

Tadeusz considered the matter of strangling.

In a cell without light he sat on a bunk, his arms still

handcuffed behind him. This made lying down too uncom-
fortable. Besides, he might fall asleep and the man who'd
whispered in his ear would tiptoe in.

Now to strangle someone the thumbs are necessary in
order to apply pressure. Fingers and palms are not enough.
When the man appeared, Tadeusz would pretend sleep. As
the hands descended towards his throat he would lunge,
get a thumb between his teeth and applying every fragment of strength his anger gave him he would bite the
thumb off. He couldn't bite through bone so he'd aim to get
the second joint between his teeth.

He would be killed anyway but that sadist would never
be able to boast about strangling a prisoner again.

Some time during the night he heard soft steps
approaching and lay down on his bunk.

If this is the end, this is the end. He thought briefly of
Zuzanna, the body he would never paint or love again. He
even thought of Tex and wondered what turning his life
would have taken if that hot summer day in 1976 she had
taken her clothes off too and they had made love out in the
open. To his surprise he caught a hint of perfume mixed
with cheap Bulgarian vermouth wafting over him as his
mother bent to kiss him.

The door opened. He saw a silhouette against the dim
corridor illumination before the door was closed. For a
few moments the cell was in complete blackness. Then the
light came on and he saw Baran's hand on the switch and
Baran's protruding lips. As if puckering for a kiss.

'You think I've come to do it?' Baran said. 'You were
expecting someone else and you aren't prepared for me.'

Baran took out his cigarette packet and put one between
Tadeusz's lips. Tadeusz spat it out.

'The condemned man refuses the ritual final cigarette.'
Baran lit one for himself. 'But I haven't come to kill you.

Your execution has been cancelled, or at any rate postponed. Maybe this is merciful, maybe not. I don't know
how your fellow prisoners will react to the murderer of a
Solidarity priest.'

Tadeusz didn't speak. He willed his brain to blankness.

Baran drew deeply on his cigarette. The tip glowed. The
tip looked angry.

'You wouldn't plead for your life in front of the judge.
You won't show gratitude now. One part of me has to
admire you. You show strength in your character that quite
frankly surprises me. I thought you were mad, the crazi-
ness of artists. But it seems you also have some of their
determination to carry things through.'

Baran did a circuit of the cell, four steps one way, five
steps the other.

'Your next cell will be smaller. You'll be in it for a long
time, fifteen years if your fellow prisoners spare you, maybe
twenty-five. Is there anyone you want to pass a message to
before they take you away in the morning?'

For the first time in over a year Tadeusz thought of
Rafat. Rafat too had had a trial, not completely secret
because Zuzanna had been present. When Rafat had been
imprisoned, Zuzanna had come to him. Who would she go
to now?

'So, no message?' Baran paused by the door. 'Oh, you
think maybe you'll be compromising the other person. But
I promise you I won't have her arrested. Or him arrested.
Not a word?'

What value was a promise made by Baran? Tadeusz
pressed his lips tighter. He closed his ears to any more lies.
He did not move so much as an eyelash. He closed the
very pores of his skin so that no more poison could seep in.

CHAPTER TWENTY-THREE

It was mid-morning and as bright as the cell was ever going to get. Later in the day there would be a patch of pale sun but it seemed to make little difference.

Cells I have known, Tadeusz thought. Here I am locked in one; I don't want to think about the one Baran sent me to. I don't want to think about the lost years. Altogether I'm thinking too much. A habit of waiting in a cell for time to pass.

There were images that not all the years of his life would erase. At first he had been put to share with a man, some petty swindler. On the second day the news reached prison of Tadeusz's crime, or supposed crime, and the absence of mercy that Baran had predicted began. His cellmate spat in his face. When Tadeusz rose slowly to his feet and grew with anger – Baran's thuggery, wrongful imprisonment, a petty crook imagining himself above him – seeming to puff himself up and his eyes to open wider and his chest to swell like a wrestler's, the swindler screamed 'Shit' in his face, then screamed for the warders, opened his mouth until it was a gaping hole and screamed and screamed. He demanded to be taken out, not to have to share with the murderer of a Solidarity priest. No one would share with Tadeusz except a large man with dangerously dull eyes who Tadeusz suspected planned to throttle him in his sleep. He got a cell on his own.

In the exercise yard the other prisoners ganged up on him, kicking him in the back of the knees to make him stumble then kicking him on the ground until warders ran to his rescue; though perhaps 'ran' exaggerates their urgency.

In the canteen queue his elbow was jostled so his plate tipped its contents down his trousers. He was taken in to get his food first, sat at a table in a corner on his own, watched by warders. Potatoes with rotten purple blotches mysteriously lobbed in his direction. Bread soaked in fat hit the wall behind him and spattered the back of his head.

If he walked past cells the other prisoners screamed at him. Screaming was an offence so it was done silently. The images fixed in his memory were of open mouths like Edvard Munch's *The Scream*, but it was hate not fear they screamed with.

The prison wing he was put in was filled with Solidarity activists. At first they were not supposed to talk to each other. But Tadeusz, in his solitary confinement, could hear the prisoners singing hymns and at midday reciting together the angelus prayer. They were sharing – he understood – and this kept their spirits high. He, isolated, could feel a stain of blackness spreading through him.

Then like the dawn of a soft summer day, the harshness faded. The swindler who'd shared his cell sidled up to him, speaking out of the side of his mouth. 'We've got the word you're okay. We've heard tell how They fitted you up. No hard feelings.'

'I am an artist,' he had said. 'Give me paper and a broad-nibbed pen and black ink.'

He drew a portrait of a pig's body with the head of General Jaruzelski. He entitled it: *The pig lives until it feels the butcher's knife.*

He drew a portrait of Hitler addressing the Nuremburg rally, on a platform before an adoring audience of Aryan zealots. It had Hitler's little jutting arse and his arm was raised in the Nazi salute. But in place of Hitler's face, he drew Jaruzelski's. He entitled it: *All leaders develop stiff right arms.*

He drew a picture of Jaruzelski lying in a coffin that was being lowered into a grave. He entitled it: *The General joins the underground.*

In the canteen was a noticeboard with exhortations to 'Renew socialism for a better Poland', 'A reformed prisoner can be an honoured citizen' and 'Report any subversive talk to a member of the prison service'. One breakfast he smuggled these portraits in under his tunic and tacked them up to roars of approval from the other prisoners.

His paper, pen and ink were taken away from him.

For a while Tadeusz closed his eyes, screwed them very tight in an attempt to squeeze out the memory of his cell from thirteen years ago. A cell is a cell is a cell, he told himself. All cells are alike. All cells are made to the same pattern of smooth walls, high barred window, spyhole in the door. All cells are made in a big factory in a Warsaw suburb and are sent to fill the blank spaces in prisons. Cells are the success story of the twentieth century. In my next life I shall go into the manufacturing of cells and export them to the big growth areas of the world which are no longer the satellite countries of the deceased Soviet empire but more far-flung territories. So I shall fly my cells to Asia, to China in particular, to Indonesia and Burma, to Africa, to Latin America if the Generals return to plague El Salvador and Panama and Argentina and Bolivia.

A cell is not just to keep a prisoner in. A cell is to keep the outside world out. In a communist country news had been a dangerous commodity that must be rationed. But even that thin and untrustworthy news had been too rich for prisoners and had to be filtered and doctored and blended and dosed with bromide. So when several cells were gathered together, rumours had spread.

'You know what they say?'

It wasn't Miler who spoke. Miler had gone, leaving blankets in a lump. The blankets looked like Miler in a sulk. A pimp can sulk, an *alfons*.

'I said, you know what they say?'

Listening very hard Tadeusz could almost swear he heard a faint echo of Roman's harsh whisper. After Tadeusz had been reinstated as a decent member of prison society, Roman had been moved in to share with him. Roman had been a tram driver and his crime had been to toss leaflets from his tram all along the route to Biskupin. The leaflets were a crude incitement to an indefinite general strike and had been printed with a child's toy press but that didn't save him from a five years' sentence.

'What do they say, Romek?'

'They say America has threatened a nuclear strike unless Lech Walesa is released. They say the bloody Russians are on red alert and the submarines are streaming out from Murmansk.'

How do rumours start? How do they spread and change? Tadeusz remembered making up a rumour of his own.

'You know what they say?' he muttered to the man in front of him in the canteen queue. This had been during the time when prisoners were not supposed to talk. 'They say that West Germany is massing its troops on the border and is going to crash through the German Democratic Republic and invade Poland.' The next day his cellmate Roman spoke when they returned from the exercise yard.

'You know what they say?'

'What do they say, Romek?'

'They say Germany is invading Poland, thirty divisions, and we're being sent up to the front line. Only, because we're Solidarity and against the government, they're not going to give us guns in case we mutiny and join the Germans.'

A few days later a voice murmured in his ear as he waited in line in the shower room.

'Have you heard? There's a thousand trucks heading for Poland. It's the biggest convoy since the blitzkrieg.'

Tadeusz imagined this was a further mutation of his rumour, except it turned out to be true. The lorries were laden with food, medicines and clothing to help the increasingly desperate Poles.

All prisoners have time to think.

'What are you thinking about, Romek?'

'Sex.'

When Tadeusz's mind wandered through the thickets of sex, he thought of Zuzanna. Oh Zuzia Zuzia Zuzia. He had never appreciated the meaning of the word 'voluptuous' until he knew her. Her body displayed all the richness of our planet: valleys, slopes, undulations, earth tremors, springs, bushes, volcanoes, caves; her belly was a sea on which to row; her breasts were mountains to climb; her toes were pebbles on a beach; her flanks were a long day's walk. His daydreams grew fevered, his images far-fetched. What was she doing now? He could not picture her knitting socks and waiting. She'd said she had money. Did this mean she had a rich 'uncle'? Was she living with him. He sighed.

'Sex, right?' Roman said.

If you didn't think about sex, you thought about food. But how could you fantasize about being released and enjoying a blow-out when all there was to queue for was potatoes? When all you could buy on the black market was powdered milk and macaroni?

Which left revenge. Tadeusz had spent long unprofitable hours turning over the matter of his arrest. He had been set up. He had been betrayed. Why him? To what purpose? By whom?

Gossip among the prisoners was that Father Michal had been planning a radical and uncompromising sermon. No sooner had Lech and the other leaders been put away than a new and more militant generation rose up. So to kill Father Michal was, for Them, logical. To carry on Their thinking, to blame another Solidarity activist for the murder shifted the opprobrium. To show Solidarity riven by dissent to the point of murder was to discredit and demoralize them. Most of the Klub were arrested or on the run. But everyone knew about the wild streak in artists. Tadeusz Lipski was perfect.

That was as far as his thinking ever got him. He sighed some more.

'Still sex, hey?'

No paper, no pen, no ink, no drawing. Tadeusz had turned to the consolations of music. No sax, no keyboard. He composed music in his head, he heard great sounds in his head, he had concepts in his head, he played music in his head he thought.

'What's that?' Roman had asked one night after lights out.

'What's what?'

'That noise.'

'What did it sound like?'

'Air raid warning. Cops chasing robbers in Chicago. Dying cow in a thunderstorm. That kind of noise.'

'I can't hear anything.'

'Not *now*. Of course not now. You were making it. On and on. Sometimes up a bit, sometimes down a bit like you were running out of steam, then up again. Why?'

'I was composing,' Tadeusz explained. 'A musical piece.'

'I thought music was something you could whistle. A tune.'

'A sound composition then. About a girl I saw on a beach once.'

'If she was as flat as your music, she wasn't worth looking at. You're driving me nuts frankly.'

Prison etiquette demanded you didn't drive your cellmate nuts, so Tadeusz kept quiet. But he held the concept in his head. Many years later it achieved a certain fame, or notoriety.

Without that sound composition would he be languishing in this cell now?

Tadeusz lay on the bunk staring at the ceiling, as he had for years. Roman had been released after two years, most of the other activists shortly afterwards. Judges, on the whole, had not been as venal or as cowed as Judge Skibska. They had handed down the minimum sentence of three years with remission for good behaviour. As one by one the Solidarity prisoners left, Tadeusz had suffered a new bout of black dog. Murder was different. Murder meant ten years, fifteen years, twenty years. Murder of a priest meant you were forgotten. Murder of a Solidarity priest meant they threw away the key.

One by one, before they were released, the prisoners had asked him: Can we pass on any message? Can we see anyone? Can we make any enquiries? But Tadeusz had been struck by a strange insight: that no member of the Klub had been imprisoned with him. No, he had said, thank you but no. To himself he had promised that one day, when he was free, no matter how long he had to wait, he had questions he would ask and answers he would demand.

'Guess what.' The warder stood at the door with a lunch tray.

'How many guesses do I get?' Tadeusz asked.

'Half a guess.'

'There's been a bomb scare in Miler's court.'

'You know what the judge did? He said the court would take an hour's recess. Everybody except for Miler would be evacuated. If Miler wasn't blown up by his friends, the court would reconvene.'

Tadeusz grinned. 'What did Miler do?'

'He swore. He begged. He appealed to his lawyer. But his lawyer was already heading for the exit. Another thing. You know you said that the houses that were robbed while Miler was holding his party might be guarded by one security company? They were. PAX. How did you know?'

'I have a criminal mind.' Tadeusz yawned. He'd dozed on and off but never had a proper sleep.

'Also, it looks like your case will be coming up this afternoon.'

The yawn snapped shut. 'You're sure?'

'The judges and jury are convening at half past one.'

Tadeusz looked round the cell. He'd been moved to a different cell. Or the same cell in a different building. He didn't want to brood about cells any more. There'd be time enough in the future.

'So what will they give me? I've already done thirteen years for a murder I didn't commit.'

'Thirteen years? How did you stand it?'

'Each morning you say: I didn't do it so this must be the

day they admit it's a mistake and let me go. When the old
regime crumbled, when Solidarity took power, when Lech
was elected President – each time I was sure I would be
out. The trouble was my fingerprints were on the murder
weapon. And there was an eye witness – a woman who
swore she had seen me plunge the knife in, though she'd
never been a witness at my original trial. She only came
forward later. Finally I saw a photo of the woman who'd
identified me. She wore glasses as thick as the bottom of
wine bottles. I asked for her optician's records to be
checked. She'd had an eye test a month after the murder
had been committed, got her glasses a couple of weeks
later. At the time she said she'd seen me wielding the knife
in a dark cathedral she was so blind she couldn't have seen
further than the hands in front of her face when she
prayed. It was just – she finally confessed – that she wanted
somebody to pay for the priest's death. The day I got
out . . .'

Tadeusz's voice had gone dreamy and he smiled at a
memory.

'You got drunk? Found yourself a woman?'

'I bought a bunch of daffodils and sat on a bench in the
spring sun. They were the first flowers I'd seen in thirteen
years. I was crying and God knows what people thought.
That I'd been jilted, I suppose.'

'And had you been? Who waits thirteen years?'

'First I had to find her.'

CHAPTER TWENTY-FOUR

Poland had become a foreign country, Wroclaw a city under occupation. The patrolling troops were boys in distressed denim and girls in pretty colours who had hatched out in the spring sun. The girls preened or feigned indifference in front of the boys. Every street corner seemed to have acquired a food stall and people ate to make up for the years of deprivation. Ice cream and slices of pizza and *zapiekanki* and Turkish pitta stuffed with salad. Bewildered by the crowds, the bustle, the laughter, the colours, Tadeusz sat on benches to gape. I'm a tourist arrived from a different era, he thought. All the years inside the prison. All the years before that in the great prison outside.

He stared at a stall where people came away biting into a bun or licking to catch juices. The doors of the stall were folded back. On one door he read DOG BURGER in English. Crossing to read the other door he saw HOT HAM.

For his first days of freedom he sought out Roman and slept on the settee in his living room. It was only marginally less comfortable than his prison bunk. Roman had a wife and two young sons. The wife watched Tadeusz closely, either because of stories her husband had told or because he was a released murderer. Never mind that he had been pardoned because the evidence of the eye witness was discounted. Other witnesses might yet come forward.

His old friends and acquaintances had become strangers who'd lived different lives. He began with Zdzislaw, who

was still at Dolmel but with a job title something like
Quality Controller. Zdzislaw had got married but was
happy to escape from domestic bliss for an evening. No,
Zdzis didn't really see anything of the old Klub members
any more. They had been brought together simply by the
urgency of the times. Witold he met for a beer on occa-
sions. Henryk had died four or five years back. Rafat –
remember Rafat? Well, Rafat had stood for election and
was now a member of the Sejm. Well, bloody politicians
were all actors anyhow.

'Zuzanna?'

There was something of a pause. People had always fid-
geted a bit at the mention of Zuzanna. She was Tadeusz's
woman. Or, the more perceptive said, he was her man and
she had seemed to possess him totally. She didn't behave
like a Pole for whom moderation was a virtue. She was a
Latin, Zdzislaw thought, with passion and sparks and daggers in her eyes for any other woman who spoke too freely
to her man.

'No. No idea what became of her. Maybe she moved
away. The bright lights of Warsaw. Or Chicago. Lot of Poles
live in Chicago. She could be there,' he finished. A foolish
remark but Tadeusz interpreted it as: it's all water under the
bridge now. She won't want to carry on as before. Or her
husband or her lover won't want it.

'Eugeniusz?' Tadeusz dropped in casually. 'Do you see
anything at all of him these days?'

'No, never run into him.'

Waldemar and Witold were no more helpful about
Zuzanna. Or about Eugeniusz.

When Tadeusz felt the time had come to talk to
Eugeniusz, to put certain questions to the man who'd sent
him to the cathedral and a staged murder, he found that
Eugeniusz had moved. The Bierut Apartments had been

renamed Luxor in an attempt to make them more habit-able. The new people in the flat Eugeniusz and Justyna had lived in had no information. Gone away. No letters ever came. No forwarding address.

Nobody had prospered quite like Natalia. Her old gallery had been gutted to make a larger space that could be used for sculpture exhibitions, musical soirées or lectures by visiting cultural luminaries. Her new picture gallery was the most flamboyant of the row of them in Jatki. 'Though frankly,' Natalia said, drawing on her cigarette holder, 'since the galleries are in what used to be butcher's shops, it would be more appropriate for a critic.' When he men-tioned Zuzanna, Natalia took an even longer pull on the cigarette holder. 'The Horizontal Woman. Try a younger model, darling. Get you going again.'

Tadeusz frowned.

'Well, are you painting?' she asked. 'Sculpting? Music? Creating anything?'

'I've got nowhere to live.'

'Have you thought of going back to where you were before?'

'After thirteen years?'

'Afraid of what you might find? Afraid of ghosts? Afraid of yourself?'

That was too many *afraids*. Tadeusz frowned again.

A burglar sniffing out a prospect, Tadeusz went first by night to what he still thought of as the Half House. He walked softly as if someone might hear his footsteps, first on the far side of the road, then crossing over he came back. A light was on downstairs, visible as a crack between curtains. A light was on upstairs, the window uncurtained just as it had been when Tadeusz and Zuzanna had lain together with the sweat cooling on their bodies, gazing at the stars or, indeed, the midday sun.

He paused at the end of the path. I once lived here, he said, trying out the idea. Lived, loved, worked, wrangled in the Klub while bloody Baran was listening in. He did not quite dare knock at the door in case it was Zuzanna's unclothed shoulders that appeared at the bedroom window, shouted down to find out who was there, then shrugged and turned away. Yes, afraid. He needed the courage of the sun.

It was a boy of five or six who answered the door. He had blond hair though Tadeusz could not see if his eyes were blue. He's Zuzanna's, he thought, with something very like a stab of despair. Husband, family, the lot. Before he could say anything the boy turned away.

'Mama, it's a man.'

The genes must have been the father's because the woman who came from the kitchen had dark hair and a stocky figure more often seen in a field humping a sack of potatoes.

'Yes?' she said. 'Good morning.'

Recovering, Tadeusz said, 'I used to live here once. In half the house. I don't know if it's still divided. My name is Tadeusz Lipski.'

'It's you,' she whispered. Some emotion passed across the woman's face and she raised a hand to her throat. 'My husband's out. He won't be long. He's just gone for cigarettes. But it's all right.'

Sensing the worry in his mother's voice, the boy had moved behind her, putting an arm round her thick thighs and peering with round eyes at Tadeusz.

'It was a long time ago. I've been away for thirteen years.'

'Yes,' she said. 'My husband will be back soon.' She started to close the door.

'I'll wait for him inside.'

She hesitated so he pushed his way in. She retreated two or three steps. She knows, he thought. She knows I'm a murderer. Also a rapist and child molester. When I've nothing better to do I steal sweets from babies in prams.

'He'll be back very soon,' she said, warning him not to try anything. She was wiping her hands on her apron as if there was dirt she wanted to get off.

'Why don't you get on with what you were doing in the kitchen.'

'It's all right,' she said. She wouldn't let him any further into the house, wouldn't let him out of her sight. The stalemate was broken by the return of the husband, a large man with blond hair crimped across his head like a perm and cheeks red with veins.

'You've got some identity?' the husband asked and scrutinized the card Tadeusz gave him, turning it over, peering at the photo, peering at Tadeusz's face. 'All right,' he said. He turned to lead the way. Somewhere upstairs a baby started to cry. 'You see to it,' he said. 'I'm sick of it bloody keeping me awake.' To Tadeusz he said, 'I haul beer crates. Do it every day. I need my sleep. Bloody kid is screaming all night.'

'She can't help it. She's teething. You used to scream when you were teething.'

'Got a clip round the ear if I did. Give her a spoon of vodka.' And to Tadeusz once more, 'Only thing keeps the bloody kid happy.'

At the door to the studio – somehow Tadeusz knew he was being taken there and that a mystery surrounded the room – the man turned again. 'Name's Jan. People call me Janek. You're Tadeusz. Do people call you Tadek?'

'Yes.'

They shook hands formally; 'Well, Tadek, I think your

stuff is all right. It's just there was a break-in a little after we
moved in so I put that on the door.'

That was a monstrously large combination lock.

'How long have you been here?'

Jan thought about it. 'Summer of '82.'

'And you've kept a room of my stuff all that time?'

'See, the Housing Department gave us this part of the
house. When we moved in two men came. They said this
room had to be kept as it was. What was in it could be used
as state evidence. Against you. They told me what you'd
done.'

'I didn't do it.'

Jan ignored this denial. 'They were very particular.
Nothing to be touched, nothing sold, nothing thrown away.
I asked Them why They didn't take all the stuff and They
told me not to try to teach Them their job. They didn't say
who They were but you could always tell. It was the way
They watched all the time.'

Some emotion passed across his face as it had with his
wife. If it wasn't fear, it was caution. For twelve years They
had made an impression on a man who drove a beer wagon
and shifted crates.

'I bought this lock. I'm the only one knows the combination.' He looked round to make sure they were alone.
'One-nine-seven-eight. Year we got our Pope. I shan't forget
but catch Them ever thinking of it.'

The door opened on Tadeusz's past life.

Jan had to go to work. His wife wouldn't dream of coming
near a murderer. Tadeusz had the studio to himself. He
stood, stupefied. He wasn't just among his past creative
work, he was confronted by what seemed the whole of his
previous life. Someone had jammed the studio with all the
furniture from the Half House. The double bed was against

one wall with chairs from the sitting room strewn across it like exhausted lovers. The big settee was jammed against the cupboard door under the window seat. The philodendron – his own bit of Bolivian jungle – had struggled towards the sun and then died from lack of water. Paintings had been stacked on a table. His saxophone was suspended from a picture hook. The Dustbin of History had been kicked over and the three heads lined up on the desk, glowering at him. With a Magic Marker someone had given Lenin a monocle – a touch Tadeusz wished he'd thought of.

He moved the chairs off the bed and sat on it, surveying the jumble. Gingerly, like a man wary of a sudden shock, he bent down to bury his nose in the mattress. He inhaled. Was there anything left of her? She'd used perfume sparingly because Moscow Nights – which was all one could buy in the end – was a heavyweight wrestler among scents. Not a trace? Not a hint of the odour of her own body? He stretched out on the mattress, leaving space beside him for her body. Or his memory of it.

Weak sun was coming through the window. It caught the dust motes he had stirred up. They floated in the air. They twirled and pirouetted, swooped and hovered. He was transfixed. The Dust Dancers. A ballet. Music by Tadeusz Lipski that he could hear in his head.

I'll stay, he told himself, settling back into his interrupted life.

'There used to be a lot more stuff in here,' Jan said. His tone of voice was accusing, though only Tadeusz was there to be accused.

'I got rid of it,' Tadeusz said.

'What? All them chairs? They were good chairs. What did you want to get rid of them for? And the settee – that's gone too. Why?'

'For *feng shui*.'

'Who's he? Live close does he 'cause all that stuff must have weighed something. Here, have another beer.'

It was a Saturday evening, a busy day for Jan, and with so many crates to deliver one was never missed.

'*Feng shui* is acupuncture for spaces. You see, this room is a space but it was so cluttered there was no room for *chi* to flow. *Chi* is good energy and you want to encourage it in your life-path area. The whole room, I decided, is my life-path area so I cleared it to let the *chi* flow. Here is my wealth and career corner, around this potted climber. To you the plant may appear dead but look at the top leaves. I've painted stars on some, a smiling sun here, and see, there's the man in the moon. It symbolizes that the sky is the limit. I've kept a small table here in the blessing zone. What are the heads of Lenin, Marx and Brezhnev doing on it? Look at what I've done to them. Painted hands across Lenin's eyes – see no evil. Painted hands over Marx's ears – hear no evil. Painted a hand over Brezhnev's mouth – speak no evil. Now here I've positioned a mirror so that the negative energy from the apartment block opposite is reflected right back at them. What I lack is a crystal or cut glass next to the easel to concentrate the positive energy flow.'

Tadeusz stopped, nodding to himself. Like the room itself, he had been reduced to essentials. Prison had melted all the fat off him and there wasn't even much flesh. Hollows dimpled his cheeks, shoulders and wrists. You felt his bones might rub holes in his skin.

'Bloody hell,' Jan said. He drank from his bottle. 'What happened to the stuff?'

'I put it out of the window.'

'Bloody hell.' He took another drink. 'Bloody hell, Tadek, what did you do that for?'

'I've been putting it out for three nights. In the morning

it's gone. Look at it this way: someone's needs are being satisfied. If everyone did what I've done, our country's
economic problems would be solved. It would be the
Polish economic miracle.'

'Bloody hell,' Jan said. He frowned a bit. 'Something in
what you say. What are you putting out tonight?'

'I need the mattress. But the bed can go. If you give me
a hand with dismantling it, we'll put that out.'

Jan laughed. 'Bloody game, isn't it?'

Spring turned to summer. Tadeusz was busy. He took to
playing his father's old saxophone and when there was a
holiday vacancy at the Monopol, he even claimed his
father's place. He was a puzzle to himself because he didn't
much enjoy being part of a band. His solos were the bright
spots of the evening. But whereas the band's soul was
rooted in the French quarter of New Orleans, his was more
Miles Davis. The clash of styles led to the maître d' making
a complaint. Tadeusz took four or five steps forward for his
solos and found that he had developed a limp. My father
and I, he thought, our lives in parallel, both deserted by
our women.

He even took a temporary mother back with him one
night. She was called Wanda and was the wife of an airline
pilot. 'He flies to Bangkok every week and I don't think it's
jet lag he's suffering from when he returns. So I decided,
right . . .' She stared round Tadeusz's studio with shock.

'You live here? Where's the furniture?'

'In the Bermuda Triangle, probably.'

'They broke in and stole it?'

'I made it easy for them. I left it outside the window.'

'There's no bed,' Wanda pointed out.

'There's a mattress.'

'You expect me to do it on the floor as if we were dogs?'

'Dogs seem to have fun.'

'And what on earth are those?'

'Ah, *haikus*,' Tadeusz said. Recently he had been to a lecture given by the cultural attaché from the Japanese embassy about the strength of tradition in their culture. *Haikus* had impressed Tadeusz: their brevity, their allusiveness. He had jotted down two *haikus* in Polish which afterwards he got the attaché to translate into Japanese.

'You see, our Western letters look like insects marching across the papers. Japanese calligraphy already looks poetic. So I came back here and copied them.'

'But you've painted them over the whole bloody wall.'

'Yes.' Bold red strokes did indeed take up two entire walls. 'That wall reads, "Music does not die. It fades away into eternity." The other wall reads, "Rise before the sun. The early worm escapes the bird."'

In the morning, when he awoke, Wanda had gone. On a piece of paper she had written, 'The early worm has flown.'

Airline pilots, he thought, and worms.

In the hot days of early August Eugeniusz came.

'How long have you been out? I've only just heard.'

Tadeusz didn't answer but studied him. How best to broach the subject? Why did you betray me in December 1981? Send me to the cathedral in the knowledge I'd be set up for Father Michal's murder? Know that Baran and his thugs and his photographer would be lurking in the shadows?

Tadeusz said, 'I thought you'd got out of Wroclaw?'

'Got out?'

'Moved away, somewhere where no one knew you. No memories. No old ties.'

'So you've heard about Justyna. She never really recovered from the fall. It was all the troubles we had at the time. She wasn't given the attention she needed. People's minds were elsewhere. Even nurses' minds. Even doctors' minds. Poor Justyna. Still, it was a long time ago.'

He was describing events of which Tadeusz knew nothing. The bone in her leg had been badly set, complications set in and it was necessary to break it to reset; she never came round from the anaesthetic. There was only the window seat to sit on and the two men were side by side. Being next to Eugeniusz and hearing details of his past troubles, Tadeusz found his hostility draining away.

'And now?'

Eugeniusz looked pleased. 'Well, I'm of a certain age, you know. By now it's usually the men who are popping off. You'd be surprised how many lonely women there are.'

A widow, he said. Got a twinkle in her eye. Had her own flat. Moved in with her – oh, ten years ago. Got two sons older than Tadeusz, even grandchildren. Hearing these domestic details, knowing it was Eugeniusz who'd come to seek him out and not the other way round, Tadeusz understood the other man had not sent him into a trap.

Tadeusz edged closer to the abyss.

'Gienek, thirteen years ago.'

'Yes.'

'Martial Law Day.'

'Never forget it.'

'I went to the cathedral to meet Father Michal.'

'I'll never forget that. Never, never, never.'

'And he was murdered.'

'No need to remind me. They hung it on you. Trying to confuse everybody, saying Solidarity was out of control, the country was freewheeling to disaster.'

'Gienek.' Tadeusz drew a breath to ask the final question. 'Who gave you the message about Father Michal wanting to meet me?'

Eugeniusz's head swung round. His brow furrowed. 'Nobody told you? Well, I suppose nobody else knew. We were all arrested or on the run. That woman of yours told me. Zuzanna. She stepped up to me on the street not far from here. She gave me the message to pass on to you.'

It was towards the dusty end of August. Wroclaw was preparing for the Cantans Festival, but posters appeared advertising an entirely different musical event.

Closing the Piano Lid

&

Girl, 5

Two sound concepts by Tadek Codename Tadek

The venue was Natalia's previous gallery which Tadeusz, on *feng shui* principles, cleared of everything except his Yamaha electric keyboard and speakers. Following Natalia's advice he staged his concert just before the main festival opened, when the critics were all bored, having written their first reports: Whither Cantans? Daggers at Director's Back.

No more than a dozen people were at the opening night, among them the renowned critic Bogdan Sadowski. The following piece appeared in his Warsaw paper.

Jesus had twelve disciples and that was the number of witnesses to an extraordinary musical event in Wroclaw. The comparison between Christ and Tadeusz Lipski may be far-fetched but there was no doubt among the privileged audience last night that we were in the presence of an artistic messiah. Picture the scene. The lights dim. The audience squats or sprawls on the floor. The maestro appears dressed in prison uniform, for he has lately been in jail for a murder he did not commit. He approaches the microphone, picks it up and tosses it in a corner. He wishes to communicate with us directly.

'My name is Tadek Codename Tadek. That is how I was known in the earliest days of our struggle to establish freedom in Poland. Tonight you will hear two sound concepts that I composed during my years in a prison cell. The first is called Closing the Piano Lid.'

The piano in question is not your Bechstein Grand but a modest Japanese import. What Tadek Codename Tadek does is what his title so graphically describes. He strides to the piano, lifts his hands as if to launch into the Emperor Concerto – and closes the lid with all his might. A resounding crack echoes through the room, fading to silence. Ah, how rightly he has judged our hunger. We are transfixed, waiting for more. There is no more. That one sound – loud and clean – is the whole of the piece. What a concept! It is a rifle shot, but no one is killed. It is the whole of World War Two in one sound and there are no mutilated bodies. He has expressed the experiences and emotions of millions of ordinary people at a time of great trauma through the brilliance of his imagination.

It is necessarily very short. But the next piece is very long. How long I cannot tell you because after three hours the approaching deadline meant I had to leave to file this piece. But the effect is already amazing, the audience swelling, debate growing, and I must return to catch the latest happenings. Read my next report for a description of this artistic bombshell.

But bravo Tadek Codename Tadek! You have
already taken the burgers of Wroclaw by the ears!

Tadeusz had slammed the lid of the Yamaha as hard as he
could. He preferred the resonance of a solid wooden instru-
ment but this was satisfactory. He waited, staring at the
ceiling, as if viewing stars or hearing a distant call. His
audience on the floor also waited, looking at him, looking
at each other. Someone coughed. Someone lit a cigarette.
They began to talk among themselves, mumbles, as if this
was a church. A man in a brown suit crawled along the
floor to confer with a man in a paisley jacket. After murmured conversation, Paisley Jacket got into a kneeling
position.

'Mr Lipski, please.'

'Tadek Codename Tadek.'

'Please, is that it?'

Tadeusz's eyes came down by degrees to stare at him.

'I mean, is there more? If not, would you do it again?
Please. So we can consider it more deeply. My colleague
says he wasn't quite mentally prepared.'

'There could be nuances I missed,' the Brown Suit said.
'One's ears are so polluted by everyday cacophony, I fear I
might have missed some of the texture of your performance.'

'Please, Tadek Codename Tadek,' said the only woman
present. Her full figure swelled inside her boiler suit. 'Do it
again. For my sake. Will you?'

Tadeusz considered her. 'Yes. Yes, I shall. I shall do it
again before the Jazz Festival next June. Now, if you are
mentally alert, we shall pass on to the second sound concept. Girl, 5. That is its title. For me it is a formidably
personal experience. I hope you have the empathetic
capacity to share it with me. When I was creating this

concept in prison, Roman, who had the other bunk in the cell, could not appreciate it. Fortunately he was released.

'The piece has its genesis in the summer before General Jaruzelski declared war on us. I was on the beach near Ustka where a family had come for the day with a windbreak, chairs, some fruit and beer. There was a girl, aged five. She took all her clothes off to play. Naked, she ran across the sand, kicked the waves as they came in, dug a moat against the flood of water, turned somersaults. What would she be like when she grew up? She had blonde hair. Would it be a mass of curls, a flowing mane, a pony tail, a braid? Would her blue eyes shine with love? The woman was already in that girl . . .' He raised a schoolmasterly finger and his eyes toured their faces to make sure he had their attention, '. . . like a woman I once knew and loved and lost. She had a mass of blonde hair and blue eyes, blue eyes with depths, most distinct. I saw the future in this Naked Girl, 5. She had no clothes, no jewels, no body hair. Just as my sounds have no clothes, no jewels, no body hair. Listen, imagine, know yourselves, learn the possibilities of which your lives are capable, the loves you will find and lose.'

Three strides and Tadeusz was at the Yamaha keyboard and lifting the lid. He produced from his pocket two household clothespegs. With each one he depressed and locked down a key. A sound was produced which didn't satisfy Tadeusz. He moved one of the pegs a note lower, listened with his eyes closed and nodded. Next he flicked a switch that set the automatic rhythm ticking. A *bossa nova* beat.

He left by a door at the back of the room.

He wanted to return at nine o'clock but Natalia restrained him. And again at ten.

'Give it time,' she advised. 'They'll be bored out of their

minds but won't dare admit it. They'll get to thinking. Not about the naked little girl, except for that disgusting pae-dophile Chmielewski. But about your blue-eyed, blonde-haired lover. You should have mentioned her tits. That always gets them.'

Natalia, who was not big in that department, blew out a lot of smoke.

Returning to the room at eleven, Tadeusz found Sadowski, Szyperski, the woman in the boiler suit and three others still there. These were the forward-thinkers, the ones not over-awed by the legacy of the past. They'd moved to one side of the room and sat on the floor with their backs to the wall as if they were the injured dragged away from some accident. At Tadeusz's reappearance they stirred collectively, like one beast, and watched while he went to the Yamaha and made an adjustment to the rhythm. It was a foxtrot perhaps or a quickstep – their musical tastes were too exalted to know.

Szyperski was the boldest one. He took Tadeusz aside. 'Could you expand a bit on your lost love. Not the girl. What the girl grows up into. You only just mentioned her but she is the key to your whole creation. So tantalizing. Were you very much in love?'

Sadowski, sensing a story slipping by, sidled up. 'Yes, what was her name? Is she someone famous? Singing in the festival, perhaps?'

The woman in the boiler suit asked, 'Was she married? Is that why you won't answer?'

'Don't be so domestic,' Szyperski told her. 'He is an artist. He's not constrained by such a narrowly bourgeois moral code. She has to be beautiful. I see her as a film star. Is she from Wroclaw?'

'We are the press,' Sadowski said. 'We could help you find her.'

'She's here,' Tadeusz said. They all turned, looking into dark corners. The room was so stark there was no hiding place. 'She's in the sounds.'

Tadeusz brought a sleeping bag in and lay on the floor. Sadowski and the woman also stayed the night, perhaps to keep an eye on Tadeusz. It was certainly for no amatory reason of their own for they took care to stretch out on opposite sides of the room.

Two plus Tadeusz was the smallest number who kept vigil. The Wroclaw press printed a story – 'The Lost Love of an Artist' – and people came to look at Tadek Codename Tadek. Passers-by were drawn in through curiosity at the wailing noise, like the drone of a bagpipe. At midday office girls brought sandwiches and picnicked on the floor. In the afternoon students came with beer and sang the words to the Beatles' 'Yesterday', but all in the one chord. A party of Polish-American women on a 'Homeland Tour' called in because they were thrilled to bits by his story. One matron, on a dare, lifted her skirt for Tadeusz to sign his name on her thigh: Tadek Codename Tadek was here.

The next night a dozen people kept Tadeusz company. Some read books, some slept, some played chess. About midnight a woman in her mid-thirties slipped through the door. A great unhappiness had taken possession of her. She sat, cross-legged, and wept. There is an embarrassment about witnessing someone else's sorrow. Finally a man sat next to her, gave her a cigarette and took her hand in his. They talked in low voices, then in still lower voices so that their heads had to be close together. Later they moved to a corner where it was darkest, took off their clothes and made love. It seemed the natural thing to do.

Around dawn a man in a sailor's peaked cap appeared. For some reason the woman found this funny and laughed and gave a military sort of salute. The man who'd made love to her in the night flew into a jealous rage, shouting. She scratched his cheek, her nails like cat's claws drawing blood. He slapped her face and walked away. She spat after him, then went to squat near the man in the peaked cap. Soon they were talking in low voices, their heads close together.

This, too, found its way into the press. Day Four it was. 'People meet', an editorial writer opined, 'they marry, they divorce. The most profound human experiences are to be found at this extraordinary event. We are absorbed by the endless sound and ponder eternity. Tadek Codename Tadek has created a phenomenon. How long can he keep it up?'

'You're famous.' It was a partly familiar figure who stood at Tadeusz's side while he ran on the spot, knees high. He did it for exercise after being shut inside for five days, in time to the rhythm which he'd set to a simple march beat. 'You're in the Warsaw papers.'

Tadeusz stopped his jogging. With one hand he masked the beard on the other man's face and recognized Renton. 'Aha! You're in disguise. You must still be on the cultural side. You've come to see me?'

Renton had a smile which always seemed to keep something in reserve. 'I'm mostly in London now. Just in Warsaw for a few days for consultations. I told people, "I must go to Wroclaw to hear some of the Cantans Festival." To myself I said: I must go to see my old friend Tadek, see how he is doing, how life is treating him. I find you have disciples at your feet.'

They looked round. It was early afternoon, a lull. A family squatted round a jigsaw of the Mona Lisa. Two women with cropped hair knelt together and seemed to be arguing about God and the Creation. A young woman and man stretched full length on their backs, sharing a cigarette.

'Has the sound been the same right from the start?' Renton asked.

'The sound has been the same. The interpretations have varied. That is the point.'

'I see.' Renton considered. 'Could we slip away for a few minutes? That would refresh your ears. We could refresh ourselves with a beer at the same time. Would they miss you?'

'There is a side exit. Fire regulations insist.'

At the end of the block was a big old café used in the evening by students but deserted now. Renton chose a table by a curtained window and sat facing Tadeusz.

'Perhaps I should grow a beard,' Tadeusz said.

'You've made a start. But a beard is not Polish. A moustache proves you are a grown man but a beard would suggest you have something to hide. You could be concealing a scar or your identity or a bomb.'

Their beers came. After the waitress left Tadeusz said, 'I have a scar but a beard doesn't hide it.'

'Exactly.' Renton drank some beer. 'I read in the papers about this woman you had loved and lost, and speculation about where she might be. I said to myself: Could that be Zuzanna? The lovely Zuzanna who so enchanted me and captivated you? Could Tadek be courting notoriety and publicity in the hope of rousing her out of obscurity?'

'I want to see her again.'

'Indeed.'

'I have questions to ask her.'

'Ah well, I didn't know that. But I can understand that you might.'

They looked intently into each other's eyes like children playing at out-staring and who will blink first.

'It is Zuzanna Raducka?' Renton said at last. 'I've remembered it right?'

'Tell me. What is it?'

Renton played with his beard the way another man might fiddle with a pipe when he had something awkward to say.

'Tadek, the world has turned on its head since we last met. Do you remember Stalin's Palace of Culture? How we sat on a bench in its shadow and you said how you'd once kicked it? Well, the whole world has kicked it now. The changes are ones we could never have dreamed of. For instance, in London where I am based one of my duties is liaison with a KGB officer at the Russian embassy. Amazing! There is a special house in the London district of Bayswater where we can meet away from the gaze of diplomats to exchange mutually interesting information. You know, drugs, arms, international gangs, all the usual. To cement relations we socialise. I took him one afternoon to Lord's to watch a cricket match. Let's call him Boris. After an hour Boris asked, "Why do you bring me here?" "So you can understand the English better," I told him. After another hour the players all walked off the field. "They are English? They go on strike?" Boris asked. "No, they go for tea." "They stop for tea in the middle of a game? No, I never understand the English." "And, Boris, the game goes on all day, sometimes three days, and some particularly exhausting matches last five days." Boris had nothing to say.'

Tadeusz raised his eyebrows. 'Perhaps I would enjoy your cricket.'

'Perhaps you would. It has something in common with your sound concept. All right, I told you this for background, so you know how good relations are. Yesterday when I read about you and your missing love, my mind began to wander over past events and suspicions began to form. I said to myself: Let's just see. So I telephoned my good friend at the Russian embassy in London. "Boris," I said, "I hope your hangover is not bad this morning because I have a big favour to ask. Does the name Zuzanna Raducka ring a bell in your archives, the early eighties?" It was only an hour later when he rang back.'

Renton broke off to take a drink of beer, which he did in small thoughtful sips. He ran the back of his hand across his mouth then smoothed the beard on his chin. When he spoke again his voice had slowed right down. The words found their way out with difficulty, regret, even pain.

'Boris said, "Robin, my good pal, you owe me a pint, I have found out about your Raducka. Born 1955 in Lwow in the Soviet Union which by a magic wave of the political wand is now Lviv in the Ukraine. And yes, she worked for us from 1975 until 1989. After training etcetera etcetera she was posted to Poland, to a city called Wroclaw. At the time of the great democratic upheavals – praise be to Allah – she disappeared. So, if you do find her again and she is still beautiful, maybe you owe me two pints."'

'Oh Zuzia,' Tadeusz whispered. 'Zuzia Zuzia Zuzia.'

Perhaps he'd always known it. Perhaps others had known it, not as a fact but a feeling. Perhaps others had felt she was just too alluring and too flush with money to settle for someone like Tadeusz. But if he had known it, it was the kind of knowledge he had put into a side room of his mind and locked the door because he had loved her too much to doubt her.

Renton spoke some more to try to rouse Tadeusz, talked of other things, of taking Boris to Question Time in the House of Commons and Wimbledon in the pursuit of understanding the English. But to no avail. Tadeusz stared into a distant corner.

Renton stood but paused a moment. He had come to help Tadeusz too late, as the British did with the Poles. Tadeusz had done a small job for him in the past which might even have added to his troubles. Renton wouldn't say he had a guilty conscience but a sense of owing something. He said, 'I have to catch a plane back to Warsaw, but perhaps we can meet again. Would you like to come to London? Lord's maybe? And I do know one or two people who run galleries. Not Bond Street, but Portobello Road would appeal to you. An exhibition. You used to be a Conspirator but maybe you've moved on. Would you be interested?'

Getting no response he decided it would be better to leave Tadeusz.

People from his past dropped in, not as a party but singly. The last was Zdzislaw.

'Stone the dogs, Tadek, if you weren't gaga to begin with, this howling would drive you gaga.'

At the time Tadek was standing on his head, with his feet against a wall, encouraging the blood to go to his brain. He came off the wall in an elegant flip and stood up.

'You were right about Zuzanna,' he said, 'and I was wrong.'

'Zuzanna?' Zdzislaw asked, and then he remembered. He seemed more embarrassed than anything. 'She led you by the balls,' he said. 'It can happen to anyone. And it was a long time ago. Time to forget, old friend. Why don't you pack it in and come with me. We'll have a drink. We'll drink to drown the past.'

'She'll come,' Tadeusz said. 'Soon.'

And it was on the seventh day, in the afternoon, that Zuzanna came. She stood in the doorway a few moments taking in the scene, the dozen or so people sprawled on the floor, a Polish flag which someone had brought with the crown restored above the eagle, the Yamaha keyboard which was now banked with floral tributes, and Tadeusz.

Tadeusz had caught sight of her through the glass of the door even before she entered, felt the stab of recognition of the most intense part of his life, saw her hesitation and willed her to overcome it, waited while she surveyed the room until she started towards him.

He crossed to the keyboard, jerked off the two clothes-pegs and switched off the rhythm. The sudden silence was appallingly loud in everyone's ears. People rolled over on the floor to stare at him. There were protests.

'Switch it on again.'

'Why did you turn it off?'

'Because it has come to an end,' Tadeusz snapped at them. 'There is nothing more to say.'

Except to Zuzanna.

CHAPTER TWENTY-FIVE

Side by side they walked down the corridor from the cell. Tadeusz no longer seemed a remand prisoner, an accused, more a colleague, even a friend one shares a secret with.

The officer said, 'We live in an age of wonders and they are called computers. You remember you said it was worth looking into – I'm talking about Miler's case, you understand.' He drew a breath and started again. 'You said, see if the houses that were burgled while Miler threw his party were protected by any particular security firm. Yes, it turned out, PAX. Remember? Well, of course you do.'

The officer stopped outside a holding cell but still talked to Tadeusz. 'Strange they chose the name PAX. My father used to talk about the PAX priests. "Fascist turncoats", he called them. Still, there you are. PAX it is called.' He slid back a panel in the door, stooping suddenly for a closer look. Tadeusz was reminded of a dentist spotting a cavity.

'Poor devil,' he said as they resumed the walk down the corridor. Stairs lay ahead of them. 'Well, he shouldn't have. Only himself to blame.'

Tadeusz half turned to look back at the cell. Was the door weeping? Trembling? What had the poor devil done? Murder? Stolen a million or three? Slandered the President? Crossed the road against a red light?

'PAX,' the officer returned to his subject. 'All four house-holders had a contract with PAX for security checks. So there are going to be security checks made on PAX. Such as: show us the logbooks of your guards' rounds. Such as: explain why the alarm systems were so easily switched off.' They were climbing the stairs and the officer saved his breath until they reached the top. 'Now here's the wild and wonderful thing. All employees of private security companies must have their names registered. PAX employs twelve men, no women except for a secretary who presumably doesn't do patrol duty. These dozen names were fed into the computer system, check on the databases, check on criminal records, check on civil status, check on tax returns – though that's a useless one – check on previous government employment and whoa! In the past they used to work for the *Bezpieka*. All of them. A nest of former Ubeks. There's going to be some fun, I can tell you. All right, here you are.'

So saying the officer opened the door, letting Tadeusz into the interview room. The door was closed and locked behind him.

Tadeusz had refused a lawyer so the court had appointed one for him. Jez, first name unknown. He was seated at a table which an open briefcase and a slew of papers had turned into a temporary office. He was scanning a document and making tiny notes in the margin. He didn't look up. Tadeusz sat in the chair facing him, waiting. Jez continued to read, suddenly frowning, pursing his lips and sidelining a paragraph.

After a couple of minutes of this Tadeusz got up and walked to the door. He was about to knock for attention when Jez looked up.

'What are you doing?'

'Leaving?'

'Why?'

'When you've finished your homework I'll come back. Or not. Depends.'

'You're not my only client, you know.' He collected together the papers, closed a folder and slipped it inside the briefcase. 'We're due in court at two-thirty.'

Tadeusz returned to the chair. He studied Jez. Built on the lines of a snowman. Large round body, small round head, hairless, white. Also, in Tadeusz's opinion, full of self-importance.

'This afternoon we hear the court's verdict,' the lawyer said. 'The sentence – that is if you are pronounced guilty – will follow. I must impress on you the importance of appropriate behaviour. Any sentence that is imposed could be increased if there are outbursts such as we had during the trial.'

'Outbursts? All I said—'

'I was there. I know what you said and I did my utmost to prevent you. It was struck from the court record because you were not yet under oath. But undoubtedly it made an impression on the judges and jury members. No more of that. I represent you. I talk. And you, unless you are called upon to speak, keep quiet. Is that understood? Your situation is extremely grave. Do you understand that? Do you understand why you are here? Do you understand anything? Perhaps,' and his voice lost its pompous hectoring tone, falling away into something like despair, 'perhaps I should have pleaded "while balance of mind was disturbed" after all.'

'This is monstrous.' Never mind waiting until he reached court, Tadeusz was intent on an outburst now. He was cut short.

The door was unlocked, the officer came in. 'The court is going into session. We're on our way.' As Tadeusz was passing out of the room the officer said in a low voice,

'Tadek Codename Tadek, I dropped in one night. I'd read about you in the paper. I don't know what Girl, 5 was about, to be honest, but I met a gorgeous girl there myself that night.' The lawyer was fussing behind them. 'Good luck.'

Luck? What else could the judges and jury make of what happened that night?

CHAPTER TWENTY-SIX

Now there was something about Zuzanna that alerted Tadeusz right from the start. Her confidence seemed dented, her assertiveness had been part of another life. Those who'd said before that he was her man would now have reversed the pull and said she was his woman.

They embraced but the passion was all on her side. Her arms were round him, holding him, her hands smoothing his back, her fingers remembering each rib, pressing into the spaces between them, finding him definitely thinner than before. She raised her face and kissed him full on the mouth but when she parted her lips, inviting his tongue in, he pulled back. He looked in her face to see what damage the years had done, how the lines had spread from the corners of eyes, mouth and nose. What caused those lines? Laughter? Tears? Staring into the sun? Staring into despair? He noted something very like a shadow cross her face, not fear but wariness. Was it life in general she was not sure about or Tadeusz?

'Come.'

It was the first word spoken.

He walked out into the street leaving behind a stunned and peeved audience. Even Natalia had appeared, attracted by the silence, and stood frowning. Zuzanna followed, running a few steps to catch up, taking his arm with both her hands.

'Tadek,' she said, 'Tadek,' trying to slow him down, 'where are we going? Where are you taking me?'

'The Half House. Or Quarter House it now is.'

'Oh lord.' She could foresee the memories that would come flooding back. 'I tried to keep away from the performance, your show. Girl, 5, you called it but I wasn't fooled. From the first time I read in the paper what you were doing, how you talked of your prison cell and your lost love, I knew the signal you were sending out. Every day there was more. I'd refuse to look at the newspaper and it would lie on the table sending out signals . . . Read me, read me, I'm speaking to you. Until I had to pick it up and see what was in the report. And then there was something on the radio. I ran across the room and swept the radio off the table. Smash it, kill it, shut it up. But the voices didn't even hesitate. They were interviewing you. You wouldn't let them broadcast the sound but I heard your voice. That was when I knew I had to come.'

She was half running to keep up and fell silent, out of breath. Strangely, not knowing her current life, whether she was married or living with someone, Tadeusz had never doubted she would come with him. Once, waiting for the traffic to let them cross the road, he took her face in both his hands and tilted it up to him. She closed her eyes, expecting to be kissed, but when nothing happened she opened them again. He stared into those eyes which had had depths where she kept her secrets. Now the eyes seemed pale and shallow.

'Come,' he said, hurrying her again.

Keep her moving, Tadeusz thought to himself, don't give her time to think. Don't let her ask questions: Why are you bringing me here? What's on your mind? Do you still love me as much? Do you remember all the places I taught you to kiss me?

To let her ask questions as she used to is to surrender to
her.

He had the front door key in his hand, he turned the
lock, opened the door, pushed her inside all in five seconds. Janek's wife looked out from the kitchen. Seeing
Tadeusz she drew back and closed the door.

'Who's she?' Zuzanna asked, as Tadeusz led the way
down the corridor. He didn't reply so she answered for
him, 'No, Zuzia, not mine. Not my wife. Not my mistress.
That is the woman in the moon.'

Tadeusz had her in his own room now, once his studio,
now his whole living area.

'That is Katarzyna,' he said, with the door safely shut,
'wife to Jan, mother to two screaming brats, and she keeps
away because she knows me as a murderer.'

There it was, like a cell door slamming shut. At the word
murderer, Zuzanna closed her eyes a moment, then opened
them and ran on again, much as she'd done in the street.
'Tadek, what have you done? Are you living in this one
room? There's a mattress on the floor and pillows but what
is this?' She stooped to look more closely at the coverlet.
Tadeusz had painted on it the body from the neck down of
a naked woman. 'Who is she? Why have you painted her
like this?' Getting no answer, she straightened and began a
tour of inspection. She nodded at the heads – See no evil,
Speak no evil, Hear no evil. 'You could add a fourth. Stalin
holding his nose. Smell no evil. Would that work? Tadek?'
She peered at the easel to see what work was in progress.
The piece of white card there showed not a painting or a
drawing but a title across the top in a neatly flowing script:
Poem for February 30th. Underneath the title the card was
totally blank. 'What is this? What nonsense? Why is there
no poem? Oh, there is no thirtieth of February. Tadek,
sometimes I don't know when you're joking or when you're

serious or if . . .' Her voice trailed into silence. She remembered through the mists of thirteen years an outburst Tadeusz had had. Someone, in a careless moment, had used the word *mad*. It was probably meant lightly but Tadeusz had reared up in anger. *After He'd rested on the seventh day*, Tadeusz had said, *God went back to work again on the eighth day creating a parallel universe that only those who are touched with genius can see.*

While she was wandering and chattering Tadeusz stood in the centre of the room, turning to keep her always in front of him. She ended her tour and stood staring up into his face. 'Tadek?' she said uncertainly. 'Tadek, why have you brought me here?'

He said, 'Take your clothes off.'

She shook her head. 'I don't want to.' But his face grew so hot with anger she began fumbling at her buttons.

'No, don't.' Now, while she was confused and uncertain what he wanted, now was the time to strike. 'Zuzanna, why did you betray me? Who gave you the order?'

'Oh no, please don't,' she whispered, her eyes fixed on his face. 'I love you, Tadek. I've come back to you. You called to me and I dropped everything and returned. Come to bed.'

She began fumbling again at the front of her blouse but she couldn't look down to find the buttons because he held her eyes with his. He made no move towards her, to undress her, to embrace her, to hit her. He simply stared.

'Oh God,' she whispered. She squatted on the mattress, her knees up, her head bowed on them. She looked up, drawing a breath. 'If you knew what it was like, would you understand? Accept?'

He kept staring.

'I was born in Lwow. My parents were ethnic Poles and we

spoke Polish at home when I was a child. Polish at home, Russian at school. I suppose now it would be Ukrainian but then it was the Russians who were the masters. Apart from speaking Polish I was an ordinary girl. Normal at school, nothing special. Not a high flier. No great brain, no Academician in the making. Normal all the way. Normal hormones when I grew older and boys noticed me.'

As if this prodded her memory, she patted the mattress beside her. 'Sit down, Tadek. It makes me nervous to see you looming up there. Like one of those cranes with a big wrecking ball that they knock buildings down with.' Unconsciously or not, she'd been fiddling with the top button of her blouse. It opened on to the swell of her breasts. Tadeusz moved himself to the window seat. He didn't want to be next to her, he wanted to be apart from her. He wanted her story – her defence as he thought of it – while his own mind was quite clear. He didn't want the warmth of her, a reminder of the past, not now.

'I was normal.' She shook her head, in amazement at her girl's ordinariness or to get herself moving again. 'I even belonged to Komsomol. I went to a summer camp – all swimming and singing songs and fumbling among the birch trees. It was there I think I got myself noticed. Anyway, after I'd finished high school a man and a woman came to see my parents and said I'd made a good impression on certain people and I'd been selected to go to a training school for interpreters. Polish speakers were needed. I remember my father saying that since I spoke Polish already, why did I need to go to a special school? Questions like that were frowned on. There are other things to learn, these people said, how to conduct herself with foreigners, special vocabularies, slang, so on. So of course I went. And of course the language school was where the KGB trawled for recruits. In 1979 I was sent here. You see the people in Moscow were concerned about Wroclaw. Here is where ethnic Poles from Lwow settled after the war. 'Forty-five, six, seven. Tens of thousands, maybe hundreds of thousands, left Lwow because the Soviet Union annexed it. Moscow felt these were unreliable people, full of resentment, a breeding ground for counter-revolutionaries.'

This was history and Zuzanna had spoken it dispassionately, almost as if she had no part in it. Now, to Tadeusz's attentive ear, she became more hesitant. As she spoke she glanced at him to judge his reaction.

'I forget the term they used. "Infiltration", "penetration", "access". Anyway I was to worm my way into opposition groups to find out what was happening. How? I asked. Use your natural advantages, I was told.' She passed a hand across her face as if to wipe out memories. 'See, I'm being absolutely open with you. I have to make you understand. Do you?' When he didn't respond she went on, 'What must I do, I asked. Sleep with them. No need to ask questions in bed, just be around at times when there is discussion. Make coffee, sit in, listen. You're giving sex, you're getting secrets. Makes it sound like export-import,' she said in a poor attempt to get Tadeusz to laugh. 'I had sessions with their psychologists. They were concerned I should not think myself dirty, a whore, or I would lose self-respect and probably defect. I was instructed this was a great honour, helping defend the motherland against fascist Western enemies just as heroic Soviet soldiers had given their lives in the Great Patriotic War.'

She must have felt she was talking too much. Or had said enough. She simply stopped. Tadeusz's gaze remained fixed on her. She was inspecting the spread fingers of one hand. Finding a hangnail that displeased her, she bit it off.

'How did you begin?' he prompted.

'What do you mean?'

'You arrived. You found somewhere to live. You had to start . . . operating. How did you know who to aim for?'

She took her time. 'I was pointed. As soon as Solidarity got going it was much easier.'

'Who pointed you?'

She seemed to take for ever. 'Baran. The KGB had recruited him. He was my boss in the field.'

'Baran. Of course. He told you: Go and seduce Rafat.'

'Tadek,' she murmured, 'please don't.'

'When Rafat was arrested he told you: Now go and seduce Tadeusz.'

'Darling, we'd already met. I was falling for you.'

'That was convenient.'

'Don't. Please don't. I loved you. Truly, truly, truly.'

'You'd love me in bed at night. You'd listen to the Klub's plans by day. And in the afternoons you'd go and report to Baran. And to think I was jealous. I thought you had another lover. Or was Baran your lover too?'

But Zuzanna's head was turned so low he couldn't see her expression. She didn't answer.

'When martial law was declared, when Father Michal was murdered, when the Klub members were being arrested, you were still working for him. When he needed a scapegoat, you carried the message and gave it to Eugeniusz. So I went to the cathedral on your instructions. I spent thirteen years of my life in prison.'

'I didn't kill him.'

'But you knew Father Michal had been murdered, didn't you? Maybe you knew it was going to happen and did nothing. Maybe you were even present.'

'Tadek, no.'

'You knew I was going to be arrested, didn't you?'

She said nothing.

Tadeusz scrambled off his seat, knelt in front of her and turned her face up so she had to look at him. 'Answer me. You *knew*, didn't you?'

She opened her mouth but no words came. He took his hands away from her face.

'Sorry – is that the word you were trying to say?'

'Please,' she said.

'You loved me. You truly, truly, truly loved me. And you truly, truly, truly betrayed me. Tossed me to the wolves. Connived at a murder and let me rot for it.'

There was a gas ring in the corner. Tadeusz made them both tea, black, with slices of lemon floating on top. While Zuzanna was sipping hers, feeling this show of hospitality must mean the worst was over, Tadeusz said, 'So we come to the present.'

'What do you mean?'

'What are you doing? Where are you living?'

She stared into a spiral of steam.

'Are you making up another lie?'

'Please,' she said. That seemed to be her answer to painful questions. After a pause she said, 'I live with Fredzio.'

'Who is Fredzio? Do I know him? He has a second name to go with the first?'

Another pause. 'Baran.'

'Jesus,' he said.

'Can't you understand? When the old system collapsed, I had nowhere to go. Who wants to employ someone who's spent fifteen years as a . . . well, as a Mata Hari for the KGB?'

'Other people faced this problem but you moved in with Baran. Where do you live?'

'He has an estate in the country.'

'Big?'

'Big enough.'

'Servants?'

'A couple. Horses. I enjoy riding. A wood. Trout stream.'

'A helicopter landing pad? A chapel? Private bishop? Art gallery? A harem? Or are you the only one?'

She frowned.

'Bloody Baran,' Tadeusz went on. 'He's seen me naked so why not you? What does he do for money? Did he get a big pay off from the Russians?'

'The Russians are misers. They only pay for results.'

'He'd been salting it away then?'

'A lot of the old guard had been putting it aside. He bought the estate and set himself up in business.'

'What's his racket?'

'Private security firm. People who used to work for him before now work for him privately.'

'Thugs. God, people entrust their property to the likes of him. What's it called?'

'PAX.'

'Peace of mind. Is that the idea?'

'Tadek.' She put her cup down. 'Tadek.' She wanted to be certain she had his attention. 'I've walked out on him. I couldn't stand it any more. He drinks with his cronies and then calls me down and makes me dance with them. All of them, one after the other. All stinking drunk. All leering and groping. "Go on, help yourself. That's all she's good for." That's why I came to you. You put out these signals and at first I resisted them. Then I got to thinking.' She took a deep breath and went ahead. 'We went well together and I want us to live together again. It can't be the same as before but we can make something new. It'll be better because this time there'll be no deception.'

'I wasn't deceiving you before.'

'We can go away. Abroad. Look.' She opened her bag to show him a bundle of dollar bills held together by an elastic band. 'I know his safe combination and I helped myself. Thousands. We can go wherever we like and start again. California, Asia, you choose.'

Tadeusz stared at the slice of lemon in the bottom of his cup. She'd seduced him, used him, spied on him, betrayed him, forgotten him and now she planned to buy him. A truly beautiful woman has her own morality. Was that it? Did that explain her? He put the cup down.

'Somewhere hot,' he said. Oh, how he'd loved her.

'Yes, yes.'

'With palm trees.' A part of him loved her still, always would, no matter what happened.

She clapped her hands. 'Where?'

'Come.' He got off the window seat.

'Now?'

'Yes. We leave this minute. Before Baran and his thugs have time to track you down. Do you think they won't look here?'

'I've no clothes.'

'It doesn't matter. It'll be warm. You won't need any.'

She laughed, perhaps a bit too shrilly.

'All right. Darling Tadek, I thought so much about you while you were away.'

Away? Away she called it? Tadeusz pressed down the urge to scream at her.

'Here.' She stuffed the dollar bills into one of his pockets. 'I feel easier now. Muggers and palm trees go together.'

They went into the corridor. Half way to the front door he said, 'Wait there. I've forgotten something.'

They turned left into the street and right at the corner,

away from the station. Were they going to run the whole way?

'Where are you taking me? The airport?'

'Hurry,' he urged.

He turned at a noise and there was a tram behind them. They raced it to the stop and boarded, breathless. There was a shine of excitement to Zuzanna's face as she pressed close against Tadeusz, taking his hand and squeezing it between her thighs. She laughed and said, 'We've escaped. We're free. Tomorrow we'll be lying under the palm trees, looking at a tropical moon.'

Tickets, passports, these were tiresome details that a wad of dollars would smooth over.

The tram went up through the city centre, past the covered market, over the river Odra. By now Zuzanna's attention had left Tadeusz. She peered through the window.

'Where are we going? Tadek?' She swung back to him.

'Here.'

He got down first, pulled her after him and crossed the road behind the tram, giving rise to a squeal of brakes and a blare on someone's horn. He paid no attention. He was rushing her across the wooden bridge and into the road leading to the cathedral. An autumn sun softened the blackened stone in front of them.

'Tadek, where are you taking me?'

'Not into the cathedral. You've done your confessing.'

He didn't give her time to protest or ask more questions, barely time to think. She stumbled but he had a tight grip on her so she didn't fall.

'Wait,' she cried out and took off her shoes. Barefoot, she trotted at his side. They skirted the north side of the cathedral, taking one of the alleys that led away from it. Ahead were the walls and railings of the botanical gardens.

'Put your shoes on.'

It was half an hour until closing time. He didn't want the ticket seller noticing a barefoot woman and then wondering where she had got to when it was time to shut the gates. Tadeusz was very quiet getting out his money, effacing himself.

'We close at six,' the woman in the booth said.

'I know.'

The path they took was bordered on one side by beds of roses, their summer flush spent. Huge chestnut trees marched with them on their right, the first yellowing leaves scattered on the ground and a few conkers gleaming like jewels among them. The path curved right and divided and Tadeusz paused a moment, looking behind. They were out of sight of the ticket booth. He opened the door leading into the greenhouses.

'Tadek, I don't understand.'

'You will.'

They were transported to a different country, a different continent. Tadeusz led the way through a succession of rooms, first warm and dry with pans of succulents and cacti. Opening a further door they entered the tropical houses. There were three interconnecting glasshouses, all hot, all humid, with sunlamps to augment the poor winter light. The furthest had a huge raised cement pond. There were waterlilies from Africa, Asia and Latin America. Some lily pads were over half a metre in size, looking sturdy enough to walk on. Small black fish darted between the lotus plants. They walked all round the pond, passing what looked like clumps of tall grass.

'Poland's rice crop,' Tadeusz said.

'Why have we come?'

'I promised to take you somewhere hot.'

'I thought we were going away.'

'Baran won't find us here.'

'We're staying the night?'

'Hush.'

The other houses had rubber trees and stands of bamboo four or five metres tall. Papayas jostled with bananas. Orchids in bloom and epiphytes clung to branches. Lianas dropped in loops like ropes abandoned by stage hands. Palm trees reached to the glass roof, struggling to break free. At the back paving stones formed a path through the luxuriant greenery and here Tadeusz and Zuzanna lingered.

When the last of the visitors left, he made her crouch among some cocoa bushes, pulling philodendrons down to add to the cover. The attendant did a tour of the three houses, calling out, 'We're closing. Is there anybody left?'

Tadeusz had hold of Zuzanna's hand and gave it a squeeze.

'Welcome to Bolivia,' Tadeusz said. 'People think of Bolivia as high in the mountains, with strange women wearing bowler hats. But it goes right down to the Amazon basin. That's where they raise the cocaine. Clearings in the jungle, little airstrip, a lab with an old Nazi chemist. Very old. That's what's lacking here – coca bushes.'

It was dark and a full moon hung in the sky. Its light came through glass that was misted with condensation.

'I'm scared.'

'Baran can't reach us. Nobody will come until the sun rises tomorrow. We're alone.'

'It's the heat. The humidity, I mean. All these jungle plants.'

'Isn't that what you were dreaming of? A tropical moon shining through the palms?'

'I'm dripping with sweat.'

'Take your clothes off.'

She was peering through the leaves of a fan palm. The moonlight through its slashed leaves lay in stripes across her face. It could have been the warpaint of some primitive tribe or the latest fashion among the tribes who go to discos.

'I said, take your clothes off.'

'And you?'

They undressed together. Tadeusz studied the temple where he had once worshipped. A little plumper at the calves, a little fuller in the breasts. The body in between was in shadow.

'You're the creation of a Conspirator,' he said.

Confused, thinking it was a reference to Baran, she said, 'I don't follow.'

'Your breasts are in moonlight and your calves and your feet. But in between I have to use my imagination.'

'Have you forgotten what I feel like?'

'In prison, lying on my bunk, I thought if I applied all my mind to it, concentrated hard, used all the power of my imagination, I would be able to feel your body.'

'Could you?'

'If a man could do that, there'd be no need for the real thing.'

'Tadek, come here, kiss me. It's been so long. Kiss me all over like you used to, every secret place. Please, oh please.'

She'd pulled him close and her hands seemed desperate as they roamed over him.

'Lie down,' she said. 'Here.' She dragged him to the earth under the palm trees and lay half on top of him. She kissed his mouth. He let her do it but didn't join in. Her hand caressed his chest, his belly, his thighs. Finding him unaroused she said, 'What's wrong? Oh, it doesn't matter. We're together now. The passion will come back.'

What's wrong? he thought. Apart from murder, betrayal,

thirteen years in prison, living with a thug, everything was fine.

She said, 'I'm so tired. I haven't slept for a week, I swear it. Ever since I read about you.'

She spread her jacket as a groundsheet and made herself comfortable, ranged at his side, with a hand on his hip. She wriggled and settled. She sighed, whispered his name, her breathing slowed.

Thirteen years. She treated it like a blink.

Tadeusz lay awake, watching while the moon swung through the sky. As the moonbeams moved over her body he saw now a hip, now the cup of a breast, now the depth of her navel, now the early warning of a roll of fat at her waist.

The time has come, he told himself, while she slept with the illusion of love and the promise of a new life in a far away place. He moved to reach his jacket. She stirred and he let her settle once more.

Not her heart. He'd loved her breast too much for that. Not her temple. His hands had held her face too often to kiss her. The back of her head, at the base of her skull. There was a rightness to that because it was how the KGB had executed its traitors.

He shot her with the Luger that had stayed hidden in the cupboard under the window seat. One bullet into the brain, and he let the pistol drop. It was the loudest noise ever, echoing in his head worse than all the artillery in all the history of man's wars. He put his arm across her and pressed her naked body close because he'd killed what he had loved.

He closed his eyes and saw a jumble of images of their past life racing in succession. After a while his brain slowed. Sleep came in waves, each wave drowning him deeper. He jerked awake once as a sinuous black beast crouched to sink its teeth into his throat. It was a jaguar, giving him a love bite.

The moon had dipped below the chestnut trees when he awoke. Her body was chilling so he rolled her up in the jacket she'd been lying on. He dressed and decided he wanted to get away from the foetid atmosphere. When he reached the front door to the hothouses he found it locked. He smashed a glass panel so he could scramble through.

It never occurred to him to climb over the wall and escape. An artist embraces the truth. He sat on a bench, waiting for the new day to start.

CHAPTER TWENTY-SEVEN

This is the High Court. This is the beginning of the end of my life. This is where misery and avarice and jealousy and cupidity and lust and rage and plain human weakness are everyday events. This is where Zuzia keeps me company in the dock, nodding agreement while the President of the High Court pronounces judgement. She turns to me and says: Tadek, you took being a Conspirator too far.

Tadeusz's head was a swirl of thoughts as he was brought into a courtroom as high and as bleak as a squash court. He was seated in the dock to the left of the judicial bench, flanked by policemen wearing caps. Ahead of him windows, quite high, gave on to the building's interior courtyard. Some panes were frosted, others were of plain glass. My last view of freedom is of chimney pots, Tadeusz thought. A few puffball clouds rode in the sky, lit by the sun. Outside it was a golden October day.

Jez, his lawyer, bustled across to lean into the dock. 'I do any talking that's required,' he said. 'Anything you say will make things worse.'

'How could things be worse?' Tadeusz asked, but his lawyer only glared.

Everybody rose as the court assembled. For a murder trial there were two judges, robed in purple. They sat, heads together, murmuring confidences. Behind them on the wall was a heraldic Polish eagle, its head turned to the west as Poles had resolutely told themselves during the communist era. Three members from the jury panel sat beside the Judges. The panel was one hundred and fifty members of the public chosen for their achievements and their experience of life. Tadeusz studied their faces. There was a woman in her late thirties and two older men. Was their experience of life even remotely similar to his own? The woman glanced at him and looked away. Does she have a sisterly feeling for the murdered Zuzanna? Has she the capacity to imagine what Zuzanna was like, her vitality, her passion, her eroticism, her boldness, her colour, her hidden treachery? One man was in his late fifties. He had the solid earnestness of a trade unionist, possibly a Solidarity official though not one Tadeusz remembered. What were his views on someone who had so comprehensively betrayed Solidarity? He was frowning but there could be a dozen reasons for that. The third member of the jury stared back at Tadeusz, which he found disturbing. Friendly people don't stare. Disapproving people stare.

The court was called to order. The more senior of the Judges was smoothing a sheet of paper flat on the desk in front of him. He nodded to the prosecutor, a woman with permed grey hair like a helmet, then to Jez.

'I trust this session will go more smoothly.'

There was a little laughter. It was polite to laugh if the Judge thought he was making a joke. Jez stood, ducked his head in the direction of the Judge, then sent a look at Tadeusz. Tadeusz stared back at his lawyer, sending him messages of hate.

After hearing the evidence and the arguments by the prosecuting and defending counsel, the Judges and jury members went away to mull it over separately. It could be for half a day, two days, three days. They looked at the facts, considered the accused's demeanour, studied precedents, consulted their consciences and drew on their knowledge of the world. This was the Polish way. Now the President of the Provincial High Court was delivering their verdict.

'In the minds of civilized people, murder has always taken a place all on its own,' the Judge began. His voice was soft and dry, the words seeming to drift out. Capital punishment was still on the statute book. Even though no one had been executed for ten years, it was still there. Tadeusz tried to concentrate. It's me he's talking about. 'Murder is abhorrent to us. The deliberate taking of a single person's life arouses more condemnation than all the horrors of war. When we – Judges and jury – retired to consider all aspects of the case, this moral dimension was foremost in our minds.'

Tadeusz glanced to the left, his eyes caught by a gesture. Natalia was perched on the edge of one of the spectators' benches. She had raised a hand to her mouth, struck by the gravity of the opening remarks. No cigarette holder, Tadeusz thought irrelevantly. Looks naked without it.

'A body is found with a single bullet lodged in the cranium. The murder weapon lies beside the corpse. The accused is sitting on a bench. He tells the police officers who are called to the scene that he did it. Obvious, isn't it?'

The Judge looked up from his papers, his gravest expression on his face. He let his eyes wander round the courtroom, his lips pursed.

'Obvious,' he repeated. He nodded before raising a cautionary finger. 'However, the duty of the court is not to accept the obvious but to seek the truth.'

When he paused again the stillness in the court was absolute. He's an actor, Tadeusz thought, he's got his pauses all marked. Out of the corner of his eye he saw movement.

Zdzislaw had pushed open the door and was tiptoeing in. He sat next to a journalist taking notes.

'We set ourselves the task of considering the gun,' the Judge continued, 'the motive, the condition of the hothouse, the history of the people involved, and what caused so much trouble when it was mentioned before – the psychological condition of the accused.' The Judge regarded Tadeusz. Jez looked his sternest. For a moment Tadeusz was the centre of all eyes until the Judge reclaimed the limelight. 'Because there is, in our opinion, the possibility of another explanation, and in a case so serious possibilities must be explored.'

Now the stillness broke. Movement, murmurs and a furious look from Jez warning Tadeusz to hold his tongue.

'Let us begin with the gun,' the Judge continued.

Tadeusz had the feeling the Judge also lectured at the university and this was how he taught students to lay out the forensic evidence. The cadaver here, the pistol just so, the accused's fingerprints smudged but identifiable but the accused has already admitted to picking up the gun – an example of carelessness you will have to contend with in your later careers.

So it was that Tadeusz's concentration slipped while the Judge's soft voice sifted through a lot of extraneous facts to do with the ownership of the pistol. But it was my finger on the trigger, Tadeusz wanted to point out. Nobody else's. Truth is precious in a world spinning out of control, where politicians and mullahs and revolutionaries and publicists of every persuasion shout at the tops of their voices, each hawking his version of paradise or threatening the burning flames of eternal damnation. Find a piece of truth, hold it in your hands like a gem, treasure it. Perhaps the truth of his finger on the trigger was too precious for everyday use. The Judge was talking about the Half House which the

Housing Department said had been in the name of Baran
and that was where the gun came from and it was reasonable to assign ownership to Baran, 'Of whom,' the Judge
said, putting down a marker, 'we shall hear more in a few
moments.'

There was a pause while the Judge selected another
sheet of paper. He had prepared carefully. Tadeusz looked
away, catching Natalia with her eyebrows raised. The Judge
seemed to be following a path rather different from the
one she expected.

'Zuzanna Raducka,' the Judge announced, putting his
head to one side like a man reading the title off the spine of
a book. He launched into a summary of her life. Ethnic
Pole, born in the former Soviet Union, recruited and
trained by the KGB, sent to spy on political targets in
Wroclaw, controlled by Baran who owned the murder
weapon, one time mistress of the accused, latterly mistress
of the said Baran, left him on the day of her murder. With
asides, parentheses, repetitions, speculations, it took the
Judge fifteen minutes.

Fifteen minutes to sum up the life of Zuzia? Fifteen minutes wouldn't be enough to sum up the colour, shape,
texture and responsiveness of her left breast let alone give
a true and full portrait of her. What mention was there of
her passion? Or her varying moods? Or her encourage-
ment of his art? Or the conflicting strands of her nature
that let her love him even as she betrayed him? How could
this Judge, whose words drifted down like dead autumn
leaves, know her? Could that sensible woman jury member
ever have turned cartwheels naked in a cornfield?

We loved each other, didn't we? It was Zuzia speaking to
him. She was in his head and would never leave him. We
could have lived on tea and love. And when the tea ran out
we could have lived on air and love. And when they'd

polluted the air so much we could scarcely breathe, we
could have lived on love alone. Could that trade unionist in
his white nylon shirt understand that?

Now the Judge was saying how Baran had come searching for them at the Half House in the late afternoon of the
murder, how angry he had been, how Baran employed
men – former Security personnel from the recent discred-
ited past – men whose speciality was tracking people
down, how Baran was the cause of the accused spending
thirteen years in prison for a crime he didn't commit, how
Baran was at this moment being investigated for allegedly
masterminding other crimes, and although that was by the
strictest judicial definition nothing to do with this case it
was nevertheless one of the wider circumstances which
needed to be taken into consideration.

'As is also the previous wrongful imprisonment the
accused endured. And the effect this had on his mental
attitude.'

NO! Tadeusz shouted. But only in his head. He'd tried
shouting it aloud before and it had had no result except to
cause a rumpus in court. He shouted it to Zuzia, but she
seemed indifferent. La, la, Tadek, she murmured, you do go
on sometimes.

Now the Judge was saying they had considered the argu-
ment suggested by the accused's counsel that the action of
a rational man who had committed a murder would be to
climb over the wall and not sit waiting on a bench; they
had pondered the possibility of other explanations; they
had done this singly and together. Was it conceivable that
having in the past been imprisoned for murder, the accused
had simply – in his emotional and mental turmoil –
assumed responsibility for this murder? Pattern behaviour
or a meta-pavlovian reflex, to use the jargon of the learned
counsel. It had seemed a far-fetched hypothesis. At first

they had discounted it. But then they considered that it was
Baran who had that day been deserted by his mistress,
Baran who had come searching for them in a rage, Baran
whose pistol was used, Baran whose career in the *Bezpieka*
had accustomed him to both violence and false accusation.
Whereas the accused had been involved in the struggle to
achieve democracy, whose many paintings of the dead
woman attested to his love for her and whose most recent
artistic performance was all to do with the purity and joy of
a little girl playing on a beach.

'We were not witnesses to the dreadful act of murder,'
the Judge said, 'we are only able to picture the moment
from such evidence as is given to us and such constraints
that we put upon it. We asked ourselves: if we had to
choose the more likely person to commit murder, which
would it be?' The Judge closed a folder on the notes he had
been consulting. He looked round the court, a long slow
tour of the faces. He seemed to be reassured that the verdict
he was about to pronounce was one that met with
approval. 'The verdict we reached, after long reflection and
discussion, was unanimous. We find there are grounds for
reasonable doubt that the accused committed the crime.
We therefore find him Not Guilty. Mr Lipski may leave this
court a free man.'

There was a lot of noise, in the courtroom and in his head.
As he made his way from the dock his lawyer was shaking
his hand. Even the police were grinning and one whispered in his ear, 'Just heard – there's a warrant out for his
arrest on that other thing.' He was almost disabled by
Zdzislaw's thumping on his back. Natalia kissed him with
more enthusiasm than she'd ever shown, kissed him full on
the mouth. There were friends spilling out of the benches
that he'd hardly noticed: Eugeniusz looking very trim with

his new wife, Dorota from the City Hall, Jan who said he'd get a couple of cases in. In his head he could hear Zuzanna and she was saying: You promised to take me somewhere warm.

'What are you going to do?' Natalia asked, taking his arm to get through the press of people.

'I'll go away,' Tadeusz said.

'Where?' she asked. 'France? Italy?'

Tadeusz knew a country. Its capital was called Peace. It had mountains up in the sky and mighty rivers through the jungle where monkeys howled and parrots flew between the palms. And he had money in his pocket – seven thousand three hundred dollars when he'd come to count it.

'Further,' he said.

'America?' she asked. 'Florida? Jamaica?'

'Further,' he said. 'Further further further.'

ON LEAVING A
PRAGUE WINDOW
David Brierley

David Brierley has written a novel for our times, a dark
and complex portrayal of the hidden side of the Velvet
Revolution, when the dreadful crimes of the heady days
of the Prague Spring were only just coming to light,
crimes giving rise to a multitude of questions. While
Father Alois Fulnek tries to find some answers – to the
mysterious death of a young journalist and the nature of
the corruption he was about to expose – the guilty are
tracking him as he tracks the guilty.

Superbly reflecting the realities of Prague after the Cold
War – with its jazz cellars and sleazy dance halls, its
joyful drunks and dangerous fixers – *On Leaving A Prague
Window* is a subtle and sophisticated thriller vividly
encapsulating the dilemmas of the new democracies, full
of moral ambiguity, tight plotting and taut excitement.

'Brilliantly evoking the joyous upsurge of hope that
erupted during that springtime – the noise, the music,
the drinking, the dreaming of new dreams – the author
catches and holds the reader's attention from first to last.
Unusual, exotic and tantalising' *Irish Times*

THE MARGIN OF
THE BULLS

Jeffrey Robinson

'Disgracefully entertaining' *Daily Mail*

In 1970, an American calling himself Bay Radisson arrived in London with no place to live and no place to go back to. Twenty years later he was riding the crest of a wave as one of Britain's brightest and most successful 'risk takers'. With charm, élan, cunning and humour, he and his British partner had built themselves a minor empire; conquering gladiators in an arena where money was the only way to keep score.

Then Robert Maxwell died – inadvertently sparking off a chain of events that sends Bay's world into a crashing nose-dive. Haunted by his yearning for success and faced with ultimate ruin – torn between the American woman he left behind, the Swiss woman who ripped his world apart and the British woman he married – Bay Radisson is forced to square off against the system in a ruthless battle to save his own life.

'(Robinson) has taken stories that the libel laws would not allow him to tell as non-fiction' *Sunday Times*

❏ On Leaving A Prague Window	David Brierley	£5.99
❏ The Margin Of The Bulls	Jeffrey Robinson	£5.99
❏ Just Cause	John Katzenbach	£6.99
❏ The Shadow Man	John Katzenbach	£5.99
❏ In The Heat Of The Summer	John Katzenbach	£5.99
❏ Gone But Not Forgotten	Phillip M. Margolin	£4.99
❏ After Dark	Phillip M. Margolin	£5.99

Warner now offers an exciting range of quality titles by both established and new authors which can be ordered from the following address:

Little, Brown and Company (UK),
P.O. Box 11,
Falmouth,
Cornwall TR10 9EN.
Telephone No: 01326 372400
Fax No: 01326 317444
E-mail: books@barni.avel.co.uk

Payments can be made as follows: cheque, postal order (payable to Little, Brown and Company) or by credit cards, Visa/Access. Do not send cash or currency. UK customers and B.F.P.O. please allow £1.00 for postage and packing for the first book, plus 50p for the second book, plus 30p for each additional book up to a maximum charge of £3.00 (7 books plus). Overseas customers including Ireland please allow £2.00 for the first book plus £1.00 for the second book, plus 50p for each additional book.

NAME (Block Letters) ....
....
ADDRESS ....
....
....

❏ I enclose my remittance for £ _____
❏ I wish to pay by Access/Visa card

Number | | | | | | | | | | | | | | | | | | |

Card Expiry Date | | | | |